Erica James is the number one internationally bestselling author of more than twenty novels. She has sold over five million books world-wide, and her work has been translated into twelve languages. Erica won the Romantic Novel of the Year Award for *Gardens of Delight*, set in beautiful Lake Como, Italy, which has become a second home to her. Her authentic characters are thanks to her insatiable appetite for other people's business and a willingness to strike up a conversation with just about anybody.

You can discover more about the author at ericajames.co.uk

COMING HOME TO ISLAND HOUSE

It's the summer of 1939, and after touring an unsettled Europe to promote her latest book, Romily Temple returns home to Island House and the love of her life, the charismatic Jack Devereux. But when Jack falls ill, his estranged family are called home and given seven days to find a way to bury their resentments. With war now declared, each member of the family is reluctantly forced to accept their new stepmother and confront their own shortcomings. But can the habits of a lifetime be changed in one week? And can Romily, a woman who thrives on adventure, cope with the life that has been so unexpectedly thrust upon her?

Books by Erica James
Published by Ulverscroft:

A BREATH OF FRESH AIR
A SENSE OF BELONGING
ACT OF FAITH
THE HOLIDAY
PRECIOUS TIME
HIDDEN TALENTS
PARADISE HOUSE
LOVE AND DEVOTION
GARDENS OF DELIGHT
TELL IT TO THE SKIES
THE QUEEN OF NEW BEGINNINGS

ERICA JAMES

COMING HOME TO ISLAND HOUSE

Complete and Unabridged

CHARNWOOD
Leicester

First published in Great Britain in 2018 by
Orion Books
an imprint of The Orion Publishing Group Ltd
London

First Charnwood Edition
published 2019
by arrangement with
The Orion Publishing Group Ltd
An Hachette UK Company
London

A catalogue record for this book is available from the British Library.

ISBN 978–1–4448–4024–7

Published by
F. A. Thorpe (Publishing)
Anstey, Leicestershire

Set by Words & Graphics Ltd.
Anstey, Leicestershire
Printed and bound in Great Britain by
T. J. International Ltd., Padstow, Cornwall

This book is printed on acid-free paper

*For Edward and Samuel, Ally and Rebecca,
and the Special One that is my grandson.*

Acknowledgements

The village of Melstead St Mary exits entirely in my head, as do all the characters, but a very real and beautiful house inspired me, and so I'd like to thank the owners who unwittingly provided me with Island House. They know who they are!

I'd also like to thank one of my readers — Naomi Veasey — for giving me Winter Cottage.

My good friend Rita Annunziata deserves a mention for helping me with the *ninna nanna* — *Fate la Nanna Coscine di Pollo* — the words of which I still struggle to make sense of!

Lastly, I'd like to thank the staff at the Suffolk Regiment Museum in Bury St Edmunds for showing me round and for being such a great help.

As always, artistic liberties are the prerogative of the author!

Part One

The Family

'Love is the crowning grace of humanity, the holiest right of the soul, the golden link which binds us to duty and truth, the redeeming principle that chiefly reconciles the heart to life, and is prophetic of eternal good.'

Petrarch 1304–1374

'Man has no greater enemy than himself.'

Petrarch 1304–1374

1

'There she is, the scarlet woman herself.'

'She's back then.'

'Back to flaunt herself right under our noses. She's no shame, that one.'

'No shame at all.'

'She's a fast one and make no mistake.'

'And just look what she's done to the running of Island House, got rid of Mr Devereux's old housekeeper, maid and cook as soon as she had her feet firmly under the table, didn't she? Brought in her own staff too.'

'We all know what that means. She has that Mr Devereux right where she wants him.'

'Under her thumb,' said three voices in unison. 'That's where.'

The three women watched with hostile curiosity the progress of the open-topped red sports car that had just been driven at breakneck speed into the market square of the village. With an abruptness that implied the driver had stopped on a sudden whim, the car skidded to a halt.

They continued to watch as the young woman threw open the driver's door and leapt to her feet with a vibrant and youthful energy. In her early thirties and undeniably attractive, she was exactly the sort to turn heads. Her clothes were

3

expensive and well cut and she carried herself with confidence and an easy grace. Tall and slender, with dark hair making a bid for freedom from beneath a silk scarf, she hooked a handbag over one of her bare arms, removed her sunglasses and entered Teal's grocery shop.

Minutes later, she emerged into the August sunshine with a paper bag from which she pulled out a peach, biting into it with undisguised delight. As she paused on the pavement to relish the moment, licking the juice from her painted red lips and smiling happily to herself, the three disapproving women sitting at their table in the window of the Cobbles Tea Room shook their heads and shuddered collectively.

'Mark my words, no good will come of that one,' said Elspeth Grainger.

'Never does when you live in sin,' said Ivy Swann.

'That's what comes of writing those dreadful books,' said Edith Lawton. 'All that blood and twisted thinking, it warps the mind.'

In full accord, the three women shuddered again.

* * *

Romily Temple was well acquainted with the coven of Melstead St Mary who daily occupied the best table in the Cobbles Tea Room in order to carry out their malicious brand of espionage. Not for a second did she doubt the depths to which they would go in order to establish everybody's business, or, more particularly, the

4

contempt in which they held her.

With a roar of engine, Romily gaily waved to the three women and, still eating the peach, drove out of the cobbled market square ringed with a topsy-turvy assortment of shops and cottages, some with thatched roofs, others with slate, all of them as neat as new pins. As she slowed her speed to turn onto the main street, she spotted Miss Gant and Miss Treadmill trudging up the road. Following a few feet behind, and as if mimicking their slightly waddling gait, was a pair of white geese, each with a green and yellow ribbon around its neck. They were as well behaved as any faithful hound trailing after its owner and were a familiar sight in the village; nobody batted an eyelid, apart from strangers.

It was a short distance to Island House, and after tossing the peach stone into the shrubbery at the entrance, Romily drove through the gates and brought her MG to a stop alongside Jack's prized 4½-litre Bentley saloon CXF 114. They had been planning to drive it down to the French Riviera next month, but now, with all the talk of war becoming a grim reality, the holiday was unlikely to happen. She had spent the last two weeks touring Europe carrying out a series of speaking engagements about her latest book, and everything she had seen and heard, particularly in Vienna and Berlin, told her that Nazi Germany was intent on spreading its vile roots, and by any means. War was going to happen — it wasn't a matter of *if* any more, it was *when*.

Out of the MG, and taking a moment to stare up at the beautiful house she now regarded as her home, she thought how exceedingly glad she was to be back. Then, with eager hands, she hurriedly gathered up her handbag and the small amount of luggage she had brought with her. She was about to let herself in at the front door when it was opened by her maid, Florence. The dear girl had been with her for the last four years, having come to work for Romily in London when she was just fifteen. Back then she had been a shy and timid thing who had jumped at her own shadow, but Romily had soon cured her of that. The girl's unswerving loyalty and devotion was matched only by her willingness to accept the unconventional manner in which Romily chose to live.

'How was your trip, miss, I mean, madam?' asked Florence, reaching out to take the heavier of the bags from her.

'Tiring, but successful,' Romily replied with a smile, amused at being called 'madam', a form of address she had yet to get used to. 'Is Mr Devereux at home?' she asked.

'Yes, he's in his study. He's been in there since after lunch listening to music and told me he didn't want to be disturbed, not for anything.'

Romily smiled again. 'We shall see about that. Could you ask Mrs Partridge to rustle up a sandwich for me, please? I'm ravenous. Oh, and here, have a peach, they're delicious.'

Taking her handbag and leather briefcase with her, she went upstairs to her dressing room, next door to the bedroom she shared with Jack.

Older than Romily by twenty-seven years, Jack Devereux was the first man she had truly loved, and the first man who had allowed her to be the woman she wanted to be. Most men in her experience had wanted to tame her and effectively turn her into something she wasn't — their social inferior. Invariably the very things that attracted these men in the first place — her independence and spirit of adventure — were what they set out to squash once they thought they had ownership of her.

Jack hadn't been like that. Perhaps that was because he was so much older and didn't feel threatened by her success as a writer, or the strength of her character.

They had met earlier in the spring at Brooklands, although she had already known of him through her love of racing. Her passion for cars had come about as a result of being invited to watch her best friend's brother compete in a race. Both Romily and Sarah had enjoyed themselves so much they had immediately signed up for racing lessons, wondering why they had reached the grand age of twenty-six and never done so before. They took to it with gusto, and after buying herself a second-hand Bugatti 35C, Romily made it to the podium in her first official race. From then on there was no stopping her, or Sarah, and together they began to race in earnest, competing against each other as much as the rival drivers on the track. They had been the same at school, always trying to outdo one another. Their exploits as solo racers took them to the circuits on the Continent, and then they decided to have a go at racing in a team and were lucky enough to be selected for MG at Le Mans.

But unlike Sarah, who had unlimited funds at her disposal — the Penhaligans had made their fortune in the tea trade, going back as far as the eighteenth century — Romily was not quite so blessed. What family money there was had been largely swallowed up by her parents, who, after the Great War ended, her father having survived the trenches, threw themselves into an extravagant lifestyle. Once they'd got through their combined inheritances, they had existed mostly on fresh air and the generosity of wealthier friends as they moved from one new home to another, ricocheting between Paris, Cannes, Saint-Malo, Beziers, Deauville, Rome and Venice, and all without a care in the world as to what tomorrow would bring.

Romily's nomadic childhood came to an end when both sets of grandparents persuaded her mother and father that it was time for her to be given a more settled environment in which to grow. At the age of fourteen, she was sent to boarding school in England. Carefully chosen by her mother, it had been an unconventional school on the South Downs with a progressive headmistress who believed in teaching the girls horticulture, dressmaking, carpentry and basic mechanics. It was also where she met Sarah.

Not long after her twenty-first birthday, her parents died in a tragic boating accident in the Adriatic. It took her a long time to get over their deaths; she simply couldn't accept they were gone. When eventually the worst of her grief had passed, she promised herself that she would honour their memory by living life to the full — as if each day might be her last — just as they had. It was a promise that made her realise that if she were to pursue her love of racing to the extent she wanted, as well as gain her pilot's licence — another expensive hobby she and Sarah had taken up — she needed a decent income, and so she seized upon the idea of writing, something she had always been good at while at school.

Her first published novel, much to her amazement, was a great hit, in the United States as well as the UK and Europe, as were the four books that had followed since. Funnily enough, writing gave her almost as big a thrill as racing or flying did; there was a freedom in it, that and an absorbing sense of control, of being solely in charge.

Fourteen months ago, when she'd met Jack at Brooklands, she had just come second in a race and had not been in the best of moods. She knew him by sight as a driver of some repute in his younger days, and for being a notorious womaniser, so when he came over to congratulate her on driving a good race, she had been less than gracious. 'But I finished second,' she'd replied, snatching off her gloves furiously.

'It's not always about the winning,' he'd said.

'The hell it isn't!' she'd declared.

He'd thrown his head back and laughed. 'Good for you! It's not a cliché I subscribe to either.'

'So why did you say it?'

'To see how you'd react. Now I'm wondering how you'd react if I asked you out for dinner.'

'Try me.'

Which he did. There then followed what could only be described as a whirlwind romance that led to Romily experiencing love — true love, the kind that made her want to sing from the rooftops — for the first time. No matter that she was thirty-two and Jack was nearing his sixtieth birthday, and that he had grown-up children not much younger than herself. None of that mattered. All that counted was the love she felt for him and the sheer joy she experienced whenever they were together. More than a year on and she still felt exactly the same way about him. She had only to think of him and her pulse quickened.

Going over to the largest of the built-in wardrobes and opening it, Romily pushed aside a row of dresses. She turned the dial on the safe door, and when it opened with a soft clunk, she took out two velvet pouches from her handbag; they contained diamond necklaces, ruby earrings, a collection of diamond and emerald rings and a pearl and diamond brooch that the owner had said meant more to her in sentimental terms than any monetary value.

From her leather briefcase she withdrew a file containing the lecture notes she had used during her book tour. At the back of her notes was an A4 buff-coloured envelope; feeling she ought to check that the contents hadn't come to any harm, she opened it and stared in wonder at the simple sketch of a young girl reading in the light of a candle. The signature of the artist was 'Rembrandt'. Handling the drawing as though it were as fragile as a newborn baby, Romily very carefully slipped it back inside the envelope and placed it with equal care in the safe. The picture had belonged to an Austrian family, having been treasured by several generations. Its clandestine journey with Romily across Europe to this small village in rural Suffolk had all the hallmarks of a gripping opening to a novel. Who knew, maybe one day Romily might write it.

Her hand poised to close the safe door, she had a sudden change of mind, and reached further in, right to the back to where a small black ring box lay. Pushing the lid up, she smiled at the sight of the three rings nestling companionably together. Two were simple platinum wedding bands; the other was an engagement ring with a central rectangular emerald-cut 2.2-carat diamond and four rectangular baguette-cut diamonds either side. Jack had surprised her with the ring, and a proposal, shortly before she departed for her book tour.

At the time, and on an impulse, Romily had suggested they marry straight away, and in secret. The ceremony had taken place at Kensington Registry Office; their witnesses were Jack's oldest and most trusted friend, Roddy Fitzwilliam, and Florence. Along with Mrs Partridge, they alone knew that Jack and Romily were now a respectably married couple and that officially she was Mrs Romily Temple-Devereux. For the sheer hell of it, she was tempted to continue with the pretence; she enjoyed fooling people, particularly the coven, who had her painted as a scarlet woman.

She put the box of rings back in the safe, closed the door and went through to the bathroom to freshen up before going down for something to eat, and to stir Jack from his lair in his study. Knowing how eager he would be to hear how she had got on with her mission, she was surprised he hadn't come to seek her out. Perhaps he had fallen asleep after eating an excellent lunch prepared by Mrs Partridge, she thought. She would pull his leg if he had. 'You have a young wife to stay awake for now,' she would tease him. 'You're not allowed to grow old and fall asleep in your favourite armchair.'

She took the stairs swiftly, her spirits high. She was quietly proud of herself for her smuggling exploits and wanted to regale Jack with how she had kept her nerve throughout the train journey from Vienna to Holland, and then on the boat to Harwich, all the while hiding a collection of priceless heirlooms in her luggage. The treasures belonged to the Friedbergs, a Jewish family who were long-time friends of the Penhaligans and were fearful of what Nazi Germany might do next. Sarah had offered to bring them to safety, but after falling off a horse and breaking an ankle, she had enlisted Romily's help.

Romily had had no qualms about carrying out the commission; after all, she was perfect for the task — who would suspect Romily Temple, a respected English novelist, of such a thing? On her return this morning, as soon as she had reached London and her flat overlooking Regent's Park, she had telephoned Sarah with the good news that all was well and she was on her way to Suffolk, where the Friedberg treasures would be kept until Sarah had organised a security box at the bank.

At the bottom of the stairs, she hesitated. Her rumbling stomach urged her to go to the kitchen and find what Mrs Partridge had for her to eat, but her heart compelled her to go to the study and see Jack.

He was sitting with his back to her when she pushed open the study door, looking out towards the garden. With its book-lined walls, comfortable armchairs covered in soft chestnut-brown leather, and French doors that led onto a small terrace, it was his favourite room in the house.

'Hello, darling,' she said, 'I'm home.'

When he didn't respond, and noticing that the gramophone player had reached the end of the record and the needle was stuck, she smiled. So he *had* nodded off, had he? Well, she would wake him with a kiss.

But when she placed her lips against his cheek, she let out a cry of shock.

2

Roddy Fitzwilliam contemplated the man lying in the bed next to him. To see his oldest and dearest friend reduced to this pitiful state was hard to bear. He wanted to believe that Jack would soon be up on his feet and giving everybody hell for making a fuss, but that didn't seem at all likely.

Roddy's own father had suffered a severe stroke some years ago and had died within days. He feared the same thing would happen to Jack. With painful difficulty, little more than grunts and mumbles through his lopsided mouth, Jack had indicated that he knew he wasn't going to live. With considerable effort, which had left him exhausted, he had also managed to state his terms: that he was not to be taken to hospital to die amongst strangers; he wanted to die here at Island House with Romily by his side. Roddy's initial reaction had been to disregard Jack's wishes and insist he go to hospital, where he would receive the best possible care and where his chances of survival might be improved. However, within minutes of his arrival this morning, he had been persuaded by the evidence of his own eyes that everything that could be done was being done for Jack right here. Two nurses had been engaged and the doctor from the village, Dr Garland, seemed highly competent.

A soft breeze blew in at the window, fluttering the pages of the newspaper Roddy had been reading to Jack before he'd fallen asleep. The news was going from bad to worse, with Nazi Germany hell-bent on adopting a stance of hostility that could lead only in one direction. For once in his life Roddy was glad he wasn't married and didn't have sons who would have to go and fight. Jack, on the other hand, had two sons who would be called upon to serve their country, although with Arthur being blind in one eye, his contribution would probably be limited.

How would Kit and Arthur, the girls too, Hope and Allegra, react to the news of Jack's stroke? If the telegrams Roddy had sent reached them in time, would they put their animosity aside and come and make their peace with Jack before it was too late? Surely they would.

In his capacity as a lawyer, Roddy had come across many a family who'd fallen out, but it had been a great disappointment to him when Jack's family had disintegrated to the extent it had. Of course, it had started a very long time ago, when in 1915 Jack's first wife, Maud, died shortly after giving birth to their third child, Kit. From that moment on Jack was a changed man. Maud's death left him heartbroken, and nothing filled the void that her passing created. In his mid thirties, with the Great War raging and his own rage burning ferociously inside him, Jack left his business in the hands of his younger brother, Harry, at the same time abandoning his children entirely to the care of what would prove to be a series of nannies, and volunteered to join the army. It was in northern France in the summer of 1916 that Roddy and Jack met and their friendship was born during the Battle of the Somme.

In January of this year, over dinner at the Connaught, they had celebrated their sixtieth birthdays together, their conversation mostly centred on the past and how they'd come from such very different worlds. Roddy's upbringing had been one of wealth and privilege, whereas Jack had grown up in the East End of London and left school at fourteen to work as a barrow boy. Wheeling and dealing was second nature to him, it was what he lived for. He was seventeen when he took himself off to South Africa and got a job in a diamond mine. Before long, he was working as a diamond trader, and on moving back to London he had invited his brother to join him in his enterprise. It was, he believed, a way of keeping the wayward young man on the straight and narrow.

Unfortunately there was no force on earth that could do that, and after Jack and Roddy were both invalided out of the war — Roddy returning to the law firm in Mayfair where he was a partner, and Jack to the diamond business he had left in his brother's care — he discovered that Harry had all but run the business into the ground in his absence.

Furious, Jack left him to it and started up a new company, relying on all his old contacts and clients. When Harry was then accused of fraud, he seemingly disappeared off the face of the earth, until years later Jack heard that his brother

16

had died of cholera in North Africa. He also learnt that Harry had fathered a child — the result of a brief liaison with a dancer from Naples. The girl was then nine years of age and had been living in an orphanage since her birth.

A change in Jack's breathing had Roddy sitting upright and glancing anxiously at his old friend, but no sooner had he wondered if he should call for one of the nurses than the laboured heave of Jack's breath settled again. Restless with myriad thoughts, Roddy rose stiffly from the chair he'd occupied for the last hour and went over to the window. He wasn't a man inclined to mawkish sentiment, but the idea that Jack might not be a part of his life any more left him feeling utterly defeated.

To distract himself, he thought of the will he had drawn up for Jack while Romily had been away in Europe. Almost as if he had had some kind of premonition, Jack had visited Roddy in London and explained that he wanted to make a new will, which was perfectly understandable given that he was now married. But what had surprised and alarmed Roddy was Jack's wish that unless his family fulfilled the terms laid down in it, they wouldn't inherit. Not a penny. Roddy had cautioned against it as being too heavy-handed and antagonistic, but Jack had insisted, claiming it was the only way he could bring them together. Since meeting Romily, it had suddenly become important to Jack that he put things right with his family. As a consequence, he had recently, and on several occasions, invited them to join him at Island

House, but they had turned him down flat each time. 'I just want them to come home so I can say I'm sorry,' he confided in Roddy. 'Why the hell do they have to make things so difficult?'

The trouble was, they probably associated invitations back to Island House with being forced to meet the latest woman Jack was seeing. The last time an invitation had been extended — Roddy had been included as well — they had made their feelings all too clear: that they regarded the aspiring actress sitting at their dining table as nothing but a vacuous gold-digger, a view that coincided with Roddy's own. The children, sensing some sport, or perhaps out of boredom, had run rings round the simpering, dim-witted young woman, making her appear even more foolish than she already was. His hackles up, Jack had hit the roof and demanded that if his family couldn't be civil to his guest they should leave. A stormy row ensued, during which even mild-mannered Kit had accused his father of never considering their feelings, and then they had all left for the station.

Roddy genuinely had no idea how Arthur, Kit, Hope and Allegra would react to the instructions in Jack's will. Would they go along with it, or would their pride — an inherently strong Devereux character trait — dictate one last act of defiance and prevent them from complying? Yet as the family lawyer, and assigned by Jack the task of creating modest trust funds for the children, Roddy knew that their pride did not stop them from taking advantage of the funds available to them.

Still standing at the window, he looked out at the well-kept garden and the lily pond beyond. It was a place of great enchantment, where Jack had felt most settled in recent years, so much so that he'd sold his lavish flat in Mayfair last summer. He had bought Island House as a country retreat when the children were young, a place where he thought they would be happy. Poor Jack. What he had never understood was that the children had wanted only two things from him, his love and his time, neither of which he had been fully able to give.

Behind him Roddy heard the door opening. He turned around and saw Romily carrying a tray of tea things. He went over to offer her his assistance, such as he could.

'It's all right,' she said, painstakingly mindful of his useless right arm and missing hand, 'I can manage.' She placed the tray on the table and gave Jack a long, searching stare. 'In spite of everything, he looks so very peaceful,' she said quietly.

Roddy thought much the same. It was when Jack was awake that his features seemed cruelly distorted. 'He's been asleep for about half an hour,' Roddy said. 'I think I bored him reading from the newspaper.'

'I'm sure that's not the case,' Romily said kindly. She poured two cups of tea and passed one to Roddy. 'If you want to stretch your legs and go for a breath of fresh air, please do. I'll sit with Jack for a while until the nurses send me away. Dr Garland is calling in shortly.'

Roddy took a sip of his tea and not for the first

time thought how composed Jack's wife was. She was one of the most admirable women he knew; he could quite understand how his old friend had fallen for her. If he were honest, he was a little in love with her himself.

When Jack had confided in him that he was going to propose to Romily, Roddy hadn't been at all surprised. There had been any number of women in Jack's life over the years, many of them wholly unsuitable, but they had come and gone without making any real impact on him. But then he'd met Romily and his life had been turned upside down. Even Roddy, a confirmed bachelor and no expert when it came to matters of the heart, had recognised in an instant that his old chum had finally found love again. 'If only I'd met her twenty years ago,' Jack had said wistfully, 'we'd have had so much to look forward to.'

'And if you had met her that long ago she would only have been thirteen years old,' Roddy had teased him.

'Any news from the children?' he asked Romily now.

She was about to reply when they both turned at the sound of Jack stirring. Hastily placing her cup and saucer on the table, Romily went to her husband. 'There you are, darling,' she said, as though he'd been out for a walk somewhere. She took his hand in hers and gave him a look of such loving tenderness that Roddy took it as his cue to leave them alone.

3

It was taking all of his strength to open his eyes. Such a little thing, but such a gargantuan struggle that made Jack feel as though heavy weights had been put on each of his eyelids. It was a thought that filled him with sudden terror. Had he been mistakenly prepared for burial with coins placed over his eyes? *No!* he wanted to yell. He wasn't ready for the boatman to ferry him across the River Styx; he wasn't dead. Not yet. Please God, not yet.

Still unable to open his eyes, he recalled the horror of another time when he had pleaded with God — a time when he had begged not to live, but to die, for his suffering to be over. He had been crammed into the back of a blood-soaked ambulance with a heaving mass of other wounded soldiers, some screaming aloud, some whimpering, and one poor devil, no more than a boy, with half his face blown away, crying for his mother. Above the din, and through the excruciating pain of his own injuries, Jack would have sworn that it had been a madwoman at the wheel of the ambulance driving them at great speed, and very little care, to the field hospital, all the while belting out the 'Ride of the Valkyries' at the top of her not so tuneful voice. He'd been conscious enough to consider it an ironic choice of music, given that the composer was German and Germany was the enemy.

For ever after he'd never been able to hear that piece of music without remembering the agony he'd been in. Singing had probably been the woman's only means of keeping her sanity in what must have been a living nightmare as she, along with countless other women who had volunteered to go to northern France, ferried bodies, or what remained of men who had been blown apart by shells, from the battlefield to the relative safety of the field hospital. Listening to her singing, Jack had welcomed death, if not from the bullets lodged in his stomach and leg, then from the wholly possible prospect of the ambulance being driven recklessly into something hard and immovable.

The pain he'd been in had been unlike anything he had ever known, and no sooner had he surrendered his will to live than he felt a lightness in his body, as if he were floating away. This was it, then, he'd thought, surprised that his prayer had been answered so swiftly. This was death. And not as bad as he'd feared it would be at the end. It was almost pleasurable. He hadn't expected that. But then, and as though she were there to welcome him into heaven, there was Maud, his dearest sweet Maud. Oh how he'd missed her since she'd died! Not a day had gone by when he hadn't thought of her and longed for her to be by his side again. And now here she was. 'Have you come for me?' he asked her.

She shook her head. 'Not yet.'

'But I want to be with you. I want to die. I'm ready.'

She pressed a cool finger to his lips. 'No,' she

said softly, 'you have to go back; our children need you. You must go home to them.'

He reached out to her, but there was nothing to touch. She was gone, leaving him to cry for her like a frightened lost child. 'Don't leave me! Don't leave me!'

The next thing he knew, he was lying on a bed in a chaotic makeshift hospital with a young nurse in an incongruously smart Red Cross uniform studiously applying a bandage to his leg while telling him everything was going to be all right. 'I saw for myself the bullets you caught,' she said brightly. 'No real harm done, so you'll soon be up on your feet.'

In the bed next to him, a man laughed. 'Nurse Wainwright says that to everybody. You could be brought in here with both legs blown off and she'd still tell you you'll soon be right as rain.'

'I'll thank you to keep your sarcasm to yourself, Mr Fitzwilliam,' the nurse said primly. She fastened off the bandage and then carefully covered Jack's legs with a blanket. 'Call me if you need anything,' she said, 'and if necessary I could find you a change of bed if Mr Fitzwilliam gives you any trouble.' This last comment was said with a friendly wink.

When she was gone, his fellow patient introduced himself. 'Roddy Fitzwilliam,' he said cheerfully. 'I would shake hands only . . .' He held up a heavily bandaged arm that stopped short just after his elbow. 'Bloody good thing I'm left-handed.' He laughed bitterly. 'Bright side and all that.'

'Jack Devereux,' said Jack. 'How long have you been here?'

23

'Came in yesterday. Only popped in for a haircut, and look what happened to me.'

Jack smiled and entered into the spirit of the exchange. 'Any chance of attracting a barman round here?' he asked. 'I could murder a whisky and soda.'

'I'm afraid the service is not what it could be.'

Their friendship was sealed that day, and afterwards, when the war was over, neither of them could quite believe they'd actually survived the hell of the Somme. Not when so many they had known had not been so fortunate.

But now Jack was facing a fresh new hell; the battle once more for his life, a life he wasn't ready yet to relinquish. He wanted one last chance to try and put things right with his family. He owed it to Maud to do that. It was what she would have wanted, and he had to do it while he still could, before it was too late.

With the certain knowledge that the sands of time were fast running out for him, he could see with unerring lucidity that stubborn pride had turned him into a dogmatic and overbearing father and uncle. Moreover, he was guilty of neglect and intolerance, of prejudice and arrogance. Even his recently made will was an act of supreme conceit. But how else to remove the battle lines and bring the children together?

He struggled again to open his eyes. He concentrated hard, forced his whole being into that one simple task. As if swimming up from the depths of a bottomless ocean, he dragged himself up, up and into the light.

'There you are, darling,' he heard a woman saying. *Maud?*

He blinked in the brightness of the sunlit room and focused on the source of the voice. No, not Maud, but another equally wonderful woman. And never had Romily looked more beautiful to him than in this moment, with the sun streaming in through the window and illuminating the radiance of her face. It was a woefully inadequate cliche, but her love for him had made him feel young again. It had also gone some way to softening many of his hard edges, awakening in him something he'd believed he'd lost — the ability to love; to love someone with all his heart and soul. In short, to care again.

He looked into the face that meant the world to him and willed himself to move, to lift a hand to touch his wife in the way that had brought him such joy. But all he could manage was a vague waggle of his fingers. The rest of him felt like a leaden dead weight.

She bent down close and kissed him on the lips. 'You look so peaceful when you're asleep,' she said. 'Can I get you anything?'

'Whisky . . . and soda,' he said. In his head, the words came out with crystal clarity, but he could see from the hesitant expression on Romily's face that she was having trouble deciphering what he'd said. Then, as if slowly making sense of it, she smiled.

'A whisky and soda, eh? Well I don't see why not. Just don't tell Dr Garland or the nurses, or they'll ban me from seeing you.'

'Let . . . them . . . try.'

Once more there was a small delay in her understanding.

She kissed him again. 'You're right, they wouldn't stand a chance against me.'

'Nobody . . . does,' he said.

She smiled and stood up. 'I'll be right back.'

He watched her leave the room. She was such a young and vibrant woman; perhaps it would be a blessing to her if he did die sooner rather than later. He hated her seeing him this way. She deserved so much more than to be married to a helpless invalid. Yet in his weakened state he could see things so much more clearly, and knowing that he would never again have the chance to do the one thing he should have done a long time ago, he resolved to ask Romily to do it for him: to reunite his family. He prayed that she would agree; it was a lot to ask of her.

When she returned, tumbler in hand, she held it carefully against his mouth. 'Nectar,' he struggled to say. 'Heav . . . enly . . . nec . . . tar.'

Whether she understood him or not, she wiped his chin with a handkerchief before offering him another sip.

'Where's Rod . . . dy?' he asked, forcing the words out through lips that no longer felt like his own.

'Taking a break. You've worn him out with your incessant chatter.'

He tried to smile. 'You're . . . the . . . best thing . . . that . . . ever . . . happened . . . to me,' he said breathlessly. He watched her face, waited for what seemed like forever for her to understand what he'd said.

'And you,' she said finally, dabbing delicately at his chin again, 'are the best thing that's ever happened to me.'

26

Her loving gentleness made him want to weep. Tears welled in his eyes and rolled slowly down his cheeks. Never had he cried in front of anyone before, and it appalled him that he was doing so now, but he was powerless to stop it.

'Oh my darling Jack,' said Romily, setting down the glass and putting her arms around him. 'We'll get through this, just you see.'

Her words, spoken so bravely, made him weep all the more.

4

The last of the guest rooms made ready for Mr Devereux's family, Florence went over to the window and watched Mr Fitzwilliam disappear inside the boathouse down by the pond. Seconds later, he reappeared with an old wicker chair and settled himself into it in the dappled shade of the willow tree. Yet as beautiful as the setting was, there was nothing relaxed about his posture; his shoulders were hunched, and his head lowered. As Florence had seen him do before, he put his left hand protectively on his useless right arm, where the fabric of his jacket sleeve hung loosely over his stump. There was something so sad about those few inches of lifeless sleeve. Something sad too about the sight of him sitting all alone at the boathouse. Poor man, she thought; obviously seeing his old friend so ill had upset him badly.

From what Florence knew of Mr Devereux's estranged family, she doubted they would feel as upset as Mr Fitzwilliam. Would they even bother to come? And if they did, how would they react to the news that Miss Temple was now officially Mrs Jack Temple-Devereux? Which was quite a mouthful, however much Florence practised it! Much easier was the less formal name she had been instructed to use when she was alone with her somewhat unconventional employer: Miss Romily.

Florence wondered what would happen if Mr Devereux died. Would Miss Romily leave Island House to return permanently to London, taking Florence and Mrs Partridge with her? Florence hoped not; she liked living here.

At first she hadn't thought she would take to life in the country, not when the church bells kept her awake at night, along with owls hooting and what sounded like a wild banshee howling in the darkness but which actually turned out to be a fox calling for its mate. To her surprise, though, in the few months she'd been here, she had grown accustomed to the strange noises, and now Island House felt like a proper home to her. It was somewhere safe where she didn't have to live in fear of her beer-sodden father and brothers finding her and dragging her back home. In London, that fear had always hung over her.

Miss Romily had been the one to offer her a means of escape from her domineering father, and Florence had grabbed that chance with both hands. Their paths had crossed, quite literally, one morning when she had stepped absently into the road and suddenly found herself thrown off her feet before landing with a heavy thud on the dusty ground. It happened so fast, but at the same time almost as if in slow motion, giving her the feeling that she was actually flying. She must have closed her eyes, for when she opened them, she found that a crowd had gathered around her. But one face stood out: the face of an elegant woman wearing the smartest red hat Florence had ever seen. Funny to think that there she was, lying in the gutter, making a spectacle of herself, the wind knocked out of her, and all she could think of was that she would give anything in the world to own a hat as smart as that.

The owner of the hat spoke; the voice was that of a posh upper-class woman. 'Are you all right?' she asked. 'Can you move? Or perhaps you'd better not. Not yet.'

'What happened?' Florence asked, the air now back in her lungs and a flood of pain making itself felt in just about every part of her body.

'I'm afraid I knocked you down. You stepped right into the road in front of my car before I could brake. I couldn't do a thing about it. I'm terribly sorry.'

Another voice joined in. 'She's right; you did exactly that. You practically walked straight into the car. You must have been daydreaming to do that.'

Mortified that she'd caused such a kerfuffle, Florence said, 'I'm very sorry. Is your car all right?'

'Oh tish and tosh, please don't be sorry. And don't give my car a second thought. Now then, do you think anything's broken?' The woman's gaze travelled the length of her, eyeing up Florence's legs and arms.

It was then that Florence realised her dress had ridden up over her thighs, and there, for all the world to see, were the livid welts and bruises her father had inflicted on her yesterday with his belt. Shame made her face flush and she pushed the dress down.

'I insist on taking you to see my doctor,' the

30

elegant woman said, a gloved hand outstretched. 'It's the very least I can do in the circumstances. Come on,' she said to the crowd of onlookers, 'let's see if we can get this poor girl up and onto her feet.'

With others rushing to do the woman's bidding, Florence was at a loss what to say. She was too weak with pain and too dazed to argue.

She had never been in an open-topped sports car before, and all she could do was sit in the passenger seat and hope she didn't wake up from this extraordinary dream. Because it had to be a dream. Maybe she had been knocked unconscious and this was all going on inside her head, and any minute now she would wake up and find herself still in the gutter. Perhaps knocked over by somebody who didn't care, rather than by a beautiful woman driving at what she now realised was an alarmingly fast speed.

More alarming still was that when the car came to a stop, she saw that they were parked outside a doctor's consulting room in Harley Street. Suddenly terrified that she would have to pay the man a king's ransom, she said, 'There's really no need for me to see a doctor. I'm all right. Honest I am. Just a bit shaken, that's all.'

'I disagree,' the woman said firmly, and helping Florence out of the car, she took her gently by the arm and led her up the steps to the black front door with its shiny brass knocker in the shape of a lion's head. 'By the way,' she said, giving the lion's head a loud rat-a-tat-tat, 'my name's Miss Temple, what's yours?'

'Florence, miss. Florence Massie.'

'Well, Florence, I'm here to tell you that whoever caused those shocking marks on your legs had no right to do such a thing. No right at all.'

'I did it to myself, miss,' lied Florence. Just as she had when a teacher at school had asked how she'd hurt herself this time. She knew better than to admit the truth. 'I tripped over the coal scuttle,' she said. 'I'm as clumsy as anything, me. Always have been.'

'Yes,' the woman replied, giving her an uncomfortably long stare, as if seeing straight through her. 'I'm sure you are.'

Their meeting proved to be the best thing that could have happened to Florence, for Miss Temple was in need of a new live-in maid. The fact that Florence had no experience as a lady's maid — she'd been working in a laundry since she left school — didn't bother Miss Temple a jot. 'I'm sure you'll pick it up soon enough,' she'd said, 'and the estimable Mrs Partridge, my cook, who's been with me since forever, will take you under her wing and give you all the pointers you need.'

Predictably, Florence's father hit the roof when she plucked up the courage to tell him that she'd found a new job and wouldn't be a burden to him any more. He told her that she would only leave home over his dead body, and threatened to beat some sense into her if she dared to defy him. But there was something about Miss Temple and the fact that she seemed to know how Florence had come by her bruises that gave her the strength, finally, to stand up to her father, to see him for what he was: a cowardly bully who was only man enough to hit a girl. She secretly packed a small bag of her belongings and slipped away without a backward glance and without leaving an address. She simply disappeared and, in so doing, history repeated itself, for just as her mother had run away, so had Florence. She felt a certain sense of pride in what she had done, and would always be grateful to the woman who had given her a chance to change her life.

And what a life she had lived in the four years since that day. With Miss Romily there was always something interesting going on, and then there was the travelling she had to do, sometimes to promote a book, other times to carry out research. Often she liked Florence to go with her on her trips abroad. Last year Florence had gone to the French Riviera and to Venice, and the year before that to Paris. Oh yes, she was quite the well-travelled lady's maid, as Billy Minton had once teased her. 'You're much too good for the likes of a simple country boy like me,' he'd said in his soft Suffolk accent. 'I've never been anywhere.'

Billy worked for his parents in their baker's shop in the village, and he always had a kind word for Florence when she passed by or called in, but then he was that sort of lad, forever with a smile on his handsome face.

Sometimes Florence had to pinch herself to make sure that her new life here at Island House was real, that it wasn't a dream. No two ways about it, she had landed on her feet good and proper the day she met Miss Romily, and in return she'd go to the ends of the earth to help the woman.

But daydreaming like this wouldn't do, she scolded herself; there was work to be done. She had promised Mrs Partridge that she would help out in the kitchen in anticipation of the family arriving. Mrs Bunch had come in especially to lend a hand with the extra work, though all she'd done so far was sit around drinking tea and sharing the latest gossip from the village.

As big a gossip as the old woman was, though, she was wise enough to steer clear of what people were probably really talking about, and that was Mr Devereux and his beautiful mistress. Little did they know, thought Florence with a smile.

5

Hope's visit to Cologne had been a mistake. She should never have invited herself, but she had thought that spending time with Dieter's parents, seeing where he had spent his childhood, might help her to come to terms with his death. It hadn't. It had made things worse.

Her parents-in-law, Gerda and Heinrich Meyer, had worn her down with their grief. They were full of angry bitterness and appeared to hold her personally responsible for their son's death from TB. In their eyes she had lured him away from the safety of home in Germany and forced him to live in germ-ridden England. No matter that Dieter had been living in London for nearly a year before Hope met him, that he had been there quite voluntarily.

Gerda and Heinrich's disapproval of their son's choice of wife was matched only by that of Hope's father. 'A German!' Jack had roared. 'You're marrying a *German*, after all they did to us? And what they're now doing to their own people?'

There had been no reasoning with her father, no explaining to him that not all Germans were merciless killers. Dieter wasn't evil; he was kind and sensitive, and his coming to England to work as a teacher had been to escape all that he detested in Nazi Germany. He had been alarmed by the growing belief within his country of birth that with the shame of poverty behind them, they were now a country to be respected, a power to be reckoned with, and feared. Poor Dieter, he had been appalled to discover that there were those in power in Britain who thought Hitler a fine leader from whom much could be learned.

Hope's brother, Arthur, had voiced a similar sentiment and praised Hitler for having taken a country from its knees and motivated the workforce and the young. 'Can you blame them for wanting to win back everything they lost?' he had said when challenged by their father's disgust, angering him further. 'Wouldn't we do the same in the circumstances?'

Now, two and a half years after her marriage to Dieter — and a year since his death — Hope was seeing for herself the evil force sweeping through the country. Life in Nazi Germany had shocked her. She was shocked too that having been so consumed by grief, she had been in ignorance of just how bad the situation had become. It made her realise that it was time to lift herself out of the trough of despair in which she had willingly placed herself, believing it to be a comfort, a means to feel closer to the man she had loved.

Without Dieter, her life these last twelve months had felt so very empty and worthless. She had tried to console herself with her work as an illustrator, but it hadn't been enough to fill the huge void. At her lowest point, having cut herself off from friends and family — especially family — she had briefly considered suicide so she could be with her beloved Dieter. But then she had thought how appalled he would have been that she could throw away her life instead of doing something meaningful with it.

Now, in the light of the suffering she had witnessed here in Germany, her grief had felt like a narcissistic act of self-pity that she had clung to for much too long. The persecution and collective hatred for Jewish people was everywhere, in the everyday casual violence they endured, but more particularly in the increasing number of laws created to make it impossible for them to live a decent life.

Even Hope had been targeted by a group of schoolboys dressed in their Hitler Jugend uniforms when she was returning from seeing Dieter's sister and husband. Her presence in a Jewish neighbourhood and the fact that her hair wasn't blonde but a mousy shade of brown was sufficient cause for the boys to jeer and taunt her. One of them had deliberately tripped her up and then laughed coarsely as she scrabbled on the ground to retrieve her bag. Another boy had spat at her.

Yet this paled into insignificance compared to what her sister-in-law, Sabine, and her husband, Otto, were subjected to. Hope was on her way to see them now, taking the tram across the city, glad to be escaping the suffocating company of Gerda and Heinrich for a few hours.

It was her last day before returning to London tomorrow and she couldn't wait to board the train that would take her to the Hook of Holland, where she would catch the boat to

37

Harwich. Yet for all her eagerness to leave, she would be desperately sorry to say goodbye to Sabine and Otto, and their dear little baby daughter, Annelise. Hope and Dieter had planned to have a family of their own one day, but now she had to make do with being an aunt to Annelise.

Otto Lowenstein was a doctor, but because he was Jewish, he was banned from working in his old hospital. Now all he could do was secretly treat Jewish patients in their own homes. Twice in the last year, since Kristallnacht last November, when synagogues were torched, Jewish homes, schools and businesses vandalised and hundreds of Jews beaten up and killed, Otto had been arrested for no real reason, and later released. It happened all the time apparently. He and Sabine had married before 1935, when a new law forbade mixed marriages. Gerda and Heinrich, both devout Roman Catholics, had been against the marriage, just as they had disapproved of Dieter marrying an English Protestant girl.

Sabine and Otto lived in a run-down area that bore all the signs of the discrimination and hatred they and their neighbours were subjected to. A number of shopfronts were boarded up and painted with the yellow Star of David, and the words 'Filthy Jew' or 'Death of the Jews' scrawled in large letters. There was nobody about, the streets as good as deserted. Remembering the route she had taken two days ago, Hope clutched the basket she was carrying and walked fast, trying not to give in to the uneasiness she felt. It was here that the group of boys had taunted her.

She turned left at the newspaper kiosk on the corner of Neuhofstrasse and became aware of an odd smell. Then fifty yards later, as she turned into Annastrasse, she stopped in her tracks at the sight that met her. The building on her left had been a bakery when she'd last seen it; now it was a burnt-out shell, a blackened carcass with smoke rising from the rubble, the warm air thick with dust and the acrid smell of charred wood. A flag with a swastika had been pushed into the blackened ruins. Shocked, Hope pressed on, stepping around the broken glass that was glinting in the sunshine. The area was nothing like the smart leafy street where Gerda and Heinrich lived; here the turn-of-the-century buildings were in a poor state of repair, with blackened walls and peeling paintwork.

With Annelise in her arms, Sabine answered the door almost immediately, as though she had been standing just the other side of it waiting for Hope's knock.

'Thank God you made it,' she said breathlessly. 'I was worried you might have changed your mind.' She spoke excellent English, just as her brother had. She hastily kissed Hope's cheeks and ushered her over the threshold of the ground-floor apartment, which had the benefit of a small garden. It also had the disadvantage of being an easy target for objects thrown through the window that fronted the street.

Hope followed her down the dingy narrow hallway with its pervading smell of damp and

39

into the shabby high-ceilinged drawing room where the paucity of furniture — the better stuff long since sold to make ends meet — testified to the daily struggle of their lives.

'Please,' said Sabine, pointing to an old couch with horsehair poking out through patches of threadbare fabric, 'sit down while I make us some tea. Or would you prefer a cold drink?' The baby began to fidget in her arms, then let out a squawk of protest.

Thinking how fraught Sabine looked — her skin had a high colour to it as if she had a fever, and her eyes were red-rimmed — Hope put down her basket of farewell gifts. 'Why don't you let me make the tea?' she said.

'No, no, I can manage,' Sabine replied. Annelise wriggled some more and began to cry in earnest, her face turning very pink, her fists punching the air.

Determined to help in some way, Hope said, 'How about I take Annelise from you?' She reached out for the crying infant, but to her horror, Sabine backed away from her and burst into violent sobs, sinking slowly to the floor, her arms wrapped tightly around her child as if protecting her from an imagined force. She knelt there on the rug, rocking backwards and forwards, her cries growing louder and louder. Not knowing what else to do, Hope knelt on the floor next to her. Clearly Sabine wasn't well. She was having some kind of crisis. A breakdown. And who could blame her, living in this godforsaken country where hatred ruled?

Sabine's wailing continued, coming from

40

somewhere deep inside her, a primordial sound that reminded Hope of when she herself had been told that Dieter had died. She was trying desperately to soothe her sister-in-law, and to get her to relinquish her crying baby, when the door opened and Otto came in, his black medical bag in his hand. Taking in the situation, he dumped the bag on the nearest chair and joined them on the floor. He spoke in German, firmly, but kindly. Still holding a howling Annelise, Sabine pressed herself against him and sobbed all the louder.

Otto continued to speak in German, and Hope understood enough to know that he was asking his wife to give him the baby, that her crying was frightening Annelise. Sabine raised her reddened tear-stained face to him and shook her head. '*Ich kann es nicht tun,*' she sobbed. *I can't do it.*

'*Bitte, mein Schatz,*' he said with a catch in his voice. For an awful moment Hope thought Otto was going to cry as well. But he didn't. Instead he somehow managed to calm Sabine, and at the same time persuade her to give him Annelise.

'I'll make us some tea,' Hope said quietly.

The kitchen was poky and dark, with a small window positioned so high it was impossible to see out of it. At the sink, a tap was dripping, and when Hope turned it to fill the kettle, it gave a metallic screech of resistance that then set off a clanking pipe. She had just found a match to light the gas on the stove when Otto joined her. He was cradling his daughter in such a loving and protective way, Hope feared he had

41

something terrible to tell her, that perhaps Sabine was seriously ill. On top of everything else they had to cope with, please not that.

'We need to talk to you, Hope,' he said. His English was good, even better than Sabine's. 'Please, forget about the tea, come and sit with us.'

She did as he said and followed him back into the drawing room, where Sabine was now sitting on one end of the couch, twisting a handkerchief around her fingers. Otto indicated the chair opposite his wife. Hope sat down and waited for him to settle next to Sabine, Annelise now perched contentedly on his lap.

'We want to ask you to do something,' he said. 'It will mean a very big sacrifice for you, and for us too.'

Hope saw the look that was exchanged between husband and wife. She swallowed. 'Go on,' she said.

'Tomorrow you return to England. We want you to take Annelise with you. That way we will know she'll be safe.'

Sabine stifled a sob, putting the handkerchief to her mouth.

Hope stared at them both with incomprehension. She tried to speak but couldn't. She knew about the Kindertransport, the hundreds of Jewish children who were being put on trains to be taken to safety in England; it had been happening ever since Kristallnacht. But for Otto and Sabine to give her Annelise to look after? It was madness. She couldn't do it.

'But I've never looked after a baby before,' she

said at length. 'I wouldn't know the first thing to do. How could you possibly trust me with your precious child?'

'The alternative is for her to go to strangers and . . . ' Otto's voice broke. He swallowed. 'We don't want that for her; she's too young and precious. And we know that you would love her. You are her Tante Hope.'

'But you don't have to give her to me,' Hope said. 'You could come to London, the three of you. You could come tomorrow. Just leave this awful place. Come with me!'

Fresh tears began to roll down Sabine's face. 'We cannot take the risk of being stopped. People like us are trying to escape all the time but are being sent back. Always the officials find some kind of problem with the passport, or the papers. But you have a British passport; you can pretend that Annelise is your child. They won't stop you.'

'But there must be some other way. Why not apply for visas from — '

Otto shook his head. 'We've tried that. The queues for visas to go to Britain are endless. It's the same at the American consulate. Besides, I cannot leave my parents.' He took hold of Sabine's hand, which lay on her lap, and raised it to his lips to kiss it. 'I've tried to make Sabine leave without me, but she won't.' He blinked. 'Hope,' he went on, 'you must take Annelise with you. You must take her tomorrow. War is coming very soon. We hear talk all the time. Soldiers are soon to be massed against the border with Poland. Once war is officially declared, there will be no escape.'

It was late when Hope finally left. Otto walked her to the tram stop. His last words to her as she climbed onto the tram were to say that he and Sabine would bring Annelise to her in the morning, but only once she was alone and on her way to the station. They didn't want Gerda and Heinrich to get wind of the plan in case they tried to put a stop to it. Not because they didn't care about their granddaughter, but because these days their loyalty lay first and foremost with the Third Reich.

The tram ride back to her in-laws passed in a daze. But Hope was in for another shock when she arrived at Kurzestrasse. Gerda handed her a telegram.

Please come home to Island House at once. Your father is dangerously ill.

6

It was a hot, airless day in Venice, and on the fourth floor of her stifling apartment overlooking the Rio di San Vio, Allegra Salvato, half-heartedly fanning herself with her hand, contemplated the telegram she had just received.

Your uncle is dangerously ill. Please come home to Island House.

Could it be true? Could Jack Devereux really be dangerously ill? And why those words — *come home?* Island House wasn't her home. It never had been, not really. Italy was the only home she had truly known. If she belonged anywhere, it was here.

Feeling nauseous with the heat, she sighed and gave up fanning herself; the effort far exceeded the benefit. A storm was on the way. She pulled absently at the fabric of her dress, which was sticking to her clammy skin. It was days like this, when Venice felt as though the very last breath of air had been sucked out of it, that she regretted submitting to Luigi's will that she move here. She had been happy in Genova, with her apartment facing out over the harbour, but Luigi had insisted, had said it would be better for her career.

At the thought of Luigi, a fresh surge of stomach-churning anger rose within her. He had betrayed her in every way possible. He'd lied, cheated and stolen from her and made her look a fool in front of everyone who mattered. Everything he'd promised her had been a lie. She was sickened at her own naivety; that she had allowed herself to trust him. Oh, how convincing he had been, promising her the world, at the same time swearing his undying love for her, when all he'd cared about was lining his own pocket by exploiting her talent. Now it looked like he had robbed her of even that.

They had met in a small theatre in Parma eighteen months ago, when he had come to her dressing room after her performance as Violetta in *La Traviata*. Introducing himself as an impresario, and her newest and biggest fan, he announced his intention to turn her into a great opera star, if she would let him. She was, he said, an artiste who needed careful nurturing and the opportunity to perform in the very best opera houses, not just in Italy but around the world. He told her he would love nothing more than to be her future manager, to share her wonderful talent with the audiences she so richly deserved.

He had taken her out for supper to explain how serious he was, and how mesmerising he'd found her performance. He had declared her a true exponent of the art of verismo; that she was a charismatic actress as well as a sublime singer. Allegra knew perfectly well that he was exaggerating, but with Alberto Ferro, her manager, safely out of the way in Genova, she had allowed this handsome stranger to charm her. With his shock of thick black hair oiled artfully into place, and his flattery and confident manner, he made a refreshing change to

Alberto's intense demeanour and strict declaration that she would only make it to the top by working hard and applying herself diligently to daily singing lessons for hours on end. It would take time, was his constant refrain, time, work and patience.

There was little room for fun in Allegra's life the way Alberto managed it, and so by the time Luigi had wined and dined her, she had made up her mind to accept his offer. Even if only half of what he promised her came true, it would be better than the never-ending run of second-rate theatre engagements Alberto had planned for her. Alberto had no vision or ambition; he was happy with the status quo. Twenty years older than Allegra, he was also very much in love with her, and by his own admission was frightened of losing her. His adoration had begun to make her feel trapped, and in Luigi, and all he was offering her, she saw her chance not just to be the star she dreamt of being, but to be free.

Within days she had cut her ties with Alberto and put her trust in Luigi as her manager. He insisted she leave Genova and move to Venice, and following intensive singing lessons with a new teacher of his choosing, her first performance under his guidance was in Rome, at the Teatro Reale dell'Opera. She sang the role of Asteria in Boito's opera *Nerone*, and to her delight received rave reviews, with special mention made of the emotional depth of her voice.

Her success there led to a busy run of bookings, with Luigi applying himself to finding her theatres in which to sing, though only those he considered worthy of her fine voice. Just as Allegra had suspected they would, they soon became lovers, despite him being married. He swore that his marriage was a sham, that as soon as he could free himself from his wife's clutches, he would marry Allegra. She just had to be patient and give him time. It seemed that she was destined to spend her life being patient.

But she willingly gave Luigi everything of herself, including her innermost secret hopes, which she'd harboured since she had been a little girl in the orphanage on the outskirts of Naples.

Her life at La Casa della Speranza — the House of Hope — had begun when she was two weeks old, after she had been abandoned there, wrapped in a blanket and put into the *ruota*, presumably by her mother. The nuns had named her Allegra in the belief that it would make her grow up to be happy and cheerful. The surname they'd given her — a foundling name — had been Salvato, meaning saved.

With the exception of Sister Assunta, who had been a pitiless tyrant, the nuns were not especially cruel, but they were driven by a quickness to find fault and mete out punishments as they saw fit, all in the name of God. Allegra was often punished for questioning something she was told to do, or for being sullen, but more often for her temper. Her closest friend from the age of five was Isabella, and such was the bond between them that they liked to pretend they were sisters. Then one day, out of the blue, Isabella's mother came for her to take her home, just as Isabella had said she always would. Allegra was eight years old at the time, and without realising what she was doing, she had expressed her sadness and loss by singing. Through song she felt an enormous release of emotion, an unburdening of her heart. She realised too that her voice had a strange power to it; it could touch those who heard her, making them cry sometimes.

Sister Maria, Allegra's favourite of the nuns, recognised her talent and encouraged her to sing as often as possible. She told Allegra that God had blessed her with a unique gift and she must never squander it; that she must dedicate it entirely to God.

With Isabella gone from her life in such a manner, Allegra could not help but wonder if one day her own mother might come to claim her. Or maybe she might be adopted, as some of the younger children were. She didn't think that very likely, as the men and women who visited the orphanage to pick out a child to take home with them did not usually want a child as old as she was; they wanted a sweet little baby they could call their own.

Shortly after Allegra's ninth birthday, Sister Maria took her aside one morning and explained that she had a visitor — a man all the way from England who was her uncle.

Allegra's first impression of Jack Devereux was of a giant of a man staring down at her. She trembled beneath the intensity of his unblinking eyes, conscious that he was scrutinising her for flaws, like the women in the market did when buying their fruit and vegetables. Scared that he might prod her with one of his large hands, she took a step back. He spoke no Italian, and so when he addressed her, she couldn't understand him. Only with the help of Sister Maria, who knew a little English, did she learn what he was saying. Apparently in England she had three cousins — two boys and a girl — who were very much looking forward to meeting her. All she could do was nod. Then the man asked her, 'Will you sing for me? I'm told you have a beautiful voice.'

Startled by his request, she was nonetheless happy to do as he asked, for here was something that might please him, and it suddenly seemed important to her to do that. But when she opened her mouth to sing, nothing came out, not a note, just an ugly croak. It was as if she'd been struck dumb. Sister Maria smiled encouragingly and she tried once more. But again she could produce nothing but a croak. Embarrassed, she began to cry, which made her feel even more foolish. From that day on, it was to become a fear that haunted her: that she would freeze on stage and be unable to sing.

Several hours later, clutching a small suitcase, she was climbing into the back of the stranger's car. She gave a hesitant wave to those who'd lined up to see her go and found herself near to tears as the car moved off. In a wild moment of panic, she realised she didn't want to leave and tried to open the car door, but the man who said he was her uncle snapped forward in his seat and put a hand out to stop her, making her feel like a prisoner.

Boisterous voices floated up from the *rio* beneath Allegra, children's voices that interrupted her thoughts and brought her sharply back to the present and the cause of her anger: Luigi.

He had finally left his wife, but not for Allegra; instead for a girl who was not yet nineteen. Worse still, he had taken all of Allegra's earnings, having put them in a bank account to which he alone had access. 'Let me worry about your finances,' he'd assured her. 'That way you can concentrate on your singing. You mustn't be distracted by the mundane.'

It hadn't only been her earnings Luigi had stolen; he had helped himself to the bulk of her trust fund. She didn't know what angered her most: his greed and betrayal, or her own stupidity. She should never have trusted him to the extent she had, but he had been so utterly convincing. Nothing had been genuine about him, least of all the supposed theatre bookings he'd put in place for the months ahead. Not a single one existed. What was more, he'd run up debts far and wide, and she was tainted by association.

He'd left her with nothing: no income, no bookings, much less her dignity. Even the rent on her modest apartment was going to be a problem, and to her disgust, the landlord, Signor Pezzo, had begun to hint there were other ways she could pay him if money was tight. His suggestion made her skin crawl; nothing would induce her to fall so low, to allow that hideous man, with his foul sulphurous breath and filthy hands, anywhere near her. A proud fascist, only last week he had taken pleasure in evicting a Jewish couple from the apartment below Allegra's. He'd claimed that they were difficult tenants and made too much noise, but Allegra had never heard a sound from them.

That sort of thing had been happening a lot since last year, when the new racial laws had been made. Jews were now forbidden from doing all sorts of jobs, and their children weren't allowed to attend Italian schools either, or go to university. What horrified Allegra most was how easily her fellow Italians had accepted the new laws, which anybody could see were just plain wrong. But even she was careful to whom she voiced such an opinion. It seemed likely that things would soon get a lot worse, with Mussolini only too keen to adopt the ideology of Nazi anti-Semitism in order to curry favour with that awful Hitler.

She heaved a long, weary sigh. She suddenly felt so very old and tired, and she was only twenty-six! She returned her gaze to the telegram and its demand for her to return to Island House. Presumably Roddy Fitzwilliam had sent it. Dear old Roddy; he'd always had a soft spot for her, and she for him. Unlike the rest of them, who never allowed her to forget that she was illegitimate — the bastard child of Harry Devereux — he treated her as if she counted for something.

But to return to England, to subject herself to God knew what? Why would Jack Devereux care if she were there by his bedside at the end? What difference would it make? Why put herself back in the very situation she had fled? All that sneering from Arthur, the mock-pity from Kit and the superior air from Hope; why return to that? Especially now that her singing career was all but over. For in the shock of what she'd discovered about Luigi, her voice had abandoned her. Every time she tried to sing, she was once again that trembling, anxious child standing before the strange man in the orphanage unable to utter more than a mortifying croak. How could she put herself through the humiliation of the family knowing that her dreams had come to nothing?

But there was something else — or rather someone else — that she might have to face back at Island House, and she really didn't think she was brave enough to do that. She had been so heartless in her treatment of him, but she had known no other way to pursue her dream. Surely he had understood that? But had he forgiven her?

Elijah Hartley. Allegra hadn't thought of him in a very long time; she had deliberately consigned him to the past, to her childhood. But he had been her one true friend in England. Would he still be there in Melstead St Mary, or had he also left?

She read the telegram again.

Your uncle is dangerously ill. Please come home to Island House.

If Uncle Jack was about to die, and given the dramatic downturn in her own fortunes, might it be prudent to swallow her pride and do exactly as the telegram instructed? Was that such a bad thing to think, that Jack's death might be an answer to a prayer?

Far away in the sultry sky, she heard the first ominous rumble of thunder. The storm was about to break.

7

Now that the other passengers who had been with him since Liverpool Street station had left the train, Kit had the carriage to himself. He stretched out his legs in front of him and settled in for the remainder of his journey to Melstead St Mary.

With London far behind him, the sight of the softly undulating Suffolk countryside stirred in him a mixture of emotions: pleasure at seeing again the familiar landscape he'd always loved, but also a feeling of trepidation for what lay ahead at Island House.

He had been away on a walking holiday in the Brecon Beacons and hadn't received the telegram until he'd returned home to his flat late last night — two days after it had been originally sent. He'd telephoned Island House straight away, despite the lateness of the hour, and had spoken briefly to Roddy, who'd urged him to waste no time in travelling up to see his father.

No matter how hard he tried to imagine a world in which his father no longer existed, Kit simply could not picture it. Men like Jack Devereux did not die; they were the toughest of old war-horses that lived forever. They were a breed apart from pathetic mortals like Kit which was how his father had always made him feel: hopelessly inadequate and incapable of doing anything right.

As a young boy, he'd suffered the ignominy of being a sickly child, rarely getting through a winter without succumbing to a debilitating chest infection, or coming down with some other ailment that kept him bedridden. When he was older, it was plain to all that he hadn't inherited an ounce of his father's hard-nosed business acumen, and not really knowing what he wanted to do, he'd drifted into reading modern history at Oxford. After graduating, he'd gone to work at a bank in London, thinking naively that it might please his father. He'd been at the bank for what seemed like the longest and most tedious two years of his life, and the thought of spending the rest of it doing something so meaningless made him feel sick at heart.

But change was in the air. It was a menacing change, but one that would give Kit the chance to do something of value, even if it meant he lost his life in the process, which the defeatist in him believed would be the inevitable outcome. Only a fool would think that war with Germany was now avoidable. It wasn't. Everybody with whom he came in contact believed the same, and perversely, he wished the prime minister, Neville Chamberlain, would just get on with it and declare war. It would be preferable to the stultifying boredom of what Kit was currently doing.

He wondered how Hope would cope with being at war with Germany. Would her loyalties be torn? Kit had always looked up to his sister, who was three years his senior. He had been fascinated as a child by her ability to draw with such skill and imagination, and he admired her hugely for having gone to art school and subsequently making a career for herself as a book illustrator. He wished he had half her talent and her clear sense of purpose.

According to old photographs, Hope was very like their mother, Maud, with wide cheekbones, and a smooth, straight jaw that ended with the narrow curve of her chin. She had been a serious child, quiet and withdrawn, losing herself in her world of make-believe, creating stories of fairies, elves, pixies and woodland creatures. Some of Kit's happiest boyhood memories, particularly when he'd been confined to bed, were of Hope telling him stories of her own devising, accompanied by exquisite little drawings.

He missed the closeness he and his sister had once shared — they'd been allies against their bully of an older brother, as well as the voice of reason when it came to their volatile cousin, Allegra. But since her husband's death, Hope had isolated herself from the family, even Kit, and the sting of it still pained him. He had thought himself exempt from her condemnation, but Hope had lumped him in with the rest of the family and rebuffed all his attempts to contact her. He wished he knew why. What had he ever done to upset her?

He held out no hope of seeing his sister at Island House. Why would she come when their father had been so vehemently opposed to her marrying the man she loved? A man he had never even met. As a consequence of that opposition, Hope, invariably the peacemaker of the family, had changed overnight and refused to speak to their father ever again. She also defied him by marrying Dieter less than a week later, inviting no one from the family to the wedding, not even Kit. Again, and despite her subsequent apology, he still felt the sting of having been excluded.

Her expression when he'd last seen her — he'd run into her by chance in London — had been one of bleak misery and reflected what he worried had become a blighted heart. He suspected that her mourning for Dieter was as devout as her sworn vow never to forgive their father for declining to give his blessing on her marriage.

She wasn't alone in harbouring a grudge, for Kit too had his reasons for keeping his distance from his family. For him, it was his brother, Arthur, whom he couldn't abide. The man's arrogance knew no bounds, nor his sense of entitlement, which explained why, three years ago, he had had no compunction in stealing from under Kit's nose his then girlfriend, Irene, the sister of one of his college friends.

Stupidly Kit had taken Irene home to meet his family, a mistake on his part because he'd only done it to show her off to his father, hoping absurdly to impress him — she was the daughter of Sir John Collingwood, a bigwig at the War Office. At the time, Kit had naively imagined himself in love with Irene, but then Arthur had made his move and that had put paid to anything further between them.

Irene and Arthur became engaged five months

later and were married a short while afterwards. On principle, Kit had not attended the wedding and had not exchanged more than a few words with his brother since that fateful day he'd brought Irene home to Island House. It was petty of him, he knew, but the hole had been dug and he had no desire to climb out of it. Perfunctory civility was the best he could manage when it came to Arthur.

* * *

At Melstead St Mary, he alighted from the train amidst clouds of steam and the slamming of doors. As the stationmaster blew his whistle, Kit spotted Arthur striding on ahead along the platform. He must have been in one of the carriages at the front of the train.

Roddy had informed Kit last night on the telephone that a car would be waiting for him, and sure enough, there was a smart-looking Bentley parked outside the station. Still ahead of him, and presumably oblivious to his presence, Arthur came to an abrupt stop when the driver's door of the Bentley opened and out stepped an exceptionally attractive woman in a large-brimmed hat. She was elegantly dressed in a pair of cream tailored trousers with a navy-blue short-sleeved top nipped in at the waist, and a pair of stylish sunglasses covered her eyes.

Whoever she was, she had the satisfying effect of stopping Arthur in his tracks.

8

When Romily had said she would drive Jack's Bentley to the station to meet Kit and Arthur, Roddy had asked if she really wanted to put herself in the firing line in that way. 'A taxi would suffice,' he'd said.

'And have them consider me a coward?' she'd responded. 'No, no, much better I go and meet them myself and break the ice.'

'How about I come with you, just in case there's any awkwardness?'

'I'd feel happier with you keeping Jack company,' Romily had said firmly.

She had also reasoned that she didn't want to give the impression that she was playing the part of lady of the house awaiting the arrival of her guests. Greeting them at the door implied a level of prerogative that she didn't feel was her right. Putting herself in the role of chauffeur suited her far better, and might make Jack's sons more favourably disposed towards her.

But judging by the expression on the arrogantly handsome face of the dark-haired man whom she recognised from photos as Arthur, she had not achieved that objective. Some yards behind him was a far more appealing-looking young man whom she took to be Kit. Tall and slim, he was dressed in a rumpled jacket and equally rumpled flannels with an open-necked tennis shirt. His hair was fair, with flecks of gold shot through it, and he had an interestingly aesthetic face. In contrast, Arthur, in a sombre dark suit, as if dressed for the office — or a funeral — had a stockier build that hinted at middle age well before its time.

If the situation weren't so grave, Romily might have felt anxious about this encounter, but Jack's state of health had worsened dramatically overnight and she didn't need Dr Garland to tell her that things were bad, very bad indeed. Her job today, and in the days to come, was to try and help bring about the rapprochement Jack desired for his family, to smooth the waters. If he were able to do it himself, Romily knew that Jack would apologise for all the mistakes he now acknowledged he'd made, but speech was beyond him. Would his family put aside their differences when they saw their father; would their hearts soften that he had been reduced to such a sorry state?

At the thought of how ill her darling Jack was, tears welled up in Romily's eyes and she had to fight hard to keep them from spilling over. She loved him so much, and the thought that she was about to lose him filled her with a sadness she had never known before. But then she had never loved any man the way she loved Jack.

Glad of the sunglasses she was wearing, she steeled herself. There would be time for tears later; now was not the time to succumb to the pain of what she knew lay ahead for her. Instead she had to rally her courage and ensure that Jack's last wishes were upheld. She pushed her shoulders back and moved away from the car to greet his sons.

61

'You must be Arthur,' she said, extending her hand. 'I'm here to take you to Island House. And this,' she said, looking over his shoulder, 'must be Kit.'

Ignoring Romily, and her hand, Arthur spun round. 'I didn't know *you* were on the train, brother mine,' he said. He sounded as though he were accusing Kit of some unpardonable offence.

'Likewise,' said Kit. 'But then I wasn't in first class. How do you do?' he said to Romily, shaking her hand and smiling with an engaging frankness. 'It's very kind of you to meet us. We'd have made do with a taxi.'

'That's what Roddy said, but I vetoed the suggestion.'

Arthur turned his hostile eyes back on her. 'Having established who *we* are, perhaps you'd care to do us the courtesy of telling us who you are?' he said.

'I'm Romily,' she replied evasively, deciding to put off a full explanation. 'Shall we get going? I'm sure you're anxious to see your father. You can throw your luggage in the boot.'

'I must apologise for my brother's rudeness,' Kit said from the back of the car once they were on their way. Just as she'd guessed he would, Arthur had opted to sit in the front with Romily.

'It's quite all right,' she said, 'I appreciate that it's a difficult time for you.'

'How is our father?' asked Kit.

She met his gaze in the rear-view mirror. 'Extremely ill, I'm afraid.'

Arthur twisted his head to look at her. 'And

just how do you know so much about our father's state of health? You don't look like a nurse; you're much too expensively dressed. Are you the latest in his long line of mistresses?'

Romily changed gear and pressed her foot down hard on the accelerator, causing Arthur's head to bounce back with some force. She decided to dispense with her plan to break the news gently. 'I'm neither,' she said. 'I'm Romily Temple-Devereux, your stepmother.'

In the silence that followed, she drove at speed, her eyes firmly on the road. So much for wanting to smooth the waters!

Until this moment, she had kept an open mind about Jack's family, but if Arthur's rudeness was anything to go by, she had an uphill struggle ahead of her. Having had a close relationship with her own mother and father, it was difficult for her to comprehend how anybody else's family could drift apart. Jack had explained to her that he knew he was mostly to blame for pushing his children away. 'I should never have abandoned them into the care of nannies to the extent I did,' he had said when she first asked him why they never visited him, 'but I thought I was doing the right thing. I was alone, and with my business interests taking up so much of my time, I thought a professional nanny would make a far better job of looking after the children than I could. But I fear now that I got it wrong.'

Romily could understand the dilemma in which Jack had found himself; it couldn't have been easy. Of course the simplest thing, and what a lot of men in his position did, would have been to marry again, if merely for the sake of the children. But as Jack had said, until Romily came into his life, marriage could not have been further from his mind.

'I fell in love with you that second evening we spent together,' he told her, 'and I knew then that I wanted to spend the rest of my life with you.'

'Only the second evening?' she'd replied. 'I'm disappointed.'

'Go on then,' he'd said. 'When did you think you loved me?'

'It was when you took me home after our first dinner,' she'd confessed. 'I couldn't stop thinking about you all night. I wanted to telephone you and just listen to your voice. You could have recited pages and pages of the dullest balance sheets and I'd have been utterly entranced.'

He'd laughed and admitted he'd felt exactly the same way.

Romily steeled herself once more not to cry at the painfully poignant memory, and in the continuing silence, she slowed her speed and swung the car sharply through the brick posts that marked the entrance to Island House.

It was Kit who spoke first. 'I've just realised who you are,' he said. 'You're Romily Temple the crime author, aren't you? I knew I recognised the name.'

'Guilty as charged,' said Romily, glancing at her stepson in the rear-view mirror once more.

'When did the two of you marry?'

'A few weeks ago. In secret. We didn't want to

make a big splash of it.'

'Well, well, *well*,' drawled Arthur, 'how very convenient for you that our father should fall ill so soon afterwards.'

Resisting the urge to respond to his vile remark, Romily brought the car to a halt alongside Dr Garland's Austin Seven. Even before she'd switched off the engine, Arthur was pushing open the passenger door to get out. His loathing for her could not have been more palpable.

'I know this must be awkward for you,' she said, out of the car and opening the boot so they could help themselves to their luggage, 'but I do hope you can put aside your surprise, and any animosity you might feel towards me, and remember why you're here.'

'That's what I'm beginning to wonder about,' sneered Arthur. 'Just why *are* we here? Other than to give our father one last opportunity to rub our noses in his contempt for us before he does us all a favour and dies.'

It was all Romily could do not to raise her hand and slap his arrogant face. How could the Jack she knew and loved have possibly produced such an odious son?

'That's a low shot, even by your standards,' muttered Kit.

At the sound of the front door opening, the group turned as one towards the house.

'Ah, the faithful lapdog is in residence, I see.' Arthur's voice took on a mocking superiority at the sight of Roddy standing on the doorstep. 'On hand, no doubt, to inform us that we're to be disinherited in favour of our new stepmother.'

'Oh do shut up, Arthur,' said Kit. 'You're not making this any easier for us.'

'I'm merely saying what we're both thinking. And if you wanted things to be easier, you should have stayed away. Take it from me, it can only get a lot worse from here on.'

9

Jack could hear distant voices. Men's voices. Was that Arthur he could hear talking to Roddy? And Kit? Were they here at last? What about the girls? Or was he dreaming?

Distinguishing between what was real and what his subconscious conjured while he slept was becoming more and more difficult. He felt trapped between continuously sliding parallel worlds, perpetually disorientated, with no idea what day or time it was. Right now, though, he knew it was daytime; the sun was streaming in through the window, causing motes of dust to dance in the shafts of light. As a child, he'd been fascinated by the sight. His mother had spun him a yarn when he'd been very young that it was magic dust sprinkled by the fairies. He'd told his own children the same story, but perhaps he hadn't been very convincing, for only Hope had believed him. Or maybe she was the only one who had felt inclined to humour him.

He wished Hope were here now. He so badly wanted to beg her forgiveness. He'd been wrong to want to deny her happiness with the man she loved. Romily had made him see that; had made him understand that there was nothing more important or powerful than love and forgiveness.

'We don't plan with whom we fall in love,' she'd said. 'Look at us; it just happens when it happens. I call it a happy collision.'

How right she was. Falling in love again at his age had seemed about as likely as him dancing on the moon, but that day at Brooklands, when he'd first approached Romily having frequently seen her about the club, he had felt something astonishing happen to him. Something he hadn't believed he was still capable of feeling. After taking her for dinner, he'd promised to go straight out and buy one of her novels. To his shame, he'd never found time to read much before; work had always consumed him.

In the days that followed, when she had been too busy to see him again, he had found it difficult to concentrate on anything; all he could think of was being with this extraordinary woman. Yet at the same time he had wanted to deny what he felt, telling himself he was too old to succumb to such absurd behaviour. But after seeing her again, he'd known that he'd been given a special gift, a second chance to love once more. And to use Romily's analogy of a collision, she had hit him absolutely with all the force of a fast-moving train.

Experiencing such a profound sense of contentment and love with Romily had made him face a harsh truth: that since Maud's death, he'd stopped himself from feeling any real depth of emotion. Everything he'd done had been through a sense of duty, never through genuine love. Regret and bitterness had played their part too — why should others be happy when he could not find the key to it himself?

But fear had also been a factor. When the children had been young, he'd lived in fear of losing them, just as he'd lost Maud. He'd veered from being too protective and flying into a furious rage if they did anything that he considered put them at risk, to leaving them to their own devices in the belief they had to learn from their mistakes. There was no halfway house for him, no middle ground of showing them how much he cared. For he *had* cared, he just hadn't known how to show it.

From the far reaches of his memory he had a sudden picture of catching Kit and Hope playing on the frozen lily pond one winter when they were little. Fear at knowing they could so easily slip through the icy surface at any moment had tipped him over the edge of mere parental anxiety into a frenzy of wrath that must have terrified them. And hardened their hearts against him.

Was this his punishment then for being such a poor father and uncle? To be a burden to the woman he now loved? If so, the sooner he died the better. Except he didn't want to die. He wanted to live. Just not like this.

He had lost track of how many days he'd been imprisoned here in bed, no longer able to control his body, a body that had become a dead weight, his arms and legs too heavy to move. Was he imagining it, or did it become more useless each time he awoke from a deep sleep?

Sometimes when he woke he forgot he'd suffered a stroke and panicked. It took him a while to remember what had happened. Other times he was convinced that he was still asleep and this was all a dream. Was it even possible that he was dreaming now? Was the nurse sitting by the side of his bed reading a copy of *Picture Post* not real at all? And was the bird singing with such obscene joyfulness in the garden beyond the open window nothing but a figment of his imagination? If so, would he finally wake up properly and be his normal self again?

His last memory of normality had been of waiting for Romily to arrive home from her book tour. He hadn't said anything to her before she'd set off, but he'd been apprehensive about the errand she had volunteered to undertake while in Europe, worried that the German authorities would arrest her and throw her into some god-awful detention centre never to be seen again.

His mind lingered over the concern he'd felt while waiting for her to return, recalling how he would have moved heaven and earth to bring her back. Hell, he'd have declared war on Germany himself!

His eyelids heavy with tiredness, he gave in and closed them. He thought of the surprise he'd had in store for Romily on her return: a motoring trip up to the Lake District to watch Malcolm Campbell in his Bluebird attempt to beat his own world speed record on Coniston Water. He was just thinking that he must ask her if the attempt had taken place when his mind became muddled. What if he'd only dreamt that Romily had returned? What if she hadn't and she'd been arrested? The thought so alarmed him, he tried to call to her. But it was hopeless; nothing came out of his mouth but a distorted grunt.

A thin, pale face loomed out of nowhere over

him and made him start. Round pebble-like eyes behind spectacles stared into his. He tried to call to Romily again and throw back the bed-clothes, but his arms wouldn't move. Or was this strange woman stopping him? Had she tied his arms down?

'It's all right, Mr Devereux,' she said. 'Don't fret now.'

She disappeared out of his sight line. Where had she gone? And who the hell was she?

Then he remembered. She was a nurse. She was here to look after him. There were two of them. But as the confusion cleared from his mind, and he relaxed in the knowledge that Romily was safely here at Island House with him, his heart gave an abrupt and agonising jolt. Some kind of reflex action made him want to clench his fist and put it to his chest, but his hand wouldn't move.

He struggled to catch his breath, gasping and gulping like a desperate drowning man. Was he having a heart attack? He tried to call for help, but he couldn't get the words out. The pain in his chest was building, as though his heart was being crushed. Suddenly raging hot, the blood rushing in his ears, he squeezed his eyes against the pain, convinced that the battle was lost. This really was the end and now he would never be able to tell his family how sorry he was.

Not yet, he wanted to cry out; let me see my beautiful wife one more time. And my family, let me make it right with . . .

But he got no further. He breathed his last choking breath and darkness engulfed him.

★ ★ ★

It was Romily who found him, Nurse Nichols having informed her as she took off her hat in the hallway after collecting Kit and Arthur from the station that Mr Devereux seemed agitated over something.

One look at his face and she knew straight away that he was dead. With a shaking hand, she felt for a pulse, her own heart beating wildly against her ribs.

There was no pulse, just as there was no sign of breath coming from his open mouth. Very tenderly she closed his lips and his eyes, then she lay down on the bed beside her husband, resting her cheek next to his, her hand placed protectively across his chest.

'Oh my darling,' she murmured through the tears that were spilling onto his face, 'why did you have to leave me so soon?'

A knock at the door made her start.

'Go away!' she cried, dreading that it would be Arthur demanding to see his father. 'Leave us alone!'

But when the door opened, it was Roddy who stepped into the room. For a moment he stood perfectly still, staring at her lying on the bed with Jack, her face wet with tears.

'He's dead,' she managed to say. 'And I wasn't here with him when he left me. I should have stayed, I shouldn't have . . . ' Her voice trailed away, and with a choking sob she buried her face in Jack's neck and wept.

10

'Dead then. Dead and buried, and the family not here in time to speak to him.'

'I told you no good would come of that fast piece moving in with him.'

'Practically half his age. It's a wonder he lasted as long as he did. Did you see that showy hat she was wearing? Quite inappropriate for a funeral.'

'And the fact they married in secret tells us everything we need to know. She must have been after his money all the time.'

'It's not like she doesn't have enough of her own. I read in the newspaper that she's a wealthy woman in her own right from those dreadful books she writes.'

The three women pondered this while they drank their tea. They had felt it only right that they do their duty and attend the funeral service for Jack Devereux; they were now reviving themselves at the Cobbles Tea Room.

At length, Edith Lawton lowered her cup to its saucer. 'Must have well and truly put the cat amongst the pigeons when the family discovered he'd married.'

Ivy Swann nodded and helped herself to a slice of seed cake from the cake stand. 'I'd like to be a fly on the wall while the will's being read.'

'Oh, there'll be ructions to be sure,' said Elspeth Grainger. 'Did you see how the children could barely look at each other? I thought

Allegra might actually slap Arthur at one point.'

'And what about him moving out of Island House and into the Half Moon Hotel with his wife? What does that say about the family?'

Ivy nodded her head again so vigorously her hat slipped to one side. She straightened it and leaned in closer to the other two women. 'I heard from my sister Cynthia that the widowed daughter, Hope, the one who married a German, arrived home with a baby. A baby no one knew anything about.'

'I heard that it's her German niece.'

'Maybe it is, maybe it isn't.'

'When did her husband die?'

'About a year ago. So it could be hers.'

'Then why lie about it?'

'Search me. But I know this much, I could believe anything of that family.'

The other two women tutted, and together the three of them shuddered in unison.

11

'I'm afraid there is no ambiguity; those are the terms of the will. It's unusual, I grant you, how he's left things, but then Jack was not the most orthodox of men.'

With a loud snort of derision, Arthur all but leapt to his feet, roughly dislodging his wife's hand, which had been resting on his forearm throughout the reading. 'Unusual doesn't come close!' he exclaimed angrily. 'The very idea is preposterous, and I for one do not have the time for such nonsense.'

His gaze still on the document in front of him, Roddy spoke in a quiet and steady voice. 'Then you will forfeit the generous inheritance your father wished for you. It's as simple as that.'

'The only simple aspect to this absurd business is that it's nothing short of blackmail from the grave. I have my principles; I will not be told what to do by Jack Devereux of all people, alive or dead! It's the most divisive and contentious will I've ever heard.'

Roddy removed his spectacles and looked steadily at Arthur with a gaze as unyielding as any Romily had seen. 'As a lawyer, I have come across far more complicated wills than this, but as you wish, Arthur. However, I'm not sure how the others will feel about your decision. As your father's will states only too clearly, the four of you must spend a minimum of seven days together here at Island House, as of now, or not one of you will inherit. Which means you can forget your share of the proceeds from the business concerns your father sold eighteen months ago, the stocks and shares too. Do you really want to let your pride stop you from benefiting from all that?'

A silence fell on the room as Kit, Allegra and Hope turned to look at Arthur. From her chair positioned at the far end of the dining table, a seat that distanced her from everybody else, Romily doubted any of them wanted to spend a second longer than necessary in Arthur's company, but she guessed they were prepared to put aside their dislike of him in order to go along with Jack's wishes. She wanted to believe that they weren't guided purely by the sizeable bequests Jack had put in place for them, but that they could see beyond that. Jack had truly wanted them to be a family again, to put the past to rest in a way they couldn't while he was still alive. In the time she had spent with him, she had come to know that this stick-and-carrot approach was typical.

The silence was broken abruptly by the sound of crying, loud crying that had been brewing for some minutes. Until now it had been an occasional grizzle of protest, probably from boredom and having to sit quietly. Romily could sympathise.

'For pity's sake, Hope, can't you keep that brat quiet? And God knows why you think it's appropriate to bring it in here for the reading of our father's will!'

'She's not an 'it', Arthur,' said Hope, lifting the child and putting her awkwardly against her shoulder in an effort to distract her. 'Her name is Annelise, and if the poor girl is crying, it's because she's picking up on your blatant hostility.'

'If I'm hostile, it's down to not being able to think straight. Why don't you take her out of the room? For the life of me I can't begin to think what possessed you to agree to have her in the first place.'

'She did it because she's a decent human being,' Kit intervened. 'Now why don't you sit down so we can decide what we're going to do?'

'Yes,' said Allegra, roused from her air of bored detachment. 'As always, you're making us all suffer your ill-temper.'

'That's rich coming from you!'

Every inch the operatic prima donna, Allegra rolled her large expressive eyes theatrically and gave a weary shrug of her shoulders — the distinctive gesture of an Italian. 'I had hoped you might have changed since I last saw you, Arthur, but you're still as obnoxious as I remember, if not worse.' She simmered with a deliciously haughty air that reminded Romily of a cat watching its prey, trying to decide whether it was worth the effort to pounce.

'Please don't talk to my husband that way,' said Irene as Arthur sat down heavily next to her, but not before glaring across the table. 'As far as I can see, he's the only one prepared to be honest here. The rest of you are cowards and too browbeaten by your father to speak your mind.'

She turned her gaze on Kit as though deliberately singling him out. Knowing their history from Jack, Romily winced.

Next to Kit, Allegra drummed her fingernails on the table. '*Va bene, cara*,' she said, her voice low and honeyed. 'If it's honesty you want, then maybe this suits you better — I'd sooner lock myself in a cold dark cellar with a barrel of scorpions for company than spend a week in your husband's company.'

In spite of everything, Romily had to bite back a smile. It was the nearest she had got to smiling since Jack's death. Until today she had shut herself away, too grief-stricken to play the part of hostess tending to the needs of her guests. Let them get on with fighting amongst themselves, she had thought miserably. It was the first time in her life she had been unable to cope; the first time ever that she had wanted to run away from something. She had been desperate to return to London, to mourn for Jack in private, away from his family. But Roddy had urged her to stay and help him arrange the funeral in the way Jack would have wanted it to be conducted — as simple as possible and not a mawkish affair.

It was seeing how devastated Roddy was by Jack's death that had helped Romily to find the strength to face each day. She had wept on his shoulder, pouring out her grief. 'Dear girl,' he had soothed, his own tears mingling with hers. Sharing their grief had helped both of them.

Florence had been a godsend, bringing meals upstairs to Romily's room — the room that she and Jack had shared as lovers, and then as husband and wife. Initially Romily had not been able to eat so much as a crumb, and no amount of coaxing on Florence's part could persuade her. But eventually, and at Dr Garland's insistence, she had forced herself to try some of what Mrs Partridge had so solicitously prepared in order to tempt her.

As well as trays of food, Florence had brought her updates on Jack's family, as had Roddy. It was no surprise to know that Arthur had immediately assumed the role of head of the household, and in so doing had offended Mrs Partridge by making unreasonable demands and rebuking Florence for not polishing his shoes as he'd instructed. So incensed was Romily by his high-handed rudeness that she emerged briefly from her room to put the upstart in his place, but was greeted with the news that both Kit and Arthur had just left for London and would return for the funeral. They had both done so yesterday — Kit to Island House, and his brother and Irene opting to take a room at the Half Moon Hotel in the village.

Their return coincided with Allegra and Hope's arrival: Allegra in the afternoon, having travelled from Venice, and Hope in the evening with the surprise of a child in her arms. The selfless act of kindness Hope had carried out in bringing this poor infant to safety from Germany had given Romily cause to think well of her. Here was someone who cared, who had a heart; unlike Arthur, who had iced water running through his veins, and a stone where a heart should be. He was probably the sort of man who, as a boy, had enjoyed taunting small animals and found pleasure in pulling the wings off butterflies. But if he thought he could treat Romily with the kind of arrogant rudeness with which he treated everyone else, he was in for a shock: this was her house now, as Roddy had informed them during the reading of Jack's will.

While he still had the power of speech, Jack had told Romily that he had made a new will while she'd been away in Europe, and that as well as leaving her an impressive portfolio of stocks and shares, he wanted her to have Island House and all it contained. At no stage had she let on to the family that she knew this, deeming it better for it to come formally from Roddy's lips. She was touched that Jack had gifted her this beautiful house, a place that she had loved on sight. But she would happily live in the meanest little hovel if it meant Jack was still alive. That their happiness had been cut short so soon, and that he had died alone and without her by his side, broke her heart.

With tears filling her eyes, she turned to look out at the garden through the open window, remembering her first visit, how perfectly idyllic it had seemed. 'But it's not actually an island, is it?' she'd said to Jack when he was showing her around.

'You sound disappointed,' he had responded.

'No, not at all, only the name suggests it is.'

'Well, I'm told some Georgian wag who had the original part of the house built decided it had the feel of an island, with the stream feeding the pond and then skirting around the house down into the next valley, and named it accordingly.'

The more Romily saw of the house, the more she came to regard it as a real island, set apart from the rest of the world, an oasis to which she and Jack could retreat.

Staring out at the garden now, and at the pond beyond with its spectacular display of flowering water lilies, she recalled the warm evening last month when Jack had taken her down to the boathouse, helped her into the wooden dinghy and rowed her into the middle of the pond. Without warning, he had thrown the oars into the water, startling a pair of moorhens. 'What did you do that for?' she'd asked, amused.

'Have I ever told you that you have the most beautiful violet eyes?' he'd replied.

'Yes, you have. And you haven't answered my question.'

'I'm going to ask you to marry me, and until you say yes, we're marooned here.'

She had laughed and watched the oars drift slowly away from the boat on the current that fed the pond. 'And if I accept your proposal, how do you plan to get us back onto dry land?'

'First tell me your answer,' he'd said, leaning forward, his expression now intensely serious.

'Oh, it's a yes, of course it is. I'm just surprised it's taken you this long to get around to asking me.'

His expression softened. 'I needed time to pluck up the courage. But are you sure you want to throw in your lot with a man so much older than you?'

'My darling Jack, I threw in my lot with you

the day we met at Brooklands. Now then, have we dispensed with the small talk? Are you going to kiss me to seal the deal?'

He had, and with a long and very sure kiss. When they finally drew apart, she said, 'On the basis that we're now officially betrothed, I'm eager to hear your plan for getting us back to the bank.'

He smiled. 'Oh, that's easily done.' Slipping off his shoes, he stood up, causing the wooden dinghy to rock precariously, then with a cry of 'Geronimo!' threw himself into the water, splashing her comprehensively into the bargain.

'You're mad!' she called out to him when he surfaced some distance from the boat.

'Mad with love for you! Are you coming in?'

'Just you try and stop me.' In seconds flat, she had stripped off down to her underclothes and dived in too.

The memory of that evening, of the two of them drying off in the boathouse and making love on a blanket on the floor in the soft glow of a storm lantern, made her close her eyes, both to recapture the moment entirely, but also to stop the tears that were once again threatening to expose her pain. When she deemed it safe to open them again, she saw a fat bumblebee buzzing drunkenly amongst the roses immediately in front of the window, the fragrant scent of the dusky pink blooms discernible on the warm air.

She sighed, tempted to go outside to escape the sniping of this querulous family at war. Behind her, and with the angry exchanges continuing around the table, she could hear Hope trying unsuccessfully to settle the crying child.

On impulse, Romily rose from her seat. 'Hope,' she said, 'why don't I take Annelise for a walk around the garden? She must be bored out of her mind. I know I am.'

Hope looked back at her with a stunned expression on her face, as though Romily had just suggested she throw the child into the pond with a heavy weight tied around her neck.

'I would have thought you of all people would want to stay here and enjoy the spectacle of our humiliation right to the bitter end,' commented Arthur, regarding her with his unpleasantly pale grey eyes.

'I imagine there'll be plenty of opportunity for that in the coming days,' Romily said smoothly. 'The bitter end is indubitably a long way off yet.' Ignoring the intake of breath from both Arthur and his wife, she reached for the fractious child. Finding no resistance from Hope, who, to put it bluntly, looked exhausted from trying to comfort the distressed infant, she settled Annelise on her hip.

She nodded at Roddy on her way out of the room. He nodded in return, the gesture implying that he would fill her in later.

⋆　⋆　⋆

In the warm afternoon sunshine, Romily took the baby round to the back of the house, through the gated archway in the yew hedge to a small private garden that Jack had especially loved. It was directly outside his study, accessed through a pair of French doors. She had not had the courage to set foot inside the study yet; it was the room they had turned into a bedroom for him, and where he had died.

Now his body lay in the churchyard on the other side of the tall beech hedge that sheltered this part of the garden. From here she could see the solid square tower of St Mary's, the pews of which had been packed full earlier today, not only with curious or well-meaning people from the village, but also with Jack's friends and acquaintances from London.

Some of Romily's friends had attended the funeral too, including Sarah, who was still on crutches nursing her broken ankle. Both Romily's agent and editor had come, and she'd appreciated their support. They knew how much she had loved Jack; knew too that he was the first man to whom she had given her heart.

Before her friends had set off for the train to London, her agent had advised her to take it easy and not to rush back to work too soon. He'd cancelled an appearance in London she was booked to do at Foyle's next week, and she was grateful for that.

She settled Annelise on the lawn and sat down beside her. The little girl looked up at her, her intensely dark eyes filled with something Romily could only guess at. At ten months old, and with silky-fine blonde hair, she was a pretty little thing, almost doll-like she was so petite. Romily thought of the girl's parents and wondered how they were coping without her. They had to be going through hell. And the worst of it was, who knew how long Annelise would have to stay in Hope's care?

Shuffling over to Romily, the baby hauled herself up onto her lap and, as if thoroughly pleased with herself, beamed a hugely happy smile. Something deep inside Romily tugged at her heart. She had never aspired to being a mother, but in that instant, she wished Jack had left her with a child. Something tangible of him, something stronger than mere memories.

A tear slid down her cheek, and seeing it, Annelise frowned, reaching up and touched it with a small finger. It made Romily cry all the more.

12

Florence was in the kitchen with Mrs Partridge and Mrs Bunch, the last of the washing-up now dried and put away, the tea brewing and a freshly baked batch of rock cakes just out of the oven.

It had been a long day and it wasn't over yet, not with Mr Devereux's family around. They were an awkward lot, especially that Arthur. Every time he summoned Florence for something, he looked down his nose at her as though she were muck he'd stepped in. His wife wasn't much better either. Thank God they weren't actually staying here.

'Come on, Flo, come and sit yourself down,' said Mrs Partridge. 'Your tea's poured.'

Drying her hands, Florence took her place at the table gratefully. She'd been on her feet since first thing that morning, and as well as helping to prepare for the expected funeral guests, she had also looked after the baby for a couple of hours. She'd had no previous contact with babies before and had been more than a little anxious when Mrs Meyer had asked if she would mind the child for her while she attended the funeral. Florence had wanted to go to the church herself and pay her respects, but she hadn't felt it was her place to refuse the request. Luckily the baby had slept for a short time, making it possible for Florence to help Mrs Partridge with all that needed doing.

At the other end of the table, Mrs Bunch let out a long exhalation of breath like a train sending a whooshing cloud of steam into the air. She rubbed at her legs — her varicose veins were the bane of her life, she frequently complained, repeatedly telling anyone who would listen that she was a martyr to the wretched things. 'I'm gettin' too old for all this runnin' around,' she said, after taking a noisy slurp of her tea.

'Get away with you, Elsie,' said Mrs Partridge, passing her a plate of sandwiches left over from the guests. 'Plenty of good years left in you yet.' She nudged the plate towards Florence. 'Better eat up and enjoy the peace and quiet before the next round of demands from that lot.' She inclined her head towards the closed kitchen door, as though Mr Devereux's family were lurking on the other side of it.

'How long do you think they'll be holed up in the dining room?' asked Florence.

'Depends how complicated the will is, I suppose,' answered Mrs Partridge, 'and if the family start arguing over who gets what. Some folk can argue over just about anything when it comes to wills. I had a cousin who rowed something awful over the ugliest of china dogs.'

'Wouldn't surprise me if they gets nothin',' Mrs Bunch said through a mouthful of sandwich. 'It's not as if they were that fond of the old boy, or he that fond of them if you asks me.'

Mrs Bunch had lived in the village all her life; there wasn't anything she didn't know about anyone, and she had a ready tongue to share her knowledge, too. 'I've told you before about my friend that used to work here,' she said, after taking another gulp of tea. 'Oh, the stories she told me! When them children came for their holidays, and more often than not without their father but with a nanny, there were troubles aplenty, let me tell you. There wasn't a nanny alive who could control them little ones; they as good as roamed free to do as they pleased. You never heard so much squabbling as they got up to!'

'Did they make friends in the village?' asked Florence.

'Young Master Kit and Miss Hope did, Miss Allegra too, but Master Arthur always saw himself as being above mere village folk. It was different when Mr Devereux came. He might not have been the best of dads, being absent such a lot, but he did try. He'd put on these big parties, invited all the kiddies from the village and all. But that was stopped after one summer when Miss Allegra got into a fight with a boy who'd lured her down to the boathouse. When she refused to kiss him and he made fun of her Italian accent, she flew into a rage and kicked and punched him like any street fighter, until finally she shoved him into the lily pond.'

'Sounds like he got what he deserved,' said Florence, feeling some sympathy for the girl.

'Maybe you're right, but the thing was, the lad couldn't swim and in places the lily pond is fair deep. If Master Kit hadn't dived in and dragged him to safety, he might've drowned.'

'Does the boy still live in the village?' asked Florence.

'He do indeed. His name's Victor, and some say it might have been better if he *had* drowned that day; he's been nothing but trouble to his family since the day he was born.'

She paused for a moment to drain her teacup, and after Mrs Partridge had filled it again, and passed her a rock cake, she continued.

'That wasn't the only time Miss Allegra's temper got the better of her. One day she'd had enough of that Master Arthur and his sneering ways and lay in wait for him in the garden.' The old woman chuckled. 'She'd got hold of Master Kit's catapult and hit her target fair and square, blinded him in one eye. She's got a real fiery heart to her, that one. Must be all that Latin blood runnin' through her veins. Makes them different to us, don't it?'

It was difficult for Florence to picture the aloof young woman she had so far encountered doing any of those things; she seemed much too grand for such behaviour. She didn't seem a very happy woman, but then maybe you couldn't be a happy person to be an opera singer; perhaps you had to have a streak of tragedy running through you. There again, she was only here because her uncle was dead; she would hardly go about with a big grin on her face, would she?

'I heard one of the funeral guests saying that Collings hardware store has sold out of wireless sets this week,' said Florence, after Mrs Partridge had topped up her teacup. 'Apparently they've sold more in the last month than the whole year put together.'

'There's always some that benefits from war,

isn't there?' said Mrs Partridge. 'Or even the threat of it.'

'Folks are stocking up on tinned food,' Mrs Bunch said. 'And you can't blame them, can you?'

Thinking of the tins Mrs Partridge had already squirrelled away for what she called a rainy day, Florence said, 'Another guest was saying that the threat of war is more real than ever now that Hitler and Stalin have formed an alliance. And there's talk of children being evacuated from London.'

'Evacuated to where, that's what I'd like to know,' said Mrs Bunch.

★ ★ ★

A short while later, after Mrs Bunch had left to go home, there was a knock at the kitchen door and Miss Romily came in. She had a frown on her face and was holding the baby in her arms.

'I think the poor thing might be hungry,' she said anxiously. 'I was playing with her in the garden but can't seem to settle her now.'

A widow who'd never had children of her own and who would have given anything to have a dozen grandchildren to cluck over, Mrs Partridge sprang into action. 'We'll soon have the little mite sorted. Florence, warm some milk for me and then make a fresh pot of tea for Miss Romily while I knock up some scrambled eggs. I've yet to meet a child who didn't like my scrambled eggs.' Within no time she had the infant contentedly sipping milk from a small cup and eating the eggs from a spoon.

'You're a miracle-worker,' said Miss Romily, sitting at the table with them and drinking her tea.

'Nothing to it,' the older woman said, smiling happily at the little girl and spooning in another dollop of egg.

'How's it going in the dining room?' Florence ventured to ask.

'You may well ask. It was cowardly of me, but I left poor Roddy to deal with them. I'd had enough.'

'What could they possibly be talking about all this time?' asked Florence. 'Sorry if that's impertinent of me.'

Miss Romily waved the apology aside. 'That's all right. You and Mrs P are fully entitled to know what's going on, as I'm afraid the outcome might mean more work here for you both. You see, Jack's will has an unusual twist to it. In order to inherit, his children and Allegra have to spend a week together here at Island House. If they don't agree to it, or if one of them drops out, nobody gets a penny.'

'Gracious!' exclaimed Mrs Partridge. 'How've they taken that?'

'Not well. Particularly Arthur. Which is why I left when I did, before I was extremely rude to him.'

'Why do you think Mr Devereux put that in his will?' asked Florence.

'I think it was his way of teaching them to realise that they're a family. And also, perhaps more importantly, that one has to pull together

91

and work as a team in life to get the best out of it.' She paused and drew a line with her finger on the table. 'I happen to believe it's a sentiment that couldn't be more true if there is a war, and it looks increasingly likely that there will be.'

'War or not, people will do all sorts for a bit of money,' said Mrs Partridge, spooning the last of the egg into the compliantly open mouth of the child on her lap. 'Doesn't mean they'll play fair.'

Miss Romily nodded slowly. 'I expect Jack understood that all too well, but he probably wanted them to have the chance to put the past behind them. I fear it may well come down to how much they want, or need, the money.'

'And what about you?' asked Florence. 'Will you have to be here with them?' Privately she thought the poor woman had suffered enough and would be better off escaping to her flat in London.

'It was Jack's intention that I should stay to try and keep the peace. And knowing how much I love Island House, he's left the place to me, so his family will have to jolly well play by my rules, or else. Moreover,' she went on, 'I don't want them taking liberties with you two if I'm not around.'

'Oh don't you be worrying about us,' said Mrs Partridge. 'We can look after ourselves. Isn't that right, Annelise?' She tickled the little girl under her chin and was rewarded with a gurgle of unfettered laughter. 'Now there's a sound we could all do with hearing a bit more round here. Nothing like a baby to put you in a good mood.'

Florence exchanged a look with Miss Romily.

'Looks like Annelise has found herself a new champion,' she said.

'Well, the poor little darling needs all the love she can get if you ask me,' said Mrs Partridge. 'Lord knows how her parents could have parted with her, and to send her so far away . . . it quite breaks my heart to think about it.'

'They did it because they had no alternative,' said a stern voice at the kitchen door, which was slightly ajar. It was Mrs Meyer, and she looked far from happy.

13

'I'm very sorry, Mrs Meyer,' said the woman who had Annelise on her lap. 'I meant no harm; I was just saying what a desperate wrench it must have been for the parents to do what they did.'

'It was, I assure you,' Hope said coolly. 'It was not a decision they took lightly.'

'I'm sure you're right.'

'I am.' And feeling she ought to, that the child was her responsibility, Hope lifted the infant up and held her against her shoulder. But then something in the juxtaposition between the little girl's softness and the harshness of her own tone of voice made her relent. 'I'm sorry,' she said, 'I didn't mean to be so short. It's just that . . . ' She broke off abruptly, not sure what to say to them. Oh, but why bother to waste what little energy she had in explaining to these people? Let them think what they wanted to. What would they know of the daily fear Otto and Sabine lived in, of the sacrifice they had made in giving up their child? What would they think if they knew just how tiring Hope found the task of looking after her, or how guilty she felt when she found herself wishing she had never agreed to it.

'I hope she hasn't been too much trouble,' she said, realising that everyone was waiting for her to go on. She looked directly at the woman who was now her stepmother — a woman with whom she had exchanged no more than a few words since arriving yesterday. 'Thank you for amusing Annelise, that was kind of you.'

'No need to thank me. I took advantage of her unhappiness to distract myself. I think being in the garden distracted her too, until she decided she was hungry. The ever-wonderful Mrs Partridge stepped into the breach. Would you like to sit down and join us for a cup of tea?'

How strange it was to be invited to sit down in what had been her family home. Hope glanced around the kitchen, at the familiarity of it, but also so much that was unfamiliar — new pieces of crockery on the dresser, the two chairs either side of the range, the colourful hearthrug, the cream walls, and the yellow and white gingham curtains at the window. The starkness she remembered of old had gone, the new brought in presumably by the new broom — her step-mother.

With some effort, Hope fought off another wave of irritation, noting the look of uncertainty passing between Mrs Partridge and the maid. But having been cooped up in the dining room for what felt like forever, she had experienced quite enough exasperation and annoyance for one day, and she refused to give in to further vexation. 'I'm sorry,' she said to her stepmother, 'but I really don't know how to address you. Calling you Mother seems vaguely absurd.'

The woman before her nodded. 'I couldn't agree more. Why don't you call me Romily?'

Sensing they had each offered up an olive branch and taken a tentative step in what would be viewed as the right direction, Hope gave a

95

small smile. 'Thank you. And likewise, so that we're perfectly clear, please call me Hope.' She turned to the older woman, who was now at the deep Belfast sink holding a pan under the running tap. 'Thank you for giving Annelise her tea, Mrs Partridge. That's why I stopped by — I knew it was time to prepare her something, but didn't want to put you to any trouble.'

'It was no trouble at all; she's a regular little darling and perfectly welcome here in the kitchen any time you need a break. Just say the word. Are you sure you don't want a cuppa? Florence here will happily oblige, won't you, Flo?'

'Of course,' the young girl said. 'There are some rock cakes as well if you'd like?'

Touched by the warmth of their friendliness — something that had always been absent from the staff here when she'd been a child — Hope was tempted to sit down and pretend that tea and cake and a cosy chat would solve all her problems. 'Another time perhaps,' she said politely, not wanting to appear stand-offish.

Since she had been widowed, Hope knew that she had become much too brusque with people. Until her visit to Cologne, she had convinced herself that being alone suited her better, that she had her work and her routine, and that was enough. But now she had Annelise, and everything had changed. Which meant *she* had to change. If she were to do a good job of taking care of Sabine and Otto's precious child, she could not do it alone; she would need help. And accepting help, or asking for it, was something she was going to have to get used to. It meant also that she would have to learn to invite people back into her life. To be more approachable. For Annelise's sake, she would have to find a way to do that.

'How are things going in the dining room?' asked Romily. 'Have you managed to find a satisfactory conclusion to . . . to matters?'

Before she had a chance to reply, Hope heard footsteps and then Kit appeared in the doorway. 'Ah, there you are, I was wondering where you'd got to. Mind if I join you all? I say, those cakes look nice; are there any going spare? All that blasted tussling with Arthur has left me quite ravenous.'

'He's not still arguing the terms of the will, is he?' said Hope, while Florence fetched a plate.

Kit let out a short laugh. 'With his customary bad grace, our dearest brother has finally caved in and accepted there's no point in challenging its legality. Which is bad news for you, Stepma, as it means you're stuck with us for the next seven days.'

Hope winced. 'Kit, I really don't think it's appropriate for you to speak in that overly familiar way to Romily. Especially not in the circumstances.'

Her brother looked at their hostess, who appeared not to mind; in fact she seemed mildly amused. 'No offence intended,' he said. 'Just trying to lighten the mood; it's been one hell of a day.' He pushed a hand through his hair, a rueful gesture Hope had seen him make a million times before and which he probably didn't realise he

97

did. 'I'm afraid it must feel like an awful imposition, the four of us landing on you, given the situation,' he continued, 'but for once we can't be held entirely responsible.' He took a bite of one of the rock cakes Florence had given him. 'Mmm . . . just the ticket.' He clumsily plonked himself down at the table, rattling the china. 'First-rate baking,' he said. 'My compliments, Mrs Partridge.'

'I must apologise for my brother and his somewhat blithe fashion,' Hope said tiredly as Annelise twisted round in her arms to look at something on the dresser. 'He seems to have misplaced his manners.'

Kit frowned. 'I say, Hope, that's a bit unfair, don't you think? After all, we're not strangers here.'

'Things have changed, Kit,' she said. 'Like it or not, this is Romily's house now and we're guests in it, and therefore we should behave accordingly.'

Once again her brother cast his glance in Romily's direction. 'It seems I'm destined to keep apologising to you if my sister has her way. Could I just bank a week's worth of apologies right now and you cash them as and when I put my foot in it?'

'Please don't worry on my account,' said Romily with an easy smile. 'We all have a period of adjustment to get through. I'd sooner we were comfortable around each other, and more importantly, honest.'

'Well then,' said Mrs Partridge with an air of taking charge, 'if you wouldn't mind finding a more comfortable place to congregate, I have dinner to prepare. Florence, you'd best see to the dining room if Mr Fitzwilliam has finished with it.'

'I expect what is required right now for everyone is a strong drink,' said Romily, getting to her feet. 'I know I could do with one. Roddy must be simply gasping.'

Following Romily and Kit out of the kitchen, Hope wished that she had the same informal and composed manner her stepmother possessed. She knew that she herself came across as awkward and surly, not to say prim. She had been the same as a child — shy and somewhat inarticulate, preferring to lose herself in her intricate world of make-believe, a world over which she had complete control. That was how she had been until Dieter's love for her had given her a new sense of who she was, imbuing her with a confidence she had never owned before. But now widowhood had robbed her of it.

In contrast, Romily's grief did not seem so apparent. Yes, she had quietly cried during the funeral service, particularly when Roddy had given the eulogy, but had those tears been an act? For her part, Hope had not cried. She had felt nothing in the church, nothing in the graveyard when the coffin was lowered into the deep hole, and nothing when she had tossed a handful of earth onto the wooden box. If that made her sound heartless, then her father was to blame.

14

'I know that you've never truly believed that Jack cared for you, but I assure you he did.'

Allegra said nothing, her gaze taking in the sheen of liquid silvery light cast across the lily pond. It was a clear starry night and she had come out here to be alone, and to think. Just as she used to. Something about the stillness of water had always had a calming influence on her. She used to feel the same in Venice late at night. Often when she was on edge, or anxious after a performance, she would go for a solitary midnight stroll, her footsteps echoing in the deserted *calle*, her erratic heartbeat slowing to the rhythm of the gently lapping water. She had come in search of that same comfort tonight, to think about the consequences of today's events, and perhaps more importantly, her future.

But within minutes of stepping inside the shadowy darkness of the boathouse, she had been startled by the appearance of Roddy, asking for permission to join her. He must have followed her out here. Had it been any of the others, she would have walked away and let them have the place to themselves. But Roddy had always been kind to her.

The unhappiness she had experienced when she'd first arrived here as a child had never left her, nor the memory of her determination to escape. In those early weeks she had silently cried herself to sleep every night, dreading the morning, when yet again she would have to face Nanny Finch. An elderly woman, stiff with bitterness and rheumatism, she had harboured a sadistic hatred for Allegra, seeing her as an additional burden thrust upon her. 'You filthy bastard child,' she would curse when no one else was about. 'You're destined straight for the fires of hell, you are.' They were almost the first words in English that Allegra learned.

It had been Roddy who had realised that Nanny Finch was making her life a misery and advised Jack to send her packing. Allegra had never forgotten that act of compassion. And now once again Roddy was being kind to her, trying to make her believe that Jack had felt something for her.

For years she had believed her uncle had regarded her as some sort of trophy charitable cause, a way for him to garner accolades for good work, for giving a home to his brother's bastard child. Surely this will of his was no more than a last attempt to salve his conscience? Or was she misjudging him? Could a person change that much? Roddy had once said that her uncle had gone in search of her in Naples because he'd known it was something his wife — his first wife — would have done; apparently Maud would never have turned her back on a child in need. Was Allegra supposed to feel grateful that she'd been plucked from the orphanage by a stranger and dropped into the bosom of a family that had resented her presence so keenly? She didn't, and never had.

'I tried to dissuade him from putting that clause in his will, you know,' Roddy said, his voice as soft as the velvety dark sky. 'But you know Jack; once he had an idea in his head, he wouldn't be swayed.'

'You sound tired, *caro*,' Allegra said, but still not turning to look at him, or responding directly to his comments.

'I am,' he replied. 'I'm dog tired. It's been a long day.'

'You should go to bed.'

'I will. Before I do, I want to talk to you on your own.'

Now Allegra did turn to regard him. 'Why?'

'Because you don't look well.'

She faltered at his perceptiveness. 'I'm in mourning,' she said. 'One isn't supposed to look well. Although Romily makes for a fine widow, don't you think? She's an attractive woman. I can quite understand how she caught Uncle Jack's eye with her *bella figura*. But then he was never short of beautiful women in his life. It was quite a hobby for him.'

'That's unfair, Allegra. Romily is the first woman Jack truly loved since Maud. That's what makes his death so hard to bear for me, knowing just how much he loved her. For almost as long as I knew him, he was looking for that elusive special person with whom to share his life, and finally he found her. He was the happiest I'd ever seen him. I'll . . . I'll always be grateful to Romily that she did that.'

Hearing the catch in his voice, Allegra put a hand out to Roddy and rested it on his forearm.

102

'You sound like you care for her.'

'I do. I have the greatest respect and admiration for Romily. That's why I readily promised Jack I would help her if required, just as I promised him I'd always be of assistance to you if you needed it, and to Hope and Kit, and even Arthur.'

'Was ever a man so lucky as to have a friend such as you?' she murmured. And then: 'It's odd, but Romily strikes me as being too young to be a widow. Whereas Hope seems more than old enough.'

'What a strange thing to say.'

'Not strange at all. Naming her Hope was in vain as far as I can see. She was born to be hopelessly miserable, to be a widow in a perpetual state of bereavement. From what I've seen of her since yesterday, she virtually revels in the role. In contrast, I predict *la bellissima* Romily Temple-Devereux will shake off her widow weeds in no time at all.'

'It's unworthy of you to speak of them in that way.'

Allegra shrugged. 'But you know it's true. You English are so afraid of the truth, aren't you?'

'You're half English yourself, may I remind you.'

'*Sì*,' she said with a sigh, 'that is the cross I have to bear in this life.'

Roddy tutted and moved his arm so that the stump within his jacket sleeve was resting on his lap. When she had been a child and met him for the first time, Allegra had been petrified of his stump, or more particularly the ugly artificial hand he had worn at the time. Arthur had made it worse for her by saying that if she didn't always do as he said, he would cut off her hand and make her wear a false one just like Roddy. She had been so relieved when Roddy had given up wearing the cumbersome mechanical device.

'What about you, Allegra?' he said, interrupting her thoughts. 'Were you born to be unhappy like Hope? And bitter?'

'Maybe so. Maybe the nuns at Casa della Speranza should have called me Mara, the Hebrew word for bitter.'

Neither of them spoke for a while. Allegra listened to the rustle of something moving in the nearby undergrowth, and an owl hooting in the trees on the other side of the pond.

Roddy was the first to speak. 'May I give you a piece of advice, Allegra, as someone who has known you for a very long time?'

'Only on the understanding that you don't make me promise to heed it.'

'Did you ever?'

She smiled into the darkness. 'Not often. But go on, try me with your advice.'

'It's a very simple piece of philosophy by which I've tried to live my own life. It's this — happiness is a choice; you either decide to be happy with what you have, or you don't.'

'And has that worked for you?' she asked.

'Yes. I decided that I was happy with the life I had. With my work, with my friends, especially with my best friend, Jack, and his family.'

'What about love and marriage? Did you never want that?'

'If the right woman had come along, then maybe yes, but it was never a priority for me.'

'So what are you trying to say, in your ever so subtly English way, *caro?*'

'I suppose I'm asking you if your career as a singer is bringing you the happiness you thought it would. Is life everything you want it to be? And what about love? Have you met a man who makes you happy?'

'*Carissimo* Roddy, what makes you ask all these questions?'

He cleared his throat. 'Because I suspect you are not happy, and that something is very wrong with you right now. Have you been overworking, is that the problem?'

But before she had a chance to reply, he went on, 'Last year, in one of those inexplicable coincidences that sometimes happen, I was in Lucca and came across you singing the role of Mimi in *La Bohème*. You sang beautifully; in fact I was moved to tears, remembering with sadness the fiercely angry child you had once been. I've never forgotten how striking you could look and how your eyes could change colour depending on your mood — dark and flashing when in a temper, soft and as sweet as molasses when quiet and lost in thought. Poor Hope, your beauty made her feel so very ordinary in comparison.'

Again Allegra tried to speak, but Roddy was clearly in the mood to say his piece. 'After the performance that evening in Lucca, I tried to find you backstage at the theatre, but I was denied access by a foppish upstart of an Italian who pompously informed me that Miss Salvato

105

never spoke to anyone after a performance, least of all an ageing stage-door Johnny. I left you a note; I doubt for a minute you ever received it.'

'What did it say?'

'That I was so very proud of you that night, because you had achieved your dream, and that is something very few people do in life. But dreams often come at a cost, and I'm wondering what price you've had to pay.'

His words filled Allegra with an enormous sadness and she suddenly felt the irresistible urge to rest her head against his shoulder. 'Dear wise old Roddy,' she said, 'how perceptive you are this evening.' She sighed. 'I *am* wretched, but not for the reason you think. Overwork is not the problem, far from it.'

'Will you tell me what is?'

Why not? she thought. 'The man who turned you away that night in Lucca had not only been managing my career; he had promised to marry me. Instead, though, he ran off with all my earnings. He owes money to theatres all over Italy and has blackened my name in the process.'

'Good God, Allegra, what a scoundrel!'

She smiled at his outrage. 'That certainly is one way of describing him.'

'But surely, in terms of work, the right people will quickly realise that what he's done is not your fault. That you're not to blame?'

'I shall be tainted by association and will be lucky even to get a role in the chorus. And . . . ' She stopped herself short. No, there was no need to admit her real fear: that she was terrified she had lost her voice and would never sing again.

Say the words aloud and it might become reality.

'And what?' pressed Roddy.

'It's nothing.'

'Are you sure? If I can help in any way, please say.'

Snatching at something to satisfy his curiosity and his need to help, she said, 'I'm ashamed to confess this, but Luigi stole from my trust fund. I put my faith in him to manage all my financial affairs. I was such a fool. Please don't tell the others. I couldn't bear for them to know that I've been so stupid.'

'My dear girl, whatever you tell me stays strictly between us. I speak as a lawyer and as a friend. But is there anything I can do meanwhile?'

'I don't think so.'

'Do you know what you'll do when your week here comes to an end? Because if I may be so bold, I don't recommend you go back to Italy. Not with the threat of war hanging over Europe.'

'Italy won't join the war,' she said with more certainty than she felt. 'You don't need to worry about me.'

'But I do. I know what you're like, Allegra, that you can be hasty, and that once your mind is made up over a thing, there's no changing it. You're just like your uncle in that respect.'

She laughed, in spite of being likened to, of all people, Jack Devereux. 'Well, for now I have no choice but to remain here at Island House with Arthur and his insufferable arrogance,' she said. 'I can't help but feel that Uncle Jack is punishing us all in some horrid way. As if we haven't been punished enough.'

'I assure you that wasn't his intention; you must trust me on that. Through loving Romily, he came to appreciate just what his family meant to him. I know for a fact that had he still been alive when you arrived, he would have asked you to forgive him for all that he got wrong. The question is, can you do that now that he's dead? Can you forgive him?'

Allegra thought of the inheritance Uncle Jack had left her, knowing that it would offer her a degree of security for many years to come. And of course now it might not just be herself she had to think of.

Her suspicions had been roused when the queasiness she had been experiencing at the shock of Luigi's treachery had worsened, and always first thing in the morning. Before she left Venice, she had gone to the basilica in St Mark's Square and prayed with all her being that she was mistaken; that God wouldn't inflict this on her, not on top of everything else.

But now she was as sure as day followed night that she was expecting a child — a child, she was adamant, that like herself would never know its father.

15

In their room at the Half Moon Hotel overlooking the market square, his duty as a husband fulfilled, Arthur lay wide awake on his back next to his wife, who was now fast asleep and emitting a rhythmic guttural snore. Irene refused point blank to believe she was capable of such unedifying behaviour, and it pleased him no end to inform her that she snorted as charmingly as a pig in her sleep.

It was a shame he didn't derive as much pleasure from the act of having sex with her. He found her about as arousing as a plank of wood, and it took a good deal of effort and imagination on his part to conjure up sufficient desire to get himself across the finishing line. If he'd been allowed to sample the goods before marrying her, as he'd tried to do, he might have thought twice about going through with the wedding, but her old-fashioned sensibilities had put a ban on anything more daring than a kiss and an occasional fondle of her breasts. She had known that he was the more experienced of the two of them and had believed that to be the natural and proper order of things. She just had no idea what he'd got up to before meeting her, and what he still did.

For the sake of his sanity, and his physical needs, he'd maintained his regular liaisons with an obliging, if somewhat mature, woman in

Wembley. He had promised himself when he married that he would put a halt to his costly visits to Pamela in her shamefully suburban little semi-detached house, but the lure of her voluptuous body, which she offered so generously to him, had put paid to his good intentions.

He had lost his virginity to Pamela on his twenty-first birthday. His performance had not been up to much, but Pamela had been an enthusiastic teacher and he'd been a quick learner. Smiling, he closed his eyes now and thought with pleasure of the myriad tricks she knew when it came to pleasing a man and satisfying her own voracious appetite.

In comparison, the only appetite Irene had was driven by the desire to have a baby. Which struck him as odd, for she was utterly self-obsessed, and determined to keep her figure matchstick thin so that she would be the envy of all her friends, who, she claimed, had badly let themselves go now that they had children. But a baby was what Irene wanted, and Arthur knew to his cost that whatever Irene wanted, Irene got. He had her family to thank for that. Money had been no object for her while growing up, and she had only to snap her fingers and her wish would be granted. She seemed to think the same was true now: that Arthur should throw cash into the bottomless pit of her spendthrift nature. He had never known a person to get through money as fast as she did. Her wardrobes were full of the finest clothes, hats and shoes, and yet she still wanted more frippery.

'Do you want me to go about town looking like a ragtag scarecrow?' she would ask if he dared to suggest she couldn't possibly need yet another new outfit. 'Don't you want me to look nice so you can be proud of me?' Frankly, he'd pay good money to see her go round in rags!

His answer had been to remind her, yet again, that money did not grow on trees, and that his work at the War Office, while well paid, was not going to stretch to the lengths she believed it would. Moreover, he had his own pleasures to fund, namely Pamela, his club and his weekly card games. He had no intention of giving up any of those so that his wife could show off a new frock to her friends.

However, it was something of a tightrope he was forced to walk when it came to denying Irene anything, because infuriatingly, her trump card was always to shrug and say she would ask her father to step in and make good any financial deficit. Which Arthur could never allow to happen. A man had his pride, after all, and it would be too galling for him to be shown to be incapable of providing for his capricious wife.

He felt undermined enough by the Collingwoods as it was, with their constant harping on their superior ancestry — all the way back to God himself, if they were to be believed — without giving them any more cause to look down on him. Being the son of a former barrow boy from the East End was a millstone of shame Arthur was never going to lose. Certainly not in the eyes of his in-laws.

He rued the day that he ever saw fit to filch

Irene from under his brother's nose, but it had been an instinctive reaction. As children, anything Kit had possessed was automatically something to be taken in Arthur's eyes; it had been a sport for him to reduce his pathetic weakling brother to a state of abject misery. Having power over his siblings, and his cousin, Allegra, had been one of the great lessons of Arthur's life, having learnt it when he'd been sent away to school at the age of five.

He had hated the school initially, so much so that he had humiliated himself thoroughly by wetting the bed, which had led to Matron stripping him naked and beating him with a long-handled brush in front of his peers. In turn this had led to him being bullied, and in very short order he had discovered that the only way to survive was to toughen up and find somebody weaker than himself to torment. Even at so young an age he had grasped the basic law of both the animal kingdom and mankind — existence was all down to the survival of the fittest.

Since then, he had regarded any trial in his life as a challenge to be overcome, and with a bit of luck his latest trial, of lack of funds, was soon to be addressed, thanks to his old man dying so conveniently.

Trust his father to have left such an absurd will, but it had certainly spiced things up this afternoon when that dullard Roddy Fitzwilliam had taken forever laying out the exact terms of the bequests. Of course Arthur had had no intention of not going along with it, but he had thoroughly enjoyed watching the reaction on the other side of the table. Once again he had gained the upper hand simply by refusing to play along, by playing by his own rules.

Everybody was greedy for money, even his po-faced sister Hope, who advocated a life of selfless restraint in the belief that it would somehow make her a better person, and so it had been fun to see the looks of horror on their faces when they thought they might not get their hands on Jack's lucre. The only face he could not read had been that of his father's widow. He sensed in her an adversary, which only heightened the fun of the game ahead.

According to the terms of the will, Arthur would have to move into Island House tomorrow morning, and so straight after breakfast he would put Irene on the train for Scotland to join her family on holiday there. Once he'd seen his wife off, his next job would be to telephone the appropriate people at the War Office to explain his continued absence. Of course, with the threat of war hanging over them, there was the chance that his request could be denied. He hoped not.

In a strange way, he was looking forward to what lay before him. One thing he knew for sure: he would be at the centre of things, manipulating the others like puppets.

Just as he had in the old days.

16

Awake earlier than usual, Florence remembered with a start what day it was — the twenty-fourth of August, which meant it was her nineteenth birthday. Not that it would be appropriate for her to celebrate it in any way, not so soon after Mr Devereux's funeral.

Last year Miss Romily had given her a pretty enamelled brooch, and the year before that a beautiful leather purse. She really was the most generous and thoughtful person Florence knew; not once did she overlook those who worked for her. Nobody ever had a bad word to say about her. Probably, and unfairly so, certain members of Mr Devereux's family might prove to be the exception.

Through the open window, where the rose-patterned cotton curtains were swaying in the breeze, Florence listened to a cuckoo joining in with the birds giving voice to the dawn chorus. After a few seconds she was aware of another noise, and after straining to make out what it was, she realised it was the sing-song chatter of the baby in the room below. She was such a sweet little thing, and Mrs Partridge had been right yesterday to say that it must have been the most awful wrench for her parents to part with her.

But it was surprising what parents were capable of doing, and nobody knew better than

Florence the truth of that. What was also a truth for her was that if she ever had a child, she would never abandon it, or treat it badly. She would treasure it as the most precious thing in the world.

When her mother had vanished without a word to anyone, Florence had convinced herself that she would one day return home from school and find Mum waiting for her with open arms. Another hope she had hung onto was that her mother had planned all along to sneak back in the night to take Florence away with her. For a long time she would lie awake in bed listening for her return, but eventually, when a year had passed and there was not so much as a letter or a birthday card, she accepted that her mother was gone forever, that she had never really loved her daughter. If she had, she wouldn't have left Florence alone to cope with her violent drunkard father.

Not wanting to dwell on the past, Florence pushed back the bedclothes; it was time she was up. She had work to do.

As she quietly descended the stairs, the happy chattering from the baby in the room below her changed; there was a fretful tone to her voice now, as if she was anxious, perhaps hoping her mother or father would appear at the door.

Florence paused, waiting for the sound of Hope's bedroom door opening, followed by footsteps across the landing, but there was nothing, only the cries of the infant now growing in volume and irritability. It seemed heartless to ignore the poor mite, so she judged it better to do something rather than have everybody's sleep disturbed.

The baby fell instantly silent at the sight of her, but then her face crumpled, maybe because Florence wasn't the person she had hoped to see. Even so, Florence leaned over the side of the cot that had been hastily found by Mrs Bunch in the village and scooped up the child. As she did so, she caught a whiff of an atrocious smell. She had never changed a baby's nappy before, but now she looked about her for what she imagined was required. Somehow she managed to wrestle the revoltingly soiled nappy off the squirming infant, clean her up, pin a fresh one in place and then dress her, all the while making soothing noises that seemed to have the desired effect. Although perhaps it was purely being rid of the foul nappy that wrought the change.

Carrying the child, Florence took the stairs carefully down to the kitchen, where she scrubbed her hands and set about warming some milk, as well as making herself a cup of tea. Both achieved, she sat to one side of the range and, with Annelise on her lap, administered the milk. At first the child closed her eyes and sucked on the bottle with intense concentration, her delicate pale eyelids fluttering, tiny bluish-pink veins visible just above her long eyelashes. With one hand resting on the bottle, the other patted it gently, her small fingers splayed.

Drinking her tea Florence marvelled at the child, in particular her trusting nature as she contentedly nestled in close. Or was it no more than a survival instinct? Either way, it gave

Florence a strange feeling, one that she had never experienced before: a desire to protect and nurture something so vulnerable.

Continuing to suck on the bottle, the little girl had just opened her eyes and was staring with an unnervingly solemn and intelligent force directly into Florence's gaze when the kitchen door opened and Hope came in. Still in her nightclothes, with a silk dressing gown tied loosely around her waist, she looked sleep-rumpled and cross. 'You really shouldn't have taken Annelise from her cot without speaking to me first,' she said with a frown. 'I was worried when I found it empty.'

'I'm sorry, madam,' said Florence, stung at the rebuke, 'but she was crying and so I thought — '

'It wasn't your place to think. Annelise is *my* responsibility, not yours!' She came over and roughly snatched the baby out of Florence's arms, knocking the bottle of milk to the floor. At once, Annelise began to cry.

'I call that a fine way to show your gratitude to somebody who was only trying to help,' said another voice. It was Allegra, and she too was in her nightclothes, except in her case, with her bare feet and scarlet-painted toenails and her long black hair, she looked far from sleep-rumpled. Admittedly she was a little pale, but the silk kimono she wore, which was untied and revealed a cerise silk sheath clinging embarrassingly close to her body, gave her the appearance of a seductive starlet luring a handsome man to her bed. 'I was tempted to see to the *poverina bimba* myself,' she went on, 'but Florence beat me to it.'

'For a woman who only thinks of herself, I find that hard to believe,' said Hope stiffly, at the same time jiggling Annelise in her arms to quieten her.

'Believe what you want, Hope, but if you ask me, you owe Florence an apology, and a word of thanks might not be out of place. The poor girl did you a favour, allowed you to sleep in. Which is more than some of us were able to do, given the racket.'

'Since I'm not asking you, perhaps you'd like to mind your own business.'

Allegra shrugged and turned her attention to Florence, who was trying her best to give the impression she wasn't witnessing the unpleasant exchange. She wished they would stop turning up in the kitchen unannounced. Why couldn't they stick to the rest of the house to air their differences? Was this how it was going to be for the rest of the week while the family adhered to the terms of Mr Devereux's will? She hoped to God it wasn't. And why was Hope so cross with her? She had seemed pleasant enough yesterday. What had got into her?

'I wonder if I might trouble you for a cup of coffee? Black and with two sugars.'

'Of course, miss,' said Florence. 'I mean *signora*. I mean *signorina*.' Oh heavens, what was it Miss Romily had said she was to call Allegra?

'You may call me Miss Salvato if it's easier for you to remember,' she said. 'Or Allegra.' Her voice might have sounded as sweet as honey, probably hoping to get on Florence's good side, but Florence wasn't going to be taken in. She knew how false familiarity could be; that more often than not it led to somebody taking downright liberties. Sometimes it was easier to cope with hostility; that way you knew where you stood. It was different with Miss Romily and the friendly way she treated Florence. Her informality had always been genuine; there was no side to her.

'Thank you, Miss Salvato,' she said politely. 'Would you like anything to go with your coffee? Some toast, perhaps, before Mrs Partridge comes down to make breakfast for everyone?'

Allegra visibly blanched at the suggestion and she shook her head. 'Just coffee. I'll have it in the garden.' She turned to go. 'You'll find me on the terrace in front of the drawing room.'

'I hope you're going to put some clothes on,' remarked Hope, 'instead of making an exhibition of yourself.'

Allegra gave her a cool look, her amber eyes narrowed, her lips slightly pursed. 'Why? Who's going to see me making an exhibition of myself, as you put it?'

Hope tutted. 'You always did have to attract attention to yourself, didn't you? You haven't changed a bit.'

'Unlike you, *cara*. You have become an embittered old woman who can't be nice to anyone, let alone yourself.'

And with that, ensuring she had the last word, Allegra closed the door behind her, but not before Florence caught a look of grim satisfaction on her face.

Gawd! Could no one in this wretched family be nice and get along?

119

17

With Roddy on the train back to London, Irene heading north to Scotland and Arthur now installed at Island House, Kit was keen to escape his brother and had seized on the opportunity to do so by offering to post some letters for his stepmother.

Before Roddy had left for the station, his parting words had been to remind them why their father had wanted them to stay here for the week. 'It's so that you can put your differences aside and learn to be the family you should have been,' he'd said.

'I'm surprised you're not staying here to put us under house arrest and act as our gaoler,' Arthur had responded. 'Or are you entrusting our stepmother to carry out that duty on your behalf?'

'I'm trusting you to act like the responsible adults you are,' Roddy had replied evenly. 'And please don't upset Romily. Do that and you shall have me to answer to.'

For mild-mannered Roddy Fitzwilliam, this had been a severe admonishment indeed, and Kit had every intention of doing what he'd been told. Unlike Arthur, who would relish going out of his way to upset Romily.

At the end of the driveway, Kit waited for a cart to pass by on the road, the horse plodding slowly in the languid warmth. The air was scented with honeysuckle scrambling through the hedgerow, birds were singing and bees humming, and away from his family — or more precisely his brother — Kit felt himself begin to relax and enjoy the loveliness of it.

The horse and cart having now passed, he turned right towards the centre of the village. He had intended to ask his sister if she wanted to accompany him, but she had been embroiled in a lengthy telephone conversation. From what he'd caught of it as he'd hovered momentarily outside the drawing room door, Hope had been trying to explain to the publisher for whom she was currently illustrating a children's book that her circumstances had altered dramatically in the last week and she could only try to do her best to meet the deadline, which had been unexpectedly brought forward. Kit could tell from the strain in her voice that it was an awkward conversation and she was struggling to provide the reassurance her publisher was seeking.

Kit himself had had an equally awkward conversation with the bank he worked for when he'd explained that he wouldn't be returning until late next week. He'd cited grief as his excuse, somehow seeing the lie as preferable to disclosing the terms of his father's will, which cast the family in an embarrassingly poor light. In many ways he didn't actually give a damn what the bank believed; he had few aspirations to be well thought of there in order to rise through its ranks.

He was keeping his fingers crossed that he and his brother and sister and cousin could stick it out for the week and therefore earn their inheritance. The money, like an answer to a prayer, would give him the financial freedom to walk away from the bank. The idea of living abroad appealed to him, somewhere warm and sunny, the south of France perhaps, or maybe inland in the hills of Provence. Or he could go further afield, to Mexico and Central America. It would be an adventure! Wherever he went, he'd live modestly, unencumbered by the tedious constraints of his life here in England; he'd be at liberty to be himself. Although if he were honest, he wasn't entirely sure just who he really was; he had yet to discover that.

It was an admission that pained him, because it meant that his father had been right: he lacked the necessary drive and ambition to seize hold of life's myriad opportunities and thereby make something of himself. He wasn't like his sister, or Allegra, who had both known from a young age what they wanted to do. Hope had been adamant that she wanted to go to art school in London, while Allegra had been born with the gift of a great singing voice and had been determined to pursue a career that would, in Kit's view, satisfy her craving for attention and the adulation only an adoring audience could provide.

As for Arthur, his talent had always been for domination and ensuring that he was the one in charge. It really wouldn't surprise Kit if in due course his brother made the transition from the Civil Service to politician, and God help them all if that ever came to pass!

Meanwhile, Kit had meandered along in his hapless way, hoping that in the fullness of time he would stumble across a signpost leading him to his own future. He'd toyed with the idea of painting, but one artist in the family was quite enough, and anyway, objectively he wasn't that good. Writing was a possibility — not poetry, he didn't have the tortured soul for that, but the thought of crafting a novel tempted him. He'd made a couple of stabs at it, but each time he'd abandoned the idea after only a few pages, disgusted at the pathetic immaturity of his efforts.

Now even that particular avenue had been purloined by somebody else in the family. How could he dare to put pen to paper when his stepmother was such an acclaimed author? Although strictly speaking, did marriage for only a few weeks to his father really qualify her as family?

She was certainly a cut above most of the women with whom the old man had got himself involved. Kit had to admit he rather liked her. There were worse stepmothers with whom he could have been landed. One in particular came to mind. She had been an actress, or so she claimed, and while Kit would never lay claim to being the slightest bit clever, she had been embarrassingly dim, with only one topic of conversation at her disposal: that of herself and the trouble she was experiencing in finding the perfect hat for Ascot that year. Kit had almost felt sorry for her; until, that was, she had singled out Hope for some tips on how to make more of her appearance.

They had been in the drawing room, drinking cocktails, waiting for Jack and Roddy to finish discussing some contract or other in the study, when their guest had slipped her arm through Hope's in what she probably thought was a gesture of friendly intimacy, but which Kit knew Hope would dislike intensely. 'There's no excuse for any woman these days not to make herself more attractive,' she had declared, adding, 'Take it from me, Hope, if you were to dye your hair blonde like mine, and use some lipstick, you'd look a lot less dowdy.' The frozen expression on his sister's face had been enough to make Kit join in with Arthur, who had been systemically firing off derisive salvos at the dreadful woman. They'd kept it up right through dinner, until their father exploded and all hell broke loose. He'd refused to accept that their rudeness was justified, and maybe he was right, but he'd also refused to accept that the simpering actress had insulted Hope. 'You always have to find fault with anything I do,' he'd shouted at them. 'You've never once approved of anyone I've introduced you to!'

With the memory of his father's angry voice ringing in his ears, Kit slowed his step as he heard another, much sweeter sound — the jangly song of a corn bunting. He looked around him for the bird and spotted it perched on a fence post a few yards ahead of him. His knowledge of birds, as well as flora and fauna, was down to his sister.

As a child, Hope had forever been dragging him off with her on nature trails, traversing meadows and riverbanks, armed with sketch pads, butterfly nets, and jam jars to fill with tadpoles to take back to the pond at Island House. Even at so young an age, Hope had had a tendency to be a bit of a schoolmarm and would insist on teaching him the names of whatever they saw and heard. Some days, when all he'd wanted to do was lie on his back and stare up at the clouds in the sky, imagining they could transport him to anywhere in the world, he would get annoyed with her and sulk.

At the bottom of the lane, he paused at the T-junction for a couple of cars and a bus to rumble past before crossing over onto the main street of the village. It occurred to him as he waited that he was still as big a dreamer as he'd been when staring up at the clouds as a child. It was a trait his father had doubtless viewed as a weakness; after all, men like Jack Devereux knew exactly what they wanted in life. Their vision was perfectly clear, whereas Kit's had always been a bit blurred.

He was just entering the market square when he spotted a familiar face amongst the shoppers, a face he hadn't seen in a long time. It was Evelyn Flowerday. Dressed in a pretty polka-dot dress, she was walking alongside two elderly women whom Kit also recognised — Miss Gant and Miss Treadmill. The former was decked out in lace and frills and a straw hat decorated with flowers, shiny red cherries and all manner of ribbons, while the latter wore sturdy corduroy breeches and a plaid shirt. Waddling behind the two women were their pet geese, each sporting a neckerchief. It was so long since Kit had seen the old ladies and their devoted birds — assuming they were the same ones and not younger replacements — he'd forgotten how perfectly normal the sight of them was in Melstead St Mary.

The last time he'd seen Evelyn had been three years ago at the village fete, when they had both been briefly home during the summer vacation. Back then Evelyn had been up at Oxford, reading mathematics at Lady Margaret Hall while he had been at Brasenose, but despite knowing one another since childhood, their paths had seldom crossed during term time, mostly because Evelyn had been such a studious undergraduate, rarely leaving her college or the library.

But their paths *had* crossed that particular August Bank Holiday weekend, when Kit had made a rare visit to Island House. Within hours of him being home, he and Jack had argued over something wholly irrational — probably Kit's poor academic results that term — and he had escaped to Clover Field to enjoy a glass of ale in the warm sunshine at the annual fete. He'd come across Evelyn inside the refreshment tent, where she had been tending to her mother, a sour and monstrous hypochondriac who treated her daughter as nothing more than an unpaid slave. Emboldened by alcohol, Kit had asked Evelyn if she would accompany him to the village dance that evening. He'd always liked her, having often played with her and her brother Edmund, during the school holidays, although as the years went by, he had begun to suspect that she found him rather lightweight in the intellectual department. To his surprise, she'd agreed, much to her mother's displeasure.

The evening had gone wrong from the start. They'd been dancing for no more than a few minutes when Kit, thinking he was demonstrating sympathy for the position in which she found herself, made the mistake of criticising her mother and suggesting Evelyn shouldn't indulge the annoying woman. To his horror, she had taken it as a personal slight, as though he were disparaging her.

'Don't think for one moment you have the right to judge me,' she'd thrown back at him. 'Not when you can't stand up to your brother or father!'

He'd been stung by her comment. 'If you think so poorly of me, why did you accept my invitation for this evening?' he'd replied.

'Because I'd hoped you might have changed; that Oxford had taught you to grow up.'

Her condemnation could not have been greater, and had caused him to behave far from well. He'd abandoned her at the dance and stomped home to Island House in a thoroughly bad mood. When he returned to Oxford, he left a note of apology in her college pigeonhole, but he never heard back from her.

Now here she was. The coward in him wondered if he could pretend he hadn't seen her — why put himself in the firing line of yet more of her disapproval? But before he could take evasive action, Miss Gant spotted him and raised her gloved hand. Miss Treadmill and Evelyn then duly turned to look. With nothing else for it, he went over to say hello. What could be the worst that could happen?

'We were so sorry to hear about your father,' said Miss Gant in her breathy voice. 'So sad to have lost him when he was still so full of life.'

Miss Treadmill nodded and joined in with her deeper staccato voice. 'Forgive us for not showing our faces at the funeral yesterday. Couldn't be helped. We had unexpected visitors. Tiresome really. But there you go.'

'It was good of you to consider attending,' Kit said, before risking a glance at Evelyn. Finding a friendly enough face looking at him, he said, 'It's good to see you again, Evelyn. How are you?'

She smiled. 'I'm well, thank you.'

'And Edmund?'

'He's very well too. He's a doctor in London now.'

'Evelyn's such a dear girl,' Miss Gant cooed. 'Since her return to the fold, she's been helping me with the children in the Sunday school. Oh, they absolutely love her!'

'You've moved back, then?' said Kit. The last he'd heard of her, she'd left the village.

'Yes,' she replied. 'My mother needed me.'

Was it his imagination, or did she raise her chin in a gesture of defiance? 'Please give her my regards,' he said politely as one of the geese began to peck at his trousers, nipping his calf muscles with its sharp beak.

'I will,' Evelyn said.

'Cecil, stop that at once!' ordered Miss

128

Treadmill, taking her boot to the goose and nudging it away from Kit's leg. 'Better get on. Lots to do. We'll leave you young folk to catch up. Toodle-pip!'

In a flurry of hand-waving and goodbyes, the two elderly women left Kit alone with Evelyn. Shuffling the letters in his hands, he sought for something to say, something that wouldn't cause offence. 'So,' he tried, 'when did you move back to the village?'

'In January. My mother had a heart attack and now requires a lot of care.'

'I'm sorry to hear that.'

'Don't be,' she said matter-of-factly. Then: 'Actually, it's me who should apologise to you. I've meant to do so for ages but never got around to it.'

'What on earth do you need to apologise for?'

'Because I was very rude to you when we last met, and afterwards I didn't have the decency to reply to your letter.'

'Oh, that,' he said airily. 'Don't give it another thought. I was my usual clumsy, idiotic self that evening at the dance. I should never have said what I did.' Feeling on safer ground now, and noting the tea room behind them, he said, 'I don't suppose you'd care for a cup of coffee, would you?'

* * *

They took the last available table and ordered coffee and a toasted teacake each. 'What were you doing before coming home to care for your

129

mother?' asked Kit, after the waitress had brought them their order.

'I was teaching.'

'Really?'

'Don't look so surprised. I was actually rather good at it. What did you expect me to do? Marry and have children?'

He smiled. 'Nothing would surprise me with you, Evelyn. Where were you teaching?'

'At St Agatha's in Kent; a prestigious boarding school for girls. I taught mathematics.'

Treading warily, Kit said, 'Do you miss it?'

She stirred her coffee slowly. 'Terribly. I miss the girls and the other teachers; they were a good crowd. And I'm well aware what you're thinking: that I've sacrificed a fine career for a rancorous woman who does nothing but complain and make my life hell.'

'I wouldn't presume to think anything of the kind.'

She smiled. 'Well it's exactly what *I* think, so I wouldn't blame you for seeing it that way. It was why I was so rude to you that night of the dance; you said exactly what I was thinking and I hated myself for it. But life has a habit of changing, so who knows what the future holds? Probably war at the rate things are going in Germany. Will you go and fight?'

'Of course, try and stop me!' His response, he realised straight away, was ludicrously glib and said in the hope that she would be impressed, or at least think well of him. 'I'll join the RAF, if they'll have me,' he said more seriously.

She took a sip of her coffee, regarded him over

the cup with a sure and level gaze. 'So you'll become a dashing pilot in a smart blue uniform. How very *you*.'

'And now you're teasing me, I do believe.'

'Only a little.' She lowered her cup into its saucer and sighed. 'I wish I could do something half so useful if war is declared. As it is, I'll be stuck here. Although, and much against my mother's wishes, I have agreed to take in an evacuee if called upon to do so.'

'Well, that would be doing something eminently useful and practical.'

She shook her head and tutted. 'Don't patronise me, Kit. Anything but that.'

'I didn't mean it that way.' He took a bite of his teacake, and when he'd finished chewing on it, he said, 'I'm glad I bumped into you.'

'I'm glad too. I saw you at the funeral and thought how well you looked.'

'You were there? I didn't see you.'

'I sat at the back and didn't linger when it was over. I wanted to say hello to you, but I didn't think the moment was right. How long are you going to be staying at Island House?'

'A week. Along with my brother and sister, and Allegra.'

She nodded thoughtfully. 'The gossip machine has been rife with talk. I heard Hope surprised you all by arriving home with a baby, a German baby no less.'

'A German baby whose father is Jewish,' he said, keen to make things clear. 'The child is her niece.'

'I imagined it was something of the sort. The

parents did the right thing; I've heard terrible stories of what Jews are being subjected to in Nazi Germany. Couldn't the parents escape as well?'

Kit told her what Hope had shared with him about Dieter's sister and brother-in-law.

Evelyn nodded again. 'I suppose, like so many, they're clinging desperately to the hope that the danger they're in will pass. So what do you think of your glamorous stepmother?' she asked in a sudden change of subject.

He shrugged, caught off guard. 'She's nice.'

'*Nice?* Is that all you can say about her? Goodness, the whole village is agog about Romily Temple, or Mrs Temple-Devereux as she is now. She's quite the brightest thing to hit us here in a very long time. The men all secretly worship her and the women view her with the utmost suspicion. They'll be hanging on to their husbands like mad now that your father's gone.'

Kit was shocked. 'That's an outrageous thing to say!'

'I may be exaggerating a little, but you have to admit she is highly unusual. I've met her several times in the village; she was charming, and I might say utterly in love with your father, and he with her. Have you read any of her books?'

'Sadly not, I'm afraid.'

'Then I recommend you do. They're excellent. I came across an interesting interview with her in which she said she was fascinated by the 'eternal why' of human behaviour. She's of the opinion that crime intrigues people more than love does.'

'What an extraordinary thing to say.'

132

Evelyn looked at him, her dark eyebrows raised. 'Do you think so? I for one regularly ponder how to go about murdering my mother, but I barely give love a second thought.'

Kit didn't know whether to laugh or remonstrate.'

'And there I go again,' she said, 'I've shocked you, haven't I? Take no notice. But I do urge you to read one of Romily's novels. She has a perceptive understanding of human nature, at its worst and its best.'

'She may well be seeing a lot of it at its worst in the coming days,' said Kit ruefully.

'Yes, I daresay your family won't make things too easy for her. However, beware. She'll get her revenge by putting you all in a book and having you bumped off one by one in the most grisly fashion.'

Now he did laugh, causing three old biddies at a nearby table to turn and stare. He recognised them as Elspeth Grainger, Edith Lawton and Ivy Swann. He had noticed them looking his way ever since he and Evelyn had entered the tea shop. He gave them a friendly smile, then, realising he was enjoying himself more than he had in quite a while, decided to confide in Evelyn as to why he would be staying on at Island House.

'So you see,' he said at length, 'as always, my father had the last word.'

'Why be so cynical?' she said. 'Why not respect your father's wishes and see if you can be friends with your family? Why not be the one to make the first step to make it happen?'

133

'I fear you imagine I'm a better person than I really am.'

As if warming to her theme, Evelyn leaned across the table, so close Kit could almost count the smattering of freckles across the bridge of her nose. 'Then why not surprise yourself by seeing just what you could be capable of. My God, Kit, if you're prepared to learn to fly and go to war, surely you can help to build bridges with your family? No, don't bother trying to answer that, I don't have the time. I'm sorry, but I must finish my shopping and get home to mother. She'll be expecting her lunch.'

Kit paid for their coffee and teacakes and they left together, Evelyn in the direction of Teal's the grocer's, and Kit to the post office, but not before Evelyn proposed they meet again at the weekend.

Which put a decidedly happy spring in his step.

18

Allegra had missed breakfast, having been disgustingly sick first thing that morning. Even now, she felt queasy at the thought of lunch.

Just how long would this go on for? she wondered wretchedly as she walked the length of the garden up to the house. Was there something she could take to stop it? Perhaps she ought to visit the doctor in the village. But what if it got out that she was pregnant? If she could only make it through the next seven days, she would then go to London and see a doctor there. An anonymous doctor who wouldn't ask too many awkward questions.

Then what? What was her big plan? As Roddy had advised her last night, returning to Italy didn't seem the most sensible thing to do in the current climate. Perhaps she should take his advice and remain here in England.

But what to do about the child she was sure she was expecting? Could she go somewhere and live unobtrusively for the next seven months, then reappear again claiming she'd rescued a Jewish baby just like Hope had? If she did that, she'd be regarded as the child's saviour, practically a saint for acting so selflessly. But it would be a lie that she would have to live with for the rest of her life, for there would be no handing back the baby, as Hope would be doing. No, this child she was carrying would be hers forever.

But to live as a liar for the rest of her life would make her as bad as Luigi. She grimaced at the thought of the man who had betrayed her so cruelly. The man who had left her in this terrible mess.

There was always the option of having the baby and giving it up for adoption. That would be the simplest solution, but knowing what she had gone through as a child herself made her reluctant to consider it as a possibility.

Yet her true nature — her wild, rebellious nature — was calling to her to be brave, to throw caution to the wind, stand defiantly before the world and claim that she was unmarried and expecting a child. And what of it! But if she did that, the poor little thing would be forever labelled a bastard. He or she would be tainted for life just as Allegra herself had been.

She had so very nearly confided in dear old Roddy last night down at the boathouse, but she hadn't had the courage. Because as long as she was the only one who knew she was pregnant, she could almost get through each day believing it wasn't true, that it was all in her imagination.

Back at the house now, she stepped into the drawing room through the open French doors. Romily was there, sitting at the walnut desk, her head lowered as the pen in her hand scratched across the lined page of a notebook. She looked up when she realised she wasn't alone.

'I'm sorry if I disturbed you,' Allegra said, deciding to assume the role of apologetic house guest. Which in so many ways was perfectly apt, given that the atmosphere was akin to a stage play of a country-house drama.

Putting her pen down and straightening her back, Romily said, 'That's all right. I really should stop for lunch now.'

'Are you working?' More acting — contriving to show interest.

Romily nodded. 'Yes. Does that seem very callous to you? Jack only buried yesterday, but here I am writing?'

Allegra shrugged. 'Not really. If it helps, why not? I wish I had something to do, other than waft about the house and garden. I'm bored out of my mind.' She made a performance of drifting over towards a small occasional table and bending down to breathe in the fragrance of a vase of sweet peas.

'We could put you to work in the garden if you like,' Romily said. 'I'm sure your help would be appreciated; there's always plenty to do.'

Allegra affected another careless shrug. 'And I'm equally sure I would be as good as useless. I have no idea what to do to make things grow.'

'I'm told gardens are like children: if fed well and given a firm hand now and then, they flourish quite happily.'

Flopping into the armchair near the open door, Allegra adopted a friendly smile, the sort to invite a sharing of confidences. 'Can I ask you a personal question?' she said.

'Of course. I'm sure you have many you'd like to put to me.'

'Had my uncle lived, do you think you would have had children?'

Romily picked up the fountain pen and twirled

it slowly between her fingers. Allegra could see she had not expected the question. But then she herself hadn't expected to ask something quite so personal either, or something so close to home.

'I don't think I know the answer to that,' Romily said. 'Not in all honesty. It wasn't something we ever discussed. Why do you ask?'

'I suppose I'm just curious,' Allegra said mildly, trying again to affect a persona of casual indifference. 'You don't appear to be the maternal type, but you seem quite at ease with Annelise.'

'I don't believe I am the maternal type, but Annelise is easy to like, wouldn't you agree?'

Leaning back in the comfort of the chair, Allegra crossed her legs, then uncrossed them. 'Maybe that's because we can't help but feel sorry for her.'

'You could be right. What about you, Allegra, do you think you'll have children one day?'

She was saved from answering the question by the shrill ringing of the telephone on the desk. 'I'll see you in the dining room,' Romily said as she reached for the receiver and picked it up.

Having been summarily dismissed, and wondering why on earth she had started the conversation in the first place, Allegra went upstairs to freshen up. She was on her way back down when she saw Kit coming in through the front door. He was whistling jauntily and looking particularly pleased with himself.

'You were out a long time posting those letters,' she said. 'Were you trying to avoid spending any time with the rest of us?'

'Perish the thought, Allegra. Actually, I bumped into someone I haven't seen in a long time. Do you remember Evelyn Flowerday?'

Allegra thought for a moment, searching back through her memory to the last time she had been here at Island House. 'Do you mean that clever girl you were always pining for?' she said eventually.

He frowned. 'I wouldn't go so far as to say that, but yes, that supremely clever girl.'

'How very agreeable for you, a romantic stroll down memory lane.'

'Once more, I wouldn't go so far as to say that. But it was certainly pleasant seeing her again. Coming for lunch now?'

They crossed the hall together, and when Kit pushed open the dining room door and stepped aside to let her through first, and she thanked him, he said, 'See, we can be perfectly civil to each other after all.'

'The question is, can we maintain that civility for a full week?'

'Oh, I think for the amount of money at stake, we can make a fair pretence of it, can't we?' remarked Arthur. He was standing at the far end of the dining room looking at the garden. 'You of all people should be able to manage it, Allegra, being such a consummate actress.'

Something about the way he held himself, one hand pushed deep into the pocket of his trousers, the other holding the cigarette he was smoking, and the way he didn't even bother to turn around and look at them, made Allegra

139

want to take a poker to him.

'I wonder how Jack's will would work if one of us died before the week was up?' she asked Kit. 'Would we still inherit, and if so, would we each then have a greater share of the pot of money?'

Arthur turned around. 'Threatening to do away with me must surely contravene the terms of my father's will. It's also hardly an example of the family accord the old man was hoping for.'

'Who said anything about doing away with you?' said Allegra. 'I was merely talking hypothetically.'

He gave a loud guffaw, but without a trace of amusement. Then he tapped his left eye — the eye she had blinded as a child with Kit's catapult. 'Of course you were, Cousin Allegra,' he said. 'It must be having a crime author in the house with us that put such a thought into your pretty little head.'

'I have it on good authority that Romily's books are very good,' said Kit, pulling out a chair for Allegra. He was doing what he always did, thought Allegra, putting on a show of blithely ignoring the undercurrent of his brother's simmering hostility.

'Oh?' said Arthur, stubbing out his cigarette in an ashtray on the sideboard behind him. 'And who might that authority be?'

'Evelyn Flowerday. I was just telling Allegra that I met her in the village earlier. She seems to think that Romily has a very insightful way of looking at people.' Kit laughed. 'Who knows, we might all come under her microscope during this week. Perhaps you'd do well to mind your Ps and Qs, Arthur. Evelyn was also saying that she's offered Meadow Lodge as a home to take in an evacuee. Do you suppose Romily will have to do likewise here?'

'It appears so,' said the woman herself, appearing in the doorway with Hope behind her. 'Lady Fogg, our newly appointed billeting officer for the village, has just telephoned to say in her inimitable way that it's all hands on deck. Apparently it's just what a grieving widow needs, a couple of children to keep me busy. She's paying us a visit tomorrow morning to discuss the details.'

'Ma Foghorn hasn't changed, has she?' said Kit, moving quickly to pull out a chair for his stepmother at the head of the table. 'Still dishing out the orders as per usual.'

Romily smiled at him and sat down. 'Her type is born to dish out orders.'

'Will you do as she says?' asked Allegra, thinking of the conversation they'd had in the drawing room, and still trying to fathom why she had instigated it. What had got into her?

'I told Lady Fogg what everyone is probably telling her: that I'll do what needs to be done and for however long it needs to be done.'

Having taken the chair at the opposite end of the table, Arthur said, 'I assumed you'd be returning to London once this week was up. To your flat.'

'A miscalculation on your part, Arthur,' Romily said lightly, unfolding her napkin.

'When are the evacuees arriving?' asked Kit.

'I gather that will be one of the details with

which Lady Fogg will provide me. I imagine it will be after you've all left.'

'Assuming we do,' said Arthur with a smirk.

At that point Florence came in with a large soup tureen. The smell of food made Allegra's stomach clench and she suddenly felt very hot. She fanned herself with her hand.

'Are you all right, Allegra?' asked Romily quietly as Florence began serving the soup.

'Just a little warm,' she murmured, still fanning herself and praying that her stomach would settle. She took a cautious sip from her water glass.

'Lady Fogg also informed me that she'd just heard on the wireless that Parliament has been recalled and Neville Chamberlain has said that we're now in imminent peril of war.'

'So it's really going to happen,' murmured Hope, staring miserably across the table.

'It would seem so,' said Romily. 'Nazi Germany is showing no sign of backing down.'

When Florence had left them, Arthur said, 'Talking of Germans, Hope, where's that tiresome charge of yours?'

'I've told you before, Arthur, please show some respect and call her by her name.'

'Very well, where is Fraulein Annelise?'

'She's had her lunch already and is now having a nap, if you must know.' Hope sighed. 'I never knew a small child could be such overwhelmingly hard work.'

'Then perhaps you should have thought twice before accepting the responsibility,' said Arthur. 'You have only yourself to blame. Please don't look to us for sympathy.'

'What a perfectly heartless monster you are, Arthur,' said Hope.

'I'm just being honest. Whereas you, as always, are too wrapped up in your emotions to see what's as plain as a pikestaff to the rest of us.'

'Oh yes,' said Hope, staring down the table at him, 'and what is that precisely?'

'That you're hopelessly out of your depth and wishing you had never gone to Germany in the first place on some fool's errand to see Dieter's family, because then you wouldn't now be stuck with a child that's draining you of all energy. Is that precise enough for you?'

'I say, Arthur, give it a rest, won't you?'

'That's all right, Kit. I can fight my own battles, thank you very much!' Hope's voice wobbled, and to Allegra's surprise, the unimaginable happened: her cousin's cool reserve faltered and she burst into tears and fled from the room, knocking over her chair as she went.

19

Hope was in the cocoon-like warmth of the Victorian glasshouse in the kitchen garden; it was where she'd always escaped to when she was upset as a youngster. More often than not, Arthur's cruelty had been the reason. On one particular occasion she had sobbed her heart out for hours on end. It still upset her to think of it. To this day she still could not understand how her brother could have done what he did.

On her seventh birthday, she had been given a tame canary. She had loved that beautiful little bird so much. One day Arthur deliberately let it escape from its cage in her bedroom. It flew straight out of the open window, but to her delighted relief returned that same evening. However, a few days later she found the cage open and no sign of the canary. She discovered it dead on the ground below her bedroom window; it had been crushed flat. She knew Arthur had done it, although he vehemently denied it. From that day on she kept her room locked and wore the key around her neck on a ribbon.

At the sound of footsteps, she turned to see Romily looking in through the doorway of the glasshouse. Her heart sank. Being found by a woman who was so sophisticated and composed, and so perfectly in control of her emotions, made Hope feel a hundred times worse; as though she was a pathetic child who'd made a fool of herself by throwing a tantrum.

'You poor thing,' Romily said. 'What can I do to help you?'

Hope tried to say something, but couldn't manage it; her throat was too bunched up with anger and tears. All she could do was shake her head and try to blow her nose on her already sodden handkerchief.

'Here,' said Romily, coming over and sitting on the dusty wooden stool beside her, 'take mine.'

Reluctantly Hope took the proffered square of prettily embroidered linen.

'Now you can tell me to mind my own business, but putting aside your brother's despicable provocation, it strikes me that you're probably suffering from a combination of exhaustion and anxiety, in the way that any new mother would. Am I right, or am I totally wide of the mark? And as I said, you could just tell me to mind my own business.'

Hope wiped her eyes and blew her nose again. 'I just feel so completely overwhelmed,' she said. 'I've never looked after a child before. I do all those illustrations for children's books, but I don't know the first thing about them. Now that I'm responsible for one, I'm failing spectacularly in every way. And there isn't any time to do anything else.' She kept to herself that the worst of it was that Arthur's provocation had upset her because it was entirely true. She *did* regret taking on the responsibility of poor little Annelise. Moreover, she was being torn apart by guilt that she could think of herself before Sabine and Otto.

'Kit mentioned that he thinks you're up against a deadline to deliver some illustrations to your publisher. Is that also what's worrying you?'

Hope nodded. 'I've promised I'll have the bulk of the drawings with them by early next week. But I have no idea how I'm going to do it. I thought I'd be able to work at night when Annelise was in bed, but I'm just too shattered to do anything of worth.'

Her lips pursed, Romily stared over at the row of neatly lined-up clay pots on the bench. Such was her concentration, Hope could have almost believed she was actually counting them. 'Well,' she said eventually, 'it's a tall order you have to contend with, but it's not insurmountable. We can easily solve part of the problem.'

'How?'

'I see two solutions. One, you could hire a nanny to look after Annelise; or two — which I favour, and would be the quickest way to help you while you're here — is that we do as Lady Fogg says and get all hands on deck. I'm sure Mrs Partridge would be the first to do what she can to help, as will Florence, and I'll do my bit too, and even Kit and Allegra if we ask them nicely. I think we can safely agree that it would be preferable to leave Arthur out of the arrangement.'

'But you have work to do yourself,' said Hope, her voice trembling with an unsteady note. She was stunned at Romily's suggestion. 'And Kit and Allegra wouldn't know one end of a baby from the other.'

'Do any of us? We'll all just have to muck in

and knuckle down.'

A fresh batch of tears pricking at the backs of her eyes, Hope pressed the handkerchief in her hand to her lips. 'Why are you being so understanding towards me?' she murmured.

'I don't like to see anyone suffering, and I think you've been quietly suffering for too long on your own.'

Suspecting that Romily was talking about more than just her inability to cope with Annelise, and wondering what she knew, and from whom she'd learned it, Hope said, 'I'm afraid I was quite rude to Florence first thing this morning. She was trying to help and I was horrible to her. And I don't even know why. Would you tell her I'm sorry, please?'

'Of course. But telling her yourself would be better, don't you think?'

Hope bristled. 'Are you trying to belittle me and put me in my place?'

Romily looked at her with a frown on her face. 'Why would I want to do that?'

Any number of reasons sprang to mind, but Hope suddenly saw how petty she was being. Here was this relative stranger doing her best to help, and all Hope could do was question her motives. 'I'm sorry,' she said. 'I've become so used to my own company and feeling wretched that I sometimes forget how to be nice to others.' She paused. 'And you're the first person I've admitted that to.'

'Then I'm honoured you felt able to say it. Now then, do you have everything you need to work on these illustrations?'

'I never go anywhere without my drawing materials.'

'Good. So what you presumably also need is a quiet room with good light. Yes?'

'My bedroom will be fine. It's where I always used to draw. But I'll need a table or a desk to put in front of the window.'

'Easily sorted. Leave it with me. Well then,' Romily added decisively, getting to her feet as if all was settled, 'why don't we go back up to the house and find you something to eat, and afterwards you can get to work — that's if you feel you want to, if you're in the right frame of mind.'

'I'd better see to Annelise first,' said Hope. 'She'll be awake from her nap now.'

'In that case, I'll go and see if she's awake while you have your lunch.'

As they walked in step along the gravel path away from the glasshouse, Hope had the strangest of feelings; as though this wholly pragmatic woman had the power to make everything right in the world. There was a powerful magnetism about her, too. You couldn't help but be drawn towards her and respond to her positivity. Was that what Hope's father had seen in her?

They were almost at the gate that separated the kitchen garden from the rest of the garden when Hope slowed her step. 'How do you do it?'

Romily stared back at her. 'In what sense?'

'Make life look so easy?'

'Don't be fooled. I'm a swan, gliding along on the surface but paddling frantically beneath.'

'I find that hard to believe. You've just lost your husband and yet you're able to show me sympathy and enormous kindness. I couldn't have done that when I was first widowed. In fact, if I'm brutally honest, I still can't.'

'You do yourself down, Hope. You could have said no to Annelise's parents, but you didn't. You did something wonderfully heroic by bringing their precious daughter home with you.'

'The trouble is, I can't stop thinking of Otto and Sabine. I should have tried harder to make them come with me. I fear for them, I really do.'

'I believe you have every right to be concerned. What I saw going on in Europe when I was recently there chilled my blood. But you did what you could. We all, in the end, have to make difficult choices, and simply do the best we can.'

Romily paused and turned to look towards the house. 'I found writing today a great comfort,' she said softly. 'It was a much-needed diversion.' She slowly switched her gaze back to Hope. 'Maybe you'll find that doing some work will help you get a fresh perspective on your new-found situation. You know, your father was immensely proud of your talent as an illustrator.'

'He never said so. Not in those actual words.'

'He probably thought you'd imagine he was patronising you. Would he have had cause to believe that?'

The pain of an old wound deep inside Hope made itself felt, made her remember how furious her father had been when she'd first told him about Dieter. She remembered too how much she had hated him for his high-handed and illogical prejudice. 'My father rarely gave praise,' she said, 'but in contrast he was always quick to show his displeasure at something.'

'Do you mean when you wanted to marry Dieter?'

'Yes,' Hope said flatly. 'My father refused point-blank to consider any view but his own on the matter. His trouble was that he couldn't accept he could ever be wrong.'

'He did, you know. He profoundly regretted his reaction to you and Dieter. If he could have turned back time, he would have.'

Hope chewed on her lip and frowned. 'What made you fall in love with him? It's a question that's puzzled me ever since meeting you. You just don't seem to be the sort of woman who would put up with a man like Jack Devereux.'

'I fell in love with him because . . . because he made my world seem so much better than it had before.' Romily stared into the distance, her gaze directed towards the church tower on the other side of the beech hedge. 'The sun was brighter when we were together,' she said faintly, 'the sky bluer, the stars and moon bigger. I can't explain why that should be, but Jack just had that effect on me. Yes, he could be dogmatic and wickedly quick-tempered, but equally he could be gentle and thoughtful. I was ill once, just with a silly head cold, but instead of driving down to London for a meeting he had planned, he cancelled it, then put me to bed with a hot-water bottle, a glass of lemon and honey and a tot of whisky, and read to me.'

'That doesn't sound like the man I know,' Hope said. But no sooner had she uttered the words than a memory from a long time ago surfaced, and she pictured her father by the side of her bed, reading to her and encouraging her to sip the milky drink he'd brought up for her.

'Perhaps he was afraid to show his softer side,' said Romily. 'It couldn't have been easy for him being on his own after your mother died. He had to be both father and mother to you; he was bound to make mistakes. Mistakes I know that he very much came to regret. He so badly wanted to make amends to you all. But he realised it too late. And now he's dead.' She turned away and resumed walking, but not before Hope saw her eyes fill with tears.

'I'm sorry if I upset you,' said Hope, and meant it.

'Don't apologise, there's no need.'

'When you feel able to, will you tell me some more about my father, the man you came to know?'

'I will if you'll tell me about Dieter.'

Hope's instinctive reaction was to refuse the request, to withhold every precious memory she had of Dieter for fear of exposing it to ridicule, or worse, losing it. But sensing she was in the presence of somebody who might actually understand, she said, 'Dieter made me feel the same way my father made you feel, he made my world feel infinitely better than it had ever been before.'

'How did you meet?'

'At a lunchtime concert at the Albert Hall. It

151

was a piano recital, Grieg. I don't know how you feel about Grieg, but after a while he palls for me.'

Romily smiled. 'I know exactly what you mean.'

Hope smiled too. 'Well, I rather rudely began to occupy my time with doodling on my recital programme, drawing a family of trolls and their little house built into the rock of a hillside. I was so absorbed that I didn't notice that the man in the seat next to me was watching what I was doing.'

'And that was Dieter?'

'Yes. When the concert was over, I apologised for distracting him from the music, and he said that he'd welcomed the distraction, that it had given him enormous pleasure to watch me and that he was envious of anyone who had such a natural gift. I'm making him sound more forward that he really was; he was actually quite a shy man.'

Romily nodded. 'But he plucked up the courage to ask you to go out with him, I'm assuming?'

'He gave me his telephone number in the hope that I might like to arrange an outing together to another concert sometime.'

'Which you did?'

'Yes. And from then on, we were more or less inseparable.'

Neither of them spoke for a few moments, not until they were almost on the terrace of the house. 'It strikes me,' said Romily, 'that we're not so very different, you and I. We've both lost the man we loved and we're in a similar line of work, with deadlines to meet with our respective publishers. Why don't we, in the days ahead, do all we can to support each other?'

Hope was surprised at the suggestion. 'I'm not sure how I can support you. Or if you really need any assistance.'

'Don't you? How about helping to make peace with your cousin and brothers?'

20

Lady Fogg arrived the following morning on the stroke of eleven o'clock, just as the last of the chimes from St Mary's rang out.

An overbearing, condescending woman of advancing years who believed firmly in the old order — the more feudal the better — Lady Fogg was comprehensively reviled within the village for her ability always to cause offence. Romily was fascinated by her, from the top of her Queen Mary styled hair to her large sensible lace-up shoes. Most assuredly, and before too long, the woman would appear as a *femme formidable* of some magnitude in one of her novels.

Villages up and down the country undoubtedly needed and relied upon this type of woman. They were the backbone of small communities; without them, nothing would get done. It was a fact that Lady Fogg had been only too quick to point out to Romily as she swept in on a gust of her own martyred self-importance.

'If one wants anything done, one has to get on with it oneself,' she'd barked. 'As if I haven't enough to do! But since nobody else was inclined to grasp the nettle and offer themselves as billeting officer, there was nothing else for it but for me to volunteer.'

Privately Romily would sooner believe that nobody else had had the courage to put themselves forward, or if they had, the move had been swiftly vetoed.

'Now then, Miss Temple,' said Lady Fogg, as though addressing a large gathering, while settling her ample posterior into the armchair opposite Romily and clasping a folder to her equally ample bosom. 'I need to check a few details with you and convince myself of the suitability of the accommodation you have here, which I'm sure — '

Romily raised a hand to interrupt the flow of Lady Fogg's words, something she warranted not many dared to do.

The woman looked at her askance.

'It's Mrs Temple-Devereux,' Romily said smoothly. 'After all, Jack and I *were* married.'

A flaring of nostrils indicated that Lady Fogg was far from pleased at being corrected. Furthermore, she probably doubted the veracity of Romily's marital status.

'I believe the accurate use of titles is so important, don't you agree, Lady Fogg?' said Romily with a smile. 'Please, do carry on.'

'I was under the impression that you were retaining your maiden name,' the woman responded.

'And so I am for professional purposes; to my readers I shall always be plain old Romily Temple. However, in my private life I was Jack's wife, alas all too briefly, and I'm proud to bear his name.' She knew that Lady Fogg had been particularly vocal on the subject of her living in sin at Island House with Jack; had even snubbed her on one occasion.

'Quite,' replied the woman with a steely tone.

Not for a second had Romily expected any

155

kind of half-hearted attempt on Lady Fogg's part to offer condolences on Jack's untimely death, and in many ways it was refreshing not to have to summon the platitudes demanded in such circumstances. It was much more fun to be sparring with the woman.

'Now if we could get on,' Lady Fogg said. 'I'm extremely busy. Yours is not the only house call I have to make this morning.'

'I suppose I would be adding to your burden if I were to offer you some refreshments; a cup of coffee perhaps?'

Lady Fogg hesitated.

'No, no,' said Romily quickly, enjoying herself, 'you have far too much to do. Silly of me to say anything, of course you need to get on. I mustn't delay you. Not for a minute.'

Her lips pursed together, Lady Fogg opened the folder on her lap and withdrew a pen from her handbag. A pen that didn't work, it transpired. She jabbed it at the piece of paper, but it refused to cooperate.

Romily went over to her desk and helpfully handed Lady Fogg a pen. 'Try this one.'

'Thank you,' the woman said, without the slightest trace of gratitude. The pen poised, she crossed her legs at her ankles, which were remarkably slim, given her bulk. 'Of course in so many ways this is all highly unethical,' she said, 'but needs must.'

'In what way unethical, Lady Fogg?'

'Well, Island House isn't strictly yours, is it? Not until probate has been dealt with, presumably.'

If she was trying to make a point that Romily did not in some way belong here, she had better think again. 'In that case, maybe this has been a wasted visit for you,' said Romily, with some heat to her voice. 'I'd hate for you to feel compromised in the name of necessity.'

'In difficult times one can always find a way round these things,' Lady Fogg replied. Her satisfied expression showed that she felt she'd scored a well-aimed blow. She then gave her attention to working through the details of what would be involved in having an evacuee to stay.

When she'd finished, she said, 'Will the house be sold off and the proceeds shared amongst the children? Talking of which, I heard they were staying on with you. It must be a trying time for you; they're not an easy family.' She gave a bizarrely sudden and loud laugh, like a gunshot being fired, which made Romily start. 'You may well rue the day you ever met Jack Devereux!'

Enough was enough. Romily rose to her feet. 'Lady Fogg, you could not be more wrong. On all counts. Do please forgive me for rushing you, but I'm expecting a phone call from my editor. Do you have time to inspect upstairs before leaving? I must ask you to respect Mrs Meyer's privacy; she's working in her room so I'd rather we didn't disturb her.'

★   ★   ★

With his eyes closed, and basking in the pleasantly warm morning sunshine on the wooden bench to one side of the open French doors of the drawing room, Kit had been listening to the exchange between Romily and Ma Foghorn, all the while silently cheering Romily on. Hearing how easily she had run rings around the old battleaxe, he'd back his step-mother any day in a head-to-head!

He opened his eyes and looked over to the pond, where his brother was rowing languidly through the lily pads. Once he was in the middle of the pond, he stopped and drew in the oars, then produced a bottle of beer and proceeded to twist off the cap. Watching his brother gulp down the beer, tipping his head back in the sun, Kit could almost believe Arthur was happy, that he was enjoying the solitude. But more likely he was plotting who to upset next.

Well it wouldn't be him, vowed Kit. There were more important things going on in the world than allowing himself to be cowed by Arthur. Following his admission to Evelyn yesterday that he was thinking of joining the RAF, he couldn't help but think he'd better get on and do something about it. Or should he wait until war was declared? No point in rushing to sign up if nothing was actually going to happen.

And there he went again, he thought crossly. Why did he keep procrastinating? Why could he not just make his mind up and get on with things?

From around the side of the house his cousin Allegra appeared. She saw him, hesitated, and then came over. 'You look as bored as I feel,' she said.

'I'm not bored at all. I was just sitting here

thinking. You're welcome to join me.'

Again she hesitated, but then smoothed down the back of her skirt and sat next to him. 'What do you think of this idea of Romily's to have us all babysitting Annelise?' she said.

'It's certainly not something I thought I'd ever be doing, but you saw the state Hope was in yesterday; she was obviously at her wits' end.'

'Yes, but I don't see why that should mean we have to be reduced to the same neurotic state. Why doesn't she simply find some girl from the village to do it?'

Kit had thought much the same thing, and for now was grateful that the maid, Florence, was occupying Annelise while Hope worked upstairs in her bedroom. 'It's only for a few days,' he said mildly.

'That's so typical of you!' snapped Allegra. 'Always sitting on the fence, not wanting to cause any fuss or bother.'

'As opposed to you, always making a drama out of the smallest of things. It must be the — '

'Oh, that's right!' interrupted Allegra, not giving him a chance to finish his sentence. 'It must be the illegitimate hot-blooded Italian in me!'

Kit was astonished, although he shouldn't have been; Allegra's mood swings were legendary. 'I was going to say it must be the prima donna in you.'

'Liar!'

'For heaven's sake!' he said, exasperated. 'Aren't you tired of always dragging out that old chestnut? Do you really think any of us gives a damn about it now?'

'Maybe it's because I *do* give a damn about it. You have no idea what it feels like never to have known your mother or father.'

'You're forgetting, I never knew my mother, and you never hear me complaining about that.'

'But you don't have the stigma I grew up with! Being labelled a bastard never leaves you. I wouldn't wish that on any child.'

Before Kit could say anything further, she leapt up from the wooden bench and marched off at practically a gallop. Baffled, he watched her go. What on earth was that all about?

21

It was a day for callers — first Lady Fogg and now the Reverend Septimus Tate, who had presided over Jack's funeral.

A confirmed bachelor, he was known for demanding strict piety and Christian charity from his flock while showing not a scrap of it himself. He usually timed his parish visits to coincide with mealtimes, when he could be sure of an invitation to join his hosts at their table.

Florence had announced his arrival to Romily just as they had sat down for lunch in the garden, Romily having decided that eating outside might make for a more convivial atmosphere, that the sun-drenched garden might temper Arthur's obnoxious behaviour and Hope might feel more relaxed with Annelise in these less formal surroundings.

'Apologies for the intrusion!' boomed the vicar, emerging from the house onto the terrace before Romily had had a chance to tell Florence to ask him to wait in the drawing room. 'I had no idea it was that time of day already,' he said, 'and that you'd be sitting down to eat.'

A compulsive liar as well as a grasping glutton, thought Romily, regarding with revulsion the corpulent red-faced man lumbering towards them. 'Perhaps you'd care to join us,' she said, observing him eyeing their plates of poached salmon, new potatoes and green beans. 'I'm sure we can stretch things to go round a little further. Kit, perhaps you'd be so good as to find another chair from the summer house? And Florence, could you trouble Mrs Partridge for some lunch for our unexpected guest?'

'How kind of you, Mrs Temple-Devereux,' the man said, removing his hat and mopping his sweating brow with a handkerchief. 'But really I don't want to intrude.'

'A bit late for that,' muttered Arthur, reaching for his wine glass and taking a large mouthful.

Fortunately, as well as suffering from gout, the Reverend Tate was slightly deaf, which enabled plenty of his flock to mutter about him without fear of being overheard.

Once the inconvenience of his arrival had been dealt with and he was seated between Kit and Romily with a knife and fork held firmly in his meaty grasp, she asked him what brought him to Island House.

'Ah yes, of course, so consumed was I by the warmth of your generosity, I almost forgot. I have a favour to beg of you, dear lady.'

'Here we go,' muttered Arthur. 'The Bank of Devereux is about to be tapped.'

'What's that, Arthur?' asked the reverend. 'I didn't catch it.'

'I was asking my sister, Hope, if it was time for Annelise's nap,' he lied smoothly.

The vicar looked at Annelise as if only just registering her presence, and grimaced at the sight of the child pushing a marble-sized potato into her mouth. Whether or not it was the effect of the vicar staring at her, Annelise chose to spit out the potato. She appeared to find this highly amusing and giggled, which revealed a partially chewed green bean on her tongue. She then, with very dainty fingers, picked up the rejected potato and offered it to the vicar. Romily couldn't help but laugh at his obvious disgust, which made Annelise chortle some more, as well as bob up and down happily in her high chair, her feet kicking the table and rattling the crockery.

'Looks like you're a hit with our youngest diner, Reverend Tate,' remarked Kit. 'What were you saying about a favour?'

'Ah yes. We — that is, the village fete committee — find ourselves in something of a fix for the fete tomorrow. As you may recall, Mrs Temple-Devereux, your husband had accepted an invitation to officiate and declare the fete open, which leaves us hoping . . . and I'm aware of the imposition, but could you possibly find it within your power to do the honours for us in Mr Devereux's place?'

Romily had forgotten about the fete, had forgotten too what Jack had agreed to do, but before she had a chance to reply, Arthur clanged his cutlery against his plate. 'It's out of the question,' he said. 'It wouldn't be appropriate given that our father is barely cold in his grave. What would people think?'

'Inappropriate to whom?' asked Romily, her hackles up. How dare Arthur think he could answer on her behalf!

'And since when did appropriate behaviour ever bother *you?*' said Allegra.

'I think you're talking about yourself, Allegra,' replied Arthur. 'I for one care deeply about the correct way of doing things.'

'Why not do it in Jack's honour?' suggested Kit.

Grateful for Kit's intervention, Romily turned to the vicar. 'Of course I shall do it. I'm sure Jack would have wanted me to take his place. What is more,' she said, glancing around the table, daring anyone to disagree, 'I think it would be good for us all to attend the fete as a family, as a way to thank the village for its kindness during this time of bereavement.' Ignoring the inhalation of breath from Arthur, she added, 'I strongly believe that this is something Jack would have wanted.'

★　★　★

'Bloody hell, I call it a bit rich when she starts bossing us around as though we're children. What gives her the right to do that? But I'll tell you this for nothing: she can count me out from providing her with a false united front to the peasants of this village!'

Arthur had been banging on in this fashion for nearly an hour following lunch and the Reverend Tate's eventual departure. With Hope back upstairs in her room working, and Romily doing some work of her own in the drawing room, Kit, Allegra and Arthur were in the garden minding Annelise while she slept on a rug in the shade of a parasol.

Allegra was fascinated by the pale smoothness

of the baby's skin; it was so enviably flawless, and so at odds with the disagreeably puce complexion her face turned when she was crying. How different that child was to the one sleeping so serenely now. How could two such extremes co-exist in one small scrap of life?

Never having seen the child sleep before, and seeing her lying so peacefully, Allegra was struck by her vulnerability. It made her think of the small life dwelling inside her, and from nowhere came a feeling of acute tenderness and the inexplicable urge to place a hand protectively over her stomach. When she realised she had actually done it, she whipped her hand away and pretended to shoo away an annoying fly or bee. It was nothing more than hormones making her react so illogically, she told herself sternly. She had to fight it, had to keep her emotions, which were fast taking over her mind and body, firmly under control. The thought of losing not just her mind but her figure, of becoming fat and ugly and unlovable, appalled her. Could she really go through with having the baby? But the alternative was unthinkable.

'Oh do give it a rest, Arthur,' said Kit, rousing her sharply from her thoughts. 'You've made your point repeatedly, and while you're perfectly entitled to your views, please bear in mind that if we don't go along with Romily's wishes, she may well report back to Roddy and that could be the end of our inheritance. Can't you just play along?'

'You might have become totally emasculated and devoid of all pride,' answered Arthur, 'but I have not. I refuse to be treated like a child by that damned woman!'

'Then stop acting like one,' said Allegra. 'And please watch your language in front of Annelise.'

This was too much for Arthur, and lighting up another cigarette, he strode off, shoulders hunched.

Allegra noticed that Kit was smiling. 'What's so funny?' she asked.

'You telling him to watch his language when Annelise can't understand a word of English.'

Allegra smiled. 'Not yet she can't, but she will very soon. I wonder if Hope knows what she's taken on.'

'In what way?'

'In all ways. Because let's face it, once war breaks out, that poor girl is unlikely to see her parents again, is she? Through no fault of her own, she's going to end up a member of this wretched family for life. Just as I did.'

Kit frowned. 'Is that how you really see it, even after all this time? That Jack adopting you was the worst thing to happen?'

No, she thought, the worst thing to happen to her was meeting Luigi and ending up in the mess she was now. Distracted by the sight of a tall, muscular man emerging with a wheelbarrow from the gate that led from the kitchen garden, she said, 'Who's that over there? There's something familiar about him.'

'Don't you recognise him?'

Allegra shielded her eyes from the glare of the sun. Seconds passed as she watched the man push the wheelbarrow across the lawn towards a

166

holly bush. Her heart suddenly lurched.

'It's Elijah Hartley,' said Kit when she didn't say anything.

'It can't be,' she murmured.

'I assure you it is. I spoke to him briefly yesterday on my way back from the village; he took over the job of gardener here when his grandfather died.'

'Did you tell him I was here?'

'He already knew you were.'

And he hadn't come and sought her out, thought Allegra sadly.

Dressed in a collarless shirt with the sleeves rolled to his elbows, a cotton scarf knotted at his neck, and a pair of loose olive-green trousers held up with a thick belt, he was now clipping at the holly bush. 'Why haven't I seen him around before today?' she asked Kit.

'Apparently he works three days here and the rest of the time he's up at Melstead Hall working for old Ma Fogg. You two used to be as thick as thieves, didn't you?' continued Kit in his infuriatingly blithe way.

As thick as thieves . . . Oh, it had been so much more than that! But how very different Elijah looked, how tall and handsome he had grown. The same age as Allegra, he'd been such a slight boy when he'd tagged along to help his grandfather in the garden here. Occasionally Allegra had gone to have tea with Elijah in the cottage where he lived. One time it had been his birthday and she'd taken him a book as a present — a book she had stolen from her uncle's study. Only later did she discover how useless a gift it was because Elijah couldn't read, something he had kept from her.

Back then Allegra had felt she had more in common with Elijah than with the family that had adopted her. Perhaps that was because his parents had both died from Spanish flu after the Great War, and his widowed grandfather, Joss Hartley, a devoutly religious man, had brought him up. His childhood had been a lonely one, just as hers was. Maybe that was why there had been such a strong bond of friendship between them, and why they had made a pact never to abandon each other.

But Allegra had broken that promise, and watching Elijah now, she accepted what she had always known but had tried to ignore: that it was one of her biggest regrets.

'I say, Allegra, where are you going?' asked Kit as, guided by an unstoppable force, she rose from her wicker chair and began to walk in Elijah's direction. 'You're not leaving me here alone with Annelise, are you?'

Ignoring the desperate plea in his voice, Allegra kept on walking, held in the powerful grip of the past — a past for which she knew she had to atone. She had treated Elijah badly and she owed him an apology. Even after all this time.

As though sensing her presence, or more likely hearing Kit calling after her, Elijah stopped what he was doing and turned around. Giving no sign that he recognised her, he stood very still and watched her approach. When she was level with him, he stared at her in unnerving silence. She stared back, at a loss what to say. Whatever she said wouldn't be enough.

It was Elijah who broke the silence. 'I thought it was you over there with Kit,' he said.

'You didn't want to come and say hello, then?'

'I didn't think you'd want the likes of me disturbing you.'

The likes of me . . . How cool and distant he sounded, not at all like the boy she had known.

'How could you think that?' she asked him.

He fiddled with the shears in his large square hands, but didn't answer her.

'You look well,' she said, grasping for something to say. 'You've grown.'

'So have you. But then it's been ten years.'

'Yes,' was all she could think to say.

'I was sorry to hear about your uncle. He was a good and decent man.'

'You've lost your Suffolk accent,' she said, noting another change in him.

He shrugged. 'That's what happens when you move away.'

'Where did you go?'

'Down to the south coast to work for a time, then when my grandfather took ill, I came back. Folks round here made fun of me, said I was no longer one of them. What about you?' With a subtle sweep of his dark brown eyes that left her feeling stripped to her soul, he looked her up and down. 'Word is you've become quite the singing star in Italy, just as you always said you would. But then I never doubted you'd achieve your dream, that nothing would stand in your way.'

She could have wept at his words.

22

The fete was held at Clover Field, at the opposite end of the village to Island House.

Florence and Mrs Partridge had been given the afternoon off so they could come and enjoy themselves along with the rest of the village, and watching Miss Romily welcoming everybody to the fete, and knowing how difficult it was for her, Florence was filled with pride. Having deliberately eschewed the wearing of black since the funeral, Miss Romily had opted today to wear an elegant navy-blue dress with a white collar, a wide navy-blue brimmed hat and white gloves. With a stylish pair of sunglasses covering her eyes, she looked like a glamorous film star.

Florence knew that under normal circumstances Miss Romily was very used to speaking in public, but this, up there on the podium, standing in for her husband, was different. Only once did she seem to lose her way and hesitate, and that was when she mentioned Jack by name, saying how much he had liked being involved with the village.

'I'm sure he's looking down on us all,' she said now, 'and thinking, 'Oh for heaven's sake, woman, do stop rambling and let everybody get on with enjoying themselves!' So that's what I shall do, but not without thanking you for supporting such a fine tradition as the Melstead St Mary summer fete!'

The crowd clapped enthusiastically and then the Salvation Army band struck up with 'It's a Long Way to Tipperary'. In the front row of the band, playing his trumpet, was Billy Minton. He looked very smart in his uniform, quite different to how he looked when he was serving in his parents' shop, or on his bicycle delivering bread around the village. Spotting Florence in the crowd, he gave her a wink. She smiled back at him shyly.

With Mrs Partridge going off to find herself a cup of tea in the refreshment tent, and no doubt to have a gossip with Mrs Bunch — a woman Miss Romily joked was head of the intelligence corps in the village — Florence went in search of the ice cream seller. She soon found him, and after waiting patiently in the queue, she handed over her 2d for a large cornet. She then wandered about looking at the various stalls of books, toys, bric-a-brac and home-made preserves. After browsing the jars of local honey, lemon curd and strawberry jam, she moved on to the plant stall run by Miss Gant and Miss Treadmill. Florence knew them to say hello to, and gave the ladies a smile and a wave, but with no need of a plant, she pressed on towards the home-produce tent. Mrs Partridge had wondered about taking part to see if she could win Best Cake, but what with having been so busy this last week, she hadn't had time. 'Next year,' she'd said, 'I'll bake a cake to knock their socks off, see if I don't!'

But from what some folk were saying, you'd think there wasn't going to be a next year. War. It was all people could talk about. And not *if*, but *when*. Yesterday they'd been issued with horrid gas masks as well as pamphlets about what to do in the case of war breaking out, but somehow none of it seemed real. How could it? thought Florence, looking about her at all the happy smiling faces in the summer sunshine.

As she finished her ice cream, she passed a crowd of children clustered around a wooden barrel, their arms lost within the sawdust of the lucky dip as they dug down deep for some hidden treasure. Florence was suddenly struck by a memory of doing the same thing a long time ago.

She had been with her mother at a fair, a rare chance for them to be alone together. Her mother had said that it was to be a secret between them, and that if Florence could keep the secret, maybe they would do it again. They'd only been at the fair a short while when they got chatting to a man Florence had never seen before, but who her mother seemed to know. He'd been very friendly and had bought them ice creams and lemonade to drink. She had never seen her mother look so cheerful or carefree. The man had asked Florence if she would like a go on the lucky dip, and in amongst the sawdust she'd found a stick of pink liquorice wrapped in paper, which she'd eaten immediately. Next he had asked if she'd like him to try and win her a doll on the shooting range; he'd said he was a crack shot, so it would be as easy as anything. To her amazement, he'd done just that. Never had Florence seen a doll so pretty or dressed in such fine clothes. But when she and her mother had been on the bus going home, she'd lost the doll and had cried.

'Please don't make a fuss,' Mum had said, trying to calm her. 'It was only a doll.'

'No it wasn't!' Florence had wailed. 'She was a special doll because that nice man won her for me.'

Mum had put her arm around her and told her that she had to remember that today had been a secret day, and she mustn't ever mention it to her brothers or her father. It was later, when she was in bed that night listening to her father yelling at her mother, that Florence remembered something important — *she* hadn't lost the doll; Mum had. Mum had been carrying it for her because Florence was so tired. Had she deliberately lost it? Would it have spoilt the secret if they'd brought it home with them?

She never got the chance to ask, because the next day her mother fell down the stairs. Well, that was what she said she had done, but Florence knew that the bruises to her poor battered face had not been caused by a careless tumble. Two days later, Mum disappeared.

In the days and weeks that followed, Florence would often hear the neighbours talking on their doorsteps about her mother. Some said she'd run off and good luck to her; others thought she was more likely dead, her old man's temper having finally got the better of him. Florence had always hoped that she had run off; that wherever she was, she was happy. Maybe she was with that nice man they'd met at the fair. But then she'd think of the misery of her own life after her mother had disappeared and her heart would harden.

Ahead of her she saw a small midnight-blue tent with stars and a moon painted on it. There was a sign attached to it bearing the words 'Fortune Teller — Gypsy Rose-Marie.' Florence looked at it sceptically. It was probably just someone from the village dressed up to look like a gypsy who you paid to stare into a crystal ball, or who would make up some rubbish from looking at your palm. Odds on Florence would be told that she would meet a tall, dark and handsome stranger — who she would marry and then discover he was nothing but a brute, and they'd have lots of children, one after the other, like her poor mother. If that was her future, no thank you!

But curiosity made her waver. What if the gypsy woman was genuine and could really see what the future held? The next thing she knew, she was parting the flaps of the tent and stepping inside. It took a moment for her eyes to adjust to the stuffy darkness, and she jumped when a cackling old voice told her to sit down. 'Come on, dearie, don't keep me waiting.'

The voice came from the other side of a small round table covered with a heavy brocade cloth. Illuminated by a single flickering candle was the most gnarled and wrinkled old woman Florence had ever set eyes on. Her head was swathed in a scarf with what looked like gold coins sewn along the edge, and draped over her shoulders was a black shawl.

'Please tell me I'm going to meet a tall, dark and very handsome stranger one day,' Florence said nervously. She might just as well enter into the spirit of the thing; after all, this old crone of a woman couldn't be genuine, could she?

The woman gave her a terrifyingly severe look in the candlelight. 'You've come in here to mock me, have you? You may live to regret that. Give me your penny, and then your hand.' She stuck out one of hers, gold bangles jangling on her scrawny wrist. She took the coin Florence offered and hid it somewhere in the folds of her skirt.

The woman's fingers were dry and rough as she snatched hold of Florence's hand, but surprisingly cool given how hot and fusty it was inside the small tent. Florence began to consider the possibility that she might actually be a real gypsy; she certainly had the sort of face that looked like it had spent most of its life outside in all weathers. She even had a gold tooth, and hooked through her ear lobes were gold-hooped rings, which caught the light from the candle when she moved.

A long bony finger traced a line on the palm of Florence's hand. 'I see a long life ahead for you,' she said in a raspy tone. 'It won't be an easy life, though. You'll have many obstacles to overcome. You'll find love and you'll lose love. Now then, this is interesting. I see . . . I see a woman . . . a woman with red hair . . . ' She raised her dark eyes to Florence's. 'Red hair just like yours.' She dropped her gaze back down again. 'This woman . . . you haven't seen her in a long time — '

175

Florence snatched her hand away. 'You're making this up!'

'Am I, dearie? And why would I do that?'

'Because . . . because that's what people like you do.'

The woman laughed scornfully. 'That's what all unbelievers say. If you don't want to hear the truth, don't waste my time. Be off with you!'

Florence couldn't get away fast enough from the old witch. She emerged from the tent into the bright sunshine breathless and close to tears. It was just a lucky shot in the dark, nothing more than that — Florence's own hair was red, so it made sense that somebody close to her would also have the same colour hair. Anyone could have guessed at that.

Her heart beating fast, she was practically running when she crashed full tilt into Billy Minton. 'Hey, what's the hurry?' he asked, catching her by the arm.

'I'm sorry,' she said, flustered and feeling foolish. 'I wasn't looking where I was going.'

'You okay?' he said with a frown of concern. 'You look properly ruffled. Did something upset you in the fortune-telling tent?'

'How did you know I was in there?'

'I saw you go in. Plain as daylight.'

'Well I wish I hadn't,' she said hotly. 'The old hag in there shouldn't be allowed to take hard-earned money and then tell lies to innocent folk. She's nothing but a charlatan.'

Billy laughed. 'She's here every year — she's a rum ol' gal and no mistake. She once told my gran that she was going to have an accident, and sure enough she fell down the cellar steps that very evening.'

'Was she all right?' asked Florence.

He laughed again. 'Yes, she was right as rain until she died quite peacefully in her sleep the following year. Fancy trying your luck on the coconut shy with me?'

'Aren't you needed in the band?'

'We've a short break before we have to play again. I'll stand you a go on the coconut shy if you come and listen to me play later. I've got a solo,' he added with obvious pride.

Her mood lightened and she smiled. 'Go on then, why not?'

'That's my girl,' he said.

The combination of his words and his taking her hand made Florence's heart, which had only just settled, skip a beat.

But then like a shadow passing across the sun, the gypsy woman's words echoed in her head: *You'll find love and you'll lose love.*

23

Arthur had been drinking steadily since his stepmother had given that toe-curlingly awful speech about his father and declared the fete open. Could she have been any more nauseatingly sentimental?

Everything about the fete was just as Arthur had known it would be; nothing had changed since he'd attended as a boy — tombola, hoopla, tug of war, donkey rides, country dancing, best dog in show, sack races. It was pathetically unsophisticated entertainment for the pathetically unsophisticated. At least the up side was that as an adult he could drink as much as he wanted instead of sneaking into the beer tent to help himself to somebody else's glass while they weren't looking.

He'd been in the tent for over an hour, observing the comings and goings. Apart from a few women, it was mostly lads, and older men in their caps and rolled-up shirtsleeves. Every one of them had eyed him warily without actually looking him in the eye, and not a single one had spoken to him; most had actively given him a wide berth. Which suited him just fine. He was in no mood for small talk.

It had been a ridiculous idea of Romily's to insist they show a united front in the village. For what purpose? Who did she think they would be fooling? It was nothing but a pointless exercise.

Or more precisely, on her part, an exercise in divide-and-conquer warfare. For there was no doubt about it, she was already showing signs of winning the others round. In fact, he'd go so far as to say they were warming to her so much she'd be lucky to be rid of them when the week was up. More fool her!

As for him, he'd be off just as soon as he'd fulfilled the requirements of his father's will, heading back to town on the first available train. Better still, he'd make a detour to Wembley. By God, after being cooped up here, he'd have earned the right for a lengthy session of pleasure with Pamela. And there'd be no need to worry about Irene. With her safely up in Scotland with her family, he'd be able to indulge himself for a few days before she rejoined him at home. But what pleased him most was the satisfying prospect of coming into a great deal of money before too long. Life was definitely looking up. 'Thank you, Father!' he said aloud, causing those nearest him to look his way. He raised his glass. 'Here's to Jack Devereux, who has proved to be a better father when dead. A shame he didn't die sooner. What?' he said when a cloth-capped old man tutted and shook his head.

His glass now empty, he hauled himself up to go and order another beer and caught his foot on the leg of the table he was sitting at, nearly knocking it over. 'Bloody stupid table!' he cursed. Forcing his way through the crowd of men, who seemed to be making his passage deliberately difficult, he very nearly lost his balance again. Bloody stupid uneven ground, he thought angrily. Why couldn't they flatten the field before erecting the ruddy tent?

He had the makeshift bar within his sights when he missed his footing once more, and, finding the ground suddenly rising up towards him, reached out to steady himself. His hand met with something pleasingly soft and rounded, and coincided with a piercing scream coming from a girl directly in front of him. To his amusement, he saw that his hand was clamped over one of her breasts. For the sheer hell of it, he laughed and squeezed it hard, eliciting an even louder shriek. As well as a slap to his cheek.

'Bitch!' he exclaimed, as much out of disbelief as pain.

'What did you just call 'er?' demanded a voice from behind him.

He turned to see a brute of a man staring down at him. He was an ugly, square-faced, square-necked Neanderthal beast who looked as stupid as he was big. 'I called her a bitch, sir, if it's any of your business,' replied Arthur, staggering slightly.

'It is my business,' the beast roared. 'She's my girlfriend!' And with that, he slammed a fist the size of a shovel into Arthur's face. His legs instantly gave way beneath him, and the next thing he knew, he was on the ground, breathing in the smell of crushed grass. He scrabbled to get up, but a vicious boot aimed at his ribs, followed by another and another, knocked the last breath of air from his lungs.

As he lay there with mocking laughter ringing out all around him, he heard a woman's clear voice cut through the raucous jeers and laughter, and at once a silence fell on the crowd. A request was made to help him up, and it was only when he was on his feet, dizzy and spitting blood, that he realised the person who'd come to his aid was none other than his ruddy stepmother.

★　★　★

'A misunderstanding,' Romily repeated sarcastically as she applied a wad of cotton wool soaked in warm water to his face. 'You really expect me to believe that?'

He pushed her hand away. 'I don't give a damn what you believe. It doesn't concern you anyway.'

'Of course it concerns me,' she said impatiently. 'You're a guest in my house. From what I hear, you were in your cups and behaved disgracefully, and you got what you deserved.'

'A guest in your house,' he repeated. 'Finally you dispense with the veneer of courtesy and reveal your true colours. I knew it wouldn't take you long to start rubbing my nose in your good fortune.'

'An unfortunate choice of words, given the current state of your nose.'

At the sound of the doorbell downstairs, Romily tossed the bloodied cotton wool into the bin beside the washbasin. 'That'll be Dr Garland,' she said.

'I told you there was no need to send for that quack.'

Ignoring him, Romily hurriedly washed her

hands and went to let the doctor in.

'So good of you to come, Dr Garland,' she said. 'I'm afraid the patient is not in the best of humours.'

'I'm sure I'll cope,' he said. 'How are you bearing up? It can't be easy having a houseful right now.'

'Oh, don't worry about me, I'm fine. Unlike Arthur. I don't think his nose is actually broken, but it's certainly swollen and he may well have a couple of black eyes in the morning.'

She led the way upstairs to the guest bathroom, where she'd left Arthur. When she pushed the door open, she found him with his shirt unbuttoned, examining the bruises on his body.

'I want those louts arrested,' he said, 'and I want you to be my witness, Garland, that this is the state in which they left me.'

'Are you sure you want to do that?' asked Romily, before the doctor had a chance to say anything. 'After all, there were plenty of witnesses in the beer tent who will all claim the same thing: that you were drunk and molested Bob Springer's girlfriend, and he was doing nothing more than defending her honour.'

Even with his horribly swollen face, the cold, hateful fury in Arthur's expression was plain to see. 'No pretence now at family loyalty and putting on a united front, then,' he said. 'I might have known.'

'Think yourself lucky I stopped the beating when I did,' snapped Romily. 'Dr Garland, I'll leave you to your patient.'

Alone in the kitchen, Romily helped herself to a glass of Mrs Partridge's home-made lemonade from the jug in the pantry and took it outside to the garden. She had lied earlier to Dr Garland. She did not feel fine. The burden of carrying on as normal this afternoon had left her completely drained. All that smiling and shaking hands and accepting yet more condolences had weighed heavily on her, and she had longed to escape back here to the sanctuary of Island House.

She had just seized what she thought was a quiet moment in which to slip away unobtrusively when Mrs Bunch, who always seemed to know exactly what was going on, sometimes before it had even happened, came and told her that there was trouble in the beer tent: that Arthur was drunk and had got into a fight. Approaching the tent, Romily could hear people saying that he had brought it on himself and deserved the pasting he was getting.

As tempting as it was to let the arrogant devil suffer the consequences of his folly, she couldn't bring herself to turn her back on him. Jack had often said that Arthur was his own worst enemy; that if he could only channel his guile and intelligence into something of real worth, he'd be a lot more likeable. And perhaps happier in himself, thought Romily as she sipped at the cool, refreshing lemonade.

It took no stretch of the imagination to conclude that the worst aspects of Arthur's character very likely stemmed from the loss of his mother when he'd been three years of age. The same was probably true of Hope and Kit. Their entire childhood had been overshadowed by bereavement, if not their own, then Jack's grief for Maud, which had left him unable to be the parent his unhappy children had needed.

But understanding, if only partially, why Arthur behaved the way he did did not make him any easier to deal with. The question was, was it too late for him to change? And why, for heaven's sake, did she care?

Jack. It all came back to Jack. Her love for him and her promise that she would try and unite the family. 'Do what I failed to do,' had been his last wish in those final days. 'Be the one to make it right.'

'Oh Jack,' she murmured tiredly, staring over towards the beech hedge, on the other side of which his body lay in the churchyard. 'I fear this might be a challenge too far for me.'

24

Kit hadn't enjoyed himself like this in a very long time. It made him realise that lately he had become too introverted, but mostly too disappointed with life. But here tonight at the village dance, with Evelyn in his arms, he felt like a man reborn. Like a man who could do anything he wanted! And it wasn't beer or rum punch that was making him think such grandiose thoughts. He'd deliberately steered away from drinking alcohol, given the memory of his previous disastrous evening here with Evelyn. No, this was sheer happiness.

During the afternoon at the fete, while he and Evelyn had been watching the dog show, he had risked asking her if she would come to the dance with him this evening. 'I promise to behave myself this time,' he'd said. She'd smiled and said she'd love to, but would have to check with her mother first. It was then that she'd let out a cry of delight at the sight of a man strolling towards them. It had taken a few seconds for Kit to recognise her brother, Edmund, having not seen him for some years.

'I didn't think you were coming until tomorrow,' Evelyn had said.

'I managed to get away sooner than I thought would be possible,' Edmund told her.

'I'm so pleased you are here. Now you'll be able to come to the dance tonight.'

The closeness between Evelyn and her brother had in many ways mirrored that between Kit and Hope as children. The four of them had always got on well together, but somehow — and it struck Kit now as a great shame — they had lost touch, gone their separate ways.

After the fete had wound up, Kit had returned to Island House and sought out Hope, who had taken Annelise home some time earlier. He had suggested his sister might like to come to the dance that evening, adding that Edmund had been asking after her that afternoon. He had included Allegra in the invitation too, but both had declined, Hope saying that of course she couldn't go, she had Annelise to consider, and Allegra claiming she had a headache. That was before Romily had stepped in and offered to mind Annelise. As Kit was fast learning, his stepmother had a persuasive way about her that people found difficult to resist, himself included. In this instance, she had been quite blunt. 'The world is about to change,' she had said, pointing to the copy of the *Times* she was reading, in particular a piece about France continuing to call up its reservists. 'My advice is to enjoy yourselves while you still can.'

'But I haven't got anything remotely suitable to wear for a dance,' Hope had remonstrated.

'You can borrow something of mine. You too, Allegra, if you'd like to.'

'That won't be necessary,' Allegra had said, her headache seemingly forgotten, 'I have something I can wear.'

Now, seeing his sister appearing to enjoy

herself dancing with Edmund, Kit felt proud of himself for encouraging her to come. Just like Evelyn, Edmund was a sharp-as-mustard cerebral type, and Kit knew that Hope responded well to that kind of fellow. And if an old friend could cheer her up for a few hours, then that had to be a good thing in Kit's opinion.

'Why are you watching my brother and your sister so closely?' asked Evelyn.

'I'm sorry,' Kit said, 'I didn't think I was being that obvious.'

'You were. Not that I'm expecting you to have eyes only for me, but a little contact would be appreciated.'

'Sorry,' he said again. 'It's just that losing Dieter seemed to destroy every last drop of Hope's optimism. She deserves to be happy.'

Evelyn looked at him solemnly. 'She will be when she's ready. You can't rush grief.'

The music came to a stop, and after applauding the band, Kit said, 'Shall we sit the next one out? I'm conscious that your poor feet can only take so much of my clumsiness.'

'You really should stop that, you know.'

'What?'

'Putting yourself down. You've only stepped on my feet the once, which is quite acceptable given how busy the dance floor is. Oh look, there's Allegra dancing with Elijah Hartley. Don't they make a handsome pair?'

Looking across the dance floor, Kit had to agree that they did indeed. 'It's funny how we're all picking up with old friendships, isn't it?' he said.

'Some friendships are meant to last.'

He looked at Evelyn. 'Do you think ours is?'

She laughed. 'Tell me in fifty years' time.'

He laughed too, and wondered if he dared pluck up the courage to kiss her before the evening was over. Why not? Wasn't he now a man who was capable of anything?

★ ★ ★

Allegra was surprised how well Elijah danced. She wondered where he'd learnt, and with whom. But what she wondered most was why he had bothered to ask her to dance.

After the awkwardness of their brief conversation in the garden yesterday, she had been left with the strongest conviction that he had no desire whatsoever to speak to her ever again. Yet, and with scarcely a word exchanged, here he was, his strong, warm body pressed against hers filling her with confusion and making her wish she could read his mind. His brooding silence was unbearable. Why didn't he just tell her exactly what he thought of her? Why put her through this torment?

Oh, if only she could turn back the clock to the time when they'd been such close friends, to a time before she threw away one of the few things that had ever mattered to her: her friendship with Elijah.

Luigi might have been her lover, but hindsight had taught her that he had not been a friend. All too easily she had handed herself over to him, mind, body and soul, to the exclusion of all else.

He had stressed the importance of her staying focused, of blocking out anything and anyone who might halt her progress. He had taken charge of every detail of her day-to-day routine — what she ate, what she wore, where she went.

When she thought about it now, she had been no better than a prisoner with Luigi's obsessive nature controlling her life, making her his, and his alone. It meant that she'd had no one to turn to, no one she could trust. Consequently she had been left to face an unimaginable mess alone. Had that been why she had responded to Roddy's telegram the way she did? Had she subconsciously thought of Island House as a temporary place of sanctuary where she might be able to sort out her life?

'You're not enjoying yourself, are you? Are you ashamed to be seen dancing with me?'

His first words since asking her to dance had Allegra tilting her head back to look up into Elijah's face. She almost dreaded what she might see.

'Of course I'm not ashamed to be seen with you,' she said. 'How could you say such a thing?'

'Because you're not the girl I once knew. Neither of us can pretend you are.'

'And you're not the boy you once were either. You're so full of anger, and I can understand why.'

'Can you? Can you really?'

'Please, Elijah, why don't you just say what's on your mind and be done with it?'

'Maybe I'm waiting for you to do the same.'

'Will you listen to me if I do?'

He nodded.

'You said earlier that I'm not the girl I once was; well, nor am I the woman you think I am now. I've made some terrible choices in life, but the worst one was to leave you the way I did, to say the things I did. Maybe I did it that way because I was frightened you'd try to stop me if I showed the slightest weakness.'

'I would never have stopped you from pursuing your dream,' he said with a frown. 'Never.'

She shook her head. 'My dream, as you call it, has been nothing but a sham. I've made some awful mistakes, but one in particular that will live with me forever.'

He tightened his hold on her, as if he were afraid she might escape. 'Are you sure it was a mistake? My grandfather always used to say that mistakes are like weeds, in that there's really no such thing as a weed, it's merely a plant in the wrong place. So maybe you need to look at what you think is a mistake from a different angle.' The tone of his voice had changed; there was a lightness to it now.

'I wish it were that simple,' she said sadly.

'Life is as simple or as complicated as you want to make it.'

'Do you really believe that?'

'I do. But then I'm just a lowly gardener, whereas the world you live in might be different.'

'Oh *caro*,' she said miserably, 'I'm not successful. Not in the way you think. In Italy, there are any number of singers like me, plenty who are a lot better.'

'You're just being modest.'

His misplaced belief in her was suddenly too much to bear. 'You don't know what you're talking about!' she said. 'You know nothing about the struggle I've had in order to succeed. You know nothing! *Niente!*' Anger and shame and disappointment all rolled into one and she pushed him away angrily, before turning and blundering her way through the other dancers.

She kept on running, not caring where she was going. On and on she ran until her breath was ragged and her heart felt like it was going to burst out of her chest. Then she dropped to her knees on the grass and sobbed, for the mess she'd made of everything, for the child she was carrying, and the mother she could never be to it. She sobbed for Elijah too, for his absurd blind faith that she was better than he was. She wasn't! She was utterly worthless. And still she hadn't had the courage to beg his forgiveness for the way she had treated him.

She was crying so hard, she didn't hear the footsteps coming up behind her in the darkness. Not until she felt the pressure of a hand on her shoulder did she know that somebody was kneeling on the grass beside her.

'I'm sorry,' Elijah said. 'I didn't mean to upset you. Forgive me, please.'

She shuddered and tried to compose herself. 'Please . . . please don't be nice. Not when it's me who needs to be forgiven for leaving you the way I did all those years ago. For having so much stubborn pride. For telling you that I was so much better than you because I had ambition and you didn't. I called you a nobody, and said that you would always be a nobody. It was a vile thing to say.' She looked up at him, tears streaming down her cheeks. 'I was wrong. I wasn't better than you. Far from it. Forgive me, please, please don't stay angry with me!'

'Oh Allegra, of course I forgive you. And I'm sorry I was angry with you. It was the shock of seeing you again after all those years. Back then, I knew you'd go one day, that I'd lose you, you were like a caged bird here, but I also knew that one day you'd come back.'

'Why? Why would you think that?'

He shrugged. 'I don't know. But you did, didn't you? You're here now.'

'I'm back because I'm a failure. My wretched ambition hasn't brought me happiness, or even success. Not on the scale you believe it has. My stupid big dream of becoming a famous opera singer was nothing more than a dream. And now it's gone. My voice has gone and . . . and I'm expecting a baby. There. What do you think of me now?'

He stared at her, then very gently pushed her damp hair away from her tear-stained face. 'Right now I feel as if the last ten years never happened.' He stared deep into her eyes. 'You're still the same Allegra to me,' he murmured. 'Beautiful and wilful, and a courageous fighter.'

'I'm none of those things. Maybe I was once, but not now. I'm beaten. Truly I am. I'm so tired. Tired of life maybe. Some days I think it would be better if I were dead.'

He took her hands in his. 'Don't say that. Not

ever. What does the father of the baby have to say about it?'

'He doesn't know. And he never will. He's out of my life now. He's taken all the money I earned and every last scrap of my reputation and dignity. I'm a pathetic laughing stock,' she said miserably.

'Not true. You're Allegra Salvato, the girl I adored on sight.' He bent his head and kissed her lightly on the cheek.

She shivered.

'You're cold,' he said with concern. 'Come with me.'

★   ★   ★

He took her home to Clover End Cottage, a thatched dwelling on the edge of Clover Woods where he'd lived with his grandfather. It seemed even smaller than Allegra remembered as she warmed herself by the range and looked around while he lit the oil lamps.

'It's not what you're used to up at Island House, I know,' he said, observing her, 'but it's home for me. One day I might even have electricity,' he added with a smile, 'and an indoor lavatory.'

'It feels comfortable,' she said, taking in the range with a battered armchair either side, where she remembered Elijah's grandfather sitting while reading his bible and smoking his pipe. Above the range was a shelf with a row of pots and pans and an iron, which made Allegra picture Elijah carefully ironing the white shirt he'd worn for the dance this evening. Over by the window was a table and three chairs; to one side was a sink with a wooden draining board and a cupboard, and to the other a tall bookcase crammed full with books. It was, she thought, the one new thing in the room; otherwise everything was as she remembered it.

Elijah saw her looking at the bookcase. 'I have you to thank for my love of reading,' he said. 'Remember that book you gave me for my tenth birthday? I still have it.' He went to the shelves and pulled out the book of maps she had stolen from her uncle. 'You wrote in it for me,' he said, opening it. ''Happy Birthday, Elijah, with love from Allegra.''

'You kept it,' she said softly. 'All these years and you kept it.'

'Of course I did,' he said. 'I must confess, I always felt I ought to return it to its rightful owner. But I never did.'

'You knew it wasn't mine to give you, then?'

He nodded and put the book back. 'I used to look at the map of Italy, the page you'd marked, and imagine you there. Would you like something to drink? I can't run to anything fancy, I'm afraid.'

'Do you know what I'd like?'

'Go on.'

'Some hot chocolate. I remember your grandfather making it for us.'

Elijah smiled. 'I should be able to manage that all right.'

'Do you like living alone?' she asked, as he uncovered a jug of milk on the draining board.

'I'm used to it,' he said, pouring the milk into a pan and setting it on the range. He opened one of the doors beneath and from a metal bucket shovelled in more coke to the glowing embers.

'What about girlfriends?'

He put the bucket and shovel down and wiped his hands on the back of his trousers. 'There've been a few, I can't deny it. I'm not cut out to live as a monk. No man is.'

'Nobody serious then?'

He spooned cocoa powder from a canister into the milk. 'Not on my part. Too choosy by half, my old grandad used to say. And let's face it, I'm not that good a catch.'

She smiled. 'A man who has his own cottage and can iron his shirts; I'd say that makes you a fine catch.'

He smiled too and set two mugs on the table. 'Sugar?'

'If you have it.'

When the cocoa was made, they sat in the two armchairs either side of the range, Elijah's long legs stretched out towards hers. For a while, neither of them spoke, the faint hiss of the oil lamps the only sound to be heard.

'What are you going to do about the baby?' Elijah asked at length. 'Will you keep it after it's born?'

'I don't think I could give it up. Unplanned or not, this child is mine. Perhaps it's the only real thing I have in my life. Or ever will.'

'How will you manage?'

She told him about her uncle's will. 'I never thought he'd leave me anything, but if my cousins and I can put up with each other for a few more days, my immediate financial problems will be solved.'

He nodded. 'Have you told anyone about the baby?'

'Only you. And for now, I'd prefer to keep it that way, so please don't tell anyone.'

'Why would I?' he asked with a pained expression.

She drank some of her hot chocolate. It was just as she remembered it, thick and creamy and very sweet. 'I'm bored with talking about me,' she said. 'Tell me something about you.'

He cradled his own mug in his large hands. 'I'm going to enlist and join the Suffolk Regiment. Just like my dad, and my grandad before him. I should have done it months ago. But I kept hoping it wouldn't come to that. Seems that things have changed now. I reckon by the end of next week we'll be at war with Germany, so me and some of the lads from the village have made our minds up to go and do our bit.'

Allegra looked at him, saddened. She remembered him as a young boy, how shy he'd been, and how gentle, how he'd rescued an injured baby blue tit and cared for it until it was well enough to fly away. The thought of him going to war filled her with dismay. To have found him again only to lose him was too dreadful to contemplate.

'Perhaps you'll write to me while I'm gone,' he said. 'I'd like that.'

She swallowed. 'There might not be a war,' she

said quietly. 'Germany might come to its senses.'

'They won't. Mark my words; there will be a war. A bloody awful one.'

25

It was Sunday morning and once again Annelise had woken early. It was what babies did, Hope now accepted; there was no way round it. But thank heavens for Florence and her cheerful willingness to help; the girl was a marvel.

Seated at the kitchen table and encouraging Annelise to eat some toast, Hope took the cup of tea Florence had just poured for her. 'Thank you,' she said, 'and thank you also for all your help.'

'That's all right, madam, it's no bother.'

'I'm sure that's not entirely true, but thank you all the same.' Hope stirred a spoonful of sugar into her tea, then decided to do what she should have done before now but had put off because she was so ashamed of her behaviour. She stirred her tea some more. 'Florence,' she began, 'I'm afraid I was very rude to you the other morning, and I'm sorry for what I said. It was wrong of me to be so short with you, and I want you to know that I appreciate all that you and Mrs Partridge are doing for me.'

'That's all right, madam,' Florence said with a hesitant half-smile. 'We're all finding our way just now, aren't we?'

Hope smiled back at her. 'I suppose we are, yes.' She took a sip of her tea. Then: 'Do you think you could call me by my name, Florence? Madam makes me feel so old.'

'Of course, Mrs Meyer. If that's what you'd prefer.'

'No, not that. Call me Hope. You see, despite the impression you might have gained of me, I don't really like an excess of formality. I'm much more of an egalitarian.'

Florence's eyes widened. 'An eager what?'

Hope nudged another square of toast towards Annelise, urging her to pick it up. 'Egalitarian means believing in everybody being equal,' she said. 'That's you and me being the same, with no barriers between us. A classless society is what we should be striving for in the world, not fighting each other, setting man against man and boy against boy.' She sighed. 'The Great War was supposed to put an end to all wars, but we haven't learnt a thing, have we?'

At the perplexed expression on Florence's face, Hope shook her head and raised a hand. 'I'm sorry, I'm going on far too much. Just ignore me.'

She went back to drinking her tea, knowing that the reason she had spoken the way she had was because she and Edmund had been discussing these things last night. Growing up, they had always seen the world through the same eyes, just as she and Dieter had. It was a shame Edmund had never met Dieter, she was sure they would have got along well together. Like Dieter, Edmund was of a serious bent with a strong social conscience. A doctor at St Thomas's Hospital in Lambeth, he had suggested that when Hope returned to her flat in London next week, she might like to get in touch with him to arrange lunch. She had made a note of his telephone number and address, but she knew that the reality of her life now would preclude having the time for anything like that.

Putting Edmund out of her mind, she asked Florence if she had enjoyed the fete yesterday, and in particular, the dance. 'I saw you dancing with Billy Minton,' she said. 'He's grown into a quite a handsome young man. I remember him when he was just a boy. I hope he was a gentleman and walked you home safely afterwards.'

Florence's face turned scarlet. 'He was the perfect gentleman all evening,' she said, suddenly busying herself with a dishcloth.

'I'm glad to hear it,' said Hope, amused.

⋆　⋆　⋆

Later, when Florence was alone in the kitchen with Mrs Partridge, preparing breakfast for the family, she wondered at the change in Mrs Meyer — *Hope*. She had been so chatty and friendly. Apologetic, too. And almost lighthearted. All the same, she'd talked a lot of nonsense. All that stuff about a classless society. As if that would ever happen! As if somebody like Hope Meyer would ever want to get down on her hands and knees and scrub the floors!

But there was no doubt, it was like a different woman had been sitting here in the kitchen with her. Maybe it had something to do with that man Florence had seen her dancing with last night. Billy had pointed him out, had said what a decent sort he was, and that he was Evelyn Flowerday's brother. Hope had been dancing with him for a fair bit of the evening; it had seemed to Florence that they were getting on like a house on fire.

The same had been true of Allegra and Elijah Hartley. Who'd have thought she would have lowered herself to dance with a gardener? Not that there was anything wrong with being a gardener, it was just that was not what posh folk did, like they didn't scrub floors! It would be like Arthur Devereux dancing with Florence. A thought that made her shudder and decide that if that was what Hope meant by an eager-whatsit society, she wanted none of it. But there was no getting away from the fact that Elijah was a good-looking man. He was a quiet sort, though, kept himself to himself. 'More to him than meets the eye,' so Mrs Partridge often said. 'Still waters run deep, make no mistake.'

In contrast, Billy Minton was an open book and never stopped talking. He was as honest and straight as the day was long, and good company. The only awkward moment yesterday between them had been when Billy had been walking her home and had kissed her. He'd fumbled it at first, clashed his teeth against hers, but then they'd both got the hang of it and had kissed and kissed and gone on kissing. His soft mouth against hers had made her feel as if a fire had been lit deep inside her.

She blushed at the memory. Did kissing Billy make her a scarlet woman? She would have to be careful when she saw him next. It wouldn't do to

201

let things get out of hand. She wasn't going to let him get her in the family way. She would have to make that very clear; she didn't want him thinking she was cheap. Even so, he would be easy to fall in love with. Quick as a flash the words of the old gypsy woman echoed inside her head: *You'll find love and you'll lose love.* What if it was true and she fell in love with Billy only then to lose him?

'I don't know, Flo, falling asleep on the job. That'll learn you to stay out dancing till all hours.'

'I wasn't sleeping, Mrs Partridge,' said Florence, banishing Billy from her thoughts and getting on with the eggs she was supposed to be cracking into a large mixing bowl. 'I was thinking. Do you believe there's any truth in what fortune-tellers — '

'Thinking indeed,' interrupted Mrs Partridge, banging a large pan down on the stove. 'As if we've got time for that! When you've whisked those eggs for me, you'd better lay the table in the dining room, and put a tray together for Mr Arthur Devereux. I expect he'll want to eat in his room this morning, like he did with his supper last night. From all that Mrs Bunch has told us about him, it strikes me it was about time somebody gave him a good hiding. A man of his standing getting drunk in the beer tent, of all places! He should be ashamed of himself. God rest his soul, whatever would his father have said? As if poor Miss Romily hasn't enough to think about!'

★　★　★

Romily was upstairs in her bedroom, working at her desk overlooking the long avenue of colourful herbaceous borders that led down to the pond.

She had slept badly, her sleep disturbed by dreams of Jack. Several times she had woken absolutely convinced he was in the bed next to her, only to realise he wasn't. When she'd heard Annelise chuntering to herself in her sing-song fashion, followed shortly by Hope going to her, Romily had given up on trying to sleep. Slipping on her dressing gown, she'd made a start on replying to the letters from her readers, which she had abandoned since Jack's death. Jack had often said that she should employ the services of a secretary to deal with her correspondence, but Romily believed her readers deserved more than that.

In need of some tea, she rang the bell to summon Florence, and within a couple of minutes the girl was knocking on her door. 'Would you like anything with your tea?' asked Florence, when Romily had made her request.

'No, I'll be down for breakfast just as soon as I've finished the last of these letters.'

When Florence returned with the tea tray and had poured a cup for her, Romily sensed her hovering, as though she had something to say. She was fussing over her apron, straightening it despite it being perfectly straight already. Worried that the girl might be feeling put upon with the extra duty of minding Annelise, Romily said, 'Is there something you want to say to me, Florence?'

The girl hesitated.

'Is it about Annelise?' asked Romily.

'Oh no, nothing like that, Miss Romily.'

'What then?'

'Do you know much about fortune-tellers?'

'A little. What do you want to know?'

'Can they look at your hand and really know things about you? Or do they just make wild guesses and hope something rings true?'

'What an interesting question. Why don't you sit down and tell me why you want to know?'

Florence did as she said, perching herself on the edge of the ottoman at the end of the bed. 'I went to the gypsy woman at the fete yesterday and she told me something she couldn't really know. About my mother. She also said that I'd find love and I'd lose love.'

Romily sipped her tea thoughtfully. 'I think we can safely dispense with the last part. Everybody is going to know love and lose it at some stage in their life, stands to reason, so I really wouldn't let that worry you.'

Florence nodded. 'But what about my mother?'

Romily knew all about Florence's mother running off; the girl had told her about it herself. 'What exactly did this so-called fortune-teller say about her?'

After she'd listened to what Florence told her, she said, 'I must say, it sounds intriguing. Have you told anyone in the village about your family? Is there some way this woman could have known your background?'

Florence shook her head. 'You and Mrs

Partridge are the only ones here in Melstead St Mary who know.'

'Well, I can assure you I've never mentioned it to anyone, and Mrs Partridge might enjoy listening to Mrs Bunch's gossip, but she would never spread it herself.'

'So do you think it was true what the gypsy told me?'

'Undoubtedly there are some who have the gift of seeing things the rest of us are unable to, but equally there are plenty who would seek to take advantage of what they perceive as a person's vulnerability. However, in this instance, the fortune-teller appeared not to know anything about you other than what she could guess from your dress, your voice and your manner.'

'You mean she would know I wasn't top-drawer like you?'

Romily smiled. 'Not how I would put it, but yes, in short she would know how to categorise you. That's hardly a talent; most people can do it. But by referring to some nameless woman you hadn't seen in a long time, a woman who had the same colour hair as you ... well, frankly, that could be a grandmother, an aunt, a sister, anyone related to you. Odds on there has to be somebody else in your family with your colouring. And, as is so often the way with how the brain works, you filled in the blanks of what you heard and leapt to your own understandable conclusion.'

Florence put a finger to her lower lip and pressed it pensively. 'Before I went into the tent, I'd remembered something about my mother that I hadn't thought of in a while. The memory of it was as clear as you and me sitting here.'

'Even more reason to conclude that what you heard from the gypsy was no more than a case of autosuggestion,' said Romily.

'What does that mean?'

'Basically you heard what you wanted to hear. Even if it was only on a subconscious level.'

'That's the second new word I've learned today,' Florence said with a smile.

'Oh, what was the first?'

'Mrs Meyer taught me the word eaglet . . . egalitarian.'

'Did she indeed? Well good for her.'

Florence rose from the ottoman. 'I knew you'd help settle it all in my mind. Thank you so much. I'd better get back down to the kitchen before Mrs Partridge blows a gasket.'

When the girl was at the door, Romily said, 'Florence, any time you have anything on your mind, you know you can come to me. By the way, Annelise isn't proving too much of a burden, is she?'

'We can cope. And it's only for a few days more, isn't it? Although how we'll manage if we're landed with a couple of evacuated children as well is anybody's guess.'

'We'll cross that bridge when we need to.'

Once Florence had closed the door after her, Romily poured herself another cup of tea, and pondered on what the girl had said about their house guests only remaining for a few more days. She wasn't altogether convinced that was what would happen. If Hope hadn't managed to finish the sketches for her publisher by then, she might want to stay on for a few more days to make use of the help available here with Annelise. And where would Allegra go if she left? Surely not back to Italy, not when the situation in Europe was so precarious. To London, then? Did she have friends or professional contacts there?

One thing was certain in Romily's mind: she would not turn either of them away if they needed help. She found them both oddly likeable, in very different ways. She admired Hope for her stoicism, while in Allegra she saw a passionate and fiercely stubborn and proud young woman who imagined offence at every turn. Her stormy paranoia was understandable; Romily could see how the girl had fought tooth and nail all her young life to gain the respect she felt she'd been denied as a child.

Before Roddy had left for London, he had confided in Romily that recently life in Italy had not gone too well for Allegra. 'I don't want to break a confidence,' he'd said, 'but I'm concerned about her. There's something troubling her, and I believe it's more than what she shared with me.'

Romily was inclined to agree. Allegra did seem troubled. She had seen the girl looking thoughtfully out of the window many times, chewing her lip or wringing her hands, as if trying desperately to resolve something in her mind. Was it to do with her career? Had she hit a difficult time and the singing engagements just weren't coming her way? Life on the stage was notoriously fickle, with its many ups and downs.

Something that had struck Romily as strange was that she had not heard Allegra singing since arriving here; not a single note, or even a casual little hum. It was possible, of course, that she was under doctor's orders to rest her voice; singers had to do that sometimes. Perhaps that was what was troubling her, a perfectly understandable case of anxiety that her voice might fail her.

Her tea finished, Romily picked up her pen and returned her attention to answering the remaining letters from her readers. She had just signed the last one when something down in the garden caught her eye. It was Allegra, appearing at the furthest end of the garden through a small gateway. The gate led to a private path that curled round the other side of the pond, hidden from sight by dense undergrowth and rhododendron bushes. Leaving the boundary of Island House, it eventually looped its way round to the church, and then on down to Clover Woods. So where had Allegra been so early in the morning? To church perhaps?

Or . . . but surely Romily was mistaken. Yet it looked very much as though the girl was wearing the same pretty floral dress she had worn last night to the village dance.

26

Arthur had slept badly. Not surprising, given the pain he was in. But he'd sooner rip out his tongue than admit that to anyone else. His plan for the day was to brazen it out, to shake off yesterday's incident as nothing more than a tiresome village fracas with a tiresome village nobody.

Brazening things out was his stock in trade. That and biding his time to plot his revenge. In his experience there was nothing quite like getting even. But unusually for him, he wasn't much in the mood for revenge this morning. He ached in too many places to summon the necessary energy to devise a way to get his own back. What energy he possessed currently he would need to put on a convincingly indifferent front.

Dr Garland had declared nothing actually broken, something Arthur could have told him himself, and had recommended he call in at the surgery tomorrow for a check-up. Arthur had no intention of doing that. What was the point?

Right now, his immediate concern was rousing himself from his bed and dressing to go down for breakfast. He had eaten supper in his room last night, but he wasn't going to repeat that and allow anyone to think he was hiding, too embarrassed to show his face. No, let them all wince at the sight of him across the table.

Wince was precisely what he did himself when he ventured into the bathroom across the landing from his room and looked into the mirror. Not since his days on the school rugby pitch had he looked such a mess. Back then, each cut and bruise had been a badge of honour. Less so on one particular occasion, however. He'd injured his arm in a scrum, and a zealous matron had ordered him out of her sickroom on the grounds that he was a malingerer. Two days later, when he'd still been in abject pain, one of the masters had had the sense to realise that the arm was broken and he needed immediate treatment. To get his own back on the matron for her total disregard for his well-being, Arthur had lured the woman's tortoiseshell cat away from her quarters and taken it down into the woods. He'd locked it inside an abandoned groundkeeper's hut, strung up by one of its legs. It was found a week later, dead.

After he'd gingerly washed himself, forgoing a shave, he left the bathroom to go back to his room to dress. At the other end of the landing, presumably coming out of her own room, he saw Romily with a stack of envelopes in her hand. 'How are you feeling?' she asked.

'Never better,' he replied.

'I'm glad to hear it,' she said. 'Will you be joining us for breakfast?'

'Of course. And then I thought I'd go to church.'

'Really?' she asked, an eyebrow raised.

'Really,' he repeated, and shot inside his room. He hadn't had the slightest intention of going to church, but for some reason the words had slipped out, as if in an instinctive gesture of defiance — he would not be cowed! As he dressed carefully, he wondered how the devil he could extricate himself from sitting through the tedium of another service conducted by the Reverend Septimus Tate.

★ ★ ★

During breakfast, and after Kit, Hope and Allegra had had their fill of gawping at him, making much of his blackened eyes and saying he had only himself to blame, Romily asked if there was anyone else who was thinking of attending church that morning. To Arthur's disbelief, Kit announced that he planned to go. 'Why don't you come?' he added to Hope while spreading marmalade onto his toast. 'The more the merrier.'

'I was going to try and do some work,' she said. 'I was rather hoping somebody might look after Annelise for a few hours.' She looked first at the child squirming in the high chair next to her, then around the table, as though seeking an offer of help. Her gaze finally settled on Allegra. Arthur let out a sarcastic laugh as his cousin refused point-blank to meet Hope's eyes.

'Oh Hope,' he said, 'do you really mean to say you'd trust a child into Allegra's keeping? More fool you! And while we're on the subject of Annelise, do we have to put up with this wholly unorthodox habit of yours of including her with us while we eat? The sight of her cramming food into her mouth quite puts me off.'

'What would you suggest I did with her?' demanded Hope. 'Lock her in her room until we've finished?'

'Sounds like a reasonable solution to me,' he said. 'Better still, confine her to the kitchen and leave the maid to see to her.'

'My maid's name is Florence, Arthur,' said Romily from her end of the table, 'as well you know, and while she is more than happy to help out, I don't want her taken advantage of.'

'I thought that was the role of a servant, to do our bidding.'

'In your world maybe,' said Hope, 'but I for one agree with Romily.' She looked across the table to Allegra again. 'Are you busy this morning, Allegra? Or are you joining Kit and Arthur at church?'

'I rather fancy Cousin Allegra may well now put her popish tendencies aside and rush to fill the pews of St Mary rather than be landed with the job of babysitting.'

'Arthur,' said Kit, 'could you possibly be any more insufferable?'

'*Sì,*' said Allegra, finally speaking, '*che peccato —* '

'In English!' Arthur said with a bored shake of his head.

Allegra glared at him. 'I was going to say, what a shame that whoever hit you did not do a better job and make it impossible for you to open your big offensive mouth.'

A sharp rap on the table brought silence to the room. 'Enough!' said Romily. 'Arthur, if you have nothing constructive or pleasant to say, kindly leave the rest of us to finish our breakfast in peace.'

Wholly satisfied with the outcome of his contribution to the proceedings, and with exaggerated insouciance, Arthur tossed his napkin onto the table, pushed back his chair and slowly stood up. 'Anything you say, stepmother dearest. Your wish is my command.'

'If only that were true,' he heard her say as he left the room at an unhurried pace.

★ ★ ★

As the bells rang out, calling the village to morning service, Arthur set off for the church, through the gate at the end of the garden. Ahead of him he could see Kit, and it wasn't long before he'd caught up with him. 'You couldn't persuade Hope to join us, then?' he said to his brother.

'It was no more than a passing thought to ask her. But I'm surprised a raging atheist like you is so keen to go to church.'

'I could say the same of you. Or are you suddenly in need of some special spiritual guidance?'

'I would have thought you'd be the one more in need of that. Honestly, Arthur, why do you have to keep goading us? Can't you take up fox hunting or some other barbaric blood sport?'

'A man must take his pleasure where and how he can.'

'Yes, but if you carry on like this, Romily will

report back to Roddy that we haven't fulfilled the wishes of Dad's will.'

Arthur laughed. 'Plenty of time yet to make a good impression on our stepmama.'

'I wouldn't count on it.' Kit came to an abrupt stop. 'Look, you may have married money with Irene, but the rest of us aren't so fortunate. Can't you just for once in your life think about somebody else's situation rather than your own?'

'Come off it, Kit, you know as well as I do we're never going to see a penny of the old man's money. The four of us being forced to spend a week together is nothing more than a charade, one last attempt by our father to humiliate us. You must surely have figured it out by now. Romily gets the lot no matter how we behave.'

'I don't believe you! Dad wouldn't do that. He was many things, but he never went back on his word.'

'I wish I had your sunny optimism. And who knows, maybe Romily and Roddy cooked this little enterprise up between them.'

'For what purpose?'

'Ah well, that may yet come to light. All I'm saying is that Roddy might not be the confirmed old bachelor he once was.'

⋆　⋆　⋆

Kit's only reason for attending church that morning was to snatch another opportunity of seeing Evelyn again. She had said last night that she would be helping with the Sunday school, and he had decided to surprise her at St Mary's.

214

What he had not bargained on was his wretched brother accompanying him.

They left the bright sunshine behind them and entered the cool, subdued interior of the church, each taking a hymn book from Cynthia Blackwood, Dr Garland's receptionist, as well as an abashed stare of scrutiny, particularly in Arthur's direction. Typical Arthur, he met the woman's eyes with bold insolence. 'Has no one ever told you it's rude to stare, Miss Blackwood?' he remarked.

Her face quivered with outrage and Kit moved his brother swiftly on and pushed him into one of the pews near the back. 'How you've reached this age without somebody murdering you, I'll never know,' he muttered with exasperation.

'The Lord looks after his own,' responded Arthur, who proceeded to drop to his knees in an ostentatious display of devotion.

Kit rolled his eyes. And then he saw Evelyn entering the church with her brother Edmund pushing a cumbersome wheelchair. Sitting bolt upright in the chair was Mildred Flowerday. To Kit's inexpert eye, the woman had never looked better, her plump, rosy-cheeked face giving her the appearance of a well-fed cat who had consumed more than its fill of the very best-quality cream. Whatever health problems she suffered, eating was plainly not one of them.

The trio, unaware of Kit or his brother, progressed up the church towards the front. It gave Kit the chance to admire Evelyn. How pretty she looked in her buttercup-yellow floral dress and cream cardigan. Her dark hair was tied back, revealing more of her profile and elegant neck, and perched on her head was a gay little straw hat with a whisper of cream veil. She looked the picture of demure modesty, and a far cry from the vivid memory he had of her late last night.

As the service got under way, with Reverend Tate droning on and on, Kit distracted himself by thinking how much he'd enjoyed being with Evelyn yesterday, particularly when he'd walked her home to Meadow Lodge and risked kissing her. The passionate fervency of her response had taken him aback. But only momentarily. Afterwards, and somewhat breathlessly, they had smiled shyly at each other and in the still of the dark night walked the remaining distance hand in hand. It had been a perfect end to a perfect day, and Kit very much wanted to find a way to experience that pleasure again.

A sharp dig in the ribs made him start, and he turned to his brother.

'Reverend Tate's giving a sermon just for our benefit,' muttered Arthur.

A few seconds later, Kit realised what Arthur meant. The vicar's theme was the return of the prodigal son.

27

It was with mixed emotions that Allegra had reluctantly agreed to look after Annelise. She could have refused; after all, what did she care about Hope's problems? Would Hope ever do the same for her if the boot was on the other foot?

But therein lay the dilemma for Allegra. Before too long she might very well be in precisely the same situation, and who would turn a hand to help her? There was also the fear that she didn't want to antagonise Romily, because without Uncle Jack's money life would be exceedingly grim in the coming year. With that fear constantly in mind, she had no choice but to comply with the terms of Jack Devereux's will, and that meant helping Hope, and appearing to do so with good grace.

She had to admit, though, there was rather more to it than just that. It had occurred to Allegra that looking after Annelise might give her an idea of what it would be like to be solely responsible for a child, even if only for a couple of hours.

With every conceivable childcare instruction laid out for her by Hope — treating Allegra as she always had, as worse than a simpleton — she had decided the easiest thing to do would be to take the infant for a walk in the pram. The fresh air would do them both good. With her stomach still churning queasily, she had barely eaten any breakfast, and what little she had consumed had not stayed down.

After Kit and Arthur had left for church, she set off with Annelise sitting up attentively in the pram and seeming to enjoy the view of the lane and hedgerow. In no real hurry, Allegra meandered along in the warm sunshine at a leisurely pace, pointing things out to the child — a peacock butterfly sunning itself on a clump of nettles, a pair of swallows wheeling through the sky, a sprawl of rosy-pink campion, and a large bumble bee busily inspecting a patch of thistles and buttercups. When they came to a part of the hedgerow that was smothered in bindweed, Allegra plucked a trumpet-like white flower and gave it to Annelise. The child studied it thoughtfully for a few seconds, then made to put it in her mouth.

'No, *cara!*' Allegra cried in alarm, snatching the flower out of her hands.

Annelise pursed her lips and looked instantly on the verge of tears. To distract her, Allegra plucked a long blade of grass and gave that to her instead — as a child she had often sucked on one, and she hadn't come to any harm, had she? The little girl looked thoroughly pleased with the exchange and waved it about as though it were a great treasure.

Disaster averted, Allegra pushed on with the pram, pausing to lean against a five-bar gate to show Annelise the tractor that was ploughing the field. Observing its progress, she turned at the sound of an approaching vehicle. As it drew near, she saw that it was a truck; a military truck. The driver, dressed in some kind of uniform, beeped the horn and gave her a cheery wave as it trundled by.

She watched it disappear into the distance and thought of Elijah and his eagerness to enlist in the army. There had been no doubt in his mind that Britain would be forced to honour its pledge to stand by Poland when — not if — Hitler invaded. His certainty had upset and unsettled her.

'I'm not the naive boy you left behind,' he'd said when she had questioned his keenness to fight. 'I know what I'm doing and it's the right choice.'

But did he really know what he was doing, what the danger would be? For that matter, did anyone ever know what they were doing and why? Allegra had begun to think her whole life had been one series of bad decisions, all made with what she believed had been absolute certainty. Now all she knew was that the life she had thought she would lead was never to be, just as she'd told Elijah last night.

Once she had a complete circuit of the village, with Annelise still happily viewing everything from the vantage point of the pram, she turned for home, back to Island House.

Home . . .

No more than a turn of phrase, she told herself. Island House was *not* her home; it never had been and never would be!

Yet for all her defiance — her instinctive readiness to reject the place that to all intents and purposes *had* been her home for seven years — she could not deny that right now, breathing in the clear warm air and enjoying the quiet serenity of Melstead St Mary was better than being stuck in a stiflingly hot Venice with Luigi's debtors hounding her, as well as the repulsive Signor Pezzo making lecherous suggestions as to how she could pay her rent.

★ ★ ★

There was nobody about when she arrived back, and after fetching a blanket from the boathouse, she laid it on the grass in the dappled shade of the weeping beech tree. She lifted Annelise out of the pram and put her on the blanket, in the hope that she might settle there. But the little girl had other ideas, and raising her arms, she leaned appealingly towards Allegra.

'Oh, all right then,' conceded Allegra, lifting her onto her lap. At once the child smiled prettily and began to bounce on her dainty bare feet, as if performing a little dance. Allegra couldn't help but laugh. 'What a funny thing you are,' she said.

Seeming to agree with this, Annelise nodded and pressed a finger to Allegra's lips. Allegra pretended to snap like a crocodile and bite her finger, making the girl laugh and then poke her finger again into her mouth. Allegra duly obliged and pretended again to bite her finger, resulting in yet more laughter. They played the game over and over until Annelise grew bored and showed signs of wanting to explore beyond the blanket.

Bent over her, and holding her by her hands,

Allegra walked her slowly down towards the edge of the pond, where she carefully dipped the child's toes into the water, eliciting a squeal. Whether it was shock or delight that made Annelise cry out, Allegra didn't know, but she tried it again and provoked another squeal, followed by a deliciously joyous chuckle. After doing this several more times, and with her arms beginning to ache, she carried Annelise back to the blanket in the hope that she might now be ready for a nap.

Initially the child resisted, but when Allegra gently stroked her soft peachy cheek, she almost instantly closed her eyes. Amazingly, it wasn't long before she was asleep. Feeling tired herself, Allegra lay down beside her and stared up at the blue sky through the fluttering leaves of the beech tree.

She was grateful for the chance to rest; she had hardly slept last night, having spent most of it talking to Elijah. It was his insistence on wanting to know all about her life in Italy that had done it, and once she'd begun to talk, the words had just poured out of her. It had come as a huge relief, an unburdening of herself, but the next thing she had known, daylight was streaming in through the window, the birds were singing and she realised she was covered with a blanket in the chair where she must have fallen asleep. Opposite her Elijah was sleeping soundly, his head tilted to one side, his mouth slightly parted.

Her reaction was not one of gratitude that he had been so kind as to put a blanket around her so she could sleep more comfortably, but one of anger — why had he allowed this to happen, and how on earth was she going to explain why she had stayed the night here? Her only thought was to leave at once in the hope she would get back to Island House before anyone noticed she wasn't there. She was almost at the door to make her escape when Elijah stirred. 'Where are you off to?' he asked, rubbing his eyes, his voice thick with sleep.

'I have to go.'

'Let me walk with you.'

'No! I can't be seen with you. Not at this time of day.'

He'd frowned. 'In that case, you'd better go.'

'I didn't mean it that way,' she'd said, regretting her choice of words.

'Just go,' he'd muttered. 'You're good at that.'

The cold accusation in his voice had followed her back to Island House. She could hear it now as she succumbed to exhaustion and drifted off to sleep.

★ ★ ★

When she woke, feeling pleasingly refreshed, she stretched her arms above her head and turned to check on Annelise.

But Annelise wasn't there. She was gone.

Allegra leapt to her feet and looked around her, frantically scanning the garden, but there was no sign of the child anywhere.

With her blood running cold and her heart beating fast, she ran to the edge of the pond where they'd been playing before.

'Annelise!' she called desperately. '*Annelise!*'

28

'I was asleep for no more than a few minutes!' Allegra wailed, the tears streaming down her cheeks. 'I just don't know how she could have moved so fast! She can't even walk!'

'But how could you fall asleep when you were responsible for looking after her?' screamed Hope wildly, her face contorted with petrified horror and furious disbelief. 'I don't understand, how could you do that?'

'Shouting at one another is not going to help us find Annelise,' said Romily firmly, trying hard to hide her own fear. 'Now please, just calm down, the pair of you.'

'*Calm?*' screeched Hope, 'You expect me to be calm when Annelise has probably drowned!'

The three of them were up to their waists in water, desperately searching amongst the pond-weed and reeds for the little girl, and God help them if they did find her, thought Romily with sickening dread, because by now, if she had fallen in, the poor wretch must surely be dead. Allegra had no idea how long she'd been asleep, so it was anybody's guess how long the child had been crawling around on her own.

When Allegra had come running up to the house, wild-eyed and soaked to the skin, and screaming like a banshee, Romily had resorted to slapping her face to get some sense out of her. The second she realised what the girl was saying, she'd shouted to Hope and Florence to help with the search, and to Mrs Partridge to call for Dr Garland. Then she'd raced down to the pond with the others chasing after her.

But now she was forced to accept that nothing would come of them thrashing about in the pond. If Annelise had fallen in and been trapped under the water by weeds, she was long since dead. As gruesome as it sounded, and it would be a grisly discovery indeed, they would have to wait for her body to float to the surface.

'I think we have to hold onto the hope that she didn't come anywhere near the water,' Romily said, clutching at the only straw she could. 'It's possible Florence and Mrs Partridge may find her playing happily somewhere on her own.'

She started to move towards the edge of the pond, willing the others to follow. Allegra did, but Hope remained where she was.

'We can't give up,' she said, her voice tight with shock. 'We have to keep looking.' She started to wade out towards the middle of the pond.

'Come back,' Romily said. 'The water's deep there.'

'I have to keep looking for her. I can't let Sabine and Otto down. I have to find . . . ' Romily didn't catch the rest of what Hope was saying, as she suddenly ducked beneath the surface of the water and disappeared from sight.

It was then that Dr Garland appeared, calling across the lawn to them. 'I came as fast as I could,' he said, breathing heavily, 'but I was over at Lower End Farm. Have you found her?'

Allegra began sobbing hysterically again, dropping to her knees dramatically, invoking God to have mercy in a stream of English and Italian. And though a part of Romily wanted to scream and shout at the stupid girl for allowing this to happen, she simply shook her head in response to the doctor's question.

'We've searched the pond as much as we can,' she said, shivering with cold, 'but only a miracle would enable us to find Annelise alive now if she is in there.'

Dr Garland had noticed that Hope was still in the water. 'She should come out,' he said, above Allegra's keening.

'I've told her that, but she won't listen.' Wringing out the lower part of her dress, Romily added, 'Perhaps you could persuade her to give up while I deal with Allegra.'

She was about to bend down to Allegra when Florence came running towards them.

'She's safe!' she called. 'Mr Devereux has her!'

To Romily's disbelief, and enormous relief, Arthur then appeared through the gate at the end of the garden. He was sauntering along without a care in the world, and with Annelise slung over his shoulder like a kitbag.

★   ★   ★

Arthur was enjoying himself immensely. He hadn't had this much fun in ages. And the best part was seeing Allegra squirm with guilt and shame.

For no more than a second he'd considered

drowning Annelise just to ensure that this was a lesson for which Allegra would pay for the rest of her life, but even he baulked at actually murdering a small child. This way he got to play the part of hero of the hour while Allegra was cast as the villain, a woman who was too lazy and self-absorbed to stay awake and look after her charge.

Earlier, when the dull-as-ditch-water service had ended at St Mary's, Arthur had left Kit simpering over Evelyn Flowerday and headed for home. He'd fancied a bottle of cold beer down by the boathouse, but when he'd come across the tableau of Allegra and Annelise both fast asleep, a cunning ruse had popped into his head.

A devilishly clever ruse!

With nobody about, he'd stealthily picked up the child and hurried away like a thief in the night, back the way he'd just come.

He'd taken her down to Clover Woods, where she continued to sleep, oblivious to the awaiting storm. When she'd woken and he'd decided sufficient time had elapsed to cause maximum alarm, he'd strolled back ready to tell everyone he'd found the child crawling along the path in a distressed state. To add credence to his story, he'd rolled her in the leaves and messed up her clothes. Which she didn't seem to mind at all.

'I'm just glad I was there when I was,' he now said, when yet again Hope thanked him for him for what he'd done. 'Otherwise,' he added with a meaningful shrug, 'God only knows what might have happened.' His words, he saw, were like a dagger to Allegra, and as she chewed her lip and visibly trembled, he relished the effect.

They were on the terrace, drinking tea — the British answer to all life's calamities — with Romily, Hope and Allegra having changed out of their wet clothes. Hope had the child on her lap and was holding her close, as though she would never let her go.

Arthur gave the child a crafty sideways glance. *Our little secret*, he said silently to her. *Something to keep just between the two of us.*

29

The next day, Dr Garland was back at Island House again.

Romily was worried about Allegra. The girl didn't seem at all well. She hadn't eaten anything since breakfast yesterday morning, and had locked herself in her bedroom, no doubt too embarrassed to show her face. Whenever Romily had knocked on the door in an effort to coax her out, her pleadings went unheeded. But then this morning she had heard the unmistakable sound of Allegra being repeatedly unwell in the bathroom and had confronted her before she could make it back to her room.

One look at her feverish high colour and her hands clutching her stomach and Romily's mind had been made up: the girl was plainly ill and needed medical attention. Perhaps she had swallowed water in the pond yesterday and caught something horrid that was upsetting her stomach? She had helped Allegra back into bed, telling her she was sending for Dr Garland. She had half expected her to remonstrate, but it was as if the spark that fired her determined and contrary will had left her. She was a pitiful sight, and despite her appalling carelessness with Annelise yesterday, Romily's heart softened at the visible pain of her suffering now.

Having shown Dr Garland upstairs, Romily went outside to the garden. Nobody else was about — Kit and Hope had gone for a walk with Annelise, and heaven only knew where Arthur was.

It was understandable that Hope could not now bring herself to entrust Annelise into anybody else's care but her own, and consequently she had informed her publisher first thing this morning that she needed more time to produce the promised illustrations. Privately Romily believed her vigilance would soon waver, once they had all recovered from the shock of what might have happened.

If Arthur had been unbearably unpleasant before, now, having adopted the mantle of heroic child rescuer, he was even harder to tolerate. He was insufferably smug about his role in yesterday's drama and clearly relished every opportunity to condemn Allegra for her negligence. Admittedly Allegra had made a terrible mistake, and one that could have ended in tragedy, but Romily never believed in rubbing salt into a wound. She suspected the girl would be haunted for a very long time by her carelessness. That was punishment enough for anyone in Romily's opinion.

Walking the length of the avenue of herbaceous borders and admiring the hummocks of lavender, the hollyhocks and delphiniums and the sweet-smelling roses, she spotted Elijah working at the far end of the right-hand border. She hadn't had a chance to speak to him since before the funeral, and so she decided to have a word about an idea she'd had for the area of garden outside Jack's study.

Jack had always had a lot of time for Elijah

and used to enjoy discussing his latest plans for the garden with him. 'You wouldn't believe what a weedy little fellow he was when he was a boy,' he had once told Romily. He'd also told her that as children, Allegra and Elijah had been firm friends. 'Of course she had no idea that I knew she was sneaking off to play with him in Clover Woods,' he had explained. 'One word of approval from me and she would have cut the friendship off in a heartbeat just to spite me.'

Florence had told Romily that she had spotted Allegra and Elijah dancing together on Saturday evening. Had they then spent the night together at Elijah's cottage?

Elijah touched his cap when Romily drew near. 'Afternoon, Mrs Temple-Devereux,' he said in his soft, temperate voice, the tone of which always surprised Romily, given that he was such a tall, powerfully built man. 'I'm sorry I wasn't at Mr Devereux's funeral,' he said. 'I wanted to pay my respects to a man who had always been very good to me and my grandfather, but Lady Fogg insisted she needed me for the day.'

How mean-spirited of the ghastly woman, thought Romily. 'That's all right, Elijah,' she said. 'These things happen. If you have a minute,' she went on, 'I'd value your opinion about an idea I've had for the garden; a sort of memorial to Jack.'

'I'd be happy to hear what you have in mind,' he said, 'only the thing is, I might not . . . ' He broke off and gripped the hoe tightly in his large hands.

'What is it, Elijah?' Romily asked him, concerned. 'What's wrong?'

'I was going to tell you later today, when I'd finished work, but the thing is, I might not be here for much longer. You see, some lads and me from the village are planning to enrol. We reckon it will only be a matter of weeks, if not days, before we're called up to fight anyway.'

Romily regarded him with renewed respect, but also with sadness. She thought of the young men in Melstead St Mary and the surrounding villages, all of whom would be thinking the same way as Elijah and volunteering, oblivious perhaps to what they were letting themselves in for, just as their grandfathers, fathers and uncles had done in the Great War. 'I believe you're right,' she said ruefully, 'but I hope with all my heart it won't come to that.'

'We can't just stand idly by while Hitler does what he wants,' Elijah said gravely. 'He has to be stopped, or where will it all end?'

'I agree, and I applaud you and your friends for your courage.'

'Thank you, Mrs Temple-Devereux,' he said with a small nod of his head. 'Now what was it you wanted me to do for you in the garden? Maybe I'll have time before I leave.'

She raised a hand. 'It's fine; don't give it another thought. You have bigger things to think about.'

'But if it's important to you, I'd like to help if I can. I'd like to do it for Mr Devereux too, seeing as I couldn't make it to his funeral. If that's not speaking out of turn.'

'Not at all, Elijah; I'm grateful for your thoughtfulness.'

'In that case, do you want to show me what you had in mind, and where?'

They were walking the length of the garden, back towards the house, when Romily saw Dr Garland appear through the open French doors of the drawing room.

'I'll be right back,' she said to Elijah. 'I must just speak to the doctor about Allegra.'

'Why, what's the matter with her? It's not anything . . . ' His words ground to an abrupt halt and his face coloured. 'I'm sorry,' he muttered awkwardly, his gaze lowered. 'I shouldn't have spoken like that. It's none of my business.'

'That's all right,' Romily said, her earlier suspicions further roused. 'Jack told me that you and Allegra were good friends when you were children, so your interest is perfectly understandable. I called for the doctor because I was worried about her. She doesn't seem at all well in my opinion.'

He raised his gaze. 'If it's not too much bother, maybe you could say I was asking after her.'

'Of course.'

'And . . . and will you tell her I'm sorry for what I said. She'll know what I mean.'

Romily smiled. 'I will. Now if you'll excuse me, I'll see what Dr Garland has to say.'

* * *

'Dr Garland says you have something to tell me,' said Romily when she came in with a tray of tea things.

'He didn't tell you himself?' replied Allegra,

232

surprised. Waiting for Romily to come upstairs to see her, she had been convinced Dr Garland would have rushed to break the shameful news of her pregnancy to the entire household, the whole of the village too.

'He's much too discreet for that,' Romily said, pouring out two cups of tea. 'Milk? Or lemon?'

'Neither. One sugar, though.'

She watched Romily drop a cube of sugar into the cup and then stir it before bringing it over with a biscuit placed on the saucer. After she'd fetched her own cup and sat in the chair next to the bed, where Dr Garland had earlier seated himself when he'd finished examining her, Romily said, 'I was talking to Elijah in the garden and he wanted you to know that he was asking after you.'

Allegra tried not to look too startled. 'Why would he do that?'

'Presumably because he's an old friend of yours and he cares about you. He also said to tell you he's sorry for what he said.'

'I don't know what he's talking about.'

Romily looked at her over the rim of her cup. 'Don't you? Really? He seemed very sure that you would.'

Ignoring Romily's remarks, Allegra said, 'What else did he say? And how did he know I wasn't feeling well?'

'I mentioned that Dr Garland was here to see you. There was no getting away from his reaction, which was one of alarm. Drink your tea, Allegra, before it gets cold, and perhaps try that ginger biscuit; you haven't had anything to eat since yesterday morning.'

Allegra took a small sip of the tea and then a cautious nibble of the biscuit. Dr Garland had left a prescription for some medicine that he claimed would stop her feeling so nauseous. She hoped he was right.

'I'm sorry I've put you to so much trouble,' she said, when she'd swallowed a minuscule bite of the biscuit. 'Especially after what happened yesterday.'

'Don't torture yourself by thinking about that; it won't help you. Best thing we can all do is to learn from it and be on our guard to prevent a similar thing happening again.'

'Why are you being so nice to me?'

'Would you rather I was as unpleasant to you as Arthur is?'

'I'd trust it more. The one thing I always know with my cousin is where I stand. But with you, I . . . I don't know.'

'That's hardly surprising. Until a few days ago, we hadn't met. It takes time to get to know a person, and longer still to trust them.'

'I've trusted very few people in my life,' murmured Allegra. 'Those I have have usually let me down.' She was thinking of Luigi in particular.

'I guessed as much,' said Romily. 'But I'd hazard a guess that you trusted Elijah when you were a child. Yes?'

Allegra risked another sip of the hot sweet tea before saying, 'You're fishing, aren't you?'

Romily smiled. 'He's an extraordinarily handsome young man. Quite the dish.'

In spite of feeling so awful, Allegra smiled as well. 'I didn't recognise him when I first saw him working in the garden the other day. He's changed so much since I last saw him. But you're right: he and I were good friends back when we were children.'

'Did you spend the night with him on Saturday?'

Allegra nearly dropped her teacup. 'Why on earth would you ask me that?'

'Because I saw you returning home early yesterday morning, and you were still wearing the dress you'd worn for the dance the night before.'

Allegra blinked. 'It's not what you think.'

'But you don't know what I'm thinking. And really it's nothing to do with me what you get up to with an old friend.'

'We just talked. We talked and talked and then the next thing I knew it was morning and I was still in the armchair where I'd been all night. And that's the truth. Though to be honest, I don't give a damn whether you believe me or not.'

Romily looked at her steadily. 'Actually I do believe you. The same thing happened to me with Jack when we met for the second time. We'd been out for dinner, and afterwards he invited me back to his place for a nightcap and we talked all night until we heard the birds singing. One thing you need to know about me, Allegra, I care not a jot for convention. Your uncle and I lived perfectly happily in a state of what certain folk here in the village considered to be sin, and we neither of us batted an eyelid. So you see, you can't say or do anything that will shock me, and I'm certainly not going to sit in judgement on you. Not ever.'

Allegra decided to put that statement to the test. 'What if I told you I was pregnant?'

Without missing a beat, Romily said, 'I'd say that explains the sickness, and the tiredness. When is the baby due?'

'In about seven months. Dr Garland advised me to tell you — he seems to think that it was too big a burden for me to carry alone. I didn't tell him I'd already told Elijah. That was one of the things we were talking about into the early hours of Sunday morning.'

'So that's why Elijah reacted the way he did when I told him the doctor was here to see you. His concern for you was genuine, you know.'

Allegra nodded, touched that despite the way they'd parted yesterday morning, Elijah cared enough to ask after her. 'According to Dr Garland,' she said, 'I'm suffering from mental and physical exhaustion, brought on by the shock of what happened yesterday with Annelise.'

'That would make sense. What does he advise?'

'Complete bed rest for the next few days, for the sake of the baby.' She sighed heavily. 'Which will ensure I die of boredom.'

'Then we shall have to do our best to amuse and entertain you. Take another bite of that biscuit if you can bear it, Allegra. Now then, what about the father of the baby? Presumably he's in Italy. Does he know? Can he be relied upon?'

Allegra snorted. 'If by that you mean can he be relied upon to lie, cheat and swindle, then yes.' She gave Romily an abridged version of the events that had brought her to this low point, and as she spoke, she felt a growing sense of trust and esteem towards this woman she had known for such a short time, a woman who seemed to possess a singularly clear-sighted and uncomplicated way of looking at life. She was beginning now to see why Roddy had said that he had the greatest respect and admiration for her. There was no superiority or judgement to her. Just a willingness to help. What was more, not a word of blame or criticism had she levelled at Allegra for falling asleep while minding Annelise yesterday.

The sickening guilt Allegra felt for her irresponsible behaviour had kept her awake for most of the night. Every time she had almost nodded off, the haunting image of a dead child floating in the pond came to her, and she had to bury her face in the pillow to block it out.

How could she ever consider herself responsible enough to be a fit mother after that? Would anyone in their right mind think she was capable of looking after a child?

30

Back from their walk, and at Kit's suggestion, they wandered through the garden to the old outhouse they used to play in as children. He'd had a sudden whim to remind himself of where he and Hope had often retreated when they wanted to steer clear of Arthur.

While Hope lifted Annelise out of the pram, Kit peered in through one of the grimy windows, but it was too dark inside to see clearly. Next he tried the handle of the door, half expecting it to be locked. It wasn't, and it opened stiffly with an arthritic creak. He stepped inside into the airless gloom, his nostrils instantly assailed with the dust of years gone by.

'Doesn't look like anyone's been in here in a very long time,' he said over his shoulder to Hope, his eyes adjusting to the opaque interior.

'Is it safe, do you think?' she asked, from the doorway.

'I'd keep hold of Annelise,' he replied. 'Don't put her down or she'll end up as black as coal.'

Together they moved further into the outhouse. 'Oh look,' exclaimed Hope, 'there's the old croquet set we used to play with.'

'Better still, look over there, there's Giddy-Up Jack, our old rocking horse. Do you remember how we'd both get on it and that foul old nanny would shout at us for making too much noise?'

Hope shuddered. 'What a witch Nanny Finch

was. Heaven only knows what on earth Father thought he was doing when he employed her.'

'I suppose he didn't have much say in it; he would simply have asked the agency to supply yet another nanny. After all, we did get through them at an alarming rate.'

Kit pushed aside a shabby wrought-iron table and a couple of chairs and ran a hand over the dusty back of the rocking horse. 'What say you we clean him up for Annelise to play on?

'I'd say that might be a tall order, given the state he's in. He might even be riddled with woodworm.'

'Think positively, Hope, think positively.' He cleared a path through the piles of junk, wondering why their father had bothered to keep any of it. Or had it been a case of out of sight, out of mind? Not unlike his attitude toward his children, perhaps. He began pulling the old rocking horse with its peeling paintwork towards the door. Behind it lurked another childhood treasure. 'Guess what?' he said. 'I've found our old toy donkey and cart, and unbelievably the cart has the wooden skittles in it we used to try and juggle with. Do you remember?'

'I do. I also remember you and Allegra coming to blows over them and her hurling the skittles, one after another, from your bedroom window.'

'She had quite a throw, if I recall rightly,' he said with a laugh.

But there was no laughter in Hope's expression. She pursed her lips and frowned. 'You know, I don't think I'll ever be able to forgive her for what happened yesterday. I just

239

can't credit that anyone could be so thought-
lessly irresponsible. Did it not cross her mind for
one second what the consequences could be?
But then when did Allegra ever think about the
consequences of her actions? She really hasn't
changed, has she? Still the same self-absorbed
narcissist with a chip on her shoulder.'

Not wanting his sister to get herself worked up
again — he'd heard quite enough on the subject
of their cousin — Kit said, 'The important thing
is Annelise didn't come to any harm. Come on,
let's see if we can clean these toys up so she has
something to play with.'

As if understanding him, the little girl kicked
her feet excitedly against Hope and pointed
happily at Giddy-Up Jack.

'I think we'll take it that she's in agreement
with me,' Kit said with a smile.

He soon had the toys out on the lawn in front
of the outhouse. With a stiff bristle brush he'd
found hanging on a hook on the back of the
door, he attacked the rocking horse, brushing
away the cobwebs and dust, before using a
handkerchief from his pocket to give it a final
rub-down. 'There,' he said, thoroughly pleased
with himself. 'Let's see if Annelise wants to go
for a ride.'

Hope settled her carefully on the saddle of the
wooden horse and wrapped her small hands
around the worn leather of the reins. When she
had the horse gently rocking, the little girl
beamed with delight, her blue eyes wide.

'If only her parents could see her looking so
happy,' murmured Hope, a supporting hand

resting protectively on Annelise's back.

'Have you heard from them at all?' asked Kit.

'No. I sent a letter a few days ago, but I'm not convinced it will ever reach Otto and Sabine. I'm equally certain that any letters they try to send out of the country will be destroyed by the authorities. The Nazis don't want the rest of the world to know just what they're doing to the Jews, how they're restricting what they can and cannot do. I never thought I'd say this, and it goes against everything Dieter and I believed in, but the sooner we go to war with Germany, the better.'

At the serious intensity of her expression, Kit put his arm around his sister. It was, he noted the first time he had done so in a very long time. And in that moment, as she relaxed imperceptibly against him, he wanted to believe that the fierce anger of her grief that had isolated her these last two years was beginning to ease. Perhaps now it was directed towards a new target — Germany — and she was no longer taking it out on those around her. Or herself, for that matter.

With this thought came the realisation that Kit was actually enjoying himself being back at Island House. The weight of dread that had accompanied him on the train in response to Roddy's telegram had gone, and in its place was a burgeoning sense of optimism.

On the face of it, his father's will had seemed a final and cruel act of disregard for anyone's feelings but his own, as if forcing the family to come together under the one roof and pitting them against each other had been planned to give him some sort of twisted satisfaction. But in all honesty, Kit could see no reason why Jack would have wanted to do that, not when, if all that Roddy and Romily said was true, he had at last found happiness.

When he thought about it, Kit could not recall a time when he had seen his father genuinely happy. It was a thought that had never occurred to him before. Was that because he had been too preoccupied with his own feelings? He was about to voice this idea to Hope, to explore it further, when he thought better of it. He didn't want to say anything that might disrupt her mood — a mood that was so precariously balanced — and so he contented himself with enjoying the tentative renewal of the closeness they had once shared. For which he found himself thanking his father. If nothing else, this enforced time together at Island House was proving to be a positive experience for Kit, and hopefully for his sister too.

Or was it the lull before the storm?

31

Arthur was at the top of the house in the stuffy heat of the attic. For the last five minutes, having taken a break from his own bit of poking about in the past, he'd been observing Kit and Hope down in the garden doing much the same thing in the outhouse, unearthing an assortment of their old toys.

Many a time as a boy he had retreated up here, both to escape his family and to spy on them from the window if they were in the area to the side of the house that led to the kitchen garden. They each had had their own not-so-secret place where they went to be alone — Hope to the glasshouse, Kit wandering the woods and meadows, Allegra to the boathouse and he to the attic — and rarely had they breached the invisible barrier each had erected to safeguard their privacy. Even Arthur, wanting to avoid the threat of retaliation, had chosen to respect the unwritten rule, wanting no one to infiltrate his personal kingdom. Only Allegra had seen fit to flout it, and all hell had broken out when he'd found her up here one day hunting through his boyhood treasures — his stamp and coin collections, his chemistry set and model aeroplanes, and the rat he'd been dissecting. He'd tied her to a chair and, penknife in hand, threatened to dissect her unless she swore never to come up to the attic again.

He took a handkerchief from his trouser pocket and wiped the sweat from his brow, then, moving away from the window, which he'd just opened, returned to the task in hand. It really was extraordinary what the old man had stored up here — side tables, wardrobes, vases, lamps, rugs, ornaments, tennis racquets too warped ever to be of use, a split cricket bat, a train set in its box, any number of umbrellas, a pair of stout walking boots, pictures, blankets, books, a gramophone player with a selection of records, a set of golf clubs, and countless box files of yellowed papers and documents. For the love of God, why the hell hadn't the stupid man ever thrown anything away?

It had been photograph albums that Arthur had come up here in search of, along with anything of worth that nobody would notice if it disappeared. He saw no reason not to help himself when Romily wouldn't have a clue what was here. As far as he was concerned, she had no claim to anything that had belonged to the family prior to her arrival. She might be his father's legal widowed wife and principal benefactor, but she had no claim to what Arthur considered his by birthright. If he had believed he stood a chance of winning, he would have contested the will; it was tempting to give it a go just to stir things up, but Roddy Fitzwilliam had made his feelings clear on that score.

He eased open the rusting catches of a large wooden steamer trunk that was plastered with luggage labels from hotels around the world — the Astor House Hotel in Hong Kong, the

Gritti Palace in Venice, the Cairo Grand, the Paris Ritz, the Grand Hotel in Monte Carlo, the Budapest Imperial, the Majestic in New York and the Grand Hotel Suisse. Each and every label was irrefutable evidence that Jack Devereux had spent more time away travelling and enjoying himself than at home with his family. He cast aside a layer of fusty old tissue paper and found several photograph albums resting on top of a thick woollen blanket, as well as a box of assorted photographs and postcards. He took his find over to the window and sank into the battered armchair there, with its broken springs and feathers leaking from the seat cushion.

He tackled one of the albums first, turning the pages with a slow and careful hand. It was foolishly sentimental of him, but being back here at Island House had made him think about things he hadn't thought of in a long time, things he had preferred not to think about.

He had been three years old when his mother died, and so any tantalising memory he had of her could not be relied upon for authenticity. Very likely anything he thought he remembered had been conjured up inside his head based on hearsay, or purely of his own invention.

But despite accepting this as perfectly logical, a wholly illogical part of him was firmly of the opinion that he most certainly did remember certain things about Maud Devereux. Firstly, he remembered her as being gentle and loving towards him, in a way that nobody since had been; and secondly, she had been beautiful. Of this he was absolutely sure, because as a child he had seen photographs of her. For a time he had possessed one, taken from an album his father had kept in his study. It had been a rare photograph of his mother standing alone — mostly she was captured arm in arm with her husband, or lost amongst a group of people.

He had hidden the photograph within the pages of a book inside his trunk when he had been sent away to school. It had become his most treasured possession, had taken on a far greater importance than it should have, but then one day, a boy he'd taken to be a friend had discovered the photograph and had taunted him with it, snatching the small square of precious paper out of reach of his grasp when he tried to take it back. Two other boys then joined in with the fun and held him down while the so-called friend took a torturer's delight in slowly tearing up the photograph, letting the pieces flutter to the floor.

Arthur learnt two important lessons that day — to trust no one, and never to treasure anything, or anyone, again. To fear losing something precious was effectively to make one vulnerable, and he was determined never to be at the mercy of another. As a consequence, he had decided that the cause of his misery — his sentimental adoration of a woman he had scarcely known — had to be revoked. Better to revile her memory than cherish it and make himself weak.

And yet now here he was, all these years on, curious to know more of the woman who had given life to him. What sort of woman had she really been? Was he like her in any way? And why, since returning to Island House, had he recalled a handful of memories of a woman sitting on the edge of his bed stroking his forehead when he was unwell; of a quietly spoken woman reading to him by the fireside; of a woman in a sage-green coat playing with him in a garden?

Were these false recollections, a confusion of reminiscences that may or may not have actually taken place; or if they had, was the woman in question merely one of the myriad nannies who came and went? It annoyed him that he could not be completely clear on the matter, because if there was one thing he craved in life, it was a sense of control over all that he did and thought.

The only way to find that clarity, he had concluded, was to revisit the past by investigating his father's photograph albums. Having searched the house downstairs and drawn a blank, he had been left with one last place to look: the attic. Should he have been surprised that that part of his father's life had been consigned to the junk pile up here?

He continued to turn the pages of the album, not recognising anyone or anything. There were men in labourers' clothes — shirtsleeves, trousers held up with string, and workmen's boots — and women in high-necked dresses; a gang of sickly-looking ruffians like something out of a Dickens novel, and then a lone boy peering out from beneath an oversized cap and with a determined jut to his chin, pushing a market street barrow. Presumably, thought Arthur, that was Jack Devereux just starting out in the world, embarking on his rags-to-riches success story.

He was about halfway through the album when he came to a picture that made him pause. Looking back at him was a smiling young woman with a baby swaddled in a lacy shawl in her arms. Beneath the photograph were the words: *Maud proudly holding our darling seven-day-old Arthur Ronald Augustine Devereux.*

He stared at the woman as if holding the gaze of the woman who stared steadily back at him. Was this the mother who had comforted him when he'd had a fever, who'd read to him and played with him in a garden? He turned another page and found the same woman standing beside a large pram: *Maud takes Arthur for a walk.* The following page showed a woman sitting on a tartan rug on an area of grass; on one side of her was a picnic basket and on her lap was a baby. *Maud and Arthur enjoying a picnic in Hyde Park*, read the caption beneath.

There followed page after page of mother-and-son photographs, interspersed with several containing Jack Devereux, who occasionally took his turn at holding Arthur. Nobody else featured in the photographs, and it would have been an easy assumption to make that this tight-knit family of three wanted for nothing but themselves.

By the time he reached the final page of the album, Arthur was left with a disturbing realisation: Jack and Maud had not only adored each other — that much was evident in the happy looks they shared — they had also adored their firstborn child. The discovery should have pleased him, but it didn't. It made him feel confused and adrift, cut off from the only reality he had ever known. He'd gone from certainty to its polar opposite. All his life he had been convinced that Jack Devereux had cared for no one but himself, yet now it seemed there had been a time when that wasn't the case.

He studied the photographs slowly, one by one, then turned to the next album. The first page showed the arrival of Jack and Maud's second child, Hope. There then followed page after page of her progress, just as his own had been charted. Occasionally he featured in the pictures alongside Hope, but there was no getting away from the fact that he was no longer at the centre of his parents' affections; Hope had taken that position and pushed him to the sidelines. Where he'd been ever since, he thought grimly.

He slapped the album shut and tossed it onto the rickety table at his elbow. It had been a mistake coming up here, snooping for verification of something he could never fully know.

Out of the armchair, and kicking aside the box of photographs and postcards he'd put on the floor, he made his way towards the stairs. He needed air. Fresh air, not this ancient dust-filled air that was suffocating him.

Cursing himself for giving in to the foolish desire to revisit the past, he slammed the door after him hard. There was nothing useful to be gained from such an exercise. Nothing whatsoever.

32

With Dr Garland's words of warning from yesterday still echoing in her head, Allegra was heeding his advice and resting. Only a short while ago, losing the baby might have seemed like an answer to a prayer, but now wholly unbidden, the pendulum of her emotions had swung and she would do all within her power to keep this child safe. And if that meant doing as Dr Garland said, then so be it.

However, just as she'd predicted, she had succumbed to boredom, and with Romily's permission she had been allowed out of bed to rest down here in the garden. The sun felt good on her face. It was good too to listen to the cheerful chattering of the sparrows and the joyous tuneful song of a blackbird in the apple tree. It was strange, and contrary to all that lay ahead for her, but she felt oddly at peace. She no longer cared who knew that she was pregnant; it would all come out eventually anyway. What did it matter what anybody thought of her? Only one thing mattered, and that was her baby's survival.

Romily had put forward the idea that Allegra could invent a fictitious Italian husband for herself as a way to give her and the child a veneer of respectability, if she so chose. 'Not that I'm implying you need to,' she had added. 'But you could pretend he's died very conveniently and no one would be the wiser.'

The thought had already occurred to Allegra, but it would take effort to maintain the lie while the child was growing up. And what then? Would she then tell the child the truth when she believed he or she was old enough to understand? She knew from her own experience that there were some questions to which there were no answers.

One thing that her child would never doubt or question would be Allegra's love. She would also make sure he or she never doubted their place in the world. What was more, Allegra would provide the kind of loving home she herself had craved while growing up. Her inheritance from Uncle Jack would see to that.

Increasingly she was beginning to revise her opinion of her uncle, and such was the turnaround in her emotions, and the extent of her calm acceptance of her situation, she wished she could thank him for his generosity. He needn't have left her a penny, but he had, even if it did come with certain stipulations. It was hard to admit, but perhaps Roddy was right; maybe Uncle Jack had cared for her after all. Or perhaps it was regret, a way to atone for how miserable her life had been at Island House.

She closed her eyes and listened to the harmonious rhythmic cooing of a dove, and before long its comforting sound had almost lulled her to sleep. Suddenly she sensed she wasn't alone. She opened her eyes and saw Elijah standing in front of her with a wheelbarrow to the side of him.

'I'm sorry if I woke you,' he said, his voice as soft and soothing as the dove still cooing.

'You didn't,' she answered him, shifting her position in the wicker chair to look up at him. 'Thank you for your message yesterday, that was sweet of you.'

He shrugged. 'How are you now?'

'I'm under orders to rest. Which, as you can see, I'm doing to the best of my ability.'

After glancing around them, he drew closer. 'Is it the baby?' he asked, his voice lower than ever.

She nodded.

'Does anyone else know?'

'Just Dr Garland and Romily. For now. She's been very good about it.'

'She's good about most things, in my experience. Is there anything I can do?'

'Yes *caro*,' Allegra said, leaning forward. 'Accept my apology for the way we parted on Sunday. My words came out all wrong. I didn't mean to sound the way I did.'

'It's all right,' he said. 'I was at fault too. But I do understand, you have your reputation to consider.'

She shook her head and rested a hand across her abdomen. 'I think it's a little late for me to be concerned about that, don't you?'

'To hell with anyone who criticises you,' he said vehemently, leaning in closer still.

Smiling, she said, 'I wish you could sit and chat with me.'

He glanced up at the house behind them, as if checking for anyone watching them. 'Best not,' he said, 'as much as I'd like to.'

A sadness came over her. 'I wish things were different.'

'In what way?'

'That we were children again. Life was so much more simple then. Although I didn't think so at the time. I couldn't wait to be grown up; I thought things would be easier when I could make my own decisions and be in control of my destiny. I've proved not to be very good at doing that,' she said with a rueful sigh.

'We can't turn back the clock,' he said matter-of-factly. 'We are where we are.' He cast another glance over his shoulder, then looked back at her. 'If you're well enough in the next day or so, would you like to go for a walk sometime? That's if you're happy to be seen with me.'

'I'd like that very much,' she said with a smile. 'And to hell with what anyone else thinks! But what about you signing up? When will you do that?'

'Soon,' he said. 'I've told Mrs Devereux-Temple that I'll be going.'

'I wish you weren't so keen to put yourself in danger. You won't disappear without saying goodbye, will you?'

'That rather depends.'

'On what?'

'On whether you'll still be here when I leave. I expect you'll go before me. Your week here will soon be up and you'll be off to London, won't you, or somewhere else?'

She shrugged. It was as much as she could manage to think as far as the next hour, never mind tomorrow or the day after. 'I haven't got very far with planning what happens next,' she said.

'Just don't do anything hasty,' he said. 'Not when you have the baby to consider.'

'That's exactly what Romily said.'

He smiled. 'Then you'd best do as she says. And I'd better get on and do what I'm paid to do.'

Disappointed that he couldn't stay and keep her company, Allegra watched him push the wheelbarrow across the lawn towards the kitchen garden. How pathetic it now seemed to her that she had been concerned what people would think of her staying the night at Clover End Cottage. Since when had she cared about such things?

Sadly, though, she suspected that Elijah did, for there was no mistaking the fact that he regarded her as a Devereux. Which was nonsense. Had they met in Italy when she'd been in the orphanage, they would have been on an equal footing; there would have been no question of them being of a different social class. But because by a fluke of birth Jack Devereux was her uncle, their roles had been defined accordingly.

★ ★ ★

As there often was, there was a queue outside the baker's shop, but Florence didn't mind; she was quite happy to take her turn in the warm sunshine. It also gave her the opportunity to watch Billy through the window as he helped his mother serve the queue of customers. Mrs Partridge had said she'd phone the bread order through and have Billy deliver it, but Florence had seized her opportunity and offered to fetch it herself. 'And no guesses why that would be,' Mrs Partridge had said, causing Florence's cheeks to flame.

But then what did she expect when nothing was secret round here, not with Mrs Bunch in the village? There didn't seem to be anything she didn't know. For instance, she knew that Allegra had been seen leaving Elijah's cottage early Sunday morning. 'Sweet as a pair of cooing turtle doves, they be,' claimed Mrs Bunch with a smug smile. 'Though what will come of it is anybody's guess.'

With her own eyes Florence had spotted Allegra and Elijah talking in the garden earlier that morning, and from the look of them, she'd bet a whole king's ransom they hadn't been discussing the best way to prune roses!

As the queue moved forward, she saw Billy looking at her through the window. He smiled and waved at her, and absurdly her stomach gave a little flip and set off a fluttering sensation as though a million butterflies were flapping their wings inside her. By the time the sensation had settled, Billy had appeared outside the shop with a full basket of bread, which he strapped onto his delivery bicycle propped against the wall. When all was secure, he came over to her. 'Can I walk you back to Island House when you've got what you need?' he asked quietly.

'Haven't you got your orders to deliver?' she whispered, conscious that they were being observed.

He smiled. 'I'll do them afterwards. I'll wait for you by the postbox at the end of Market Lane.'

When he'd gone — whistling merrily to himself — Florence kept her gaze fixed firmly on her shoes, diligently avoiding any speculative glances. Who among them in the queue, she wondered, would be the first to report back to Mrs Bunch?

At last she made it inside the shop, with its invitingly sweet and yeasty smell, and was served by Billy's mother, Ruby Minton. Ruby was never the friendliest of women, and there was nothing remotely inviting about the cool look she gave Florence over the counter. Florence knew what the look meant — *Leave my son alone; you're not good enough for him!* She also knew, thanks to Mrs Bunch, why just about any girl in the village would be on the receiving end of such a look. Ruby Minton had had so much difficulty in delivering a healthy baby that from the day Billy was born, she had guarded him jealously, rarely letting him out of her sight. The story Mrs Bunch told was that in the garden at the back of the baker's shop was a fruit tree planted for every baby the Mintons had lost; they numbered half a dozen.

With the bread wrapped, paid for and placed in her basket, Florence politely wished Ruby Minton a good day. After receiving no more than a sniff of dismissal, she stepped back out into the bright sunshine. Poor woman, she thought, her life had probably been overshadowed by a never-ending cycle of sadness. Was it any wonder she was scared of losing her one and only child to a girlfriend or wife?

The market square behind her, Florence saw Billy waiting for her just where he had said he would.

'You look fair pretty today, Flo,' he said, leaning over to kiss her smack on the lips. 'As pretty as a picture.'

'And you, Billy Minton, are taking liberties,' she replied, her stomach turning somersaults as she looked anxiously about them to make sure nobody was around to see.

He laughed. 'I promise that's the only liberty I'll take with you today.'

'I'm very glad to hear it,' she said primly.

He walked alongside her down the narrow lane, pushing his heavily laden bicycle, and then together they crossed the main road. 'Can I ask you something?' he said when they were on the other side.

'That depends on what it is you want to know.'

'I'd like to establish things between us,' he said. 'You know, make things official, like, so there's no misunderstanding.'

'That sounds very formal,' she said. 'What exactly is it you have in mind?'

'You know jolly well what I have in mind, but if I have to say the words, so be it. I want us to be officially stepping out, Miss Florence Massie.'

'Do you indeed?' She sounded much more in control than she actually felt. Inside she was all a-quiver, her heart beating double fast, the butterflies flapping their wings again.

'Don't tease me, Flo. You must know how I

feel about you. And I'm pretty sure you feel something for me, so why not say you'll be my girl?'

Florence thought of Mrs Minton and all those trees planted in her garden. 'Do you think that's such a good idea?' she asked. 'I don't believe your mother would take too kindly to me, do you?'

'Take no notice of her. She's just, well, you know, a bit over-protective; some mothers are like that.'

Florence decided to be honest with him. 'She was quite off with me just now in the shop. Like she was warning me off you.'

'Pay her no heed. She's too cautious for her own good. She'll come round, you see if she don't. So how about it, shall we step out together?'

Her head said no, but her heart — her treacherous heart — said yes, yes, *yes!* 'If that's what you really want,' she murmured, 'then yes.'

He laughed. 'You could sound a bit more enthusiastic about the idea,' he said. 'Anyone would think you would sooner court a rattlesnake!'

She laughed too. 'Like your mother, I'm naturally cautious. And don't you be thinking you can get away with anything, William Minton. I'm not that sort of a girl. I'm really not.'

'And I'm not that sort of a boy. So don't you go making assumptions about me.'

'I'm sorry.'

'As well you should be. I'll never make you do anything you don't want to. And that's a promise.'

Such was the forcefulness of his tone, Florence believed him. She slowed her step and put a hand on his arm. 'I'm sorry for doubting you,' she said. 'You're the nicest lad I've ever known and I really enjoy your company, and . . . and I'm not going to say anything else or it'll make your head grow too big for those shoulders of yours.'

He smiled. 'I'll have you know my shoulders are strong enough to support the biggest of heads. I'm not a weakling baby, you know. Oh, and talking of babies, I've got something to tell you, something I saw in the woods at the back of Island House on Sunday.'

When he'd told her, and after Florence had asked him if he was sure, she knew it was something Miss Romily should hear about it.

33

'I hope you don't think I'm speaking out of turn, Miss Romily,' said Florence. 'I'm not one for telling tales, I never have been. But I thought this was important and you should know about it.'

Romily put down the pen she'd been writing with and turned away from her desk to give Florence her full attention. 'It's not about that gypsy fortune-teller, is it?'

'No. It's about Mr Arthur Devereux. The thing is, Billy — Billy Minton from the baker's . . . '

'Yes, I'm well acquainted with Billy,' Romily interjected with a smile. 'He's your young beau if I'm not mistaken.'

Florence blushed. 'I wouldn't say that. I mean we're only . . . '

'I'm teasing you, Florence, which is naughty of me. I apologise. Do carry on.'

'Well the thing is, it's what Billy saw on Sunday. He'd been with his parents down at the Sally Army hall, and afterwards he and his mate Tommy Fisher from the butcher's decided to go rabbiting in the woods at the back of here. Tommy can be a bit pushy, so Billy says, and well, he insisted they take the short cut along the private path around the pond; he said the bushes were so overgrown there nobody would see them, so nobody would be any the wiser, because strictly speaking they were trespassing, and Billy was worried about that.'

When the girl drew breath, and sensing she was going to go into rather more detail than might be necessary, Romily sat back in her chair and made herself more comfortable. She couldn't help but be intrigued. 'Go on,' she said encouragingly.

'Billy says it was when they were skirting round the furthest side of the pond that he peered through the bushes, through the bit where they're not so thick — he was afraid they might be seen across from the garden — and that's when he saw Arthur bending down to the sleeping baby and carrying her off. So he wasn't telling the truth when he said he found Annelise on the path heading towards the woods. He lied, didn't he, to get Miss Allegra into trouble?'

'And you're absolutely sure Billy isn't making this up?' asked Romily.

Florence shook her head vigorously. 'He's not like that. He doesn't say things for effect like some lads do. And for what it's worth, and because I knew it was important, I made him swear he was telling the truth.' She paused and fiddled with her apron. 'I have done the right thing in telling you, haven't I?'

'You did entirely the right thing in coming to me,' said Romily. 'I'm very grateful to you, Florence, and to Billy for sharing with you what he saw. What made him tell you, by the way?'

'He'd heard about Annelise going missing, and that Arthur was the one to find her — probably Mrs Bunch had the news all round the village by teatime yesterday — and he just thought it didn't add up.'

'He's an astute young man,' Romily said thoughtfully.

Florence smiled shyly. 'I'm sorry I didn't say anything before now, but there hasn't been time since yesterday when he told me, what with everything that's been going on and looking after Annelise.'

'That's all right. I know now, that's the important thing.'

'It's none of my business, but I can't help but think Miss Allegra has been treated badly by that cousin of hers. He deserves stringing up for putting her through all that torment, especially as she's not well. Is she feeling any better?'

'Rest is what Dr Garland says is best for her,' Romily said evasively. 'But I think this news you've shared with me may well help.'

* * *

Left on her own, Romily contemplated just how loathsome a creature Arthur was. What a twisted mind he had to carry out such a scheme. And why? To pit Hope against Allegra and divide them yet further? What satisfaction did he gain from such a ploy?

But Florence was right. A great wrong had been committed against Allegra, and Romily was determined to see that it was put right. Arthur would be shamed for his plotting and scheming.

She returned to the chapter she had been writing before Florence had knocked on the door, but try as she might, she could not settle. Her mind kept dwelling on what Arthur had done, in particular the awful minutes spent searching for Annelise in the pond, fearing the worst. She remembered too how distressed Allegra and Hope had been, the terror on Allegra's face and the hopeless misery on Hope's. What sick delight Arthur must have taken knowing that he had caused such a commotion and instilled such panic. What drove him to want to be always in control, to be the consummate puppet-master pulling the strings to manipulate others to his amusement? Roddy had warned Romily that there was a dark side to Arthur and that he was capable of almost anything, but she had underestimated that warning.

It was exactly a week ago that Jack's funeral had taken place, and this evening Roddy would be arriving to inform the family whether they had fulfilled the terms of the will to his satisfaction. His decision would be made tomorrow morning, after he'd spoken with Romily.

Whatever the final decision was, Romily strongly suspected the connection between Island House and Jack's family would not be broken immediately. Free as they were to go their different ways, she was not sure everyone would leave. Kit and Arthur would probably return to London and their jobs, but Allegra and Hope would be in no rush to go. In fact, Romily felt bound to urge them to stay on. She would be happy to extend the same invitation to Kit, but not Arthur. The sooner that malign influence left, the better.

She put down her pen, abandoning the idea of

work, and switched on the wireless to listen to the latest news on the ultimatum Hitler had sent Poland regarding Danzig. With still no word on the outcome, it was as if the world was holding its breath, the future as they knew it hanging precariously in the balance. In many ways it was a reflection of their own little world here at Island House, the family waiting to hear the outcome of their week spent together.

With a heavy heart, Romily switched off the wireless and went and stood at the open French doors, where a gentle breeze blew in, carrying with it the milky-sweet scent of freshly mown grass. It was late afternoon, and in the golden sunlight the garden's exquisite loveliness had the power to touch her. But despite the warmth and beauty of the day, a shiver of fear ran through her.

★　★　★

It was later, after Roddy had joined them and they were having dinner, that Romily chose her moment to confront Arthur, when she sensed he was taking his final chance to rile everybody around the table. There was no getting away from it: the man enjoyed a captive audience and manipulating it for his own warped pleasure.

She waited for Florence to finish serving their dessert, and when the girl had left the room, Romily raised her wine glass. 'I think a toast is in order, wouldn't you agree?'

Everyone looked at her uncertainly.

'What are we drinking to?' asked Arthur

pompously. 'The fact that we've survived a week cooped up together and not resorted to murder?'

'There's still time,' muttered Allegra.

Arthur snorted. 'That's rich coming from you, the woman who very nearly caused Annelise's demise.'

Before Allegra could reply, Romily said, 'I was going to suggest we drink to truth and honesty. And regarding that, I have something I'd like to share with you all.'

Roddy looked at her, puzzled. He was as much in the dark as everybody else; Romily had decided not to tell him of Arthur's deceit before the others learnt of it.

'Here we go,' said Arthur. 'This is the bit where our beloved stepmother informs us that we won't see a penny of our inheritance because we've fallen foul of some legal clause or other. I knew this would happen.'

'Do be quiet, Arthur!' snapped Hope. 'Don't you ever get tired of your own voice?'

'Don't you ever get tired of being such a sanctimonious bore?'

'As I was saying,' interrupted Romily, 'I have something I'd like to share with you. It concerns Arthur in particular.'

With her eyes firmly on Jack's elder son, and her voice perfectly steady, she recounted what Florence had told her of what Billy and his friend Tommy had witnessed. A deathly hush fell on the room, and as one they turned to look at Arthur.

'I'm appalled that you would believe a couple of common trespassers over me,' he said witheringly. 'Plainly they've fabricated this absurd story to avoid the risk of being hauled up before the magistrate for poaching on our land.'

'*My* land, I think you'll find,' said Romily, 'and frankly, I'd believe their word over yours any day.'

'So you're calling me a liar?' Superficially Arthur appeared fully in control, with a suitable measure of outrage thrown in, but there was no mistaking the guilty darting of his eyes, and the reddening of his face, which still bore the bruises from the fight he'd got into at the fete.

'If the cap fits,' said Romily coolly. 'But actually I'd go so far as to call you a lot worse than just a liar. As would Allegra and Hope, I'm sure. At the very least I'd say they deserve an apology from you.' The two women were regarding him with identical expressions of horrified disbelief.

'Hell will freeze over before I do that!' he exclaimed. He tossed his napkin onto the table and pushed back his chair to get to his feet. His manner had suddenly altered; now he wore the chilling expression of a man who was prepared to fight in any way he had to.

Opposite him, Hope also rose from her seat. She walked slowly around the table, passing behind Roddy, and when she was directly in front of her brother, she slapped his face hard. In retaliation, and revealing himself for the craven creature he was, Arthur raised his hand ready to strike her back, but next to him, quick as a flash, Kit jumped to his feet and with impressive bravado had his brother's arm twisted behind his back before he knew what was happening.

'Apologise now to Hope, and to Allegra,' said Kit. 'Do it, or I'll break your arm.'

Arthur rolled his eyes. 'Oh please, save the tough talk for those who mean it.'

Kit yanked his arm further up his back, causing Arthur to wince. 'All right,' he gasped, 'I'll do it. Hope and Allegra, I'm sorry. Satisfied now?'

As if knowing that was the best they would get out of him, Kit released his hold. Straightening his jacket, Arthur stared defiantly at Hope and Allegra. 'You have to admit, what I did proves that neither of you can be trusted to look after a child. God help Annelise is all I can say.'

'And God help you,' murmured Allegra, who until now had remained silent. 'May you be forgiven for being such a vile monster.'

At that, Arthur laughed. 'Is that the best you can do, Allegra? I'm disappointed. I'd have expected more from you.'

'I wouldn't waste my energy,' she said, turning her back on him.

'I think you should leave us now,' said Roddy, 'so we can finish our dinner in peace and quiet.'

Arthur smirked. 'I'll be outside if anyone wants me.'

'I wouldn't hold your breath,' said Kit.

When the door had closed after Arthur, Romily sighed. 'I'm sorry about that,' she said.

'You're sorry?' said Hope, resuming her seat. 'Why?'

'I should have been less dramatic about it, perhaps confronted him on his own.'

'No,' said Roddy, 'you did the right thing having us all here. Heaven only knows what he might have said or done to you otherwise. You saw how he meant to strike Hope.'

'Well I for one think it's time to make that toast now,' said Kit, also now sitting down again. 'To truth and honesty!'

Romily shook her head. 'No,' she said quietly. 'To Jack. To Jack for bringing us together.'

'To Jack,' they echoed.

Part Two

The War

*'We have a clear conscience,
we have done all that any
country could do to establish peace.'*

Neville Chamberlain in his Declaration
Of War transcript
11.15 a.m. 3rd September, 1939.

34

3rd September, 1939

This was it then, the waiting was over: they were at war now. No more talk. No more shilly-shallying. No more misplaced hope that Hitler would do the decent thing and climb down. But then really, the moment Germany had invaded Poland two days ago on the 1st September, all doubt had been removed, with Britain duty-bound to honour the treaty to support Poland. It had been all anyone could talk about.

Now, as Neville Chamberlain's address to the nation drew to a close and Mrs Partridge rose stiffly from her chair and switched off the wireless, Florence felt a mixture of emotions — relief that the thing was finally settled, but also a churning sickness in her stomach that Billy would now have to do his duty and maybe never come back to her. And as never before, the words of the fortune-teller echoed loudly in her head: *You'll find love and you'll lose love.*

'Well that's that then,' said Mrs Partridge with finality. 'Now we know what's what and we can get on with showing that ruddy Hitler what we're made of. Just who does he think he is!' She spoke as if she would like nothing better than to box Hitler's ears. Given half the chance, she probably would! Putting her apron back on — she had removed it as a mark of respect for

271

the Prime Minister's announcement — she resumed what she'd been doing, weighing out the ingredients for an apple and blackberry pie.

'I suppose this means we'll have to start carrying our gas masks around with us like those pamphlets say,' said Florence, getting on with peeling potatoes at the sink. War or no war, there was still Sunday lunch to prepare.

Mrs Partridge snorted. 'Much good they'll do us! A waste of paper all those pamphlets, if you ask me. Still, they'll come in handy for helping to light the fires when the weather turns.'

As Mrs Partridge continued with her grumbling, Florence wondered if Billy had heard the news. Probably not; more likely he was at the Salvation Army hall with his parents. Poor Ruby Minton, how on earth would she cope with letting her precious son go off and fight? For that matter, how had she taken the news when yesterday Billy and Elijah and all the other lads from the village had taken the bus to Bury St Edmunds to enlist? Florence had hoped Billy might call in to see her afterwards to let her know what he'd been told, her hope being, God forgive her, that he might have been declared unfit for duty.

'Open that window, will you, Florence? I'm sweating like a pig in a glasshouse! It's fair sweltering in here.'

'It's already open, Mrs Partridge,' Florence said. 'Shall I open the back door and see if that will set up a through-draught for you?'

Fanning herself, Mrs Partridge nodded. 'If you would, otherwise I'll melt to nothing but a puddle on the floor.'

Florence went through to the scullery and down the few steps to the back door. When she opened it, she started. There on the step was Stanley Nettles, their evacuee, sobbing his little heart out. 'Whatever is the matter?' she asked him.

Lady Fogg had delivered the poor lad to them in person the very day Germany invaded Poland. A pale, sickly boy with bony legs and arms and a disagreeable smell about him, he had cowered beside the terrifying woman looking like he'd make a run for it any minute. Although the stick-thin legs poking out from his dirty shorts hadn't given the impression they would carry him far. Without further explanation, other than to give his name and age — he was nine years old — and that he was from Bethnal Green, Lady Fogg had handed over the bewildered boy as if he were nothing more than a parcel delivery. He'd even had a luggage label pinned to his ragged old jersey. His belongings, such as they were, had been put in a pillowcase, which he'd held tightly against his chest. He'd made a sorry sight indeed.

With both Miss Romily and Kit in London that day, and Allegra out walking with Hope and Annelise, it had fallen to Florence to take the boy in. She had led him through to the kitchen, where Mrs Partridge had been enjoying her customary late-afternoon nap in her favourite chair. Florence had put a finger to her lips indicating to the boy that he keep quiet, and poured him a glass of lemonade. He'd drunk it thirstily in one long gulp, only then to be thoroughly sick all over the floor. The noise had woken Mrs Partridge with a jolt. 'Lord have mercy, whatever is going on here!' she'd exclaimed. Whereupon the boy had burst into uncontrollable sobs and thrown himself under the kitchen table as though he were a dog about to be severely punished.

Florence's heart had gone out to him; she had recognised the fear of his reaction all too well. Later, when she'd prepared a bath for him, adding a generous dose of disinfectant to get rid of the lice he'd brought with him, she'd caught a glimpse of the bruises and sores on his back and shoulders.

She had been all for burning his filthy threadbare clothes, including his underwear, which he'd been sewn into, but that evening, when Miss Romily returned from London with Kit, it was agreed that it would be better to wash and mend the rags as best they could to give the boy a degree of familiarity, in the hope it would make him feel more at home.

But now, as he sniffed and smeared the tears across his pale face with his skinny bare arm, Stanley looked anything but at home. Florence sat down on the step beside him. From her apron pocket she pulled out a handkerchief and tried to wipe his face, but he jerked away. She gently placed the handkerchief into one of his hands. 'So what's all this about then?' she asked. 'What's upset you?'

He pursed his lips and shook his head.

'Have you hurt yourself?' she asked.

He shook his head again.

'Do you feel unwell?'

Another shake of his head.

'Has somebody said something unkind to you?'

Once more he shook his head.

'Are you homesick?'

This time there was no shake of his head, just a sniff. To Florence it didn't make sense that he would be homesick. Why long to be somewhere you were treated so badly? But Miss Romily had explained that that was often the way; that home, even when it was a place of violence and cruelty, was better than being somewhere strange where you didn't know anybody. Florence had never felt that way; once she'd left home, she'd never longed to be back there. But then she was older than Stanley when she'd made the break.

She put a hand on the boy's bony knee. 'If you are missing home, Stanley, that's okay. I'm sure you won't have to put up with us for too long. Just as soon as the dust has settled, you'll be home before you know it.'

He looked up at her. 'D'yer mean that, missus?'

'Yes,' Florence answered him, hating herself for the lie. War had just been announced, and here she was telling the lad he'd soon be home. Well, who knew, maybe he would be? 'Meanwhile,' she said, 'why don't you try and enjoy yourself? Island House is not such a bad place to be. Would you like to come blackberry picking with me again later? You enjoyed that yesterday, didn't you?'

He gave a small shrug of his pitifully thin shoulders. 'Maybe.'

'And then there are all the other children in the village to get to know when school starts,' she said cheerfully. 'That'll be fun, won't it?'

At the mention of school, Stanley's lip trembled. 'I don't wanna go to school,' he muttered.

'I'm afraid you won't have much choice in the matter. You went to school back at home, didn't you?'

'Not much. Me mum said she needed me at 'ome.'

His lower lip trembled again and he jammed the handkerchief Florence had given him against his eyes. Florence put her arm around him and gave him the hug she'd wanted to give him ever since he'd first arrived.

★　★　★

In the drawing room, the wireless now off, Kit was pouring out glasses of sherry and passing them round.

'I don't know about the rest of you,' he said, 'but I feel as if an enormous weight has been lifted from my shoulders. The bank will soon be a thing of the past for me!'

'How can you talk like that?' said Hope with a shake of her head. 'War is not a game, Kit. Thousands of lives are going to be lost, possibly even yours, so please don't make light of it. I can't bear it.'

'I agree with Kit,' said Allegra. 'I'd sooner perish honourably and in action than die of boredom in a job I hated. And let's face it, joining the RAF and learning to fly has to be a lot more thrilling than working in a bank.'

Kit smiled. 'Thank you, Allegra; I'm glad somebody understands my point of view. I just hope I don't have to hang around as a reservist for too long. I'm itching to get going with my training and then do my bit.'

'War is not supposed to be thrilling,' said Hope with exasperation. 'You've been like a dog with two tails ever since you came back from the recruiting centre in London.'

With the conversation going on around her, and Annelise on her lap — for some reason the little girl had taken a peculiar liking to her — Romily thought how unreal the situation felt. She almost didn't know how to react. Somehow she had expected to feel completely changed by the announcement they had all been waiting for. But she felt no different to how she'd felt when she woke this morning. Perhaps she was inured to shock, still numb from losing her dearest Jack and unable to feel any real depth of emotion. In which case perhaps it would simply take some time for the reality of the news to sink in. She had only been a young child when the Great War began, and her memories were patchy. She remembered more vividly the day her father was invalided out of the war, the joy at seeing him again, and later the day peace was announced.

She listened to Kit, Hope and Allegra as they agreed and disagreed with each other. It came as naturally to them as breathing, this constant wrangling, even on a light-hearted basis; they didn't seem able to help themselves. Yet far from annoying her, Romily found it mildly diverting, for there was no malice in their exchanges. The three of them were much more comfortable around each other without Arthur in their midst stirring things up. Had he not been around, could they have come together as a family a lot sooner? Who knew? But as Roddy had said, often there was no obvious reason why a family fell apart other than a gradual unravelling over the pettiest of matters. For as far as Romily could see, it really hadn't taken much for Hope, Kit and Allegra to form an alliance, even if it was a fragile one. Putting Arthur aside, was it too soon to believe she had almost achieved what Jack had wanted her to do? His will had seemed so very draconian in its instructions, but undoubtedly it had led to something positive.

It was three days now since Roddy had formally declared that having complied with Jack's wishes, his children and niece would duly inherit as specified under the terms of the will and were free to leave Island House. His case already packed, Arthur had set off for the station straight away, without saying goodbye. Which surprised no one. The surprise was that he hadn't left at once after that disagreeable scene at the dining table the evening before.

In the wake of his departure, an undeniable sense of calm and liberation had descended upon Island House. Hope duly apologised to Allegra for being so angry with her over Annelise, and in return, Allegra apologised for providing Arthur with the opportunity to play such a cruel trick. It was with this new level of accord firmly in place that Romily had made it clear that if they wanted to stay on at Island House, they were more than welcome. Kit too was welcome any time he wanted to come. She had told him this when he'd taken the train with her down to London on Friday. He had decided immediately to return with her that evening to spend the weekend with them all.

Only a short while ago, Romily's life had been so very different; now it was as if she were suddenly responsible for a house full of people who needed a guiding hand. There was Hope, who was *in loco parentis* and struggling to cope; Allegra who had yet to share the secret of the baby she was expecting as well as decide what to do next; and Kit, who with his boyish exuberance seemed badly in want of a rock on which to lean. Every now and then Romily saw through his act of acute cheerfulness and glimpsed a young boy eager to impress and be loved. She had no doubt that that was what Evelyn Flowerday also saw, and who knew, maybe level-headed and assured Evelyn was just the person he needed in his life.

Romily would never describe herself as having a truly altruistic nature, but something in this trio roused in her the need to stand by them, to be the dependable adult amongst them. Not exactly a mother figure — after all, she wasn't much older than they were — but perhaps a big sister, a figure they could turn to in their hour of need. They were also, apart from Roddy, the only real connection she had to Jack. They might not have seen the best of him, but they had known something of him that she never had, and deep down her heart yearned to know more of the man she missed so desperately. She hoped that in the days and weeks ahead, she could get them to open up more about Jack, and she in turn would share with them what she had known of him.

'Here's to giving Herr Hitler what he bloody well deserves!' declared Kit, interrupting Romily's thoughts and raising his sherry glass, a gesture that reminded her again of that awful evening last Wednesday when she had confronted Arthur.

How many other families in the village, and in the country, would be doing the same? she pondered as she reluctantly went along with Kit's bullish sentiment.

35

To her very great relief, Allegra had now made a full recovery from the lethargy that had struck her so profoundly, as well as the worst of the nausea. Occasionally first thing in the morning she felt a little queasy, but it was nothing compared to what she'd experienced before. At Dr Garland's encouragement, she was also enjoying a daily walk.

Out walking now, she thought how good it was to escape the frenzy of activity at Island House that had gone on for most of the day. *Mamma mia*, such a commotion over putting up a few blackout curtains! And such a fuss made over her remembering to carry her gas mask when she left the house. It was hard to imagine needing it when the sky was crystal clear and the afternoon so delightfully tranquil and warm.

With her, trailing a few yards behind, was their evacuee, Stanley. He was a strange and somewhat charmless boy who scarcely spoke a word and was practically terrified of his own shadow. They were blackberry picking for Mrs Partridge, except so far the berries were few and far between — the wicker basket Allegra was carrying contained no more than a cupful.

In an effort to get Stanley to talk, she kept pointing out wild flowers to him in the hedgerow, as well as butterflies and birds. 'Look,' she said now, 'can you see that?'

He looked at her blankly, then up into the sky to where she was indicating.

'It's a swallow,' she said. 'It'll be leaving soon, flying home to somewhere warmer.'

Getting no response from him, she walked on. All her knowledge of birds, wild flowers and trees came from Elijah. He'd taught her when they'd been children, when he would take her to some of his favourite places. Initially she had had no interest in what he was showing her — not when Hope was the botanist of the family, and who wanted to be like Hope! — but gradually she had picked up on his enthusiasm and somehow it had all stuck.

She pointed out some willowherb, and then, just as she spotted a large and plentiful patch of blackberries, Stanley spoke. 'I wish *I* could fly away,' he said. Such was the mournful tone to his words, Allegra came to a stop and looked down at him.

'Do you hate it here so very much?'

He nodded.

'I felt the same way when I first arrived at Island House,' she said. 'Come to think of it, I was the same age as you. I hated the house and everyone in it. I was as miserable as anything. Maybe even more miserable than you.'

'But you like it now, missus?'

'Funnily enough, I do, and I never thought I'd say that. What is it about being here that you hate so much?'

'I dunno.' This was his standard reply to most questions.

'Name one thing.'

He shrugged and stared back at her blankly. She looked at him with a frown of impatience, but then suddenly she saw her nine-year-old self in him. How stark and lonely her world had been back then, until she had found a friend in Elijah. Perhaps when Stanley started at the school in the village later in the week, he too would find a friend; after all, there were plenty of other evacuees here with whom she might feel he had something in common.

After they'd picked as many of the blackberries as they could reach, Allegra suggested they walk further along the lane in search of more. The boy's response was his habitual shrug of indifference as he fell into step alongside her.

'Don't you like the countryside?' she asked after some minutes had passed.

'S'awright.'

'Have you been to the country before?'

'Me mum took me to the 'op fields in Kent once.'

'And what did you do there?'

'Whad'yer think, missus? We picked 'ops.'

'What are 'ops?'

'Doncha know?'

'I wouldn't be asking if I did.'

''Ops is what goes into beer.'

'Oh, you mean, *hops?*'

'That's what I said, missus.'

Who'd have imagined it? Allegra thought with amusement as she popped a juicy ripe blackberry into her mouth. Me trying to make small talk to convince an angry little boy that he might enjoy being at Island House. Oh the irony!

And how ironic was it that she, who had always been so concerned about maintaining her all-important *bella figura*, had regained her appetite and was suddenly eating like a horse and not caring one little bit about the weight she was gaining. Under Luigi's ever-watchful eye, she had starved herself at times to please him. But her own vanity had played its part too — to be fat had been anathema to her. Now, at almost three months pregnant, she knew she had little choice in the matter and had accepted that the baby growing inside her was dictating the terms of her life; her body was no longer her own to do with as she pleased. There was, she had come to appreciate, a freedom in that acceptance.

This shift in her attitude was nothing short of extraordinary, but it was fuelled by a fierce instinct to protect the vulnerable child within her. It was an instinct she had never thought she would possess, and in some way it gave her the courage to admit to Hope and Kit, without a shred of shame, that she was expecting a baby. It was almost a disappointment to her that Arthur wasn't around to share in her news; how she would have enjoyed standing up to his attempts to humiliate her.

To their credit, Kit and Hope had displayed only the merest trace of shock — well-brought-up girls in their world did not get themselves into this kind of trouble. But she *had* got herself into exactly that kind of trouble, and what was more, she was going to hold her head up high when the time came, when there would be no disguising the swelling that was already pressing against the fabric of her skirts and dresses.

Perhaps what amazed her more than anything was that Romily had been so understanding. Another woman might have been only too keen to get rid of Allegra in her so-called disgraceful state, but Romily had stressed that there was no hurry for her to leave Island House; it was Allegra's home until she had sorted out where to go next. And that was her priority: she had to find a home of her own. Thanks to Uncle Jack, that would now be possible, and without too much trouble. Originally London had been her first choice, but now, two days after war had been declared, people were leaving the city in their droves, all seeking a place of safety. Even Hope wasn't sure about returning to her flat there, but then she was the most timid of things. No, that wasn't fair. Hope had a child she was now responsible for, she had to think of Annelise, not just herself.

The search for blackberries all but forgotten, Allegra quickened her pace in pursuit of the real reason she had chosen to walk in this precise direction. She was on her way to see Elijah, and it was he who had suggested that she bring the evacuee with her. She had gone in search of Elijah in the garden earlier that morning, wanting to know if he had received his call-up papers yet, and had found him in the kitchen garden in amongst the raspberry canes. Stanley had been there with him, the boy's mouth and hands revealing telltale signs of the fruit he'd picked and eaten. When Allegra had asked Elijah if he had a moment to chat, he had invited her to visit him at Clover End Cottage when he'd finished work for the day. Glancing at the boy, he'd said, 'Maybe Stanley would like to come along too. As your chaperon,' he'd added with a wry smile.

'Is it much further, missus?' asked Stanley now as they passed a freshly ploughed field where the earth was deeply furrowed. The boy was starting to get on her nerves, puffing and panting and making a great performance of lagging some yards behind her.

'A little further,' she said over her shoulder. 'We'll soon be there.'

'I'm thirsty, missus.'

'I'm sure if you ask Elijah nicely, he will give you a drink.'

'Why's 'e your friend, missus, if 'e's just the gardener?'

Allegra came to an abrupt stop and turned angrily on her heel to look at the boy. 'Don't you ever talk about Elijah like that! Do you hear me? Gardener or not, he's as good a man as any I know! Probably the best! And just you remember that!'

She walked on fast, not caring if the boy could keep up. Who did the little *moccioso* think he was to refer to Elijah as *just* a gardener? she muttered furiously. How dare he!

'I'm sorry, missus,' said a plaintive voice behind her. 'I'm sorry I upset yer.'

She whipped round. 'Then you should be more careful with what you say. If you can't be polite about Elijah, you'd better go back to Island House.'

286

'I can't go back. I dunno the way.'

'In that case, I suggest you remember your manners. Or better still, keep quiet.' She marched on ahead, still furious.

A few minutes later, the same plaintive voice called out breathlessly. 'Please missus, please slow down. Me feet hurt.'

Reluctantly she did as he requested. 'For heaven's sake, what's wrong with your feet?'

'It's me shoes, missus.'

She looked down at his scruffy shoes and saw gaping holes where his toes were pushing through. 'You'll have to have a new pair,' she said absently.

He stared at her, shocked. 'New shoes?'

Her temper cooled. 'Yes,' she said, remembering the first time she herself had been bought a new pair of shoes. Within days of her arrival at Island House, Nanny Finch had been instructed to take her shopping. Allegra had never been in a shoe shop before and had been overwhelmed by the sheer quantity of shoes in the window, and all the many boxes stacked in neat shelves. At the orphanage she had only ever had hand-me-downs, but even those she had worn with pride, knowing that there were children on the streets with no shoes at all. The shoes she had left the shop with that day had meant the world to her — she had actually slept with them under her pillow that night, and for the following two nights, terrified that somebody might sneak into the room and steal them from her while she slept. But when Nanny Finch discovered what she was doing, she made fun of her in front of the others.

'Whoever heard of such a stupid thing?' Arthur taunted her.

Perhaps glad that they weren't on the receiving end of Arthur's baiting, Kit and Hope had joined in, asking her what else she kept under her pillow. From then on, the three of them used to play a game of hiding her shoes from her. In the end she had refused to wear the shoes, had walked around in bare feet to show her cousins she didn't care.

'But I don't 'ave no money,' the boy murmured, rousing Allegra from the past. He was staring at her, his eyes brimming alarmingly with tears.

She bent down to him. 'While you're here at Island House, it is not for you to buy your shoes or clothes,' she said gently. 'We'll go shopping tomorrow before school starts later this week.'

★ ★ ★

Elijah was waiting for them at Clover End Cottage. He'd changed out of his work clothes and was wearing a collarless white shirt with the sleeves rolled up. She guessed it was his one good shirt and was touched that he had put it on for her benefit.

He greeted Stanley with a friendly smile and offered him a drink at once. 'Glass of ginger beer all right for you, lad?' he asked.

Stanley nodded.

'Say please,' said Allegra, then chided herself. She sounded so pedantic, almost as prim and pedantic as Hope!

Elijah winked at Stanley. 'No need to stand on ceremony here. And no need to stay inside on a fine day like this. Let's go out to the garden.'

'Am I not to be offered a drink?' asked Allegra.

Elijah winked again at Stanley. 'What do you think, shall we let her have one? Mind you, she has to say please, doesn't she?'

Stanley smiled shyly.

'I thought we weren't standing on ceremony here?' said Allegra.

Elijah laughed. 'She's got me there, hasn't she?'

When they all had a drink, they went back outside, where the late-afternoon sun was casting long shadows across the garden, which was just as Allegra remembered it as a child. There, directly in front of her, was the old wooden shed, with its walls and sagging roof draped with a cascade of honeysuckle as well as the branches of the elderberry tree. Elijah's grandfather used to retreat to the shed whenever he could, smoking his pipe while potting on the tender young plants he'd grown from seed.

To one side of the shed was an uneven brick path that led to the rest of the garden and then eventually down to the River Stour, which skirted the village and fed the pond at Island House. 'Do you still have your father's vegetable patch?' Allegra asked.

'Of course, I wouldn't be without it. Fancy a look, Stanley? Though don't be running away with the idea it's as grand as the kitchen garden up at Island House,' Elijah added.

The boy nodded and obediently followed him.

'Am I allowed to come?' asked Allegra. She was feeling horribly left out. It was she who'd wanted to spend time with Elijah, not Stanley!

Elijah must have caught the irritable tone to her voice. 'You go on ahead, Stanley, I'll catch you up. Go on, off you go. I think you'll find something you might like at the end of the path, the other side of the privet hedge.'

When the boy had disappeared out of sight, Elijah came and stood in front of Allegra.

'Do I detect jealousy?' he said, his voice low, his gaze boring into her.

She stared back at him, mustering defiance. 'Don't be ridiculous. Of course I'm not jealous.'

'Are you sure?'

The intensity of his words, and the powerful presence of him standing so close — so close she could smell the soap he must have washed with — did away with any more defiance. 'I'm sorry, *caro*,' she said. 'It's just that we don't have much time and I want to talk to you.'

'And I want to talk to you too.'

'You do? You could have fooled me.'

He sighed and shook his head. 'The only person I might be fooling is myself.'

'What do you mean?'

'There's something I've wanted to do ever since the night of the dance.' He put a hand to her chin and raised her face to his, then very lightly kissed her. Without a moment's hesitation, she kissed him back, but he pulled away. 'We're not children any more, Allegra,' he said gravely. 'Our actions have consequences. If I kiss

290

you, it's because it means something to me. I need to know that it means the same to you. I don't want to leave here without knowing where I stand with you.' His eyes were dark with an emotion she had never seen in him before, and his voice was thick.

'Then kiss me again and you'll know.'

'No. I want to hear you say the words.'

'What words?'

'That I matter to you.'

'Elijah, how could you ever think you didn't?'

'Because you're you and I'm me. We come from different worlds.'

'*Non è vero, caro.* It's not true.'

'You might not have been born directly into the world that your cousins were, but like it or not, you're one of them; you're a Devereux.'

It was just as she'd feared: something that hadn't bothered him as a child now did. 'I've never felt as if I were,' she said adamantly.

His expression softened. 'And I've never felt this way about a girl before. I can't stop thinking about you. We've spent hardly any time together since you came back, but you fill my every waking thought. Every time I see you at Island House I want to stop what I'm doing and be with you.'

'How can you think so well of me? I left you all those years ago, I said such terrible things, and now I'm carrying another man's child. I'm completely unworthy of your — '

'I don't care about that,' he interrupted her.

She put a hand to his cheek. 'Oh Elijah, whatever am I going to do with you?'

He turned his head and kissed the palm of her hand. At the touch of his lips, she trembled. 'I wish you hadn't suggested I bring Stanley with me.'

He smiled. 'I did it because I didn't trust myself to be alone with you.'

'What if I came back later tonight? Alone.'

'Are you sure you want to?'

She was about to say yes when Stanley reappeared behind Elijah. 'Look, mister!' he cried excitedly. 'Look what I found!' In his arms was a small black-and-white dog, its face upturned towards Stanley's and looking adoringly at him. 'Is he yours, mister?'

'He's only been with me a couple of days,' Elijah said. 'His owner . . . well, Mr Russell isn't around any more to look after him, so I said I'd find a new home for him.'

'Why can't you 'ave 'im, mister?'

'Because I'll be leaving very soon.'

Allegra's heart clenched. 'How soon?' she asked.

'Tomorrow,' Elijah said, turning to look at her. 'Me, Billy and Tommy, we've had our call-up papers and have been told to report to barracks by six p.m. sharp to begin our training. Which means Bobby here,' he went over and stroked the little dog's head, 'needs a new home. What do you think, Stanley? Do you think you'd like to take care of him while I'm away?'

The boy's eyes nearly popped out of their sockets. 'Me?'

'He needs a good friend and I thought you might fit the bill. If you're worried about Mrs

Temple-Devereux and what she might say, I've already spoken with her and she said it would be fine, that it would be good for you to have your very own new friend here.'

Her heart filled with a tender love, Allegra smiled to herself, seeing just how thoughtful Elijah had been, and how effortlessly he had befriended Stanley, just as he had her when they'd been children.

36

That evening at Island House, after dinner was over, Kit took Evelyn out to the garden. Knowing that it would offer them a degree of privacy, he led the way down to the boathouse. Dusk had yet to fall and the evening air was still warm. Clouds of gnats hovered over the end of the wooden jetty and a dragonfly skimmed the surface of the lily pond.

It was Kit's last night here at Island House; he would be leaving with Hope in the morning to go back to London. He ought to have returned on Sunday evening, but he'd been unable to face the prospect of being cooped up in his dingy little office at the bank and pretending he gave a damn. To delay his return, if only for another two days, he'd telephoned them yesterday morning to say he'd gone down with a terrible cold. He'd pinched his nose and adopted a croaky voice, the verisimilitude of which he hoped would convince his colleagues he was practically at death's door. He'd told them hoarsely that he planned to be back at his desk by the middle of the week, but secretly he was hoping that in the meantime he'd receive his call-up papers, and would be summoned to start his RAF training without having to set foot over the threshold of the Imperial Bank ever again.

It could still happen, he thought, stranger things and all that, because let's face it, who would have thought he'd come back to Island House and be here in the garden with of all people Evelyn Flower day?

He'd asked Romily if she would mind an extra guest for dinner this evening, and in her usual generous manner she had said Evelyn would be more than welcome, adding, 'While she's here, she can meet young Stanley and see if she can make him feel more positive about starting school in the village.'

Kit was aware that there were plenty of families in the village who had been pressured by Old Ma Fogg into accepting an evacuee — more than one in some cases — but he was impressed by Romily's fortitude, that so recently widowed she had not only coped with Jack's family, but now a nine-year-old boy, and not forgetting Annelise. When she'd first arrived at Island House, she could not have imagined this would be the situation in which she would find herself.

As for his own situation, Kit had not foreseen how strongly his feelings for Evelyn would develop in so short a time. He was hoping she might agree to stay in touch and write to him when he embarked on his training. Other than his sister, there wasn't anyone else who would bother to put pen to paper. He pictured himself composing long, interesting letters describing scenes that would make him appear wonderfully brave and persuade Evelyn to fall madly in love with him. Somehow he couldn't quite imagine her doing anything madly, let alone falling in love with him. But he could hope.

'It was very kind of Romily to invite me to

dinner,' Evelyn said once they were settled in the boathouse. 'You know, she's a remarkable woman; you're lucky to have her as a stepmother.'

Kit laughed. 'When I recall some of the absolute horrors the old man brought home over the years, I'm inclined to agree with you. Although I still find it hard to think of Romily as my stepmother. I don't think she approves of the title very much. But never mind Romily, it's you I want to talk about.'

'Oh yes?'

'Don't sound so alarmed.'

'You're not going to do something rash like propose to me, are you?'

'God, no!'

'That's a relief, because for an awful moment I feared the worst when you suggested we go for a walk in the garden.'

'I'm crestfallen that you think so poorly of me that you would regard the idea of a proposal as so repellent.' He put a hand to his heart for dramatic effect.

She laughed and took hold of his other hand. 'It would be hugely embarrassing, Kit, so don't go getting any thoughts along those lines. We neither of us are ready for marriage. Least of all you.'

'Perish the thought,' he said, giving her hand a squeeze. 'But why on earth would you even raise the subject?'

'Because so far this week, since war was declared, there's been a rush to the altar in the village; the Reverend Tate's never been so busy.

Which naturally means there'll be a good number of babies born early next summer for him to baptise. And talking of babies, I can't help but admire your cousin Allegra for her courage.'

'Gosh, and there was me thinking you'd be shocked.'

'Just goes to show how little you know me. But I think we can safely leave the element of shock to my mother. Naturally she's appalled, but then she would be appalled by just about anything.'

'I still can't believe you heard the news before I did.'

'You can thank Mrs Bunch for that. Apparently she had her suspicions, and since she lives next door to Cynthia Blackwood, Dr Garland's receptionist, and therefore is more or less privy to the entire village's every diagnosed cough, sniffle and bowel complaint, there was no chance of Allegra keeping the pregnancy secret.'

'Do you suppose Dr Garland has any idea that his receptionist has such a loose tongue?'

'I doubt it, and if he did suspect anything, he'd be too scared to confront the old dragon. She probably knows some terrible secret about him that means he's firmly under her thumb.'

Kit shook his head. 'I can think of no man less likely to have a terrible secret.'

She gave a short laugh 'Come off it, Kit, we all have something we'd rather keep quiet about.'

'I don't,' he said, turning to look at her. 'Do you?'

'If I did, I wouldn't be telling you about it, would I?'

Kit smiled. 'And there was I thinking you would trust me implicitly.'

'Sorry to disappoint you.'

In a more serious voice, he said, 'So meanwhile poor Allegra is the talk of the village. The only good thing is, if I know my cousin, she won't give a tinker's cuss.'

'And that,' said Evelyn, 'is why I admire her. Do you suppose she'll stay and have the child here?'

'I have no idea what she'll do,' Kit said with a shrug. 'Besides, how would I know? I'm always the last to hear anything important.'

'Well here's something else you might like to know, and I say this not as malicious gossip, but because I rather hope something comes of it.'

'What have you heard?'

'That Allegra and Elijah are seeing each other.'

'In what sense seeing each other?'

'Oh Kit, what a chump you are! Where do you think she was in such a hurry to go just now?'

He remembered back to dinner, when Allegra had excused herself before dessert had been served. 'She mentioned something about needing some air and that she had a letter to post,' he said.

'And for that she had a rosy glow to her cheeks and her eyes were all lit up?'

'I . . . I don't know what to say.'

'I'd say be happy for her, and Elijah. Goodness, Kit, I do believe you look as scandalised as a Victorian spinster. Do you need me to fetch you some smelling salts?'

'I think a glass of brandy would be more

effective. But how do you know all this? Oh, don't tell me, Mrs Bunch?'

Evelyn shook her head. 'In this case, no. Unlike you, I keep my ears and eyes open, plus I'm good at reading people. Something you could do with learning. For instance, what do you think I'm thinking right now?'

'That I'm an idiot?'

She laughed. 'We'll take that as read. Try again.'

'I'm no good at guessing games, you should know that.'

'True. How about I give you a clue?'

'Go on.'

'If I closed my eyes and tilted my head up, what do you think that would mean?'

'That you were tired and needed a rest?' he said with a smile, admiring her charmingly pretty face while she couldn't observe him. 'Or that you were listening to something in the distance and concentrating on — '

'Oh do get on with it!' she said, opening her eyes. 'A girl can't sit here forever practically begging to be kissed.'

He kissed her as he had the night of the village dance, and she responded with the same passion that had so surprised him then. It stirred in him the desire to lift her in his arms and lay her gently on the floor, and then explore every soft line and curve of her body. It made him want to feel the warmth of her smooth skin against his and to . . . But no! He daren't rush things; she meant too much to him. He would be led by her. He had sufficient wit to know that with a girl like

Evelyn, there could be no other way.

'You're thinking about something other than kissing me, aren't you?' she said, pushing him away from her so she could look into his eyes. 'What is it?'

Caught off guard by her perceptiveness, he tried to explain himself, but couldn't find the right words. Instead he stroked her cheek. 'I was thinking that given I'm such a chump, I'm at a loss to know why you would show the slightest interest in me.'

She raised an eyebrow. 'I'd call you a chump with potential, and with the right sort of handling I might be able to turn you into very nearly the genuine article. I make no promises, mind.'

He smiled happily and put his arm around her. 'I don't know why I put up with your constant mocking.'

'You do it because you like me and I like you.'

'Foolishly I was under the impression that when a person cared for another, it involved being nice to that person. Or have I got that completely wrong?'

'My dear Kit, you have so very much to learn.'

'I'm beginning to realise just how much. What about another lesson in kissing you?'

She laughed. 'You see, you're getting the hang of this already!'

'And now for the serious part,' she said, when again they parted. She took both of his hands in hers, and clasped them firmly. 'I will write to you as often as I can in the weeks and months ahead, if you'd like me to, but on one condition.'

'What's that?'

'That you promise not to do anything silly once you get yourself involved in this war. No unnecessary heroics just to impress me. Do you understand?'

He nodded. 'I'll do my best.'

37

After looking in on Annelise and finding her sleeping soundly, Hope was now in her own bedroom and studying the illustrations she had finished for her publisher.

Nobody was more critical of her work than she was herself, and to her highly judgemental eye one or two of the pen-and-ink drawings were not her best, but given the circumstances, she was amazed she had managed to draw anything at all. She placed them carefully on top of each other with a layer of tissue paper between, then began to wrap them in brown paper ready to take to London in the morning. Kit had offered to deliver them for her, and she had almost been prepared to trust him with the task, but then she had received a letter from Edmund in that morning's post inviting her to have lunch with him.

To her shame, her immediate reaction on reading Edmund's letter had been to accept the invitation, but then she had remembered she couldn't just go off and leave Annelise. And then she had thought of Dieter. That her husband had not been her first consideration shocked her. How could she be so disloyal to Dieter? How could she think of enjoying herself having lunch with another man? Even if it was only Edmund, a childhood friend. She had stuffed the letter into her skirt pocket and blinked back the tears, but not before Romily had seen her. 'Bad news?' she had asked. 'It's not your publisher making unreasonable demands on you, is it?'

'No, nothing like that,' Hope had answered.

'Anything I can help with? Other than maybe mind my own business?'

And then, because she had suddenly felt so wretched, Hope had blurted out the nature of Edmund's letter and her reaction.

'Ah, I see,' Romily had said, her expression instantly one of empathy. 'I understand completely. I would have the same reaction. But one thing I know, Jack wouldn't want me to be miserable for the rest of my life, and if lunch with an old friend might cheer me up, he would want me to do it. Do you think Dieter would have felt the same way?'

'Even if I answer yes to that,' Hope had said, 'there's still the matter of Annelise, I can hardly take her with me.'

'Of course not, you must leave her here with us. I rather think she'll enjoy herself getting to know our latest arrival.'

That was when Hope had learnt that they were acquiring a dog courtesy of Elijah, and mainly for the benefit of their evacuee. She wondered what sort of dog it would be; all they knew was that it had belonged to an elderly man in the village who lived alone and who had just died. Hope had always hankered after owning a dog, but her father had refused to consider the idea. She had been so upset, she had decided to teach him a lesson and run away. After packing a few things into a small canvas bag, along with a hunk of bread she'd taken from the pantry and a bit of cheese wrapped in some greaseproof paper, she'd set off. Her intention was to walk to the station and catch the first train that stopped there, but in the end she only got as far as Clover Wood, having chosen a densely wooded spot as her new home. It had soon grown dark, and her vivid six-year-old imagination conjured up all manner of prowling beasts hiding amongst the trees. She had wanted to go home, to be lying comfortably in her own warm bed, but fear, even when it started to rain, made her incapable of moving. Her father, drenched to the skin, had found her and carried her back wordlessly to Island House. All she could think of was that his terrifying silence, and the fact that his arms seemed to be trembling with rage as he held her tightly, proved just how cross he must be with her.

Now as she recalled the memory, and knowing how panic-stricken she had been when Annelise was missing, she wondered if she had misinterpreted her father's silence. What if he had been genuinely concerned about her running off and had been unable to articulate his feelings when he'd found her safe and well? Relief affected people differently, and at so young an age she had had no real way of understanding what she had just put her father through.

The illustrations now all carefully wrapped and securely tied with string, Hope retrieved Edmund's letter from the drawer of her bedside table. Silly to read it through again when she knew perfectly well what it said, and when she had already telephoned the number he'd given her in order to confirm what time to meet and where. But she couldn't resist it; Edmund wrote so beautifully. As a teenager he'd spoken grandly of one day becoming a poet. His ghastly mother had treated his claim as though he'd professed an interest in pursuing a life of crime. More dutifully, he'd fulfilled her aspiration for him to study medicine, presumably so that she would have a convenient expert on hand to diagnose her many ailments. Just what every hypochondriac mother desired, a doctor for a son! Why, thought Hope, did the good people of this world — people like Dieter — die when a self-obsessed woman like Mildred Flowerday was allowed to live?

As sorry as she felt for Edmund having the mother he did, at least he had been able to escape to London, unlike poor Evelyn, who'd had to make the sacrifice of giving up her teaching job in a prestigious girls' school and return home to care for that cantankerous mother. A small mercy perhaps that she had just secured a teaching post at the school in the village.

Well, they all had to make sacrifices now that they were at war. And none bigger than the one Otto and Sabine had made in handing Annelise over into Hope's care. Stanley's parents, and thousands like them, had also been forced to make a difficult decision.

Hope had written to Otto and Sabine again, the day before war was declared, even though she was sure they wouldn't receive her letter. She

305

had sent it anyway, wanting to assure them that their precious daughter was perfectly happy and being well cared for here at Island House. She had tried to write a letter to Dieter's parents, but had given up on the task. What could she possibly say to them? They probably hated her now; saw her as the enemy who had smuggled their granddaughter to England. With the views Gerda and Heinrich held, believing Hitler was a force for good in Germany, it scared Hope to think what lengths they might go to in their loyalty to the Nazis.

Her mood darkening, she changed the direction of her thoughts and contemplated being back in London tomorrow. After delivering the illustrations, she would meet Edmund for lunch, and then go and check on her flat in Belsize Park.

She wanted to believe it would feel good to be back there, but she knew it wouldn't; it would be a return to a million and one reminders of Dieter, of coping with the pain of knowing he would never again walk through the front door and surprise her with a posy he'd bought from the flower seller on the corner of their street. At least being at Island House, a place where Dieter had never been, she wasn't haunted by memories of him. But she couldn't stay here indefinitely; she had to stand on her own two feet, even if it would be extraordinarily difficult.

With her bedroom window open, leaning out to look at the garden in the shadowy darkness of dusk and watching the swallows swooping through the cool September air, Hope knew that to do the best she could for Annelise, staying here, where she had so much help on hand, was the right thing. Why uproot the poor girl yet again — and deliberately put her in harm's way in London — when she had Mrs Partridge who doted on her, and Florence who was so good with her? Yet it wasn't the right thing for Hope. She had to prove to herself — and maybe to everybody else — that she could do this alone. Perhaps it was no more than stubborn pride that dictated her desire to leave Island House, having initially thought she would stay, but she could not ignore the feeling that it would be cowardly to remain here. She had to show some backbone.

Romily had suggested that her father would have wanted her to make Island House her home while the world was in such a precarious state, and a part of Hope wanted to believe that was true, that he had summoned his family back here because he had somehow felt there would soon come a time when they would need a place of sanctuary.

There were those who were firmly of the opinion that the war they had just got themselves into would be over by Christmas, and seeing her brother and Evelyn emerging from the boat-house at the other end of the garden, Hope wanted to believe with all her being that that was true.

38

December 1939

It was the day before Christmas Eve and the war was far from over. Five British ships and a number of foreign ones had recently been sunk by mines in the North Sea, and the pride of the German fleet, the *Graf Spee*, trapped by British warships in the South Atlantic near Uruguay, had scuttled herself on a direct order from Hitler. The ship's captain had shot himself in the head, according to the newspapers. There had even been an attempt to assassinate Hitler.

But for all that, the way some people viewed it the war had hardly got going, and maybe never would, not properly. 'It's nothing but a phoney war,' was what Florence regularly heard in the village.

It seemed the government was forever saying what people couldn't do and what they couldn't have — coal and petrol were rationed, and if you didn't obey the blackout regulations you could go to prison, while old Bert Cox, the ARP warden, would love nothing better than to shoot on sight anyone who let so much as a chink of light show! Every day, as soon as it was dark, around the village he'd go, yelling, 'Put that light out!'

But it didn't seem like there was much reason for what they were doing, and to hear the way some folk grumbled, you'd think they were disappointed not to be bombed out of their homes or gunned down in the street. They should think themselves lucky that nothing was happening, in Florence's opinion.

Many of the evacuees who'd come to the village in September had returned home, despite the government advising against it. Stanley's mother, who hadn't written to him once since his arrival, had not requested he should go home. Nor had the boy shown any desire to leave.

After just three months, he bore little resemblance to the lad he'd been when he'd first pitched up. Under Mrs Partridge's vigilant eye he'd put on weight, got some colour in his cheeks and gained confidence. He was also doing well with his lessons, and every day when he came home from school, he'd sit at the kitchen table with his exercise book and stubby pencil doing the extra work Miss Flowerday set him so he could catch up with the others. Miss Flowerday had guessed that the reason for his reluctance to go to school was because he couldn't read and write. Well he was getting there now. Florence helped him when she could, as did Miss Romily.

But the real reason for the change for the better in Stanley was down to Bobby, the dog Elijah had given him. They were inseparable and went everywhere together, apart from school, but the minute Stanley was due home in the afternoon, the dog was waiting for him at the end of the drive with his tail wagging. They were out together now, delivering Christmas cards for Miss Romily.

For Florence, Christmas had seemed like it would never come. She had literally been counting the days, willing the day to arrive when she would see Billy again. A private in the Suffolk Regiment, he was home on leave this afternoon, along with Tommy and Elijah, their basic training now over. They'd been based at the barracks in Bury St Edmunds, which was only a thirty-minute train journey away, but with no leave allowed until today, they might just as well have been in Timbuktu.

With each day they had been apart, Florence's feelings for Billy had deepened, and with each letter he'd written she'd felt she was getting to know him better. His letters had often made her laugh, especially when he wrote about the lads he was training with — 'a great bunch' — and what they got up to when they weren't carrying out drill practice, or learning how to use a Bren gun and anti-tank rifles. The way he told it, being in the army was one big lark, coupled with an impatience to get the job done to show the Hun what he had coming to him.

Florence supposed that sort of bravado was part and parcel of being turned into a soldier, but had it changed Billy? How could it not, as otherwise how would he cope when he did go and fight? He could not remain the same tender-hearted young man he'd been when she'd got to know him. And maybe that would mean he would see her through different eyes; maybe now she would be just a very dull girl to him.

The day Billy had left to start his training, he'd surprised Florence with a silver heart-shaped locket, which he'd told her had belonged to his grandmother. As he'd put it on her, taking forever over fixing the catch on the necklace chain, he'd kissed the nape of her neck, making her shiver. 'I don't expect you to feel the same way about me, Flo,' he'd said, turning her round, 'but before I go, I want you to know something important. It's this: I think you're pretty special.'

'Well, Mr Billy Know-It-All,' she'd said, 'I have news for you. I think you're pretty special too.'

'You do?'

'Don't sound so surprised. Why wouldn't I think that?'

'I can think of half a dozen reasons.'

'Then I'd advise you to keep them to yourself.'

She hadn't taken the locket off since he'd given it to her. Every night she fell asleep with a hand pressing it against her heart, praying that Billy would never come to harm. She chanted the prayer over and over to ward off the gypsy's words — *You'll find love and you'll lose love.* Oh how she wished she had never stepped into the old witch's tent, for those words — that curse — had haunted her ever since!

The last of the mistletoe and ivy that Stanley had fetched for her that morning from Teal's now used up in decorating the hall, drawing room and dining room, Florence glanced at the grandfather clock. Another forty-five minutes and she would change out of her maid's uniform to go and meet Billy. Her heart fluttered at the prospect of seeing him again.

311

In his last letter he'd told her he would tell his mother he was catching a later train than the one he'd actually be on; that way he would be able to see Florence for an hour before his parents expected him. They both knew that if his mother had her way, he wouldn't be allowed to leave her side for a single minute while he was home.

Florence went and checked that the fire was still burning in the drawing room. Miss Romily would be back soon with Hope and Annelise, and Florence wanted everything to be perfect for her. She had been away in London at her flat for a few days doing her Christmas shopping and catching up with friends, as well as her agent and publisher. She had asked Florence if she wanted to go with her for a change of scene, but Florence had declined. London was part of her old life; she had no interest in going back. This was where her life was now. And anyway, in the run-up to Christmas, there was so much to do here. Mrs Partridge couldn't manage on her own, and Mrs Bunch was the laziest woman Florence had ever known. She did about an hour's work and then spent the rest of her time nursing a mug of tea by the range while dishing up the latest round of gossip. She claimed constantly that she was on borrowed time, what with her varicose veins and what she proudly called her dicky ticker. Dicky ticker, my foot! thought Florence every time the annoying woman mentioned it.

'It be a wonder to me every morning when I wakes and finds the good Lord has spared me for another day,' Mrs Bunch often said.

No, thought Florence, the wonder was that Miss Romily didn't get rid of her. But maybe it was a case of keeping her close to be sure of staying up to date with what was going on in the village.

After throwing another log into the grate and giving it a shove with the poker, then rearranging the tinsel on the Christmas tree — Stanley had been a little ham-fisted with it earlier when Florence had asked him to help — she went to see if Mrs Partridge needed anything doing.

'All in hand,' the older woman said cheerily. 'The steak and kidney pudding is made and waiting to be steamed for supper, the mince pies are in the pantry and the trifle is all done. Why don't you go and get yourself ready? I know you must be fair itching to see that young man of yours.'

Blushing, Florence didn't need telling twice. She thanked Mrs Partridge and was about to go upstairs to her room and change when she heard the sound of the front door opening, followed by voices.

'That must be Miss Romily back already with Hope and Annelise,' she said, surprised.

'Well, better look lively; I'll put the kettle on and put a tray together. Doubtless they'll be ready for a cuppa. The house is going to feel a lot jollier now with a few more people in it.'

* * *

'Look who we came across on the Melstead Road!' exclaimed Miss Romily, shrugging off her

313

fur coat and throwing it on to a hall chair. 'Doesn't he look handsome in his uniform?'

Framed in the open doorway, a blast of freezing cold air rushing in around him, was Billy. And yet it wasn't Billy. He looked so very different in his uniform, taller and broader, and somehow older. But oh how handsome he was! Florence's heart thumped so hard in her chest that she struggled to speak.

'Hello, Flo,' he said, removing his cap. 'Cat got your tongue?'

'You look well,' she finally managed to say while bending down to Annelise as the child tottered toward her with a wide toothy smile on her face.

'Flo, Flo,' the little girl said. 'Flo, Flo.'

'Look at that,' said Hope. 'All this time since we were last here, and she remembers you!'

'Course she does,' said Florence. 'It's because she's such a clever little poppet.' She picked up the child and hugged her, using her to hide behind. This wasn't how she'd wanted Billy to see her, not in her uniform and in front of other people. She had planned to put on the new dress she had saved up for and style her hair better. She had planned to throw her arms around him and give him the biggest welcome-home kiss imaginable.

As if sensing her awkwardness, Miss Romily said, 'Florence, why don't you take Billy through to the kitchen and find him something to eat and drink while Hope and I sort ourselves out?'

'First let me help with your luggage,' Billy said. 'It's the least I can do after you giving me a lift, madam.'

314

'Thank you, Billy, that's very kind of you.'

'I'll give him a hand,' Florence said, regaining her composure and lowering Annelise to the floor. 'Meanwhile why don't you go on into the drawing room? The fire's lit, so it's nice and warm in there. Mrs Partridge is making some tea for you.'

As soon as they were alone, and standing in the shelter of the porch, Billy swept Florence up in his arms. He kissed her long and hard, his cold lips pressed firmly against hers, and any niggling worries she'd had about him viewing her differently vanished. She kissed him back, and then when she began to feel light-headed with love for him, she said breathlessly, 'You'll get me sacked carrying on like this. I thought we were meeting at three o'clock?'

He smiled. 'I managed to get away even earlier. Seemed like a good idea to me. Of course if it's not convenient, I could always go away and — '

She tapped his chest with a finger. 'You're not going anywhere, not until you've helped me get the luggage in!'

'Then what do you plan to do?'

'Then you can have something to eat and we'll go for a walk.'

He grinned. 'Somewhere quiet and secluded, I hope.'

Florence tutted. 'I hope you haven't picked up any bad ways while you've been away, Billy Minton.'

★ ★ ★

315

'It's good to be home,' Romily said with a contented sigh as she warmed herself in front of the fire. 'It was lovely catching up with everybody in town, even if half the time we couldn't see where we were going in the blackout and kept falling into the road, and nearly killing ourselves! But all the time I couldn't wait to get back. London isn't the same without Jack; it's here where I feel closest to him.'

'It's good that you have that,' said Hope. 'It might seem strange, but being with Annelise makes me feel closer to Dieter. Sometimes,' she added with a slow smile that softened her face, 'I look at her and I see something of Dieter in her features. I didn't see it at first, but I do now as she's growing. I can't believe she's already fourteen months old. She's just started to call me Tante. I'm probably biased, but I think she's an extremely bright child.'

'She's a credit to you, Hope,' said Romily with a fond smile. 'She seems such a happy little girl.'

With Hope kneeling on the floor next to Annelise, who was staring in rapt wonder at the Christmas tree, Romily thought what a heart-warming sight they made. She was glad she had invited Hope to join her for Christmas.

Just as Romily had suspected would happen, since making the decision to return to London in September, Hope had devoted herself entirely to looking after Annelise. She had given up all idea of working, unable to concentrate for long enough to produce the detailed sketches she once had. Romily had urged her to hire a nanny to help look after Annelise so that she could work, but Hope had found herself checking everything the woman did, and at times strongly disagreeing with the regime she seemed to think was suitable. *It made me think of some of the ghastly nannies we had to suffer as children*, she had written in a long letter to Romily, *and I just couldn't inflict that on Annelise.*

Romily was placing another log on the fire and thinking how changed London had been — huge silver barrage balloons filling the sky, sandbags everywhere, Hyde Park dug up and Eros removed to safety from Piccadilly Circus — when the door opened and Florence came in with a tea tray. Following behind her was young Stanley, his faithful dog Bobby at his side. Which reminded Romily of the present she wanted to give the boy, and for which she needed Hope's help.

'Hello, Stanley,' she said. 'You remember Mrs Meyer and Annelise, don't you?'

He nodded. Then, bending down to Bobby, and pointing at Hope and the little girl, he said, 'Remember your manners, go and say 'ello.'

To Romily's amazement, the dog trotted obediently over to Hope and Annelise, then sat down and held out a paw to them. Annelise giggled with delight. 'Woof, woof,' she said excitedly, rocking back on her heels and patting the dog on his nose.

'Did you teach him to do that, Stanley?' asked Hope.

Stanley nodded again, this time with obvious pride. 'Yes, missus,' he said. ''E's a real quick learner.'

'Like somebody else I could mention,' said Romily with a smile. 'Did you deliver those Christmas cards that I left on the hall table before I went to London?

'Me and Bobby did them this afternoon, just as you asked. And Miss Gant and Miss Treadmill gave me some eggs for you as a Christmas present.'

'That was generous of them.'

Stanley smiled. 'D'yer wanna 'ear a joke Miss Treadmill told me?'

'Certainly I do,' said Romily, amused at the mischievous expression on the boy's face.

'What did 'Itler say when a bomb dropped on the roof of 'is 'ouse and he fell through the bed?'

'I don't know,' answered Romily, exchanging a look with Hope and Florence 'What did he say?'

The boy sniggered. 'Now I'm in Po-land!'

Florence tutted and cuffed him lightly round the head. 'Stanley Nettles, how dare you tell such a rude joke!'

'It can't be that rude if Miss Treadmill told it me,' he remonstrated.

'That's all right,' said Romily with a laugh. 'I've heard worse. Far worse. Now Florence, it's time you went and chatted to that young man of yours; he's waited quite long enough. And Stanley, perhaps you'd like to take Annelise to Mrs Partridge, who I'm sure is champing at the bit to see her again.' She quickly checked herself. 'If that's all right with you, Hope?'

'Of course it is,' Hope replied without a hint of the hostility that had characterised their first encounters back in August. 'In fact I'm eager to see Mrs Partridge again myself. I've missed her cooking.'

★ ★ ★

At Winter Cottage, on the other side of Clover Wood, Allegra was waiting anxiously for the sound of footsteps on the path.

For the last hour she had been unable to sit still for more than five minutes without going to the window that overlooked the small front garden. The afternoon light was fading now, the day shrouded in a misty gloom, and as she moved away from the window to add another log to the fire, she felt the baby give a wriggle of movement inside her.

Sometimes the child moved with such energy, Allegra would swear that it had ambitions to be a dancer like her own mother. On this occasion, however, the movement was no more than a slight shifting, as if the baby had briefly woken from a deep sleep and was trying to get comfortable again.

With all her being Allegra hoped and prayed it would be a girl; she didn't want a boy who might remind her too much of Luigi. She felt she could love a girl more than a boy. At night when she couldn't sleep, she would sing a lullaby to the baby — her *piccolina*, as she thought of her. It was the *ninna nanna* that Sister Maria used to sing to the babies at the orphanage, and which in turn Allegra had learnt to sing to the little ones when she was old enough. 'Fate la Nanna Coscine di Polio' was the only song she had allowed herself to sing since leaving Venice. It had come so naturally to her, without even thinking about it, yet she hadn't dared to explore her voice further for fear of discovering she had lost her full range and power.

Although what did it matter whether she had or not? She was never going to sing again, not on a stage. Her professional career was over. All those dreams of singing at La Scala in Milan, and all the other prestigious opera houses around the world, seemed so ridiculous now. She had never been good enough to be a truly great singer. But it was only now her life had changed so dramatically that she had the perspective — and the courage — to admit that her talent had not measured up to her ambition.

What was important to her now was being the best mother she could possibly be. She had another three months to go before the baby would be born, and it was beyond her to imagine how much bigger she could become; as it was, she felt as enormous as a whale, and about as ugly.

Whenever she wished that March was here already, and the waiting was over, she would worry just how she would manage. She had seen the effect Annelise had had on Hope, how exhausted and overwhelmed she had been, and she dreaded the same happening to her. Romily had assured her that just as Hope didn't need to face the challenges of motherhood alone, Allegra didn't either.

At the beginning of October, not long after Hope had returned to London, Allegra had left

Island House and bought Winter Cottage. Roddy had helped her by arranging for an advance on the money that would be coming to her once Uncle Jack's will had been finalised. It was a mystery to her why these things took so long, but patience was one of the many things she was being forced to learn.

Just a short distance from Elijah's house, her new home, a modest timber-framed cottage with a thatched roof and slanted walls, was more than adequate for her needs, and with each day that passed, it felt more of a home to her. At Romily's suggestion she had had one of the bedrooms upstairs turned into a bathroom and had the place redecorated throughout. She had even tried her hand at painting the nursery, with pleasing results, realising that she was more artistic than she'd previously given herself credit for. She had chosen a colour scheme of sunny yellow for the walls and duck-egg blue for the ceiling in an effort to mimic the sky. Onto this she'd painted some fluffy white clouds and, as an afterthought, a trio of swallows. In her mind, the three birds were Elijah, her and the baby. At the small diamond-paned window she had hung a pair of pale green and white gingham curtains, which she had sewn by hand. She often liked to go and sit in the nursery and stare out at the garden and its grassy bank that sloped down to the stream.

Mrs Bunch had offered to come in and clean for her, but Allegra had refused to have the gossiping old biddy over the threshold. Instead, she looked after the cottage herself — all those years of learning to clean and polish and scrub floors at the orphanage had not gone to waste! She would probably find a girl from the village to help with the heavier work when the baby was born. But for now she was enjoying having the cottage all to herself.

In idle moments of daydreaming, she pictured herself next summer lying tranquilly on a rug in the garden listening to the soothing sound of birdsong and tinkling water from the stream while her baby slept contentedly at her side. But then she would remember there was a war on, and who knew where any of them would be next summer. There was an airfield on the outskirts of the village of Shillingbury, some five miles from Melstead, and every day aeroplanes could be seen and heard flying overhead. The first time she had been woken by a night-time flying exercise, she had bolted out of bed as the windows rattled and the walls of the cottage seemed to shake. Convinced it was the Luftwaffe, and bombs were about to fall from the sky, she had grabbed her dressing gown to run out to the garden and the Anderson shelter Romily had had built for her.

Now when she heard the noise of the aeroplanes in the night, she felt no fear, only an awareness of her cousin Kit, for whom she would send up a silent prayer for God to keep him safe.

Bored of waiting to be called up to begin his training with the RAF, Kit had taken matters into his own hands and crossed the Atlantic to begin pilot training in Canada, his hope being that when he returned to England, he'd be fast-tracked and put to good use. A letter had arrived from him yesterday, a short communication revealing his obvious pride in what he was doing. Allegra guessed he'd never been happier, that finally he was doing something worthwhile and, perhaps more importantly, something his father would have been proud of. Poor Kit, all those years of wanting to please Uncle Jack, and only now achieving it when it was too late.

She was just about to go and look out of the window again when she heard a knock at the front door.

Elijah, at last!

39

His kitbag at his feet, Elijah held Allegra at arm's length, his eyes slowly taking her in from head to toe.

'Don't, *caro*,' she said, 'don't look at me too closely, *sono grassa e bruttissima*. I'm so fat and ugly now.'

He shook his head. 'No you're not. You're beautiful. Even more beautiful than before. Your skin is glowing and your eyes are clear and bright.'

She groaned. 'You make me sound like a horse being sold at auction.'

He laughed, then threw off his overcoat and drew her close, holding her firmly within his strong embrace, his hands pressing into the small of her back. He looked down into her face, his gaze intense. 'You never could accept a compliment, could you? Would you accept a kiss instead?'

Inhaling the masculine smell of him and the warmth of his body through the woollen serge of his battledress jacket, she nodded. His mouth was hard and sure against hers, and with her arms wrapped around him, she returned his kisses with a fervour that was filled with longing for him. All the time he had been away she had ached for his touch, to feel his muscular body against hers, to lose herself completely in his passion for her. She had never known such an acute sense of loss and loneliness without him. Her head swimming with desire, her legs felt ready to buckle beneath her. As if realising this, he held her even more firmly, but then suddenly pulled away and gazed down at her once more, his breath ragged. 'I'm sorry,' he said, his voice thick.

'Why?'

He touched her cheek lightly. 'I should be more gentle with you, given your condition.' He lowered his gaze to the unborn child between them.

'I'm not made of glass, Elijah.'

'I know, but . . . '

'But what?' And then she knew, and her heart sank. It was obvious — oh, so blindingly obvious, even to a fool like her — her swollen body repulsed him. She should have known better than to think she would still be sexually attractive to him. Before, when they had made love in his bed at Clover End Cottage, her body had gained hardly any weight at all in comparison to now, but in the weeks since he had been away, it had altered dramatically. Back then, they could both pretend that she wasn't carrying a child — another man's child — but now there was no ignoring the grotesque reality of that fact. She stepped away from him, sickened by her selfish greedy desire, and by her naivety in the believing — hoping — that he would still want her.

'It's all right,' she said. 'I understand completely.' She bit her lip in quiet rage.

He looked at her with a frown, his head tilted.

'It's fine,' she asserted with an attempt at indifference. 'Why on earth would you find me attractive when I look like an enormous barrage balloon? I'm so hideous I can barely bring myself to look in the mirror these days, so I understand perfectly that you would not be able to view me — '

'Allegra,' he interrupted sternly, his frown deepening, 'be quiet and listen to me, will you? I love you unconditionally. That means I love you and your body whatever shape it is.' He put a hand to her swollen abdomen. 'I just don't want to hurt you, or the baby. I would never forgive myself if I did anything to cause you harm. Now why don't you put the kettle on and show me round the cottage? I want to see all the changes you wrote about in your letters. I particularly want to see the bathroom.'

★ ★ ★

Later, much later, after they'd shared a bath together — the first Elijah had experienced that wasn't in a tin bath in front of the fire — they made love. Afterwards, lying in euphoric silence with her head resting on his chest, Allegra listened to his heart thumping while tapping the rhythm of it with her fingers. '*Ti amo tanto*,' she murmured in a rare moment of what felt like true happiness.

He took her hand in his and kissed the tips of her fingers softly. 'What did you say?'

She lifted her head and looked at him. 'I said I love you.'

He gently rolled her off him and raised himself up on his elbow, staring at her for the longest moment. 'That's the first time you've said that to me. Do you mean it? Because please don't say it unless you do.'

'It's true; I do love you. And in a completely different way to how I've loved anyone before.'

'Why's that?'

'It's simple. You want nothing from me. I'm not something that you see as being useful to you and which you can put to your advantage.'

'Are you thinking of the father of your child?'

She nodded.

'I would never treat you that way, Allegra. You must know that. Just as you must know that I've always loved you, even when we were children.' He smiled. 'I adored you on sight. I thought you were the most beautiful girl I'd ever seen.'

'I wasn't beautiful, I was just different.'

With a smile, he ran a finger along the curve of her chin. 'What was it I said earlier about you not being able to accept a compliment? To me you were beautiful, and so very fierce. I'd never come across anyone like you before.'

She said nothing as a wave of great sadness came over her. 'I wonder what my life would have been like if I hadn't left here when I was sixteen.'

'You wouldn't have been happy. You had to leave. And then,' he added solemnly, 'you had to come back to me.'

She pressed herself closer to him. 'But now it's you who's leaving me,' she said. 'When will you have to go and fight?'

'Shh . . . ' he said, brushing his lips against hers. 'Let's not talk about that now. Let's enjoy this time together.'

Yes, she thought, for who knew what tomorrow would bring.

40

Meadow Lodge,
Melstead St Mary
10th December, 1939

Dear Kit,

I can't believe it will be Christmas in less than two weeks and the school term will come to an end. Our classrooms have more or less resumed their normal numbers after most of the evacuees returned to London. Many of them hated being in the countryside; they found it too quiet, with nothing to do, and couldn't wait to leave and go home. We never did have an evacuee ourselves — I suspect they'd all got wind of Mother!

Talking of not being able to wait . . . I'm still surprised that you weren't prepared to wait it out as a reservist for your call-up papers. But when I really think about it, I may well have done something equally rash, had I the opportunity and the financial wherewithal to relieve myself of the boredom of the status quo and travel halfway round the world to do it. So I salute you, Kit, for your impatience, and your good fortune in being able to afford to do what you've done.

How are the flying lessons going? I have it on good authority that it's perishingly cold there in Winnipeg, so I hope the enclosed present will come in handy for you. And yes, I knitted it myself; not very well, admittedly, but I defy you to be so impolite as to find one single fault with it. (You decide whether to open it before Christmas or not.)

Never did I think I would turn into one of those women who sits at home knitting while listening to the wireless and humming along to Gracie Fields singing 'Wish Me Luck as You Wave Me Goodbye', but Lady Fogg issued a dictat that we must all do our bit and knit for our brave troops. It's a sentiment I fully endorse, but I pity the poor fellows who receive anything I make them. You included! (If my effort doesn't fit you, use it as a tea cosy!)

I hear from Edmund that he's seen Hope occasionally in London and is concerned about her. He seems to think that she's tired and anxious as a result of fretting over Annelise, and would, in his opinion, benefit from returning to Island House. I'm not sure whether this is my brother speaking in a professional capacity as a doctor, or as a friend who cares deeply about Hope. Either way, I know him well and wouldn't question his judgement.

Mother continues to be Mother, which means I continue to grit my teeth and square my shoulders. She has some absurd notion that she should be exempt from rationing, that others can go without coal or petrol, or whatever else will be rationed in due course, in order for her to carry on as normal. I have explained to her until I'm blue in the face about the ration books with which we've been issued, that everybody has them, but as I say, she seems to think her needs should not be affected in any way.

We've lost the lad who had been working in the garden for us this last year — he's joined the navy — and Jean, who'd been cleaning for us, has joined the Women's Land Army. I can quite see the attraction of working from dawn till dusk on the land in preference to putting up with Mother's infernal griping over the silver that hasn't been polished to her liking. For that matter, I should like to do the same myself!

Well, I think I've grumbled on quite enough and should stop now if I'm going to stand any chance of getting this off to you in time for Christmas 1939!

I hope you're well and keeping your promise not to do anything silly in the way of heroics. Leave the heroics to me as I battle on with these wretched knitting needles while tangling myself up in life-threatening balls of wool!

With warmest best wishes,
Evelyn

PS I apologise for the frequent use of exclamation marks, a habit I deplore in others but which I seem to have slipped into with lamentable ease in the writing of this missive. It must be you — you bring out the exclamation in me!

Kit had read the letter three times over, and each time he had smiled, hearing Evelyn's acerbic tone so clearly. The picture of her with knitting needles in hand, her lips pursed in concentration, her brow furrowed with irritation, amused him greatly.

On the nightstand next to his bed was the three-page letter he had written to her late last night, and before hers had arrived in this morning's post. Now, with just enough time before Charlie came to give him a lift to the flying school, he took it up to add a postscript so he could thank her for the present, which he was keeping to open on Christmas Day. Then he read the whole thing through one more time, just to be sure he hadn't made any mistakes, or used the exclamation mark too frequently!

119 Sunny Ridge,
Winnipeg,
Canada
22nd December, 1939

Dear Evelyn,
Thank you so much for your letter, it made me quite homesick for dear old Mel-stead. I found your account of Miss Gant

332

and Miss Treadmill acquiring a pig and taking it out for a walk on a lead along with their geese hilariously funny. In fact I laughed so much I nearly choked on my supper. My landlady, the wonderful Mrs Medwin, had to thump me on my back!

The countryside here in Winnipeg with its vast prairie could not be more different to the softness of the Stour Valley that surrounds Melstead. It's like nothing I've ever seen before. The landmarks of grain holders and the transcontinental railway line ensure that it's just about impossible to get lost when up in the air.

Another huge difference is the weather — it's freezing, far colder than I've experienced before. It gets deep, deep into your bones and sometimes, if I stand still for too long in the wind, it feels as if my eyeballs might actually freeze and become stuck in their sockets, never to move again! One of the instructors told me a story about a boyhood chum of his who nearly lost his ears to frostbite when he forgot to wear his hat. When he got to school, the teacher boxed his ears; apparently that was the best way to stop them dropping off. The boy never forgot his hat again!

Training continues well, both on the ground and in the air. When the weather's too awful, we're grounded and confined to the classroom at the flying school. The instructors are excellent, really know their stuff and put us through our paces. My group is only small, but I must confess to a glimmer of pride the other day when I came top in both a navigation and a night-time flying exam.

But the time I most enjoy is when I'm up in the air. The Tiger Moths we've been training in so far are old bone-shakers in every respect, but they're sound enough and do the job. It might seem odd, but these single-engined bi-planes, which leave us exposed to the elements, are marvellous for making us trainee pilots at one with the aircraft.

Of course, this type of machine is a long way from the fighter planes I aim to fly. My first solo flight was one of the best experiences of my life and came after just ten hours of flying time. The sense of free-dom when up in the sky on my own with the world beneath me is powerfully exhila-rating — it's all that I hoped it would be, and more. My only frustration is that I haven't been able to fly as frequently as I'd like, but that's down to the snow. Never have I shovelled so much of the stuff! We're often called upon to help clear the runway — the exercise keeps me fit and warm, so it's not all bad.

Outside of the flying school, my life is fairly quiet, but when I do go out it's usu-ally with some of the other trainee pilots. I've discovered the delights of eating out in the local diners. I'm now a connoisseur of egg, ham and chips — never has the humble potato tasted so good! I've also developed a fondness for dill pickle, as well as waffles with maple syrup, though not at the same time! I shall be spending Christmas Day with Mrs Medwin and some of her family who will be visiting — my landlady's an excellent cook and spoils me rotten.

I hear from Romily that their evacuee, Stanley, is doing well under your expert tutelage. As a work in progress under your guiding hand — a distant guiding hand — I like to think I'm also doing well!

It's funny, but I don't miss London at all, but I think of Melstead St Mary often, probably because I think of you there. And before I say any more and make you roll your eyes, I shall sign off.

With fondest regards,
Kit

PS 23rd December now . . . Your letter and present arrived this morning — whatever it is, I know it will be perfect and I shall wear it always. I hope by now you've received my little Christmas parcel, which I sent in haste and without much of an accompanying letter, I'm afraid.

After a moment's thought and scanning the letter once more, Kit added another postscript: PPS. I apologise for the excessive use of exclamation marks — seven in all. Then, looking at his watch and seeing the time — Charlie would be here any minute — he folded the pages and slid them inside the envelope with Evelyn's address already written on it. He sealed it and put it ready to take with him to post on the way to the flying school.

They were a good crowd he was learning to fly with, and Charlie was the best of the bunch. Like Kit, he'd come over specially from England to gain his pilot's licence. It was actually Charlie's cousin Dickie, who had been at Oxford with Kit, who was responsible for Kit being here.

Quite by chance, Kit had run into Dickie in London, and over a drink he had explained how frustrated he was at being stuck as a reservist, even though the Royal Air Force was urgently in need of pilots. 'The trouble is,' Dickie had said — he was now a journalist, so had his finger on the pulse — 'there aren't enough instructors on hand, or sufficient equipment available to teach the numbers required.' He had then gone on to explain about his cousin, who was hell-bent on speeding up the process of receiving his call-up papers. 'I could ask him to get in touch with you if you like,' he had said. 'Canada isn't the only place you can go, South Africa is another option.'

Kit had leapt at the idea, and within weeks, it was all arranged; he'd handed in his notice at the bank, shut up his flat and was crossing the Atlantic.

From the quiet street outside came the sound of a car horn. Gathering up his things, and the letter for Evelyn, Kit shot downstairs before

Charlie beeped again and disturbed the peace of the neighbourhood. 'A quiet and respectable neighbourhood,' as the woman next door often liked to point out to Kit when their paths crossed.

'See you this evening, Mrs Medwin,' he called out to his landlady, pulling on his thick overcoat in the hallway. 'Anything I can pick up from the grocery store for you on my way home?'

Mrs Medwin appeared in the doorway of what she called the front parlour, a duster in hand. She was a widow, a motherly sort of woman with the faint trace of a Scottish accent — she was originally from Edinburgh but had emigrated when she married a Canadian. Kit was always happy to help her when he could. 'That's all right,' she said. 'I'm going there myself later.'

'Are you sure there isn't anything heavy I can bring back for you? It's no trouble.'

She smiled. 'I'm very sure, thank you. Say hello to Charlie from me, and tell him he's more than welcome to join us on Christmas Day. I know his landlady of old and she'll be too mean to give him a decent Christmas lunch.'

'He won't need asking twice,' Kit said with a laugh.

Then, hearing the car horn being pipped again, he opened the front door. The dry icy air hit him like a physical blow, but he stepped outside with a happy smile on his face. It might be freezing cold, but the sky was clear, which meant it would be a perfect day for flying.

41

'I hope you're not rushing off, darling.'

Already out of bed and pulling on his trousers, Arthur looked at Pamela standing in the doorway of the bedroom. Back from the bathroom, she was wearing the scarlet robe with fur trim she had asked him to buy her for Christmas, letting it gape at the front to reveal the fullness of her naked body. It was the first time she had asked him to buy her anything, and he hoped it would be the last. He'd felt such an idiot in the shop paying for the robe, convinced that the woman serving him knew that it wasn't a gift for his wife.

The thought of Irene wearing anything so gaudy was laughable. Such things were not for the Irenes of this world; they were for the Pamelas of Wembley, uncultured women who lacked style and taste. But then it wasn't Pamela's style or taste that he visited her for; it was for sexual pleasure and nothing else.

'It's Christmas Eve,' he said. 'I have to go. I'm expected at my in-laws' for dinner.'

She pouted, which she was much too old to get away with, and leant against the door frame, her hands behind her back, her breasts thrust forward in the manner of a vampish film starlet posing for the camera, a role she liked to play. He felt as he always did at this stage in the proceedings: impatient to be on his way. He pushed his feet into his shoes, began tying the laces.

'Can't you stay for a drink?' she said, her voice low and purring. It was her seductive voice, the one she used while leading him upstairs to the bedroom at the back of the house overlooking the small garden, where there was now an Anderson shelter. They never used her own room at the front; that was out of bounds, even to him. A woman needed her own private sanctuary, she claimed.

'Just one drink,' she pressed, her voice even lower and more sensual. 'To celebrate Christmas.'

What she didn't understand was that those seductive tricks of hers had no effect on him once the act had been completed, once he'd got what he came for. He was tired, too, too tired to play games at any rate.

'I can't,' he said tersely, his patience wearing thin. It wasn't like Pamela to drag things out, or to be obtuse. She knew his moods, knew how to respond and to make him feel better. It was one of the things he'd valued in her, the fact that their arrangement was all about him and his needs, for which he paid her handsomely. And just as she had never allowed him into her private sanctuary, he didn't speak about his family or his work; their lives ran on entirely separate lines.

Recently, however, he had broken that rule and had talked about his family, as well as venting his frustration that all he did at work was spend his days shuffling paper. It seemed to him that if the war was going to be won with an army of civil servants running up and down corridors with files in their hands, then Whitehall had it sewn up.

He'd made a stupid mistake in October when, in a moment of boredom, he'd asked Irene if her father might fix him up with something more useful to do at the War Office. He'd assumed he might be found a senior position of some standing, but — and maybe it was deliberate on his father-in-law's part — as far as he could see, he was doing nothing more significant than overseeing a chaotic typing pool of women. 'Temporary billeting,' he'd been told by an effeminate man in a tweed suit who reeked of cologne. 'Soon have your talents put to greater use, old chap. We're all finding our way now that we're actually at war. I recommend you bunk down as best you can meantime and bear in mind that we're cogs in a colossal machine; we all have our part to play.' Such was the man's cheerfully demeaning manner towards him, Arthur had wanted to drive a fist through his girlish face.

While it was true that Arthur had no appetite for enlisting and putting himself in physical danger — being blind in one eye conveniently ruled him out of active service — he still wanted to do something constructive towards the war effort. Was it too much to expect a role that came with some prestige and respect?

To make matters worse, Kit was in Canada learning to fly, and would probably contrive to make out he was some kind of bloody war hero before he even donned a service uniform!

'But I have something for you,' Pamela said, breaking into Arthur's thoughts. 'A gift. After all, you gave me this lovely present, so it's only fair I should give you something in return.' She flung wide the front panels of the robe, exposing the whole of her fleshy contours, which only minutes ago had been his for the taking. Now Arthur felt faintly revolted by her sagging breasts, swelling stomach and spreading hips. In the stark light of post-coital satisfaction, when his head rather than sexual need guided him, Pamela's age was all too obvious. No amount of powder, lipstick or rouge could disguise the lines at the corners of her eyes and around her mouth. And a satin robe could only conceal so much when it came to a forty-year-old woman.

He stood up and began tucking his shirt in. 'Go on, then,' he said. 'What have you got for me?' He might as well play along and please her. She need never know that the minute he left here, he'd chuck whatever it was she had bought him straight in the nearest bin.

As he put on his jacket, he watched her go over to the chest of drawers in front of the window and take out a large envelope. A Christmas card, he thought, taking it from her. Hardly much of a present. He was almost disappointed. He ripped open the envelope and put his hand inside, then froze when he saw what it was.

'What's this?' he demanded, staring at two black-and-white photographs, one showing him entering Pamela's house, the other showing him

341

leaving, and with Pamela's hand on his shoulder as she planted a kiss on his cheek. He remembered when she'd done that the last time he'd visited, he'd warned her never to do it again, that they had to be more circumspect or somebody might see. Somebody clearly had.

She tied the satin robe around her with the belt and smiled. 'I think it's called an insurance policy, darling.'

'Are you sure you don't mean blackmail?'

'You can call it whatever you want,' she said. 'We're both intelligent enough to know what the situation is.' She picked up the packet of Player's Weights from the nightstand next to the bed and lit a cigarette. She inhaled deeply, then removed a loose bit of tobacco from her lip with the long red nail of her little finger before blowing a curling ribbon of smoke into the air. All the while Arthur stared at her.

'Why?' he said eventually, hardly able to get the word out.

'Why not, ducky?' she replied with a nonchalance that incensed him.

'But . . . but after all these years, I thought our arrangement . . . I thought you cared about . . .' He stopped himself short, horrified at what he'd almost blurted out.

Pamela's eyes narrowed like those of a cat and she pounced. 'What?' she said, her tone mocking. 'You thought I cared about you? Oh, of course I cared about you coming here and using my body for your greedy selfish pleasure as and when the mood took you. But you know, I also care about your poor dear wife and how upset she would be to know what you get up to when you're not with her. How you like to tie me to the bed and take out all your nasty, sadistic frustration on me. And I'm sure your colleagues at the War Office, including your father-in-law, would love to know what you get up to in your private time.'

Arthur looked at her with loathing, seeing her for what she really was: a cheap whore. A fat ugly whore who would stop at nothing. Would he never learn that all women were devious bitches, not to be trusted? 'How much?' he said. 'How much to buy your silence?'

'That's more like it, ducky. Well then, shall we call it a nice round figure of say, one thousand pounds?'

His jaw dropped. 'You can't be serious. I don't have that kind of money to give away.'

'Yes you do. Your father's left you a small fortune. You told me the inheritance would put an end to all your financial worries. And a thousand pounds will help buy me a sweet little cottage that I can turn into a tea shop. That way I won't have to sell my body to foul men like you.'

'I haven't received my inheritance yet,' he said quietly, hardly able to believe what he was hearing. 'It's still tied up with the process of probate.' Which was true. Not that the truth mattered right now.

'You can borrow against it,' Pamela said. 'Don't take me for a fool, Arthur, I know how these things work.'

'Don't you just?' he muttered through

343

clenched teeth. His anger, which had been partially masked by shock, he realised, was now coursing through him with a fiery heat, making him want to show this woman that she'd made a big mistake in trapping him. How dare she think she could have a share of his inheritance!

After making an elaborate show of flicking the ash from her cigarette into the glass ashtray on the nightstand, she inhaled again, looking for all the world as though she were enjoying herself. As though she had it all worked out.

'I'll make it easy for you,' she said. 'I'll take a cheque, but if you do anything underhand and the money doesn't clear because you've put a stop to it, copies of those photographs will appear on your wife's breakfast table. I can just picture the look on her sweet little face. I'll fetch you a pen, shall I?'

It was her smug expression as she turned away that was too much for Arthur. He snatched up the heavy glass ashtray and crashed it down on the side of her head. She seemed not to react at first, but just as he was about to smash it down again, she slowly dropped to the floor and lay there in a great inert pile of red satin.

'Happy Christmas,' he said with savage satisfaction as he stepped around her.

42

'Are you going to make a New Year's resolution?'

'I've thought about it,' said Hope in answer to Edmund's question, 'but frankly it feels absurd to make one when heaven only knows what 1940 will bring us.'

'I know what you mean. All that talk of war being over by Christmas was just nonsense. I don't suppose you've heard anything from Annelise's parents, have you?'

Hope shook her head. 'Nothing. But then I wouldn't expect to, not now. I fear for them, I really do. If they've been detained and put into a camp, then . . . well it just doesn't bear thinking about, not when I recall what Otto told me of his experience of being taken away in the night to be questioned. They held him in a cell for two days without food or water, then released him covered in bruises. And all for no reason other than he was Jewish!' She suddenly realised her voice had risen above the sound of the music coming from the gramophone, and that Lady Fogg, sherry glass half raised to her mouth, was looking at her disapprovingly.

'Sorry, Edmund,' she said, 'I'm making a spectacle of myself and spoiling the mood. It's New Year's Eve and we're supposed to be enjoying ourselves. But really, how can we?'

'You have no need to apologise to me,' he said, leaning in closer, his eyes focused directly on hers. 'I've heard similar stories in London. I treated a Jewish woman the other day who'd escaped here with her husband from Czechoslovakia. Both classically trained musicians, they left their home with nothing but their passports and what little savings they had. Her husband had had his fingers broken so badly while being interrogated, he can no longer play the violin the way he once did. Now he has to make do with teaching schoolchildren.'

'The poor man,' said Hope. 'But what frightens me most is that this is only the beginning. There is far worse to come. For all of us.'

'I agree. I just wish there was more I could do.'

'Are you thinking of enlisting? I'd have thought you'd be needed as a doctor in London.'

'That's what I keep being told,' he said ruefully, moving aside to let a man and a woman Hope didn't recognise squeeze past him. Romily's idea to throw a big New Year's Eve party had gone down so well that just about everyone from the village had shown up. Hope had never seen Island House so full.

When Edmund had resumed his place in front of Hope, he said. 'I keep being told that I'm in the right place ready for when the bombs do start dropping on London. There's also the worry that at any minute great numbers of wounded soldiers from the British Expeditionary Force could arrive back from France and Belgium. So I'm stuck for the time being as a reservist.'

'Your mother would have a fit of apoplexy if you enlisted.'

He smiled. 'But at least I'd be out of range of

her cries of hysteria.'

Hope smiled too. It was always on the tip of her tongue to ask Edmund what he really thought of his mother, but good manners prevented her from doing so; that and the feeling it was an unfair question. After all, nobody knew better than she did that family relationships were complex and not what they might at first appear.

As her gaze drifted around the crowded drawing room, observing all the cheerful faces, Hope spotted Edmund's sister deep in conversation with Romily. Noticing the apparent ease between them, Hope thought how similar the two women were, not in looks, but in temperament; both were confident and capable, as well as clear-sighted and fearless. They were the kind of women Hope had secretly always wished she could be like.

'I know exactly what you're thinking,' Edmund said, catching the direction of her gaze.

'I very much doubt that,' she said.

'You're wondering why Evelyn puts up with things the way she does when she could have stayed in Kent where she was happy. Yes?'

'No, that wasn't what I was thinking right then, though I have done many times before. Since you've raised the matter, why has she made such a huge sacrifice?'

'It's mostly because she has a strong sense of duty, but she also possesses something far stronger: a need to take on the impossible. And our mother, as I'm sure you'll agree, is impossible.'

'Meanwhile, you're only too glad you were

born a boy and therefore not expected to shoulder the responsibility of your mother when there is a daughter on hand to do it.'

Edmund frowned. 'That's a bit harsh.'

'But wholly true,' Hope said, softening her tone. 'I feel sorry for Evelyn. She deserves better.'

'She would hate your sympathy.'

'I know,' said Hope, draining her glass of punch. 'Which is why I'd never show it. Have you really never heard from your father in all these years?'

Her question evidently took him by surprise, as much as it did herself. Edmund and Evelyn's father was an enigma to her, a man who as good as never existed.

'Where did that come from?' he asked.

'I don't know. It just occurred to me that perhaps because it would be different for Evelyn if your father had never left your mother. Is the subject out of bounds? If so, I apologise.'

'Not particularly,' he said, still frowning. 'It's more that I don't give my father much thought these days.'

Hope, who had given her own father a lot of thought recently, said, 'What would you do if he did show up out of the blue?'

'I'd ask him why. Why he agreed to the terms my mother specified for their separation: that she would only allow a divorce if he agreed to support us financially but never saw us again. It seems cowardly on his part to have walked away without more of a fight.'

'Perhaps he was actually being brave,' Hope

said after a moment's thought. 'It couldn't have been an easy decision to make. One thing I've come to realise is that we really don't know how we'll react when we're faced with our worst nightmare. Or confronted with a challenge we think is beyond us.'

'You're thinking of Dieter, aren't you?'

'And Annelise.'

'This may be an indelicate question, but have you thought what you'll do if her parents don't make it through the war?'

'Some days it's all I ever think of. And then I think, what if they do make it and I have to give Annelise back? She's become such an important part of my life now. I'd miss her terribly.'

'You'd get back to drawing again, though, wouldn't you?'

Hope smiled shyly. 'And that's where you're wrong. I've been drawing since Christmas Eve.'

'You dark horse, you!'

Her smile broadened. 'It's down to Romily; she asked me to produce a sketch of Stanley's dog for him as a Christmas present, and the funny thing was, although I started it reluctantly, once I got going, I couldn't stop. I've drawn so many pictures of Bobby now, Stanley has practically wallpapered his room with them!'

Edmund smiled. 'That's wonderful. I hated the thought of you casting aside your talent. Are you going to let your publisher know that you're back in the saddle?'

'There's not much point. Once I return to London, I'll be solely responsible for Annelise again and won't have time.'

Edmund stared at her, his blue eyes serious. 'It needn't be that way,' he said. 'After all, you trust Florence, Romily and Mrs Partridge to look after her here; why not find somebody you really like and trust in London?'

'I told you, I tried it and it didn't work. I just couldn't settle. I kept worrying about Annelise.'

'Then there's only one solution as far as I can see: you have to stay here at Island House.'

Hope rolled her eyes. 'Oh don't you start. I've had Romily slyly suggesting that ever since I arrived. She seems to think London doesn't suit me.'

'I'm inclined to agree with her,' Edmund said with a small smile.

'So that's what the two of you were discussing earlier when I was trapped in the hall with the wretched Reverend Tate! Did she put you up to this? I might have known.'

'Not at all,' he said with a laugh. 'It was Kit we were discussing. I was saying how envious I was that he was learning to fly, and Romily surprised me by saying she holds a pilot's licence herself. Did you know that?'

'Yes, I did, and surely by now you must have realised that there's nothing about Romily that should surprise you.'

'That's true. She was also saying that a friend of hers is hoping to join the Air Transport Auxiliary. Apparently after much persuasion, the ATA have accepted that they're going to have a shortage of pilots, and so women with the right amount of flying time under their belts will be allowed to ferry military aircraft around the country.'

'Do you think Romily might leap at the chance to join her friend?' Hope could well imagine her stepmother doing exactly that. She could also imagine how different Island House would feel without her presence. It was strange how easily the house had become hers, and odder still, how right that felt. It was as if Romily had somehow made it into the home it had never before been.

'You know her better than I do,' answered Edmund, 'but I wouldn't be surprised if she did. But never mind Romily. I have to say this to you, Hope. Whenever I saw you in London, you didn't look well or happy to me. Whereas here, you look infinitely better, much more your old self, like the girl I remember when we were children and running amok in the meadows!'

Hope smiled. 'Is that your professional diagnosis, Dr Flowerday?'

'It's my opinion as an old friend. Why not consider staying at Island House until the war is over? Would it be so very bad?'

'This is Romily's house and I'm a guest here,' she said, thinking that Edmund wasn't only an old friend; he was one of her very few friends. As a child, she had always preferred the solitude of her own company, or that of Kit, a habit she had maintained into adulthood. Dear Kit, she thought with a sudden rush of affection, wishing he was here to see the new year in with them all.

Since her brother had left for Canada, Hope had regretted not doing what she should have done a long time ago, and that was apologize to Kit. She should never have treated him the way

351

she did, it had been cruel and unnecessary. Kit had never done anything other than be a good brother to her, and yet when she had perhaps needed him most, she had cut him out of her life. Even knowing that it would upset him, she hadn't been able to relinquish the need to isolate herself, to bury herself yet deeper in her grief.

Several times in the weeks since he'd left, she had planned exactly what she wanted to say in a letter to him, but somehow each attempt failed to express just how sorry she was for cutting him out of her life. It left her wanting to say the words to his face, for him to know that she meant them. His forgiveness would be automatic, she knew, he was that sort of person, but she wanted him to know that while she had been in that horribly dark place, she had never stopped loving him. It was only now that she sensed a glimmer of light at the end of the long tunnel through which she had been travelling that she understood that herself.

Aware of Edmund's gaze on her, she realised he was giving her another searching look. 'London might feel safe now,' he said, shifting her thoughts back to what he'd been saying before, 'but I'm convinced we've been lulled into a false sense of security. If the Luftwaffe do start filling the skies over our cities, you'll be in great danger. Wouldn't you want Annelise to be somewhere safer than a bombing target?'

'Are you trying to scare me?' she said.

He put a hand on her forearm. 'I'm trying to tell you that I care about you and want you to be safe. Promise me you'll think about it.'

She looked down at his hand, then back up into the intensity of his beseeching eyes. 'I will,' she said. Then, more cheerfully, 'And that's my New Year's resolution!'

43

It was gone eleven o'clock and Romily thought she would never get away from Sir Archibald Fogg. Many a time Lady Fogg had looked across the room, her face resembling a thundercloud, as though Romily had deliberately cornered her husband and was playing the femme fatale.

For what seemed an eternity the man had stood so close to her that his bushy whiskers all but brushed against her face while he shared his opinions — Stalin: a thoroughly disgusting man; the neutrality of America: a detestable country; conscientious objectors: he'd have the damned cowards publicly horsewhipped, would happily do it himself; the war would be over in six months: a tap to the side of his nose indicated he knew people in high places who *knew* such things.

But his particular grievance, which he was keen to share with Romily, and on which he had much to say, was his view that the country was going to the dogs: people no longer knew their place, the old order was in danger of being lost forever, and that was the real battle they were facing. He had questioned Romily's prudence in the way she had arranged this party. 'Capital idea of yours to throw a bash like this,' he'd said. 'Just what was needed to raise morale. But take it from me, it's never a good idea to invite every Tom, Dick and Harry into your home.' He'd looked pointedly at George and Ruby Minton and their son, Billy, who were chatting to Evelyn.

Romily had now reached the stage when, if forced to listen to another word, she would gladly shoot herself, and so to bring matters to an immediate halt, she applied her most charming smile. 'I really can't help but wonder whether one morning we'll all wake up and decide we deserve a Bolshevik regime to put right the wrongs history has laid upon us and redress the balance,' she said.

Sir Archibald goggled at her, his face brick red, his bearded jaw momentarily slack. Seizing her chance, she touched his arm. 'Do excuse me, I really ought to attend to my other guests. They must think me a very poor hostess monopolising you for so long.'

She turned on her heel and left him to deal with his shock, not caring that he would now regard her as an untrustworthy viper in the nest. *A commie, right here in Melstead St Mary!* she imagined him telling Lady Fogg later. By lunchtime tomorrow she would once again be the talk of the village, perhaps elevated to the status of a Nazi propaganda agent!

The prospect pleased her no end. Because lord knew she had grown tired of the status quo. Yes, she had been pleased to return to Island House after a brief stay in London, but as soon as the excitement of Christmas was over, she had grown restless, unable to settle and resume the novel she was working on. With talk of paper being rationed, she wondered why she should bother; it also seemed in poor taste to write a murder mystery when so many lives were genuinely at risk. Melvyn, her agent, was of the opinion that books would be needed even more as a distraction. 'Whatever is going on in the world,' he had said, 'people still want to be entertained. More so if there are further restrictions on petrol, and opening hours for theatres and cinemas come into play. Reading will be one of the few pleasures left to us.'

In many ways that was why Romily had decided to throw a party, an open house for anyone who wanted to come. Hope had been unsure about the idea. 'What if everyone comes?' she had said, concerned. 'Where will we put them?'

'The more the merrier!' had been Romily's response, which would have been exactly what Jack would have said. In fact, this party was her private way of honouring Jack, for she knew it was exactly the kind of thing he would have done to lift everybody's spirits. She just wished with all her heart he was here to join in with the fun.

After going upstairs to check that the noise from the guests wasn't disturbing Annelise and Stanley, she went through to the kitchen to see if there was anything she could do to help Mrs Partridge who had done such a sterling job creating delicious party food. Reassured that everything was under control, she rejoined the party, taking with her a tray of mushroom vol-auvents to pass around. It was something to do, especially if it meant she could avoid getting stuck again with Sir Archibald.

It wasn't so much that she was bored at her

own party; far from it, it pleased her enormously to see her guests enjoying themselves — the old boys from the village who had brought the piano up from the church hall and were gathered around it with their glasses of beer, and the younger guests dancing in the dining room, the rugs rolled back, music playing on the wireless — but there was no getting away from it: she was filled with a restless energy, a sure sign that she needed something new with which to occupy herself.

She'd been like it as a child, had driven her parents mad with her constant antics of daredevilry, climbing trees that no sane person would attempt, or swimming underwater for longer than anybody else. It was what drove her to take up challenges like learning to fly, or getting behind the wheel of a car at Brooklands. She had always enjoyed the thrill of pushing herself to the limit. Only trouble was, each new thrill had to out-thrill the last.

Earlier in the evening, she had been chatting to Edmund about Sarah's determination to join the Air Transport Auxiliary. 'Once the silly old duffers realise women can fly aircraft just as well as any man,' her friend had told her, 'I'll apply to join. You should too, Romily. You need to be active; you can't sit at home dwelling on Jack while waiting for the war to end. I don't need to tell you we've all got to do our bit.'

Romily had taken offence at hearing her friend describe her in this way, and had defended her position, listing all that she did — running Island House, trying to keep to her writing schedule, looking after Stanley, keeping an eye on Allegra, and joining the WI so she could learn to knit socks and balaclavas for the troops, a skill she had yet to grasp with any real aplomb.

'Yes, yes, yes,' Sarah had said dismissively, 'all of which you could do standing on your head while juggling a couple of eggs! You could be doing so much more, Romily.'

'But I can't just abandon my post,' Romily had countered. 'I have commitments, namely an evacuee. I'm responsible for him. Why should you expect me to be doing more?'

'Because you're Romily Temple!' cried Sarah.

'I'm Romily Temple-*Devereux*,' she'd replied staunchly. 'I'm not the same woman now.'

But Sarah was having none of it and continued to insist that Romily should be out in the field rather than resting on her laurels at Island House. 'You could at least volunteer to drive an ambulance, like Rosalind Chapel has signed up for. You remember her from school — beaky nose, large hands? Or better still, join the ATA with me. Lord knows it will be fun putting all those men in their place!'

Maybe it would, thought Romily as she caught sight of Sir Archibald staring across the drawing room at her with a look of undisguised mistrust on his face. Amused, she gave him a false smile of acknowledgement and continued offering around the tray of vol-au-vents. When the last one had been taken, she returned the tray to the kitchen and suggested it was high time Mrs Partridge joined the party. 'It's almost midnight; come and sing 'Auld Lang Syne' with everyone else,' she said.

'But I've got all this washing-up to do,' the older woman replied.

'I'll give you a hand later when everybody's gone.'

'You'll do no such thing. Florence and I will see to it.'

'I shall help you both, and that's an end to it, Mrs Partridge. Another word of remonstration and I'll insist on doing it all myself.'

With a magnificent display of reluctance, Mrs Partridge finally took off her apron and hung it on the back of the door, where she and Florence kept their gas masks, now contained in the Christmas presents Romily had given them — smart new cases, one a shade of magenta, the other navy blue. 'Very well, Miss Romily, I'll do as you say, and with as much good grace as I can muster.'

Romily smiled, catching the twinkle in the other woman's eye. 'I'm very glad to hear it. By the way, have you seen Florence?'

'If you can find Billy,' Mrs Partridge said with a chuckle, 'you'll find Florence. They've been joined at the hip for most of the evening.' She gave Romily a half-smile. 'I don't know what they find to talk about, I really don't.'

*　*　*

Out in the bitterly cold garden, hidden from sight behind the big old cedar tree, with raucous voices giving vent to 'Auld Lang Syne' from inside the house, Billy and Florence weren't talking; they were kissing as though their lives depended upon it. Florence often felt that way, that she needed to absorb as much of Billy as she could while she had the chance. It wouldn't be long before he would be returning to barracks, and when he did, she didn't have a clue when she would see him again. With a heavy sigh, Billy released her from his grasp. He shuddered and closed his eyes. 'What is it?' Florence asked, alarmed. 'Are you unwell?'

He opened his eyes. 'I'm not unwell,' he said with a rasp in his voice.

'What then?'

He grinned, revealing his uneven white teeth in the silvery moonlight that was shining down on them from a cloudless starlit sky. 'Can't you guess?'

She hesitated. And then she thought of what had been pressing hard against her while they'd been kissing. The very first time she had been aware of it, she'd been horribly embarrassed, scared too that Billy might insist on putting it where she didn't want it to go. She might be naive compared to some, but she knew that was how she'd end up pregnant, and not for anything, not even Billy, who she loved with all her heart, would she let that happen.

'If you're talking about what I think you are,' she said, 'then my answer is still no.'

He shook his head with a smile and put a hand to her cheek, cupping it gently in his palm. 'I'm not asking that particular question,' he said softly. 'All I'm saying is that that's how you make feel. I love you, Flo. In fact, I love you so very much, I think it would be only right and proper that we should marry.'

She stared at him, shocked. '*Marry?*' she repeated. 'You mean *us* get married?'

He laughed. 'Who else would I mean?' And then dropping to one knee, he looked up at her. 'Florence Massie, will you make me the happiest man alive and agree to marry me?'

★ ★ ★

In the boathouse, Allegra sat in the crook of Elijah's right arm, while his left hand rested gently on her stomach beneath the blanket that covered them both. 'I can feel it moving,' he said.

'*She,*' Allegra corrected him. 'I've told you before, it's a girl.'

'And I've told you before, you have no way of knowing. It could be a boy; a handsome boy just like me.'

'And presumably just as modest as you, *caro,*' she with a smile.

He moved his hand lightly over the baby as it continued to wriggle around. 'Will you promise me something?' he said finally.

'Depends what it is you want me to promise.'

'Promise me that if you're wrong and it's a boy, you'll still love him.'

She sat up straight, dislodging his arm from around her shoulder. 'Why would you say that?'

'Because I'd hate to think of this poor child not being loved just for being a boy.'

'It's a girl,' she said adamantly, 'so it's an unnecessary promise to make.'

'Allegra, don't be stubborn. Just say the

words, 'I'll love this child whatever.''

'And since when have you become the one who tells me what to do?'

'Since I decided that we should get married.'

She stared at him, stunned, not quite believing what she'd heard him say. But then quickly recovering, she said: 'And you think marriage would give you that right over me?'

He laughed. 'Not for a minute. But the thought of it did stop you in your tracks, didn't it? So how about it, Allegra? How about we put an end to all the talk in the village and surprise everybody?'

'Would that be the only reason for us to marry?'

'Oh, my darling Allegra, of course not. We should marry because I love you and you love me. And then the beautiful daughter you're going to give birth to, or the handsome son, will have a father in its life. The child could have my name on the birth certificate to make everything nice and respectable.'

'You've given this a lot of thought.'

'Are you saying you haven't?'

Of course she had. Being with Elijah, whether it was at his cottage or hers, had made Allegra feel happier than she could ever remember being. Any time spent apart from him dragged, and the thought of him leaving to return to barracks and then being sent to fight God knew where chilled her to the marrow. If she could, she would keep him safe with her at Winter Cottage, never to let him go again.

But even marriage wouldn't keep him by her

362

side where he would be safe. Married or not, he would still have to go and fight, and she would still be left alone in Melstead St Mary with her child. For herself she didn't care a fig about marriage providing her with a veneer of respectability, but as husband and wife, would they spend the rest of their lives fighting prejudice, because in the eyes of some people they came from different worlds? Surely Elijah deserved better than that.

'This long silence from you is not filling me with hope that you'll say yes,' he said.

'Are you sure you know what you'll be taking on?' Allegra responded. 'It's not just me you're marrying; you're taking on a child as well. Another man's child.'

'Allegra, don't you think I've worked that out for myself? Now for the love of God, it's gone midnight and it's the first day of 1940. Give me your answer before it's 1941! Yes or no, will you marry me?'

44

January 1940

'Darling, I think it's time we bought a bigger house, don't you?'

'Is that a statement of intent or a question?' responded Arthur indifferently to his wife as he prepared for bed.

It was two o'clock in the morning, New Year's Day, and he was standing at the side of the large four-poster bed debating with himself whether to put on a scarf as well as keep his dressing gown on. Their north-facing room caught the worst of the wind. He'd damned near frozen to death last night in this mausoleum of a house to which Irene's parents insisted on retreating for New Year.

The very first time Irene had proposed visiting her parents in their Scottish house overlooking Loch Leven, he'd been more than happy to make the long journey; a week of shooting and fishing, and then hunkering down in a comfortable chair in front of a log fire with an endless supply of locally produced whisky and the newspaper had sounded just the ticket. But the reality was quite different. Yes, there was shooting and fishing to enjoy, but the log fires and whisky were always in short supply, the latter being kept practically under lock and key by the dour, miserable-faced housekeeper.

Irene's family was bred from hardy puritanical stock — freezing-cold winds rattling through windows that didn't fit properly in the casings were apparently good for one, put some backbone into a person. And then there was the endless socialising — it was Liberty Hall with people coming and going all hours of the day, the laird of this, the laird of that calling in to say hello. There wasn't a moment of peace to be had. And as for all that blasted Scottish dancing and bloody bagpipes . . .

Of course, this wasn't the first New Year in Scotland Arthur had been forced to endure, but somehow he'd hoped the tedium of it all would lessen with each returning visit, that he would become inured to it. No such luck!

'It's a statement of intent,' Irene said, regarding him steadily in the mirror as she applied yet more face cream. 'I just think that we've outgrown our present home. And' — now she did turn round to look at him properly — 'we're going to need more space very soon.'

'What for?' Oh God, he thought, she hadn't gone on a spending spree behind his back and bought a lot of new furniture, had she?

Her expression softened and she looked coy. 'I'm going to have a baby. At last, darling, we're going to be parents.'

The news took him off guard. Myriad questions flew to the tip of his tongue, but the one that came out was: 'How long have you known?'

'Since before Christmas, after I saw Dr Osborne.'

'You didn't tell me you were seeing him?'

She screwed the lid back on to the pot of face cream and placed it amongst all the other pots, tubes and bottles that cluttered the dressing table. 'I didn't tell you because I wanted to surprise you,' she said, 'and judging by your expression, I have.'

'You're right, you have. Why didn't you tell me before, though? Why wait until now?'

'Because I wanted to keep the news until this very moment, to mark the coming of the new year. I wanted 1940 to start with something positive. I'm sick of all the talk about the war. It's so depressing. You are pleased, aren't you?'

He tried to think how he really felt, but could summon nothing genuine that he could put into actual words. He went over to her; clearly that was expected of him. 'Of course I'm pleased,' he lied.

'You don't look it.'

'That's because I'm worried what kind of a world our child will be born into,' he said smoothly.

She grasped his hands. 'Don't say that. Not a word about the war. I'm so very tired of it. It's all Daddy and his friends talk about. You are pleased that you're going to be a father, aren't you? Only you've seemed so distracted lately. All Christmas I kept thinking there was something you weren't telling me, that there was something bothering you.'

'It's work,' he lied again. 'It's damnably boring. I had hoped your father would find me a role with more responsibility.'

'Would you like me to speak to him? I'm sure he could arrange for something better for you to do if I asked him. Especially now that you're going to be a father.'

'Best not,' he said, thinking of the tedious job his father-in-law had found for him following Irene's last intervention. But then, and not without a trace of irony, realising that an important role with more responsibility had now been unexpectedly thrust upon him in the form of fatherhood, he said, in a more conciliatory tone, 'You should get some sleep, Irene. You need to look after yourself. I don't know what you thought you were doing dancing all night in your condition.'

She rose from the dressing table stool and giggled, which was very unlike her — Irene wasn't a giggler; she was always too poised for such behaviour. 'That's just what Mummy said to me.'

'You told her before me?' Arthur said, vexed that he wasn't actually the first to know, although it shouldn't have surprised him. Irene and her mother came as a pair; nothing happened to one that the other didn't know about.

'She guessed,' Irene replied. 'She noticed that I wasn't eating breakfast, that the very thought of it made me feel queasy.'

Arthur hadn't noticed that, but then he had been somewhat preoccupied. 'I suppose your mother told your father?' he said.

Irene pulled back the heavy eiderdown and got into bed. 'Naturally she did. But I swore them both to secrecy until I'd told you.' She giggled again. 'And now that I have, the whole world can know!'

★ ★ ★

Later, when he had put out the light and the wind was howling and making the curtains sway at the draughty window, Arthur tried to take stock.

A baby. He was going to be a father.

He still could not work out just how he felt about it. He wasn't exactly unhappy, but neither did he feel particularly pleased or excited. It would just be another burden to carry. As if he didn't have enough on his mind.

The events of Christmas Eve were never far from his thoughts. Daily he'd searched the newspaper for a report of the death of a woman in Wembley, but had found nothing. Had Pamela's life been of so little consequence her death wasn't worth mentioning? Ironically, he could almost feel sorry for her, but then he would remind himself of what she'd been prepared to do.

It was possible that her body had not yet been discovered, that it was lying where he'd left it on the floor of that poky back bedroom, the curtains drawn. She had never spoken about family, or the neighbours, so perhaps there was nobody who would miss her, or mourn her passing.

In the moments immediately after bringing that ashtray crashing down on Pamela's skull, Arthur had sat on the edge of the bed and

368

gathered his wits. That was when the reality of what he'd done had hit home and he'd had to force himself to breathe deeply to combat the shock.

Murder; he'd committed murder. He hadn't intended to. All he'd wanted to do was ensure the wretched woman wouldn't extract a penny piece from him. Not ever. But looking at the gruesomely lifeless body on the floor at his feet, blood staining the rug beneath her head, he'd had to accept that this was not something he could now undo. What was done was done.

Once the worst of the shock had passed, he quickly set about covering his tracks, but more importantly, finding where Pamela had hidden the negatives of the photographs that had been taken of him on her doorstep.

It hadn't been difficult. He'd found them in her private sanctuary, in a wooden box at the bottom of the wardrobe. They were not the only photographs he discovered. He also found a notebook containing a list of men's names, his included. It was a client list. How sickeningly methodical she had been. Any qualms Arthur had experienced at having taken a life existed no more. In fact he'd go so far as to say he had done the world a favour in ridding it of such a vile woman.

His conviction was compounded as he continued to search through Pamela's things and found her bank statements neatly stored in another box. A look through them showed regular amounts of money being deposited into an account for the last six months. She had been systematically blackmailing half a dozen poor devils who would very likely sigh a massive sigh of relief when they realised they would no longer be at her mercy. They would thank him if they only knew who had brought about an end to the extortion.

He could see from the bank statements that the initial request she had made of him would very probably have been only the start. It puzzled him why she had left it until now to blackmail him. Had the other men been easier targets? He would never know, and frankly he didn't care.

He'd thought hard about his next step after sorting through Pamela's things. Should he remove all evidence of the other men who had been blackmailed, or leave the notebook so that her death would be pinned on one of them?

In the end, and deeming it a necessary insurance policy — an echo of Pamela's own words — he had carefully removed the page from the notebook that contained his name, putting it safely in his briefcase along with the photographs. He then went around the house meticulously wiping any surface he might have touched.

It was dark when he left, and with the brim of his hat pulled down and his coat collar up, he strolled away from the house as nonchalantly as he could in the direction of the train station.

The only fly in the ointment was that the photographer who had taken the incriminating pictures was an unknown quantity. There was no way of knowing who it was; Arthur had been unable to find any reference to him in amongst the carefully kept records. Would the partner in crime have kept copies? He had no way of knowing, and there was little point in worrying about something he had no control over.

But he'd learnt an important lesson. There would be no more visits to women to satisfy those urges that Irene would recoil from in horror; he would have to turn his back on them and satisfy himself with what his wife could provide.

It would be his New Year's resolution, not to stray. Moreover, from here on, he would look upon the whole sordid business as a warning, and a lucky escape. If he so much as allowed a single thought to step out of line, he would have to remind himself of the wholly apposite proverb that one of the masters used to quote to the boys at school: 'The lips of a forbidden woman drip honey, and her speech is smoother than oil, but in the end she is bitter as wormwood, sharp as a two-edged sword.'

45

A week after Billy's proposal, Florence woke to a beautiful morning with a low sun sending long shadows stretching across the glittering hoar frost that covered the garden. Whitened cobwebs hung like delicate lace doilies amongst the bushes and a blackbird pecked hungrily at the ruby-red berries on the holly.

It was truly the most glorious of mornings, and within a few hours Florence would no longer be Florence Massie, she would be Florence Minton. She could say the words a hundred times over in her head and still it wouldn't seem real. Glory be, she was actually marrying Billy Minton!

Once she had said yes to Billy's proposal and he had told his parents, everything had moved at lightning speed for them to be married before he returned to barracks. He would be gone tomorrow and he didn't have a clue where he would be sent. But for now, all that mattered was that they made it through the day without Billy's mother finding some just cause and impediment as to why her son should not take Florence as his lawful wife.

Miss Romily had been delighted at the news, but was anxious to know that Florence would still want to work at Island House. It simply hadn't crossed Florence's mind that she wouldn't carry on as normal. At this stage, she and Billy both agreed, that there was no point in finding anywhere else to live, they would deal with that when they needed to.

They weren't the only ones who were going to be married, Allegra and Elijah were also tying the knot, and with two ceremonies taking place, and at only a week's notice, Reverend Tate had somewhat pompously taken it upon himself to propose that since there was a war on and there were economies to be made, they might like to consider a joint wedding. 'Lazy old devil,' Mrs Partridge had muttered. 'The man's too idle to conduct two weddings at such short notice, more like it.'

Florence hadn't thought Allegra would agree — after all, she was a Devereux and had probably expected a grand affair — but she was all for it, even joked that she would be able to hide behind Florence so people couldn't see just how big she now was.

With a growing sense of excitement, Florence began to get dressed, slipping on the lovely dress Miss Romily had bought for her. It was going to be the most perfect of days, she told herself. But even as she thought this, a small part of her longed for her mother to be here to witness her marrying Billy.

At once she chased the futile thought away and wondered instead how Allegra was getting on at Winter Cottage.

★   ★   ★

Allegra was in tears. '*Sono brutta! Non posso farlo!* I can't do it! I can't!'

373

Hope shook her head wearily. 'Allegra,' she said as patiently as she could. 'You don't look ugly; far from it — you look beautiful, just like every bride does.'

Allegra snapped her head up and stared at Hope, her eyes flashing angrily. '*Madonna*, how can you say that! Just look at the size of me! I look ridiculous in this dress! This heart-shaped neck was a terrible mistake; my bosom is more out than in! I swear the dress fitted when I bought it. How could I have got fatter since only a few days ago? Oh, *la mia vergogna*!'

'You look lovely, Allegra, and by the time you have Romily's fur stole on, your breasts will be perfectly hidden.'

'Don't patronise me, Hope!' Allegra screeched, stamping her foot. 'I'm not a child!'

Her patience wearing thin, Hope sighed. 'Can I say anything that won't lead to me having my head bitten off?'

Allegra glared at her, her eyes dangerously wide, her hands on her hips. Then, as if slowly loosening the tightly wound coil inside her, she composed herself. 'I'm sorry,' she said. 'It's just that I want to look my best for Elijah.'

'And you will, I promise you.'

Hope had been here with Allegra since breakfast to fulfil her role as bridesmaid, a role that she was dividing between her cousin and Florence. Annelise was playing her part too, as a flower girl, but wisely Hope had left her back at Island House in Romily's care.

Glancing at her reflection in the mirror once more, Allegra shook her head in disgust.

'It might help if you stopped looking at yourself,' Hope suggested.

'I have to know the worst,' Allegra muttered dismally, before whipping round to face her. 'Tell me honestly. Do I look very awful?'

'I've told you many times already, you look beautiful. I wouldn't lie to you. Now stand still while I do your hair.'

Amazingly Allegra did as instructed and allowed Hope to finish pinning up her dark hair. As she worked, Hope risked giving her cousin some advice. 'Allegra,' she said soothingly, 'please be happy on your wedding day. Don't spoil it by worrying about how you look. Elijah loves you. He'll take care of you no matter what. Your vows today will include the words 'in sickness and in health', which means that pregnant or not pregnant, fat or thin, Elijah will love you. He's a good man.'

Allegra looked back at Hope in the mirror. 'He is, you're right. I am the one who is not good; we both know that. I wish with all my heart the baby was his.'

'To all intents and purposes it will be. The child will grow up always believing Elijah is its father.'

'I hope you're right. I really don't deserve him. I just hope he knows what he's doing.'

'I'm sure he does,' Hope said firmly. God help him if he didn't!

Seconds passed before Allegra said, 'May I ask you something, Hope?'

'Of course.'

'Were you as nervous as me on your wedding day?'

With a stab of pain, Hope thought back to that day in London when she and Dieter had married. Neither of them had had any family members there to support them, and though she had fought back the pang of regret that she had not invited Kit, she had stood by her decision. This was about her and Dieter and their love for each other. And no, she had not been nervous, not one little bit. She had never been surer about a thing than she was that morning as she dressed herself and did her hair. But to put her cousin at ease, she said, 'Nervous? Oh, I was as skittish as a kitten. I could barely remember my own name I was in such a state.'

Allegra frowned. 'I would never have thought that of you.'

Glad that her lie had seemed to reassure her, Hope smiled. 'Just goes to show, one can never know a person completely.'

'There now,' she said a short while later, 'you look as beautiful a bride as any I've seen. And if you hold your flowers in front of you, like this,' she added brightly, 'nobody would ever know you were seven months pregnant.'

Allegra looked at her dubiously, but obediently took the proffered arrangement of pink roses and white carnations and held them so that they draped over her stomach. Hope placed the borrowed white fur stole around her cousin's shoulders, but there was no getting away from it: Allegra's swelling bosoms had a mind of their own and were determined to have their day.

As if reading her thoughts, Allegra smirked. 'I hope the sight of me won't be too much of a distraction for the Reverend Tate.'

'His eyes will be practically out on stalks the whole time,' said Hope good-humouredly. 'You'll be a war bride he won't forget in a hurry.'

The two women, who for most of their lives had been unable to find any common ground between them, smiled, and when Allegra put her arms around Hope, and thanked her for all that she'd done, Hope found herself hugging her cousin back with genuine affection.

★   ★   ★

The two wedding parties gathered at the Half Moon Hotel after the combined marriage ceremonies.

Resplendent in their battledress uniforms, Elijah and Billy both looked so very young to Roddy. He felt sad at the sight of their youthful vitality, knowing that tomorrow they would be returning to barracks to hear what their fate would be. He could not look at the two fresh-faced men without thinking of how he and Jack had met in the field hospital during the bloodiest of wars that was supposed to end all wars.

'You did a wonderful job earlier, walking Allegra down the aisle.'

He turned to see Romily at his side. 'It was easy,' he said. 'I just put one foot in front of the other and held onto Allegra.'

Romily smiled. 'I didn't mean that, and you know it. You looked as proud as any father could standing in the church.'

'I was proud, and I'm proud of the way Allegra has finally allowed herself to be happy. But . . . ' He let the word hang in the air, unsure whether to say more.

'But what, Roddy?' Romily pressed.

'I can't bear the thought of her suffering, should anything happen to Elijah.'

Romily slipped her arm through his. 'We'll be there for her. You and me. We'll pick up the pieces if we have to. If she'll let us.'

He smiled admiringly at Romily. 'You had no idea what you were getting into when you fell in love with Jack, did you, taking on his family?'

'That's life for you. You think you have it perfectly licked, but somehow it has a way of going its own way.'

'And now you have Hope living back here with Annelise. I'm so pleased you persuaded her to leave London.'

'It took some doing, I can tell you! But just as I knew it would, being here has relaxed her and she's drawing again. Don't say a word, Hope swore me to secrecy, but she's begun working on a children's book based on Stanley and his dog Bobby. She's actually writing it as well as doing the illustrations.

'Did you have a persuasive hand in that?'

'I may have suggested something along those lines, but if there's one thing I've learnt about Jack's family, it's that they're as stubborn as hell and have to do things their own way and in their own time.'

Roddy laughed. 'Just like Jack himself, in that case! And maybe you, if I may be so bold.'

'You may,' she said with a laugh. 'Have you heard anything from Kit or Arthur?'

'I had a letter from Kit just after Christmas, but not a word from Arthur. Though after that stunt he pulled on you girls in the summer with Annelise, I have no desire to speak to him ever again. He's a rotten apple through and through.'

'I can't help but think that when a man loathes the world as Arthur does, and with such an intensity, really it's himself he detests. But come on, this is a party, not a wake. And any minute now you'll be called upon to carry out your last duty of the day: the wedding speech on behalf of both brides.'

Roddy groaned. 'How did I ever let you talk me into doing that?'

She kissed his cheek. 'You'll be fine.'

He was just about to ask her when she thought she would be next in London, and if she might find time to have dinner with him, when he heard the sound of glass breaking. Across the crowded room he caught sight of Florence with Billy and his parents, and she had the oddest expression on her face. She looked quite literally as if she had been turned to stone.

46

Her brain told her that she was seeing things, but her heart said otherwise, and not caring that the glass she had been holding now lay in pieces at her feet, Florence crunched over it and rushed to the small window that looked out onto the market square.

Yes, there in the fading afternoon light was the woman she had caught sight of through the window! She was walking across the cobbles, a basket of shopping in each of her gloved hands. She was wearing a tailored navy-blue woollen coat with a scarf at her throat and a knitted cream-and-blue tam-o'-shanter pulled to one side of her head, from beneath which hair the same colour as Florence's could be clearly seen. She was striding briskly in the direction of the war memorial.

'What is it, Flo?' asked Billy, at her side now. 'What's wrong?'

She didn't answer him; instead she pressed her face against the cold glass, trying to get a better look, willing the woman to turn around.

Several times as a young child Florence had been in this very same situation, convinced that she had seen her mother, even calling out to her. But each time she had been proved wrong. Afterwards she would feel crushed with disappointment and would vow never to make the same mistake again, no more would she be subconsciously looking out for her mother who had abandoned her.

But here, surely, was a woman who could not be anyone but Ernestine Massie. It wasn't just the colour of her hair that made Florence so sure; it was the tam-o'-shanter she wore. Florence had such a clear memory of her mother knitting one for her just like that.

Across the square she noticed the bus trundling up Meadow Lane, its destination the bus stop by the war memorial. What if the woman got on it?

'Flo?' said Billy again. 'What is it?'

'I'll explain later,' she said, pushing past him. She had only one thought in her head now: she had to speak to that woman before it was too late. Frantically she barged her way through the startled wedding guests and made it outside onto the pavement, where cold wintry air sliced through the thin fabric of her dress, straight to the bone. But Florence didn't care. Only one thing mattered.

Over by the war memorial, the bus had now stopped and passengers were spilling out into the square, chatting and laughing and infuriatingly getting in the way of Florence being able to keep track of where the woman in the tam-o'-shanter was heading.

In desperation, she called out her mother's name: '*Ernestine! Ernestine Massie!*' When she got no response, she set off at a run, her eyes fixed firmly on the woman.

She didn't see the truck, not until it was too late and her ears were filled with the deafening squeal of brakes, and she felt the impossibly hard impact of the vehicle slamming into her.

47

The nurses had told her she'd drifted in and out
of consciousness for the last twenty-four hours,
since she had been brought to the cottage
hospital; to Florence it had felt no more than a
blink of an eye. But each time she had floated up
from the depths of a deep sleep, another piece of
the jigsaw had slotted into place.

Now she could remember almost everything,
especially leaving the church on Billy's arm and
thinking she was so proud and happy her heart
might burst with love for him. She remembered
too the moment at the Half Moon Hotel that
had stopped her in her tracks — seeing the
woman who looked like her mother through
the window — but what was still a blank was
how she had not seen the truck she ran into.
Apparently it was a military vehicle that had
taken the corner faster than it ought to have, but
the blame lay entirely with Florence; she simply
hadn't been looking where she was going.

Very gingerly, she sat up, knowing that any
sudden movement would result in excruciating
pain, not just to her head, which felt like it was
being repeatedly shaken, but all over her battered
body. The doctor had told her it was nothing
short of a miracle that she had got off as lightly
as she had. Her injuries included two cracked
ribs, more bumps and bruises than could be
counted, and a blow to her head that had

concussed her and given the doctor the most cause for concern. To her mortification, she had been sick several times, once very nearly on poor Billy. What a way to start married life!

She was looking at the empty chair by the side of the bed and wondering if Billy was still around to visit her when he magically appeared through the doorway at the other end of the small ward she shared with five other women, all of whom had visitors with them.

'You're awake,' he said softly when he drew near.

'Yes,' she said.

He sat down, moving the chair closer to the bed. 'How are you feeling?'

'I've felt better.'

'Me too.'

'I'm sorry.'

'Don't apologise.'

'But I spoilt our wedding day.'

He smiled. 'You made it memorable, that's for sure.'

'And I've robbed you of your wedding night,' she said shyly.

He took her hand in his. 'Plenty of chances for that another time,' he said.

Whenever that might be, Florence thought sadly. 'Shouldn't you have returned to barracks by now?'

'Trying to get rid of me, are you?'

'I've been trying to do that ever since we met,' she said with a smile. Then more seriously: 'You mustn't worry about me, I'll be all right when you've gone.'

'But I'm your husband, it's my job to worry about you.'

'No,' she said firmly, 'your job now is to come back to me safe and sound from wherever you're posted.'

'And *your* job,' he said, 'is not to go running after strange women.'

Embarrassed, Florence lowered her gaze from his. 'I was so sure it was my mother,' she said quietly.

Before Billy could respond, Florence saw the familiar and striking figure of Miss Romily enter the ward; she looked marvellously glamorous in her fur coat. Trailing in her wake was a sour-faced nurse who could not have looked more disapproving. 'Be sure to keep the noise down,' she said sternly. 'I won't have my other patients disturbed.'

When the nurse had gone, Miss Romily removed her coat and gloves and rolled her eyes. 'Goodness, she's a bit of a tartar, that one, isn't she? What does she think we're about to do, have a wild party? Now then, how are you feeling, Florence?'

'Foolish,' she said. 'I've put everyone to so much trouble.'

'Nonsense my dear, we're all only too delighted you're going to be up and about before too long.' She pulled out a cake tin from the basket she'd brought with her. 'This is from Mrs Partridge, she thought some cake would be the answer to getting you back on your feet. I'm inclined to agree with her. Everyone else sends their love, including Stanley. But I have to tell you, if you're thinking of making this a habit, throwing yourself in the path of oncoming vehicles, I'd rather you stopped as of now.'

'I promise twice is enough,' Florence said with a small smile.

'I'm very pleased to hear it, and I want you to know that you're not to worry about a thing — you too, Billy. In your absence, Mrs Partridge and I will take the best of care of Florence.'

'I appreciate that, Mrs Temple-Devereux. I really do. Flo means the world to me.' Billy pushed the cuff back on his battledress sleeve and glanced at his watch. 'I have to report for duty in the next two hours, so I should get going. I'd give anything to stay.'

'In that case, I'll step outside and let you two say your goodbyes.'

Florence watched Miss Romily go, and despite her earlier brave words, she suddenly felt overwhelmed with sadness. This was no ordinary parting; Billy was a trained soldier now, ready to be sent somewhere dangerous where his life would be put at risk.

Perched on the edge of the bed, he rested his hands lightly on Florence's shoulders and stared deeply into her eyes. She tried to be cheerful, to make it easier for him. 'Billy Minton,' she said, 'you be sure to stay out of trouble. Do you hear me?'

'The same goes for you. No more crossing roads without looking.'

She blinked. 'I love you so much it hurts.'

'That'll be your broken ribs,' he said with a tight smile. 'And since you owe me a wedding night, you can be damned sure I'll be home quick as a flash to claim my prize.'

* * *

She was crying when Miss Romily came back, and kept on crying even when she held her close. 'There, there, you cry all you want, you'll feel better for it.'

'I'm so sorry,' Florence snivelled when finally she could speak. 'I keep thinking of what that wretched gypsy said about finding love and losing it. What if it comes true with my Billy?'

'Hush! That was all a lot of twaddle; you're not to think about it ever again. What I want you to concentrate on is making a full recovery.'

Her lips quivering again with the threat of more tears, Florence swallowed. 'You're so good to me,' she murmured. 'You always have been, and I really don't deserve it.'

Miss Romily tutted. 'Tommyrot, you deserve all the happiness and kindness the world has to offer. Now,' she said more briskly, 'is there anything I can do for you?'

'Yes, take me home, please.'

48

Four days later, with a sudden drop in temperature and bitterly cold winds sweeping in across East Anglia from the North Sea, snow began to fall.

It was not much more than a fine dusting when Romily set off for the hospital after lunch to fetch Florence home, but by the time they were driving back, they found themselves caught up in a blizzard with visibility down to just a few yards.

Twice now Romily had almost lost sight of the road and come close to skidding off into a ditch. A competent driver behind the wheel of a racing car, she had no fear of extreme conditions, but in this instance, with Florence in the passenger seat next to her, she was taking no chances and was keeping her speed low in Jack's Bentley. She also kept her eye on the petrol gauge, knowing there was no hope of being allowed to purchase any more fuel until next month.

They'd covered less than a mile, crawling along at a snail's pace, when Florence said, 'I haven't apologised for putting you to so much trouble.'

'What trouble is that precisely?'

'Managing without me, what with Annelise and Stanley. I'm sure I could have come home sooner.'

'If you had, I would have banished you to your

387

room to rest.' Romily turned to glance at Florence, sensing there was something the girl wasn't saying. 'What's really bothering you?' she asked. 'And don't deny there's something on your mind; I've known you long enough to know when you're hiding something.'

A few moments passed before Florence answered her. 'I feel such an idiot,' she said quietly, 'spoiling my wedding day by imagining that I'd seen my mother. What was it you called it when I asked you about the fortune-teller, about hearing what we want to hear?'

'Autosuggestion,' said Romily.

'Yes, that was it. I suppose I stupidly wanted my mother to be there to see me marry Billy, so I imagined her in the market square.'

'There's nothing stupid in that, Florence. I felt much the same way when I married Jack. I would have loved for my parents to be there, to know that finally I'd found a man with whom I wanted to spend the rest of my life. You see, my mother and father had the happiest of marriages, and so I know it would have pleased them greatly to see me equally happy.'

She kept to herself how devastated they would have been for her at Jack's death. Instead she took her hand off the steering wheel and patted Florence's leg beneath the woollen blanket. 'So how does it feel to be a married woman, Mrs Minton?' she said in an effort to lighten the mood.

'I'm not sure, if I'm honest,' said Florence. 'It's almost as though I dreamt marrying Billy.'

'It'll take some getting used to,' Romily said,

again keeping to herself the sorrow she felt that she had been robbed of that chance. 'It's a shame you've got off to such a poor start,' she added, 'what with your accident and Billy back in barracks waiting to hear where he'll be posted.'

'That's the worst of it,' murmured Florence, 'not knowing where he'll end up and what kind of danger he'll be in.'

So much for lightening the mood, thought Romily, pulling over towards the hedge in order to give a wide berth to an army convoy passing them on the other side of the road. These days it was a regular occurrence to come across military vehicles on the roads. The same was true of the sky, it was now a common sight to see a squadron of bombers flying overhead.

★ ★ ★

'It's good to be home,' Florence said when Romily finally turned in at the entrance to Island House and came to a stop as near to the front door as she could manage. The driveway and garden were already completely covered in snow, drifts of it forming against the bushes.

'It's good to have you back,' Romily said, stepping out of the car into the full force of the blizzard and hurrying round to the passenger side of the Bentley to help Florence out. 'But under no circumstances are you to do any work until you're quite well. As I told you before, I am laying down the law, and if you defy me, I shall take you straight back to the hospital, where you'll have that sour-faced nurse to deal with.'

'But I'll go mad if I have to spend another day in bed. I'm sure I'm well enough to help around the house now. Just little things. Let me do that at least.'

Romily tutted. 'Absolutely not. Here, lean on my arm, it's treacherous underfoot. And don't think about arguing. You're my responsibility, Florence, as I promised Billy, and I fully intend to take the task of looking after you very seriously.'

They'd made it as far as the snow-covered steps when the front door opened and Mrs Partridge appeared in her apron. 'Well God bless you both, there you are at last!' she exclaimed, ushering them inside. 'I was getting worried when I saw how fast the snow was coming down. They're saying on the wireless that we're in for a real spell of this weather. Come along in now; let's get you both in the warm. I've got some milk warming for hot chocolate and a ginger cake fresh out of the oven. Here, let me take your hat and coat, Florence. Mercy me, you look half starved to death. I'll soon put that right!'

Neither of them had a chance to get a word in as Mrs Partridge took their coats, hats, scarves and gloves, all the while keeping up a steady flow of talk about the weather and the awfulness of butter, sugar, bacon and ham now being rationed. 'And as for that disgraceful Unity Mitford,' she chuntered on, 'well, I'm just appalled. If it had been left to me, and seeing as she's such a big fan of Hitler, I'd have left her there to stew in her miserable traitor's juices.

Pity she didn't make a better job of shooting herself, in my opinion.'

Romily winked at Florence and led the way to the inviting warmth of the kitchen, where they found Hope and the children waiting for them. Annelise immediately slipped down from her chair and greeted Florence with a beaming smile.

'She's been asking after you every day,' Hope said. 'She's missed you terribly.'

'And I've missed her,' Florence said, bending stiffly to give Annelise a hug. 'And you too, Stanley. What have you been up to while I've been away?'

'I've taught Bobby a new trick. D'you wanna see it?' the boy answered eagerly.

'How about you let Florence get comfortable by the range first?' suggested Romily. 'And I'll help Mrs Partridge with making some hot chocolate.'

'There's no need for that, Miss Romily,' interjected Mrs Partridge. 'I can manage. Why don't you sit down as well? Can't have us all bumping around into each other, can we now?'

'Which is your polite way of telling me to get out of your way, isn't it?' said Romily with a laugh.

'Not at all, perish the thought. I just want you to relax in the warm after driving through all that snow; it must have fair taken it out of you. Hope, perhaps you'd like to give me a hand by cutting the cake, please? And go sparingly with it, I used the last of the butter and sugar to make it.'

Both Hope and Romily did as they were

instructed — it never failed to amuse Romily how they all did what Mrs Partridge told them to do — then settled themselves down to enjoy the sight of Bobby standing on his hind legs and mimicking Stanley as he stepped first to the right, then to the left, before turning around on the spot.

'You could take that act on tour,' smiled Florence. 'Stanley and Bobby, the Amazing Duo!'

'It has a certain ring to it,' agreed Romily as boy and dog lapped up the attention and began chasing each other around the table. Annelise, squealing with delight, tried to join in on her little legs.

'That'll do, Stanley,' warned Mrs Partridge above the din. 'Florence needs peace and quiet, not a rowdy hullabaloo from the likes of you. I swear you're becoming more of a nuisance than that wretched Lord Haw-Haw!'

'Sorry,' said Stanley, bringing Bobby instantly to heel with a single click of his fingers. 'Can I go outside now?'

'And what, pray, are you going to do out there, other than catch your death of cold?'

'I promised Annelise I'd build 'er a snowman, she ain't never seen one before.'

They all turned and looked dubiously out of the window at the rapidly falling snow. 'Have something to eat and drink first,' said Mrs Partridge, 'then be sure to wrap up warm, I don't want two invalids in the house to look after. I've got quite enough to do as it is, young man.'

'I'm not an invalid,' protested Florence. 'Far from it.'

Mrs Partridge shook her head and wagged her finger. 'You'll consider yourself one until I say otherwise.'

'I wouldn't fight it,' said Hope with a smile. 'Just accept you're up against a superior foe.'

'Yes,' agreed Romily, 'we've appointed Mrs P as our first line of defence against the Germans.'

Mrs Partridge huffed and puffed and rolled her eyes. 'And there's me just doing my best for you all.'

'And very well you do it too,' said Hope, putting her arm around the woman.

How changed Hope had become, thought Romily; she was so much happier now, and had grown surprisingly attached to Mrs Partridge. Her stay at Island House was now officially extended until such time as London was no longer deemed to be a target for the Luftwaffe. It was anybody's guess when that might be. Every day the situation grew more grave, with Britain gearing up production of war materials. More than two million nineteen- to twenty-seven-year-olds had now been called up, and hundreds of young women were volunteering to be Red Cross nurses or Land Girls. Meanwhile, poor Finland was fighting hard to block the advance of Soviet troops. To her shame, all Romily had managed was a first-aid evening at the church hall. She really had to do more. But what? She had never been this indecisive before, but then she had never had this level of personal commitment before.

After Stanley had gulped down his mug of cocoa and finished cramming cake into his mouth, offering the last bit to Bobby, he went to find his coat, the ever-faithful hound hot on his heels. 'And don't forget your hat and scarf,' Mrs Partridge called out after the pair of them.

'And your gloves!' added Florence. She now had Annelise on her lap, the little girl tracing a small curious finger over her bandaged head.

'Be gentle, won't you, Annelise?' said Hope anxiously.

Florence smiled at the child and stroked her fine blonde hair, then tickled her lightly under her chin. 'You wouldn't hurt me, would you? Not an angel as sweet as you.'

Annelise giggled, and with a butter-wouldn't-melt expression on her face, helped herself to a bite of Florence's cake.

'She's certainly not slow in coming forward these days,' said Hope.

'No bad thing in my book, especially for a girl,' remarked Romily. Then, turning to Mrs Partridge, she said, 'No sign of Mrs Bunch this afternoon?'

'No, she's not been in, and if the snow's bad tomorrow she won't make it then either.'

'Not with her legs,' said Hope and Florence in unison, making them all laugh.

'Oh, before I forget,' said Mrs Partridge, getting up from the table where she was sitting and going over to the dresser, 'a letter came for you in the last post, Florence. Addressed to Mrs Minton it is, with a Bury St Edmunds postmark, and if I'm not mistaken, it's your Billy's handwriting. And there's one for you too, madam.'

Just as Mrs Partridge handed Florence her letter, the telephone rang and Romily went to answer it. It was Allegra.

★   ★   ★

Allegra replaced the telephone receiver in its cradle and tried not to give in to the feeling that she was an utter failure. Could she get nothing right? Why did everything she attempt turn into such a mess? What sort of mother was she going to be? A mother who couldn't even take care of herself without asking for help!

The trouble had started when she'd woken in the night to the sound of something scratching and pattering about in the attic above her bedroom. *Rats!* Thanks to Arthur letting one loose in her bedroom when they'd been children, she was terrified of them. She'd leapt out of bed and, dragging the eiderdown with her, fled downstairs, stumbling on one of the steps and landing with a heavy thud at the bottom. When she'd caught her breath and picked herself up, praying in earnest that she hadn't harmed the baby, she'd made herself comfortable on the sofa. But sleep had eluded her. Every time she had been close to nodding off, she'd imagined hundreds of rats swarming down the stairs from the attic seeking her out. She'd become so hysterical with fear, she'd started to cry.

In the cool light of day, and after sleeping for no more than an hour or so and waking stiff with cold, she could see that she had overreacted, but with the dawn had come the realisation that in falling on the stairs she'd hurt her back, and the slightest movement sent pain shooting down her right leg.

She'd managed to get hold of Dr Garland, but he hadn't been able to come out to see her until the afternoon, the snow delaying him on his rounds. His diagnosis was that once again she needed bed rest and should not be on her own. He'd made light of her teary belief that the attic had been invaded by an army of rats, telling her that it was more likely to be a couple of tiny field mice in search of shelter from the icy cold. Not a word of which she'd believed; two small mice had not created the awful noise she'd heard.

She'd hated telephoning Romily to ask for help, but Dr Garland had insisted that if she didn't make the call, he would do it for her. 'Or would you rather I whisked you off to hospital?' he'd said.

Neither was her preferred option, but for the sake of the baby, she knew she had to be sensible. She knew also that it would be what Elijah would want for her. She had received a letter from him this morning, the very sort of letter she had dreaded. He was at last on the move. He couldn't say where exactly, but it was to join the British Expeditionary Force in either France or Belgium. *At last me, Billy and Tommy will be doing what we signed up for,* he'd written. *There isn't one of us here who isn't ready. Keep me in your thoughts, Allegra, just as you and the baby will be constantly in mine.*

Wincing with every step, and listening out for the sound of rats overhead, Allegra set about packing a case to take with her to Island House. She placed Elijah's letter, along with his previous ones, carefully within the pages of a bible he had given her. It had belonged to him as a boy, a present from his grandfather, even though he hadn't been able to read it at the time.

The suitcase closed, she left it on the bed and cautiously made her way downstairs to wait for Romily to arrive. It seemed in that moment that she would forever be destined to return to Island House.

49

The snow was coming down so heavily now, the wipers were making a poor job of keeping the windscreen clear. What worried Romily more was that the petrol tank of the Bentley was nearly empty. Very helpfully, the twin SU carburettors ticked a warning about a mile before the car would run completely dry — the ticking had sounded the moment she'd turned out of the drive.

She had only ever run foul of an empty fuel tank once before, and that had been in France with Jack. They'd taken the Bentley across the Channel on the ferry and spent the weekend in Paris at the Ritz. They'd had the most glorious time staying in a suite overlooking the Place Vendome, surfacing from it only when hunger drove them downstairs to the restaurant, that and the desire for a cocktail. It had been a perfect few days, and even running out of petrol and grinding to a halt some two miles from the ferry port had not put a dampener on their spirits. They'd hitched a ride on the back of a farm truck to the nearest garage, sharing the straw-strewn space with a couple of piglets, one of which, with no encouragement, had settled itself on Romily's lap. Jack had thought it the funniest sight and had offered the driver of the truck an extravagant fifty francs to buy the piglet from him. The man had looked at the proffered money, then at the piglet, and shaken his head. 'Non merci, monsieur.' He'd given no reason for refusing the deal, but Jack had slipped a wad of franc notes into his hand anyway and thanked him for his trouble. 'What on earth would you have done with the poor little piglet if the man had agreed to sell it to you?' Romily had asked. 'Given it straight back to him, of course,' Jack had replied.

She had known that day that she loved Jack, that she loved his impetuous nature, which in so many ways mirrored her own.

A furious loud blaring of a horn roused her from the poignant memory. It was followed by a thundering great clunk as metal met metal, and Romily's head hit the windscreen with an impact that rocked her violently backwards in her seat. Her hands flew up from the steering wheel, and the car zigzagged over the snow-covered road before coming to an inelegant stop.

★ ★ ★

'Are you all right?'

Disorientated and feeling as though every ounce of air had been punched out of her, Romily opened her eyes and found herself staring into the face of an unknown man. A man dressed in a smart coat that was unbuttoned and revealed the blue of an RAF uniform beneath.

'I'm fine,' she said, thoroughly embarrassed at causing an accident, knowing that her mind had not been where it ought to have been. 'Is your car very badly damaged?'

'Oh don't give that a second thought. It's not mine; it's a staff car and tough as old boots. I'm afraid your beautiful Bentley has come off worse. I tried to avoid colliding with you, but you came straight at me. You must have skidded on the ice. Come on, let's get you out before the car slides any further down the bank and you vanish without trace into the depths of the snowstorm. I've never seen a blizzard quite like this before. There you go, take my arm. That's it, I've got you.'

'There's really no need,' she replied, vexed that he was treating her like a child. 'As I said, I'm perfectly all right.' No sooner were the words out than a gust of wind blew what felt like an entire snowdrift into her face, and she missed her footing and all but tumbled into the stranger's arms. 'I'm sorry,' she muttered, her tone anything but apologetic, almost as if she held him responsible for her predicament.

'Best hang on to me,' he asserted. 'Don't want you coming to any more grief. If you'll take my advice, you'll see a doctor pronto; you've given your noggin quite a bash.'

Mention of a doctor made Romily remember the reason for her being in the car in the first place. *Allegra!* She had been on her way to fetch the girl back to Island House. She turned to look at the Bentley, to see if it would be possible to drive it to Winter Cottage, but she could see from the precarious angle it rested at that it was going to take some help to get it going again. She peered through the blizzard to where the stranger's vehicle stood. 'Do you think you could give me a tow?' she shouted above the blast of another gust of wind. 'Only I need to be somewhere.'

The man brushed at the snow that was settling on his face, particularly his eyebrows and moustache. 'I'd advise you to go straight home,' he said, 'via a doctor. I'd be happy to drive you. Really, if we stand here a second longer arguing, we'll both end up dead from the cold.' He took her by the arm, his grip sufficiently firm to dissuade her from resisting. 'Hop in,' he said, 'and I'll take you where you need to be, if you're sure that's what you should do.'

'It is,' she said.

Once they were out of the howling wind and snow, and he'd turned the key in the ignition, he introduced himself. 'Anthony, known to my friends as Tony. Once I've turned us around to head in the direction you were going, you'll need to give me further instructions.'

'How well do you know the roads around here?' she asked.

'Not very well; I only arrived a few days ago. I'm based at the airfield over at Larkshall. Do you know it?'

'Of course. We're all very well acquainted with the squadrons of Wellington bombers flying over us. You'll need to take the next right.'

He dropped a gear and took the turning slowly. 'And am I going to have the pleasure of knowing your name?'

'Romily,' she said. 'Romily Temple-Devereux.'

'And is there a Mr Temple-Devereux?'

She paused, taken aback at the directness of

his question. 'No,' she said at length, and with no wish to elaborate further to a stranger. Even a stranger who had come to her rescue. 'Next left,' she said, 'then follow the road. Winter Cottage is on the right, look out for a green gate.'

'Which will probably be completely white now, if not buried deep beneath a snowdrift,' he said with a crunch of gears before finding the right one. 'Sorry I can't provide you with a smoother drive. This car might be as tough as old boots, but it's also a frightful old crock. You'd think we'd have better staff cars available to us, wouldn't you?'

'Would I be right in thinking you're a pilot?' she asked, although she knew that he could not be anything else. She had met enough RAF pilots over the years to recognise one a mile off — without exception they were all extremely charming, with a jovial bravado that came with the uniform.

'Guilty as charged,' he said. 'Wing Commander Tony Abbott, to be exact. By the way, sorry if I offended you in some way with my frankness; I'm always being told I'm overly familiar. Especially around women. Comes from growing up with an immensely bossy older sister and two bossier-still aunts. And that's another character trait of mine, I talk far too much.'

He looked too young to be a commanding officer, she thought, far too young. When she didn't say anything, he turned to look at her. 'I've annoyed you, haven't I? I'm sorry for that.'

'Eyes on the road, please. One accident in a day is quite enough for me.'

He laughed. 'Now how on earth am I going to get you to like me, I wonder?'

'Do I need to?'

'Well, it would be a great disappointment on my part if you didn't. Any particular reason why we can't be friends?'

Off the top of her head she could think of any number of reasons. 'What makes you think you'd like to be friends with me?' she said.

'Because' — he gave her a quick sideways glance — 'I'd rather have you on my side than against me. I think you'd make a formidable adversary.

Something about the way he looked at her and the tone of his voice made her laugh unexpectedly. It made her realise also that she had thus far behaved appallingly. She blamed it on her bruised ego, that she of all people had caused an accident.

'That's better,' he said. 'Now I feel on much firmer ground with you, and almost glad you ran into me.'

'I'm sorry,' she said. 'I've been shockingly rude to you and you've gone to all this trouble on my behalf.'

'No trouble at all. Least anyone would do in the circumstances.'

'You're very kind, and I don't deserve for you to say yes, but I wonder if I could ask another favour of you. You see, I was on my way to collect someone and take her home with me. She's expecting a baby in a couple of months and so there's no way we can trudge through the snow to — '

'Consider it done,' he cut in. 'I'm happy to play the part of knight in shining armour.'

She suspected that was a role to which he could more than live up to if given the chance. 'We're here now,' she said, leaning forward and pointing out of the windscreen. 'That's Winter Cottage on the right.' The thatched roof of the house was hidden by a thick layer of snow.

'How very aptly named,' he said as with another crash of gears he slowed his speed and came to a juddering stop in front of the small gate.

She pushed the passenger door open and was instantly met with a blast of icy wind and snow. 'I'll be back in a jiffy,' she said.

'Shall I come with you?'

'That's all right, no need for you to get cold again. You'll want to turn the car around so we can go in the direction we've just come.'

'Right you are.'

With great care, Romily negotiated the path, which was lost beneath a good six inches of snow, crunching it underfoot with each cautious step of her sturdy gumboots. Before she'd made it to the front door it opened and Allegra stood there in her coat. 'I was getting worried,' she said. 'I telephoned again and Hope said you'd left ages ago. Oh, what have you done to your head? You have a bump the size of an egg on it.'

'I'm sorry, I had an accident on the way and a stranger came to my aid.' Romily pointed back towards the car, which was now in the process of being manoeuvred by its driver. 'Have you got everything you need?'

Allegra indicated the case at her side. 'I think so.'

Romily reached for it. 'Good,' she said. 'Lock up and then let me help you to the car. It's lethal underfoot.'

Despite her instruction, Wing Commander Anthony Abbott had now stepped out of the car and was coming towards them to help. If truth be told, Romily would have been disappointed in him if he hadn't, and she smiled at him gratefully as between them they assisted Allegra to the car. Once they were under way and Romily had given directions to Island House, she introduced their good Samaritan to Allegra. 'We're very much in your debt,' she then went on to say. 'You must let us repay you for your kindness.'

'Not necessary. Not necessary at all. Only too glad to be of service.'

'At least stop for a hot drink when you drop us off.'

'I'd like nothing better, but I ought to get back to Larkshall. Another time maybe, if the invitation is open-ended. And if I'm passing this way again.'

★ ★ ★

'If I didn't know better, I'd say that man has taken a fancy to you,' remarked Allegra after they'd waved him goodbye from the front door of Island House.

'Don't be ridiculous,' said Romily. 'The snow's addled your mind. He was merely being chivalrous.'

405

Allegra snorted. 'Take it from me, he'll just happen to be passing here again before the week is out.'

50

It was a bitterly cold afternoon two days later, with the village deep in snow and more on the way, when Hope answered the door to Wing Commander Anthony Abbott.

She had heard a much-embellished account of the wing commander from Allegra, who, knowing how thoroughly it was exasperating Romily, had inflated her description with each telling of the tale to the point that when the unknown man on the doorstep introduced himself, Hope was almost disappointed, having half expected a combination of Rudolph Valentino and Errol Flynn to come calling.

Nonetheless, while Allegra might have exaggerated matters, the man staring back at Hope was certainly not without charm or looks. He was tall and slim, with a head of thick dark hair swept back from a broad forehead. He had an open and engaging face, but it was difficult to pin an exact age on him; his apparent youth seemed to contradict his being a commanding officer. Yet what struck Hope most was his hands; they were artistic hands; with long slender fingers and clean nails cut short.

'Come in,' she said. 'I'm sure my stepmother will be delighted to see you. My cousin also.' She couldn't resist adding, 'Presumably you were just passing?'

He hesitated, but only for a fraction of a

second. 'Well, yes,' he said, 'that's right. I thought I'd call in and check all was well.'

'How kind of you,' she said. She took his cap and coat and hung them on the stand, then led him through to the drawing room.

'Look who's here, Romily,' she announced gaily.

Romily turned around from her desk, where she was working at her typewriter, a distracted look on her face.

'I do hope I'm not intruding,' their visitor said, 'only I was just — '

'He was just passing,' Hope finished off for him, keeping her expression deadpan as Romily flashed her a look of irritation.

'I thought I'd call in to see if you'd managed to have your car rescued,' he said.

'That was very thoughtful of you,' said Romily, rising from her seat. 'The garage in the village collected it this morning and will have it for a while to carry out the repairs. I still feel incredibly foolish about the accident and putting you to so much trouble; I'm normally such a careful driver.'

'My stepmother's not being wholly honest with you,' said Hope. 'She's an expert behind the wheel of a car; she's raced at Brooklands and in Europe. She's quite the daredevil champion.'

Romily tutted. 'Really, Hope, now the wing commander is going to think I go tearing about the lanes in an altogether reckless manner.'

'Please,' he said, 'can we dispense with the formality? Just call me Tony. And perhaps you'd tell me about your racing exploits; I'm beginning to see you in a whole new light.'

'Why, did you have me down as a quiet little countrywoman who sat at home twiddling her thumbs?'

He laughed. 'Far from it.'

'Would you like a cup of tea?' asked Hope, surprised that Romily hadn't yet offered.

'Thank you,' he said, 'so long as I'm not putting you to any trouble.'

'I'm sure our hospitality can run to providing a cup of tea, can't it, Romily?' said Hope.

'Of course,' replied Romily with a brittle smile. 'But be careful not to wake Mrs Partridge; it's her time for a nap.'

★ ★ ★

In the kitchen, Hope tiptoed round Mrs Partridge, who was indeed having her customary mid-afternoon nap. On the hearthrug at her feet Bobby was curled up fast asleep and snoring loudly. Hope took a moment to study the pair of them — it would make an ideal little vignette to go in the children's book she was writing. This latest book, she had told her publisher, apart from being a totally new departure for her, was a heart-warming story of a young evacuee called Freddie finding happiness in the countryside through the companionship of Ragsy, a plucky mutt who rarely left his side. Hope was beginning to foresee all manner of adventures in which the two could become involved. Not that she had said this to her publisher, but in many ways the book had its roots in her own story of rediscovering happiness here at Island House.

As she filled the kettle at the sink, she looked out of the window. There, bundled up in their thick overcoats and hats, scarves and gloves, were Allegra, her back now recovered from slipping on the stairs at Winter Cottage, and Florence, standing either side of the impressive snowman Stanley had built, They were watching Stanley pull Annelise along on the sledge he had found in one of the outhouses — it was the old sledge Hope and Kit had played on as children.

One winter, when the lily pond had frozen over, they had ventured onto the icy surface to play with the sledge, Kit declaring it would be quite safe and much more fun, as the ice would send them skidding along at top speed. From the drawing-room window their father had seen what they were up to and had run outside and ordered them inside the house, clipping them both around the ear. He'd been livid and yelled at them until he was red in the face and his voice quite hoarse. Sent to their rooms, they were banned from playing in the garden until the snow and ice had thawed. At the time Hope and Kit had seen it as another example of tyrannical unfairness from their father, his determination always to spoil their fun.

Now, as Annelise's guardian, Hope saw things in a different light. Her father's angry reaction had been fuelled by fear — fear at what might have happened had the treacherous ice cracked. And of course, Kit had not been the healthiest of children, always catching colds, which went straight to his chest and confined him to bed for prolonged periods. Their father had merely acted with their best interests at heart, Hope now understood.

She also understood that she had been repeating the pattern of mistakes her father had made. It seemed as clear as daylight to her now that they had both, in the aftermath of their grief, turned themselves into strangers, to themselves and to those around them. A short while ago she would never have believed that she had something like that in common with her father, but she saw now that they had both allowed heartache to dictate their lives. Having Annelise in her care had made Hope realise just how fierce was the instinctive urge to protect a child, and by any means. She had also realised how challenging it was to be a parent on one's own, and that for her father that must have been doubly difficult. Hand in hand with that new knowledge came the understanding that so many of her father's apparently unfair and dogmatic actions had been carried out through nothing more than his wanting to keep his family safe.

She reflected on this now as she considered the stern lecture she had given Stanley about not going anywhere near the lily pond should it freeze over. 'And heaven help you if you go near it with Annelise!' she had warned him, her finger wagging just inches from his nose.

The memory of how recklessly she and Kit had put themselves in danger sledging across the ice reminded Hope that she hadn't replied to Kit's latest letter. He sounded like he was having the time of his life in Canada. With the clear sense of purpose he now had, she could detect in him the change that he'd plainly been in search of. She just hoped that when he returned to Europe to enter the fray, he wouldn't be too full of brio. There was a fine line between bravery and sheer stupidity.

Hope had thought she was showing bravery of a different sort when she had stubbornly insisted on returning to London, but now she could recognise how foolish it had been. Accepting Romily's invitation to regard Island House as her home for as long as she and Annelise needed it had been the answer all along. Here she could provide the child with a true sense of home and all the love, care and fun she deserved. In contrast, in London, Hope had woken every day with the feeling she was failing her charge, failing Otto and Sabine too.

A peal of laughter from outside broke into her thoughts, and looking out of the window again, she saw Allegra and Florence having snowballs thrown at them by Stanley and Annelise, the four of them thoroughly enjoying themselves. It was good to see Allegra and Florence laughing together so happily, especially when they must both be so concerned about their husbands.

The kettle came to the boil and Hope took it off the hob quickly before its whistle woke Mrs Partridge. She filled the teapot and set it on the tray, then went to the pantry to fetch the cake tin, which Mrs Partridge practically kept under lock and key now that sugar and butter had become so precious.

* * *

In the drawing room, Romily wondered what on earth was keeping Hope. How long did it take to rustle up a cup of tea? She felt stifled by all this absurd small talk of the weather. Another minute of agreeing with their guest that it was difficult to remember a winter like it and she wouldn't be responsible for her actions.

All of which was quite out of character for her. She was never fazed by anyone or anything; it had always been a trait she was proud of. Oh yes, throw anything at Romily Temple and she could not only catch it but throw it back clean over the boundary. But here she was at a loss to know how to deal with the simplest of things, that of conversing with a pleasant enough man who had done nothing wrong other than commit the crime of being overly familiar while rescuing her in her hour of need. And as for him just passing by, did he take her for a fool?

Their small talk having now run aground, she went over to the fireplace to add more logs to the grate. It was time, she decided, to take matters by the scruff of the neck and clarify her position before this fellow made an ass of himself. 'I didn't explain things entirely clearly the other day, Mr Abbott,' she began.

'Please,' he interrupted her, 'call me Tony.'

'Tony,' she said, obliging him politely. 'As I was saying, the other day I — '

'There's no need for you to apologise again. I understand completely. Your feathers were

413

ruffled by the accident and not surprisingly you weren't yourself.'

She spun round to face him. 'Please don't patronise me as though I'm so feeble I don't know my own mind.'

He looked back at her, startled. 'Seeing you with that poker in your hand, I shouldn't dream of it. You look as fierce as Boadicea!' He grinned. 'But a lot more beautiful.'

She pursed her lips, returned the poker to its holder next to the log basket, then faced him squarely again. 'I just want you to know that I was recently widowed, which I'm sure you can appreciate makes a remark like that last one of yours wholly inappropriate.'

He stared at her, his eyes wide, and then rose slowly to his feet. 'I'm most terribly sorry. I . . . I had no idea. I asked if you had a husband . . . and you . . . ' His voice, full of contrition, fell away.

'I answered your question honestly,' she said, 'and saw no reason to have to explain myself further to a stranger.'

'I wish you had. I feel awful now, blundering on the way I have. What a bumptious oaf you must consider me.'

As his gaze moved from her face to her left hand, she raised it to show the rings Jack had given her. 'I was wearing gloves the other day,' she said, as if that explained everything.

He groaned. 'Oh Lord, I should have noticed while we were talking with such painful dreariness about the weather just now. In my defence, I was too bound up with the thought of how I was ever going to make you like me.' He sighed. 'I think we can safely say that I've thoroughly cooked my goose in that respect. Should I leave now before I make things any worse?'

At the sight of his obvious discomfort, and relieved that he now knew where he stood, she offered a small conciliatory smile. 'There's no need for that. You deserve a cup of tea at the very least. I'll go and see where Hope has got to with it.'

Just as she was at the door, it opened and Hope came in with a tray. Their guest was immediately across the room offering to take it from her. It was when he was looking for a place to put it down that he said, 'Oh my goodness, are you Romily Temple, the author?' His gaze had been caught by a US copy of her latest book, which her American publisher had sent her that morning.

'I am,' she said, making space for the tray on the table between the two sofas.

'Have you read any of her novels?' asked Hope.

'I certainly have,' he said, picking up the book to take a closer look at the jacket, which was a little too lurid for Romily's taste. 'And now I feel even more of a fool.'

'Don't give it another thought,' Romily said, pouring the tea. 'Milk? Sugar?'

'Neither, thank you, I take it black.'

'We'll all be doing that before too long if milk is rationed the same as sugar,' said Hope. 'So where had you been in order to be passing us?' she asked.

If Romily didn't know better, she'd swear

Hope had asked the question out of sheer devilment, which was much more Allegra's style. 'Hope, I really don't think we should be so inquisitive,' she said.

'That's all right,' Tony said, 'I'd been to the Athenaeum Club in Bury St Edmunds. Do you know it?'

Hope nodded and Romily said, 'I know of it, it's near the Angel Hotel, isn't it?'

'That's right. I went to have a look at the abbey and cathedral and afterwards called in for some lunch. They provide a jolly good feed there for servicemen and women.'

'Where's home for you, then?' asked Romily, passing him his cup.

'I'm from nowhere really. My parents moved to Singapore when I was a baby, and then when I was twelve they sent me to school in England, along with my sister. Our holidays were spent mostly with our two aunts in a village just outside Oxford. I joined the RAF to fulfil a boyhood dream to learn to fly; I've been very much on the move ever since. I have a small flat in London as a base, but since just before war was declared I've been renting it to a couple of refugees from Austria. So for now RAF Larkshall is my home.'

'Are your parents still in Singapore?' asked Hope.

'No. My father died some years ago and my mother remarried and lives in Canada now. My sister and I haven't seen her in quite a while . . . ' He paused. 'She was a lot younger than our father and now that she has a new life and a new family, we've drifted apart, you could say.'

'Families are good at doing that,' said Hope. Then: 'My brother's in Canada at the moment. He was too impatient to settle for being a reservist in the RAF, and so took matters into his own hands and is learning to fly in Winnipeg. From all that we hear, he's having a ball.'

Romily was just about to offer some cake when the door flew open with a crash and Stanley, Annelise and Bobby came barrelling in with Allegra following behind. They were all in their stockinged feet, their faces flushed from being outside in the cold.

'Sorry,' Allegra apologised, 'I didn't know you had company, Romily. Oh, it's you again!' she said brightly when their guest got to his feet. She smirked at Romily, and Romily flashed her a warning look in return.

'Hello,' Tony said politely. 'How nice to see you again. And who do we have here?' he asked, bending down to stroke Bobby's head.

'He's mine, mister,' piped up Stanley, 'and his name's Bobby.'

'And who might you be?'

'I'm Stanley, and this is Annelise.'

'Well, I'm very happy to meet you all. My name's Tony.'

'Are you a pilot, mister?' asked Stanley, taking in the uniform. 'Do you fly them Wellington bombers.'

'Indeed I do.'

'Our guest is a commanding officer, Stanley,' explained Romily.

'Does that make you important?'

417

He laughed. 'Chance would be a fine thing!'

'I wish I could be a pilot.'

Tony smiled. 'Who knows, maybe one day when you're old enough you could be one. No reason why not if you work hard enough at school. Do you like school?'

Stanley nodded. 'I do now. I didn't in London.' He shrugged. 'I didn't go much. Me mum weren't keen on it.'

'Well take it from me, stick to the lessons and you'll go far.'

'Stanley,' said Romily, approving greatly of Tony's encouraging attitude, 'do you think you could fetch another cup and saucer and a plate for Allegra, and if you'd like some cake, bring some plates for you and Annelise.'

When he'd scooted off at his usual breakneck speed, banging the door shut after him, Romily explained to their guest that Stanley was their evacuee.

'I guessed as much,' he said.

'I can't ever see him going home,' said Allegra, warming herself in front of the fire. 'His mother's all but forgotten about him; she hasn't been to see him once, she never writes.'

'He's lucky to have found such a welcoming home here then,' said Tony. 'Is Annelise your daughter?' he asked Hope as the little girl climbed up onto the sofa where she was sitting.

'I'm her guardian,' Hope said. 'She's the daughter of my German sister-in-law who lives in Cologne and is married to a Jew. They thought she would be safer with me here in England.'

Tony shook his head. 'The world's turned into

418

a very evil place,' he said quietly, staring sadly at Annelise. 'God knows how it's all going to end.'

It was, Romily noted, as she observed their guest over the rim of her teacup, the first time he had shown a more mature and serious side to his personality.

51

Dearest Flo,

I've been here for two weeks now and never known such cold. It's freezing, proper brass-monkey weather. Some of the lads who've been here since the autumn reckon the cold is better than all the rain and mud they had to cope with when they first arrived. They also reckon we've got off lightly because they did most of the digging that had to be done. The joke is when they're back in Civvy Street, they'll be the best navvies going!

I enjoyed reading your last letter; it lifted my spirits a treat. It's a great weight off my mind knowing you're so much better now and have been well looked after. You landed on your feet when you started work with Mrs Temple-Devereux; she's a good sort.

Tommy is becoming quite the joker amongst the pack here and regularly has me and Elijah in fits, along with all the other lads. Turns out he has a good ear for mimicking people and can do our sergeant to a T. Everyone says he should go on the stage when the war is over. Funny that all

420

these years I've known him, he's never shown this talent before. Just goes to show, you never really know a person, or yourself.

Thanks ever so for knitting the socks for me; they do a fine job of keeping the cold out. If you have time, I wouldn't say no to some gloves as well.

I miss you so much more than I can put down on paper, Flo. I think of you every day, just as I always have since the first day we met. I miss your smiling face — and your tough scolding one too!

With all my love,
Billy X

★   ★   ★

3rd February, 1940

My dearest Allegra,

Thank you for your letter and the photograph you included of us on our wedding day. I still can't believe that we're actually married, that you agreed to be my wife. Sometimes when I wake in the night and think I imagined it, I look at that photograph and tell myself it really did happen. It's my most treasured possession and I keep it safe in the pages of a small notebook in my pocket at all times.

I'm glad you accepted Mrs Devereux-Temple's invitation to stay on at Island

House during the cold weather while you wait for the baby to come. You don't know what peace of mind that brings me. I expect it was only mice in the roof, and not rats as you thought, but maybe get old George Wiggins in to deal with them. Mrs Bunch will know his address.

It's not so bad here. Some of us have been billeted on a farm and we actually sleep in an old barn, which sounds worse than it is. The farmer's wife made us a great rabbit stew the other day. It tasted better than anything I've eaten in a long time.

We have snow just like you; everywhere is covered with it. I don't think I've ever seen so much. I wear three pairs of socks at night — don't suppose you could knit me some, could you?

Last night we went on a march on ice-covered roads. One lad slipped and it wasn't until we got back to our barn and he took off his boot that we realised he'd broken his ankle. God knows how he marched on it.

Please don't worry about me, I'm fine. The nearest to danger I've come is laughing to death over some of Tommy's antics when he's mimicking our sergeant, who has the strongest Yorkshire accent you've ever heard.

Write soon and tell me all your news. And don't forget, a pair of socks would be very welcome!

Longing to hear from you,
Your loving husband, Elijah

PS I hope that RAF bloke who you say keeps calling in isn't making a nuisance of himself. And yes, I don't mind admitting I'm jealous that he gets to see you and I don't!

★ ★ ★

25th February, 1940

Dear Romily,

I said I'd do it and I have — I'm now a member of the women's section of the Air Transport Auxiliary, a second officer no less! I had to do a flight test in Whitchurch in a Gypsy Moth, which, without being big-headed, was no test at all. We're a small band of determined women and I feel hugely honoured to be one of the group.

You should see the look of disgust on some of the faces of our male colleagues when they encounter us — they're the sort who think we should be at home cooking dinner for our husbands. Well, in the absence of a husband, I'd much rather be doing what I am. Maybe even if I had a husband, I'd sooner be doing this! I should say that not all of our male colleagues treat us this way; some are all for us.

For now our job is to help ferry training

planes — Gypsy Moths — from the de Havilland factory at Hatfield to RAF training bases in Scotland and northern England, but I suspect our remit may well change in the coming months.

On a perfectly superficial note, I have to say I think I look rather good in my uniform, which has a blue service tunic, a pleated skirt and slacks (I much prefer wearing the latter!), black shoes (serviceable rather than elegant!), a black tie and a blue shirt. Our flying suits have a quilted liner and the sheepskin leather flying jacket is jolly useful when flying in the freezing cold, as are the fleece-lined flying boots.

It's tiring work, but I can honestly say it's the most satisfying thing I've ever done. So come on, Romily, hurry up and finish your latest novel and then apply to the ATA. You won't regret it, I promise you.

All my love,
Sarah

52

On a lovely mild day nearly two months after her wedding, and fully recovered from her accident, Florence turned out of the drive and set off down the lane towards the village. As she walked along in the March sunshine, swinging the basket in her hand, all around her birds sang and sparrows cheeped happily, fluttering busily in and out of the hedgerow, where fat buds were swelling. Spring was in the air and it couldn't come a day too soon.

Winter had dragged on for far too long; it had made them all restless for change. Allegra was particularly restless, and very irritable with it. Florence didn't blame her; being the size she was must be awful. She was having trouble sleeping and Florence often heard her going downstairs in the night to make herself a drink. It worried her, Allegra taking the stairs in the dark on her own, and many a time she forced herself to stay awake until she heard the sound of her lumbering footstep on the stairs returning to bed.

After waving to old Ted Manners from Dawson's Dairy as he passed by with the milk cart, his horse raising his head in alarm as a noisy oncoming military truck approached, Florence made for the main street. Ted's brother

Bob had recently started work in the garden for Miss Romily. When he'd applied for the job to replace Elijah for the duration of the war, he had freely admitted that though he might lack youthful energy, he more than made up for it in experience and knowledge. A small, wiry man with bandy legs and a bushy beard and protruding ears, he reminded Florence of a gnarled old leprechaun.

As she crossed the main street, observing the shoppers and tradesfolk going about their business, Florence thought, not for the first time, how few young men were left in the village. It was why Miss Romily had taken on Bob Manners; there simply had not been the luxury of choice. Most of the lads who were left were too young to be trusted to tie their own shoelaces, never mind take charge of a large and beautiful garden.

How many more boys would they lose? Florence pondered sadly. How many more mothers and fathers, wives and girlfriends were going to be left to fret? And for what? Still nothing had really happened, and what had gone on seemed too far away to be of real interest. Many people, believing they'd been conned by the government and that they'd never been in any danger, had begun to flout the blackout, letting lights shine through badly covered windows. Gas masks weren't being carried like they once had been either; even Florence had forgotten hers today. Mrs Partridge would give her hell when she got back; she was a stickler for keeping to the rules.

A thunderous roar that rumbled right through to the pit of her stomach had Florence looking skywards. The source of the noise came from the east: a squadron of Wellington bombers, presumably from over the North Sea. When the shadow of their formation fell across her, she gave an involuntary shiver, out of awe mostly. The sight of such strength and power never failed to stir her, to make her feel proud of the brave men up there flying those incredible machines. Who knew, she thought, one of those pilots could be Wing Commander Anthony Abbott.

In the weeks that had followed his first visit to Island House, the wing commander had become a regular caller, always bringing with him a present of some sort, whether it was flowers, a pat of rationed butter, a box of chocolates, a book about aircraft for Stanley or a toy for Annelise. During one of his visits he'd rolled up his sleeves and unblocked the sink in the kitchen for Mrs Partridge. From then on she wouldn't have a word said against him. Prior to that day, she had been hugely suspicious of his visits. 'He's got his eye on a wealthy widow, that man, mark my words.'

Florence had thought the same thing initially, but seeing how good he was with the children, especially Stanley, she had decided he simply enjoyed time away from the airfield, and being part of a family, such as it was at Island House.

As for her own family, or more specifically her mother, Florence was determined to push her from her mind; her subconscious mind too. She wasn't a child in need of a mother; she was a married woman with a husband to care for. A husband who she loved with all her heart, and who loved her.

She passed along Market Lane and turned right for the wool shop. Every spare minute she had was spent knitting, and not just for Billy. At Miss Romily's suggestion they regularly all sat together in the kitchen of an evening knitting socks, gloves, scarves and balaclavas for the troops. Allegra had surprised them all by being the most proficient; apparently she'd been taught to knit in the orphanage as a young child. She had made some beautiful bonnets, bootees and matinee jackets for her baby, which was due in a matter of weeks. Last night Florence had finished knitting a pullover for Stanley as a surprise present for his tenth birthday today.

A fresh batch of wool bought, Florence pressed on towards Minton's Bakery. Her mother-in-law's frosty attitude towards her had not improved, but George Minton was always friendly.

To her disappointment, George wasn't behind the counter when she pushed open the door. Unusually, there wasn't a queue, and after finishing organising the trays of buns in the window, taking forever over doing so, Ruby Minton finally turned to face Florence as if she were a stranger.

'Hello,' said Florence as cheerfully as she could manage. 'It's a lovely day, isn't it? It really feels like spring is on the way now.'

'It'll be a lovely day when Billy comes home,' Ruby said coldly. 'And not before.'

The way Ruby went on, anyone would think

she held Florence personally responsible for her son joining the Suffolk Regiment. As though she'd wanted him to go! It didn't matter what Florence said to her mother-in-law, it would always be met with a caustic response. She was quite used to it now and had learnt the knack of not reacting. If she did ever feel herself rising to one of Ruby's unpleasant remarks, she thought of the fruit trees planted in the Mintons' back garden, each one commemorating the loss of an unborn child. Who was to say Florence herself wouldn't turn into a sad and bitter woman if she ever suffered the same amount of heartache?

'Have you heard from Billy this week?' she asked. 'I had a letter from him only yesterday. He sounded very . . . ' She broke off, realising her mistake. If Billy had written to his wife in preference to his mother, Ruby would be furious, especially as it might look as though Florence were crowing about it.

But her mother-in-law appeared not to hear her. Instead she said, 'I've been thinking about your marriage to my Billy.'

'Oh yes,' said Florence warily.

'It isn't a proper legal marriage, is it?' Ruby said, pushing her hands into the pockets of her apron. 'Because you never consummated it, did you, what with being in hospital the night of the wedding? Which means Billy could divorce you if he had any sense.'

The sheer nastiness of the woman's words was too much; she had gone too far this time. 'Mrs Minton,' Florence said, incensed — fruit trees and lost babies be damned! — 'your pathetic

429

attempts to split Billy and me up won't work. Billy loves me and I love him, and nothing will part us. Not even your vile tongue. Now if you'll get on and serve me, I'll be on my way. I'll have a large sandwich tin and a crusty white. Thank you.'

Five minutes later, she was back out on the street and making her way at speed across the cobbled, her anger increasing with every step. By the time she let herself in at the back door of Island House, she was thoroughly steamed up. She plonked the shopping basket down on the table and shook off her coat. Mrs Partridge looked up from the pastry she was rolling at the other end of the table. 'What's got into you?' she asked.

'Ruby ruddy Minton!' Florence snapped. 'That's what! She only went and said my marriage isn't real because . . . because Billy and I didn't . . . well . . . you know, because I was in hospital the night of our wedding. Which means in her eyes, Billy could divorce me.'

Mrs Partridge brought the rolling pin down on the table with a sharp bang. 'What a wicked old bat she is! Will you tell Billy?'

'No! He's got more important things to think about than his poisonous mother.' Florence sighed. 'Why does she hate me so much?'

'It's not you, love. That woman would hate any girl who stole her precious son's heart. Now sit down and I'll make us both a nice cup of tea. And don't you go giving that Ruby Minton another thought. Pay her no heed whatsoever. Billy loves you and that's all that counts.'

★　★　★

Later that afternoon, just as Stanley arrived home from school and Mrs Partridge and Florence were putting the finishing touches to his birthday tea in the dining room, there was a loud ring at the doorbell. Followed by another. And another. From upstairs, Bobby barked.

'Somebody needs to learn some manners,' remarked Mrs Partridge with a sniff of disapproval.

Florence stopped what she was doing and went to see who it was. But as she stepped out into the hall, an awful thought occurred to her. What if it was the boy bringing a telegram, a telegram with bad news about Billy?

53

'That's all right, Florence,' said Romily. 'I'll see to whoever it is who's disturbing the peace so rudely.'

As if to prove just how rude the person was, the bell rang again and with greater impatience.

Romily tutted and drew herself up, shoulders back, chin out, then opened the door, adopting her best Lady Fogg impersonation.

On the step before her stood a shabbily dressed woman of indeterminate years. The expression on her face, however, was much easier to read. Eyes narrowed, red lips pursed, she exuded indignant hostility from every pore. Interesting, thought Romily, a complete stranger on the doorstep who was plainly here to take somebody to task. Who could she be? And who did she imagine was culpable for whatever offence had been committed?

'Where's my Stan?' demanded the woman. 'It's time he came 'ome. 'E's needed.'

Ah, all was now clear! This was Mrs Nettles, come to play the part of aggrieved and doting mother. Romily had wondered what sort of woman she was to be able to wash her hands so cleanly of her son all these months. 'Come in, Mrs Nettles, please,' she said hospitably, conscious of Florence moving behind her. 'You must have some tea with us.'

'That won't be necessary,' the woman said,

bristling on the doorstep. 'Just give me my Stan and we'll be on our way.'

Thinking of the effort Mrs Partridge and Florence had gone to with Stanley's birthday tea, and how much he had been looking forward to it — rushing back from school and being shooed away to his room until all was ready for him — Romily urged Mrs Nettles over the threshold and closed the door after her. But as she turned around, she saw Stanley standing at the top of the stairs looking down at them, faithful Bobby by his side.

'Look who's here,' said Romily brightly, 'and perfectly timed to celebrate your birthday.'

'Birthday?' repeated Mrs Nettles. 'It ain't his birthday.'

'Yes it is, Mum,' Stanley said in a faint voice. 'You just never remember it.'

'None of your cheek, young man,' said Mrs Nettles. 'Now get yourself down 'ere. I'm taking you 'ome, where you belong.'

'But I don't want go 'ome, I want to stay 'ere.'

'Why you bleedin' little devil! Get down 'ere before I'm tempted to tan your hide!'

'Come on, Mrs Nettles,' intervened Romily. 'Let's go and sit down and sort this out calmly over a cup of tea, shall we? You must be thirsty after your journey.'

'There ain't nothing to sort out,' snapped the woman, 'and I ain't thirsty.'

'You can sort it all you like,' cried Stanley, 'I ain't going nowhere. I like it 'ere! This is my 'ome!'

'We'll see about that!' With a swiftness that

took Romily unawares, Mrs Nettles shot up the stairs towards her son. Dodging out of her grasp, Stanley turned and went crashing into Hope, who had appeared with Annelise on the landing, Allegra close behind them; clearly they had heard the noise and had come to see what was going on. They weren't the only ones to appear. Mrs Partridge had now joined Romily and Florence in the hall, just as Bobby bared his teeth and began to growl warningly, his head low, his eyes glinting. Suddenly it seemed as though they had all been caught frozen in time, with nobody moving or appearing to know what to do next.

It was Florence who spoke first, in an admirably authoritative voice, the like of which Romily had never heard from her before. 'Lay one finger on that boy, Mrs Nettles,' she said, 'and I shall telephone for the police. And don't think I won't. Now come down here and leave Stanley be.'

With Bobby still growling, and perhaps realising they'd reached an impasse, and that to continue in the same manner would leave her looking more foolish, Mrs Nettles made no further attempt to grab hold of her son.

'Stanley,' said Romily, 'perhaps you'd like to go and wash your hands and then come down for your tea. We'll be in the dining room waiting for you. Won't we, Mrs Nettles?' she added pointedly.

With her mouth set in a red hard line, the woman retreated down the stairs, but not before throwing Stanley a look that shook Romily with its venomous hatred. The thought of letting the boy leave with such a gorgon filled her with despair, but they could hardly stop a mother taking her own child back to his real home, could they? The law was most definitely on her side.

* * *

In the end, and after the most excruciating tea party Romily had ever known, letting Stanley go was what they had to do. Clutching the pillowcase he had arrived with, packed with the few things he'd brought with him, he stood in the hall to say goodbye, staring grimly down at the floor.

Other than the shoes and clothes he wore, there was no question of Mrs Nettles allowing him to take any of the other clothes Romily had bought him, or the birthday sweater Florence had secretly knitted for him. The gifts of books and games, including those from Tony Abbott, were abandoned upstairs in the room that had been Stanley's since September. Even the wrapped remains of the birthday cake Mrs Partridge had done her best to bake with so little butter and sugar had been refused. Her son's ration book stuffed into her handbag, Mrs Nettles made it clear she wanted no reminders of his time spent at Island House, and poor Stanley went along with it without a word of argument. There was no repeat of the brief display of defiance they'd witnessed earlier on the stairs. He probably knew that his mother was a force to be reckoned with, that it was pointless to fight back or reason with her. Romily observed him sadly, feeling as if all the joy and zest for life he'd acquired while in their care had drained out of him. His face was blank; his body stiff and detached.

It was only when he bent down to say goodbye to Bobby that Romily saw his expression soften with a glimmer of emotion. His lower lip wobbled and he buried his face in the dog's neck. Around him, Allegra, Hope, Mrs Partridge and Florence looked on in silent distress. Annelise was not so silent, though, and suddenly started to sing 'Happy Birthday' in a bright sing-songy voice. It was the last straw for Romily and with a sorrow that clutched at her heart, she willed herself not to cry.

'Well, Stanley,' she said with forced heartiness, 'best you go now or you'll miss that train. And remember, please write to let us know how you're getting on. We'd love to hear from you. As I'm sure would Miss Flowerday.'

Stanley let go of Bobby and looked up at Romily, his eyes brimming with tears. She would have given anything to change the situation, but she knew she couldn't; instead she tried one more time to offer to drive him and his mother to the station.

But Mrs Nettles shook her head adamantly. 'We can manage on our own. We don't need the likes of you shoving your charity down our throats.'

From the doorstep, with Romily holding Bobby by his collar, they watched Stanley and his mother walk the length of the drive, then disappear from sight. There was no last wave from Stanley, not even a backward glance.

'It's not going to be same without him here,' said Mrs Partridge, wiping a tear from her eye.

'We should have stopped that awful woman taking him,' Florence muttered as they turned to go back inside the house.

'How?' said Romily despondently. 'What could we have done? She's his mother.'

'A mother who doesn't deserve him,' said Hope quietly.

'I don't disagree with you,' Romily said tiredly. 'Rarely have I encountered a person so full of vindictive bitterness.'

'Other than Ruby Minton,' murmured Florence.

'Other than Arthur,' added Allegra.

54

Arthur looked around the dinner table at their guests and wondered if he'd ever been more bored.

Strictly speaking, they were Irene's guests; she was, after all, the one who fancied herself a great society hostess, which, no matter how hard she tried, she would never truly be. Ironically Irene was too pretty for her own good; she was all froth and no substance. So far in life she had got by on her appearance, and to a degree she had been successful in gathering a coterie of friends around her. Or so-called friends. For what poor stupid Irene didn't realise was that these women she counted as close associates were the very ones who thwarted her attempts to be truly accepted.

His proof of this was during a weekend house party at the home of Diana and Claude Charleston. While Irene had been lying down with 'one of her heads', Arthur had been in the garden and had overheard the women discussing her behind her back. 'If it weren't for her prettiness there really would be very little of worth to her,' the ringleader, and their hostess for the weekend, had said with malicious pleasure.

'Oh yes,' another had joined in. 'Beneath the superficial gloss and fluttering eyelashes one always suspects there's nothing but a very dull and vacuous woman staring back at one.'

'They make an odd match, don't you think?' a third had remarked.

'Who?'

'Irene and Arthur.'

'Not odd at all. He was looking for a wife to give him status and breeding, and Irene wanted a husband who didn't care how stupid she was.'

Someone in the group had laughed and said, 'I can never quite put my finger on what it is, but there's something just a little bit mysterious about Arthur Devereux, isn't there?'

'I know exactly what it is,' Diana Charleston had replied. 'There's a hint of danger about him. One never truly knows what he's thinking.'

'Do you suppose he beats Irene? Lord knows I should like to sometimes; she drives me mad with her prettiness!'

Arthur had been tempted at that moment to make his appearance from behind the yew hedge where he'd been listening, just to see how these catty women would react, but he'd done what he always did, and stored the knowledge away for a future time when he might use it to his advantage.

He could almost pity Irene having such two-faced friends if it weren't for the utter tedium she put him through on evenings such as these. 'Just a few friends, darling,' she would say, and then spend days planning the extravagant menu with their cook and fussing over the smallest detail of how the table should be set. She read countless periodicals on how best to present the perfect dining table so that guests would leave so impressed they would at once rush to imitate what they'd seen and eaten.

For this evening's dinner her lavishness had fortunately been tempered by rationing, although it hadn't stopped her from employing the services of an expensive florist to produce a centrepiece in the style of Constance Spry. But right now Arthur felt he could refuse his wife nothing. She was the mother of his unborn child, and to that end her happiness was of paramount importance to him and the well-being of the baby — a baby he strongly believed was a boy.

He viewed the arrival of a son as the start of a new life for him. He'd carelessly allowed matters to gain a momentum of their own recently and as a consequence things had got out of hand, but the baby symbolised a fresh start.

If somebody had told him that fatherhood would make him feel this way, so fiercely protective of the child that would be his to nurture and mould, he would not have believed them. He would not make the same mistakes his own selfish father had, of putting himself first. No. He intended to be an abiding presence in his son's life, a father who could be relied upon and who had time for his child, a father who would guide and advise.

They had just had their fish course served by their new maid, a marked improvement on the old one, who'd been so cack-handed she spilt the soup every time she served it, when the girl returned to the dining room and hovered like a moth at Arthur's right shoulder.

'Yes?' he said. 'What is it?'

She leant down and whispered in his ear. Such was her discretion, he couldn't make out what she'd said. 'What?' he responded irritably.

'There's a man at the door, sir,' she answered, this time more audibly. 'Says he has to see you.'

'Tell him it's not convenient.'

'He was most — '

'Did I not make myself perfectly clear? I said tell him it's not convenient.'

'Yes, sir,' she murmured, her face anxious. 'Sorry, sir.'

'What was that about, darling?' asked his wife from the other end of the table.

'Some man or other at the door wanting to see me.'

'Probably one of those ghastly travelling salesmen,' Diana Charleston said. 'I hear they can be terribly pushy these days.'

'Surely not at this hour of the day,' disagreed her husband, a rather pompous barrister. Claude had the infuriating manner of a middle-aged man despite being only in his early thirties. Correcting people was his stock in trade.

'Did Jane say what he wanted?' Irene asked.

'No.'

'How strange.'

Arthur had only taken a few mouthfuls of his fish when he saw the dining room door open and Jane come in again. She walked the length of the room, and not bothering to whisper this time said, 'Begging your pardon, sir, but the man insists. He says he won't leave until he sees you. He says it's very important, that he has something for you.'

'Oh for heaven's sake!' Arthur threw his napkin onto the table and stood up abruptly. 'It's come to something when a person can't enjoy his dinner in peace!'

'Who could it be?' asked Irene, her expression one of faint alarm.

'Maybe it's the police,' said Raymond Corby with a hearty chuckle. 'Have you been a naughty boy, Arthur, got yourself on the wrong side of the law?'

'Yes,' joined in Claude, 'if this were a play, that would be an inspector in your hall waiting to arrest you.'

'Very droll,' said Arthur. The smoothness of his words belied the churning in his stomach, however. In the weeks after Christmas, he'd lived in fear of a visit while at work, or a knock on the door here, from a policeman investigating Pamela's death. But as the weeks slipped by and he heard nothing, he'd begun to relax, his confidence growing that he'd got away with it, that he'd left no evidence in the house that could connect him with the woman.

Yet now, and with a strong sense of foreboding growing within him, he was gripped with a chilling certainty that whoever this caller was, he could only be the bringer of bad news.

The man was waiting for Arthur in the hall. He was staring intently at a particularly large oil painting of a herd of Highland cattle, standing no more than a few inches away from the canvas as though studying it hard. In his hands was an envelope. A gut feeling told Arthur that it contained something he'd hoped never to see again.

The man turned his head at the sound of Arthur's footsteps on the black-and-white-tiled floor. 'Ah, there you are, Mr Devereux. Finally we meet.'

'Do I know you?' Arthur replied with steely detachment.

'No. But I know *you*. Indeed, we once had a mutual friend. Pamela Mills. The name ring any bells for you?' The man smiled, revealing two rows of badly stained teeth. With an air of sickening amusement, he held out the envelope towards Arthur. 'This will make everything very clear to you.'

Arthur made no attempt to take the proffered envelope. 'I can't imagine what you're talking about. You must be confusing me with somebody else. Now if you'd kindly like to leave, I have dinner guests who — '

'No mix-up, I assure you,' the man interrupted. 'If you'd just take a few seconds to look at what I've brought you, we can settle matters and you can get back to enjoying dinner with your guests. Guests who I'm sure you'd rather didn't know the nature of our business. If you know what I mean.'

'I don't think I care for the tone of your voice.'

'Come, come, Mr Devereux, please don't waste my time by playing games. We're both adults.' He pushed the envelope towards Arthur, then inclined his head towards the closed door of the morning room. 'Perhaps you'd prefer some privacy?'

His heart beating like a drum in his ribcage, sweat pooling beneath his shirt and dinner

443

jacket, Arthur knew he had no choice but to do exactly what this odious man said. With resignation, he led him into the morning room, which was primarily Irene's domain, the room where she wrote her letters and planned memorable dinner parties. Certainly this evening would not be one Arthur would forget in a hurry.

The door closed firmly behind them, he looked inside the envelope and pulled out two black-and-white photographs of himself arriving and leaving Pamela's house in Wembley. In each of the pictures his face was perfectly visible; there was no question of being able to claim a case of mistaken identity. They were the very same pictures Pamela had shown him on Christmas Eve, and which had led to this moment — a moment he had feared because he'd always known that the involvement of a photographer in Pamela's deceit was the one thing he could not control.

He slid the photographs back inside the envelope and tossed it carelessly onto Irene's writing desk.

'I know what you're thinking,' the man said.

'I doubt that very much,' replied Arthur drily.

'I beg to differ. You're wondering what other photographs I might be in possession of. You're also wondering whether I suspect you had anything to do with poor Pamela's sudden and very unexpected demise.'

'I'm afraid you're bestowing more knowledge on me than I possess. I didn't know Pamela was dead. What happened to her?'

'You know very well she's dead. Otherwise

your . . . your association with her would have continued. But it stopped as unexpectedly as her death occurred.'

'You're right,' Arthur said, thinking fast. 'I did curtail our association, as you put it, around Christmas time, when I discovered my wife was expecting our first child. I realised then that things had to change.'

'Well,' the man said with a sneer, 'they certainly changed for Pamela.'

'While this is all very interesting, I would prefer you to get to the point of your visit. What precisely is it you want from me? Or should I say, how *much* do you want?'

'There now, that's more like it, and do bear in mind that I'm only doing this to honour Pamela's memory. I should add that this is also an insurance policy for you, because by keeping the matter strictly between us, I shan't feel the need to share with the police any of the private details of Pamela's busy and unconventional life, and more importantly how it came to such a dramatic end.'

Arthur knew the man had no real evidence to pin Pamela's death on him, and he'd be damned if this cheap blackmailer was going to get away with implying he had had anything to do with it. It was time to take control of this wholly disagreeable encounter.

'You're clearly here on a fishing exercise.' he said. 'I have nothing to fear from the police regarding Pamela's death, only the embarrassment of having my regrettable association with her made public. So keep your veiled threats for some other dupe. Now I've kept my guests waiting long enough. Get to your point and then do me the courtesy of leaving. But firstly tell me how the devil you knew where to find me. I never once disclosed my address to Pamela.'

The odious man tapped his nose. 'Ways and means,' he said, 'ways and means.'

★ ★ ★

His temper and breathing back under control, and after downing a quick tumbler of neat whisky in the drawing room, Arthur made his entrance back into the dining room. 'Sorry about that,' he said, resuming his seat. 'But it really couldn't be avoided.'

'You were gone an awfully long time, darling,' said Irene. 'What on earth could the wretched man have wanted?'

'What, no handcuffs?' remarked Claude before Arthur could reply to his wife. 'So we can discount our host getting himself arrested. How very unsatisfactory.' Everybody laughed.

'Sorry to disappoint you, Claude, but it was a colleague from the office. Very hush-hush, I'm afraid, so I can't say any more. Careless talk and all that.'

'Ah, one of your fellow desk Johnnies wanting to know which way he should push the pile of papers next, was it?' said Raymond, in what presumably he thought was a joke.

'Raymond,' Irene chided him, 'you're such a tease to poor Arthur. You know jolly well he does an important job at the War Office.'

'Yes,' commented Claude with a sly glance, 'he's one of Whitehall's many unsung heroes.'

Arthur could have picked up his fish fork and happily shoved it through the man's neck. 'And what exactly would your contribution to the war be, Claude?' he asked, clenching his fists on his lap. 'You too, Raymond?'

'Actually,' answered Raymond, exchanging a look with Claude across the table, 'we weren't going to say anything tonight, but since you ask, we've both volunteered and heard today that we've been accepted as commissioned officers in the army. We report for duty next Monday in Aldershot.'

Their wives looked on proudly, and in his own wife's face Arthur detected the unmistakable expression of envy that she wasn't married to a brave chap like her friends were. 'In that case,' he said, raising his wine glass, 'here's to Claude and Raymond. May they bring great honour and pride upon their families.' And may they achieve that by getting themselves killed on the battlefield as soon as possible, he added silently.

★　★　★

In bed later that night, while watching his wife go through her lengthy ritual of tending to her face and hair in front of the dressing-table mirror, his thoughts returned to the odious man who'd come here this evening to blackmail him. His name was David Webster, and in handing over a cheque to him, Arthur had had no choice but to accept that it was the first payment in what would be a regular drain on his bank account. Admittedly the amount was not a large one, but for how long would that be? How soon before David Webster became greedy and upped the sum? And would Arthur ever be able to put a stop to it?

'You know, darling, I don't believe you enjoyed yourself this evening, did you?'

'No,' he said simply, 'I can't say that I did particularly.'

Irene stared at him in the mirror. 'It's my friends, isn't it, you don't much care for them?'

'Is it that obvious?'

'I'm afraid it is, my dear. You were really quite rude to Claude and Raymond.'

'Only because they provoked me. They know perfectly well I can't volunteer to fight, not with being blind in one eye.'

She turned around to face him. 'Do you mind awfully about that?'

'Of course I do. Don't you think I'd give anything to be able to do my bit for the war? You know I hate being stuck behind a desk doing nothing of any great significance.'

'I'm sorry, my darling. I do so wish things could be different for you; that you could be happier with life.'

'What on earth makes you say a thing like that?'

She shrugged and went back to applying yet more cream to her face, all the time looking at him steadily in the mirror. 'I don't think you know how to be happy.' She gave another little shrug. 'I might go so far as to say I doubt you've ever really been happy at all.'

So much for his wife being stupid, he thought.

55

In the weeks that followed Stanley leaving them, Bobby was the one who missed him the most. The poor dog whined continuously while pattering about the house searching for his beloved companion, pacing the landing just outside the room that had been Stanley's as though guarding it until the boy returned. Even when Romily's wing commander turned up one day with a parcel of lamb bones from the butcher's, he showed no interest. Nothing was the same for him any more without Stanley. Allegra didn't think she'd ever seen a more pathetically sad creature.

Here for tea with them this afternoon, Evelyn Flowerday was saying how she'd regularly found the dog waiting at the school gate for Stanley in the days following his departure.

'The children all wanted me to bring him inside to the classroom,' she explained. 'I must say, I was tempted to do just that, especially when he kept up his vigil in the pouring rain.'

'I'm sorry if he's been a nuisance to you,' said Romily.

'Heavens no, I rather admire his steadfast loyalty.'

'He's settled now for patrolling the garden and keeping watch at the gateposts,' said Allegra, standing at the window and watching the dog as he slowly circled the pond, his tail between his legs, his tread weary. *For heaven's sake*, she wanted to shout bad-temperedly at him, *Stanley's not coming back! He's gone! Just accept it and get on with life!*

God help her, but in her current crabby state she could find nothing to be happy about. At the mercy of violent mood swings, she was contrary for the sake of it and could find no way to stop it. She was even more of a fidget than usual, finding it increasingly difficult to get comfortable. She could only sit down for a few minutes before hauling herself to her feet again and cursing the day she ever met Luigi, blaming him for destroying her once beautiful slim body and turning it into this loathsome, fat, cumbersome carcass. Never again would she make the mistake of falling pregnant. *Never!* If Elijah wanted children, he had married the wrong woman. She wasn't going to put herself through this torture a second time.

The baby was late, only by two days, but each day felt like an eternity and Allegra felt as though she had been pregnant all her life. Her ankles had started to swell up and her skin had stretched and felt painfully tight, as if it might burst. In fact her whole body felt like it might burst.

For some weeks now she had had moments when she was absolutely convinced something was wrong with the baby. Other times she was equally convinced that her body wasn't capable of delivering it. She had a recurring dream of the baby crying to escape her womb only to be trapped, finding no way out of the stifling darkness. Everyone said it was quite natural to feel anxious, but she was not persuaded by their assurance.

To compound her fears, Dr Garland was away on holiday in Cornwall and the doddery old doctor standing in for him was as good as useless, his only advice for her to go into hospital for the remainder of her pregnancy. Allegra had refused point-blank to do that. All she wanted, now that spring had come and the trees and hedgerows were unfurling their tender new leaves, was to be alone at Winter Cottage, but Hope and Romily had begged her not to leave Island House at this crucial stage. She knew they meant well and were probably right, but their constant attention made her feel like a prisoner.

She sighed and rubbed at the small of her back, wondering miserably if there was a greater punishment for a woman than to be pregnant. There was at least one good thing in all this: Elijah hadn't seen her in this disgustingly repulsive state. In his letters he said he would always love her, that he always had and no other woman came close. He had written of the place where he was now billeted, of the farmer's wife who cooked for them occasionally in the evening, and of her two daughters who flirted outrageously with the soldiers while trying to teach them French.

The thought of two young, attractive girls flirting with her husband drove Allegra mad with jealousy. Would he be tempted? Miles away from home, living with the daily threat of his life being cut short, could he be trusted not to stray into the welcoming arms of some petite French tart with a flawless body, all lissom legs, a perfectly flat stomach and pert breasts?

From behind her, she heard Evelyn ask if Stanley had written to them.

'No, and that worries me,' answered Romily. 'I'd just like to know that he's all right. When he first came to us, he was covered in bruises,' she went on. 'I can't bear the thought of that awful mother of his subjecting him to that all over again.'

'I suppose there's no reason we couldn't visit him, is there?' asked Hope. 'Just to see if he's all right.'

'Funnily enough, I had wondered that myself,' said Evelyn.

'What would be the point?' muttered Allegra, absently, still staring out of the window. 'It would only upset the boy. Anyway, he was only ever going to be with us for a short time; we weren't supposed to get attached.'

The room went deathly quiet. She turned around. 'I'm just speaking the truth.'

'Which is all very well,' remarked Hope stiffly, 'but knowing when to do so is something you've yet to learn.'

Allegra rolled her eyes at the priggish tone of her cousin's voice. 'Always so quick to put me right. Nothing changes, does it, *cara?*'

Romily raised a hand. 'We know you're as tetchy as a bear with a sore head, Allegra, so we'll forgive you that comment. Come and sit down and have a cup of tea.'

'Tea, that's your answer to everything!' cried Allegra. 'As though tea is going to make any of this dreadful nightmare better! You'll be suggesting next that we offer Hitler a cup! God, how I wish I . . . ' She was suddenly seized by a gripping sensation deep within her stomach, and snatched at her breath. Then to her horror, something wet and warm flooded out of her. She stared down at the floor. '*Dio mio*,' she murmured. '*Arriva . . . finalmente.*'

Quick as a flash, Romily was at her side. 'Right,' she said matter-of-factly, 'the baby's decided to put in an appearance, has it? About time too.'

Allegra gave a yelp as another pain ripped through her, and with it came the enormity of what she was about to go through. '*O Madonna*,' she cried. 'I'm not ready! I can't do this. I can't be a mother! *Non posso! Non posso farlo!*'

Hope and Evelyn were also up on their feet now.

'Time to get you to the hospital,' Romily said calmly.

'Shall I telephone for the doctor?' asked Hope.

'Do what you bloody well want!' screamed Allegra.

'That would be very kind of you,' said Romily with a smile that thoroughly infuriated Allegra. But before she could summon the strength to make a suitable riposte, her body felt as though it was being torn in two, and she would have fallen to the floor if Romily hadn't caught her by the arms.

'Something's wrong,' she gasped when the pain had passed. 'This can't be right. The pain's too awful.'

★   ★   ★

Hours later, Allegra was still calling out the same thing. 'Something's wrong! Something's wrong! Why won't the baby come?'

It was hard to listen to the poor girl crying out in such pain and distress. The longer the wait went on for Hope and Romily as they sat in the small waiting room just a couple of yards from where Allegra was struggling to bring her child into the world, the more Hope feared something might genuinely be wrong. What if Allegra's instinct was right?

'I feel awful now for the way I spoke to her earlier,' she said. 'I knew she was just being crotchety, but I couldn't stop myself.'

Romily patted her hand. 'I'm sure she'll forgive you.'

'It doesn't exactly encourage one to have a child, does it?' Hope said, as they listened to Allegra crying out once more.

Romily nodded. 'It certainly doesn't. Do you think you and Dieter would have had children?'

Hope had noticed that the better she and Romily got to know each other, the more they each asked the other about the men they had loved and lost. It was, she supposed, a bond between them. It intrigued her to hear Romily talk about a man whom Hope felt she had never really known, despite Jack Devereux being her father. It saddened her that she had missed out getting to know him properly.

'Yes,' she replied. 'We planned to have a family one day. What about you and my father?'

'Funnily enough, Allegra asked me the same question, and as I told her, it wasn't something

Jack and I ever discussed.' Romily paused before adding, 'But who knows, given time, it might have been something that became important to us.'

'You'd make a good mother,' said Hope. 'You're always so patient with Annelise, more so than me at times, and Stanley practically worshipped the ground you walked on.'

'Perhaps it's easier when the full responsibility is borne by another. I doubt I'd be that good as a real mother. I'd probably get the poor child into all sorts of scrapes, lead him or her totally astray. I think I'd also be worried about becoming bored.'

'What an odd thing to say.'

Romily seemed to reflect on this. 'I lose interest easily, that's my problem. It's why I never married until I did; previous boyfriends had bored me to tears in no time.' She smiled. 'Jack never did. We were two of a kind, always in need of some new challenge, the next big thrill. In many ways, I was his last challenge. And he,' she added softly, 'was my greatest.'

At the sadness in Romily's voice, Hope squeezed her hand gently. Then, as another blood-curdling cry filled the air, she closed her eyes, not to block out her cousin's suffering, but to focus her thoughts on willing Allegra through her ordeal.

When it went quiet again, she said, 'Romily, would I be right in thinking that life at Island House must seem very dull for you now without Jack?'

'I wouldn't say that exactly. After all, having

you and Allegra around has not been without its moments of drama.'

'But you need more, don't you? You're not the kind of woman who sits at home waiting for something to happen; you're proactive, not reactive.'

'How very perceptive of you.'

'I thought it when I first met you, the way you took charge of us all after the funeral. Especially the way you handled Arthur.'

'It had the bonus of keeping me busy. Of not dwelling on Jack.'

'But you can't have us under your feet as a distraction for ever, can you?'

'Is this you saying you want to move back to London? You mustn't ever feel you have to leave, that you've outstayed your welcome. Who knows, maybe it will be me who leaves to go and do something more useful than I'm currently doing.'

'I don't think life would be half so much fun without you at Island House,' said Hope. 'And what,' she added with a teasing smile, 'would your charming wing commander do if you left? The man is clearly besotted with you. Do you care for him at all?'

'He's not *my* charming anything. But I'm happy for him to visit; he brightens up the day when he calls. Now tell me how your children's book is coming along. Are you pleased with it?'

'I'm afraid that without Stanley on hand, I find I'm at a slight loss. It's almost as if he were my muse. Him and Bobby.'

'What can you do to resolve matters?'

'I don't know. Other than wait for further inspiration.'

'It'll come. You just need to be patient. Don't force it.'

Another howl of agonising distress made them both flinch. But unlike previous cries when poor Allegra had succumbed to yet another contraction, this one went on and on and chilled Hope to the core of her being. How could anyone go through that amount of suffering and survive?

★   ★   ★

An hour later Hope left for Island House to put Annelise to bed.

Alone in the waiting room, Romily thought how she had not been entirely truthful with Hope. She had indeed grown bored recently. On the home straight with her latest book, she was planning to apply to the ATA, just as Sarah had been nagging her to do ever since January. Her friend had written to her only yesterday urging to get on with her application. YOU'RE NEEDED! she had written in large capital letters, just in case Romily hadn't got the message.

Romily had also been somewhat economical with the truth over the way she felt about not having children of her own. She had never before had much contact with young children and so had not thought that motherhood was something that would interest her. But then along had come Annelise and Stanley and their presence at Island House had provoked an emotion she had previously not experienced. She now strongly

458

believed that she and Jack would have seriously considered the possibility of having children together one day, even so late in his life.

As for Hope teasing her about Tony Abbott, well the girl was way off the mark there. Once Tony had realised his error, which was due in part to Romily not putting him in the picture right away, he had become a very acceptable addition to the household. Having a man around occasionally helped to offset the balance of so many women living under one roof.

The appearance of a steel-grey-haired man in the waiting room interrupted her thoughts. 'Mrs Temple-Devereux?' he said, his expression severe. 'I'm Dr Longman.'

Romily stood up hurriedly. 'How is Allegra?' she asked anxiously, aware that she hadn't heard her cry out for a while now.

'I'm afraid Mrs Hartley is very weak. Her labour was not without complication.'

'But she's all right, isn't she?'

The man shook his head. 'She's weak,' he repeated. 'She's lost a lot of blood.'

'And the baby?'

'A girl.'

Just as Allegra always said it would be, thought Romily with a small smile.

'Mrs Hartley was asking for you,' the doctor said. 'I wouldn't normally allow it when a patient has undergone such a difficult birth, but in this instance I think it wise.'

The smile gone from her face, Romily said, 'What do you mean, *in this instance?*'

His face unreadable, he indicated that she

459

should follow him. 'Please,' he said, 'come this way.'

At the sight of Allegra, Romily tried hard to hide her shock. Propped against the pillows, she lay inert in the bed, her eyes closed, her face, normally so animated and vibrant, a blank mask. The stain of dark violet smudges beneath her eyes was the only colour to her lifeless pallor. For a heart-stopping moment Romily thought she was dead. But then her eyelids fluttered open, and in a rush of relief, Romily bent over the bed and kissed her cheek.

'You poor dear girl, how are you feeling?' she asked.

'Glad it's over,' Allegra said, her voice no more than a breathy whisper. 'Have you seen her? Didn't I say I would have a girl? I knew all along.'

'Indeed you did. I can't wait to meet her.'

'She's a pretty little thing.'

Straining to hear, Romily drew up a chair. 'I'm sure she'll prove to be just as beautiful as her mother.'

'I hope she won't have my temper. I'm sorry I've been so horrible to you and Hope.'

'Don't be ridiculous; you were more than entitled to be as rude as you wanted. Has the doctor said when you and the baby will be allowed home?'

Allegra swallowed, and as though the effort was too much for her, she closed her eyes. When she opened them, they glistened with tears. 'I want you to promise me something.'

'Of course.'

'I want my daughter to be called Isabella; it

was the name of my best friend in the orphanage.'

'That's a lovely name.'

'You will make sure that's what she's called?'

Alarm growing within her, Romily said, 'I won't need to, you'll do that yourself.'

'Listen to me, Romily, this is important. You mustn't let her go to an orphanage if Elijah decides he doesn't want to look after her. Or if he doesn't come back.'

Romily's throat tightened with fear. 'Don't wear yourself out thinking about things that won't happen.'

'I have to, Romily, I'm dying.'

'No you're not. You're talking this way because you're exhausted. You're going to be fine. Just fine. I'll make damned sure you are.'

With the slightest of movements, Allegra shook her head. 'Will you tell Elijah that I'm sorry?'

'Sorry for what?'

'For leaving him. For leaving him all those years ago and for leaving him now.' A ghost of a smile parted her pale dry lips. 'I'm so unreliable. But then I always was such . . . ' she took a breath, 'such a disappointment to everyone. I can never get things right, can I? And I did try. I really did.'

'Don't talk any more,' said Romily. 'Just concentrate on resting. You need to get your strength back, that's all.'

'There's something else you must do for me,' Allegra murmured. 'Elijah said I was to put his name on the birth certificate. Will you do that for

461

me? I want Isabella always to think he was her father.'

'I'll do whatever you say. Now stop worrying about everything, you must rest, you're worn out.'

Allegra closed her eyes. 'You've been very good to me,' she said in a faraway voice. 'Better than I deserved.'

A rustle of movement had Romily turning. It was Dr Longman. 'If you don't mind, I'd like to speak to you again, Mrs Temple-Devereux,' he said.

Romily followed him out of the room. 'Tell me the truth,' she said. 'Allegra thinks she's dying. Is she?'

'I'm afraid she is,' he replied gravely.

'But she can't be!'

He said nothing.

Shock and anger combined to fuel Romily's next question. 'Why?' she demanded. 'What the hell went wrong? And why couldn't you stop it?'

'We did our best, but Mrs Hartley's body just wasn't prepared for the fight it faced. Once she started to haemorrhage, there was nothing we could do.'

Unable to believe she was uttering the words, Romily said, 'How long does she have?'

'I doubt she'll last the night.'

Her eyes filling with tears, she turned away. With one hand clenched into a tight fist, she pressed it hard against her mouth to stop a cry escaping. Oh God, this couldn't be happening. Not Allegra. Not dying.

56

Allegra's funeral took place on a bright and sunny spring day, just as the first of the daffodils burst into flower. Reverend Tate took the service and droned on in his monotonous, self-satisfied voice about the renewal of life and how Allegra's indomitable spirit would live on through her child. And what would he know about Allegra's spirit? Florence wanted to know.

Those closest to Allegra were now gathered around the grave, a small, mixed group of mourners — Miss Romily, Hope, Miss Flowerday, Mrs Partridge, Mr Fitzwilliam, Dr Garland back from his holiday, Wing Commander Abbott, and the biggest surprise of all, Arthur Devereux. Nobody had expected to see him today, but here he was, large as life and just as unpleasant. Florence wanted to think well of him for coming, but somehow she just couldn't bring herself to believe that he had done it for an unselfish reason.

The casket was now being slowly lowered into the gaping hole. Florence couldn't bear to look at the wooden box that contained the body of a young woman who had been so vibrantly full of life. What a dreadful waste. And what of poor Elijah? God only knew how he had taken the news.

Miss Romily had volunteered to be the one to write and tell him what had happened. How she had found the right words was beyond Florence.

She had found it hard enough telling Billy, even though he didn't really know Allegra. All her letters to him so far had been written with the sole purpose of keeping his spirits up and to let him know that she loved him and was planning for their future when the war was over. Not one word of complaint or pessimism had she written, not even when his mother had been so rude to her.

In so many ways Allegra had been an enigma to Florence. In the blink of an eye she could switch from being full of fiery temper to being funny and warm and gentle. Many a time she had reminded Florence of a cat — purring contentedly one minute, but when provoked, showing her claws. Life had never been dull with her around, that much was true.

To the left of Florence was Hope. She had cried when Miss Romily had returned from the hospital in the early hours of the morning with the awful news. They had all waited up for her to come back, eager to hear that the baby was born safely. Never had it crossed Florence's mind that Miss Romily would come home to tell them Allegra was dead.

And now there was a motherless baby to care for. One thing Florence knew for sure, the child would not be short of love and attention here at Island House. The infant was now installed in the bedroom next door to Stanley's old room. The arrival of a baby confused Bobby at first, and then he adopted the air of a protective guard dog and patrolled the landing outside her door. If she so much as whimpered, Bobby barked and

464

came looking for someone to see to her.

Mrs Bunch had offered to mind the infant along with Annelise while the rest of them attended the funeral today, but she had made it clear that she couldn't take on any regular sort of commitment to looking after either child.

Last night and unable to sleep, Florence had padded quietly down the stairs to make herself a drink and had found Miss Romily in the kitchen, Isabella in the crook of her arm taking milk from a bottle. 'I was just thinking how like Allegra she looks,' she'd said to Florence. She'd stroked the baby's cheek tenderly. 'Whatever am I going to do with you?' she'd murmured.

Those words had stayed with Florence, and she thought of them now as the mourners took it in turns to throw a handful of earth onto the coffin. *Whatever am I going to do with you?* Had it been no more than a turn of phrase, or did it mean more: that Miss Romily would take on the full responsibility of the child?

* * *

The funeral over, and back at the house, Roddy still couldn't believe that Allegra was gone. How could anyone so vital and full of promise be dead?

It pained him that for so much of her young life the poor girl had experienced more than her fair share of unhappiness and disappointment, and that when finally she had found contentment in marrying Elijah, a happy ending was to be denied her.

She had actually said on her wedding day, when Roddy had been alone with her preparing to walk her into the church, that ever since she was a child she had somehow believed she wasn't worthy of knowing real happiness. 'It's my fate,' she'd said, 'to be denied a happy ending.'

At the time he had dismissed her comment as nothing but an example of her characteristically Latin melodramatic nature, but it had remained with him for days and weeks afterwards. Then last month, when Allegra had contacted him to request he draw up a will for her, that conversation had returned to haunt him. He'd told himself that he was overreacting, that she was only doing what was sensible now that she was married and had a child on the way, as well as an inheritance to safeguard. Yet now, as he sat in the drawing room with Romily and Hope to explain the contents of Allegra's will, he couldn't help but believe she'd had a genuine premonition of her death.

★　★　★

Arthur hovered outside the closed door of the drawing room. Had it really been necessary for Roddy to exclude him from the reading of Allegra's will? Fair enough, it was unlikely his cousin would have left him anything, but Roddy had been gratuitously high-handed in his manner, treating Arthur like a badly behaved schoolboy instructed to wait outside the headmaster's study.

With one ear listening out for Florence or Mrs Partridge, he kept the other to the door, hoping to catch the gist of what was being said. To be honest, he wouldn't have guessed at Allegra being sensible enough to put a will together, but then neither had he imagined her dying so young.

Other than surprise, he had felt scant emotion when he'd heard from Hope that their cousin was dead. He'd made all the right noises, of course he had, had even said he would come for the funeral, but he'd merely applied himself to going through the motions of what he knew was expected of him. Had he behaved differently, Irene might have made a fuss. While his wife accepted there was no real bond between the members of his family, she still favoured an old-fashioned approach of upholding the pretence that one cared, no matter how superficially. In actual fact it suited Irene perfectly that their involvement with his family was so cursory, as she would forever be tainted within the Devereux clan — what was left of it — as the girlfriend who had treated Kit so badly by jumping ship to attach herself to Arthur.

Understandably, Irene had been alarmed at the news of Allegra's death — dying in childbirth was a subject she did not want to dwell on — and for some unaccountable reason she had declared that she would accompany Arthur to the funeral. He'd vetoed that at once. 'I don't want you putting yourself, or the baby, through any unnecessary strain,' he'd said, brooking no argument. 'A funeral's no place for a woman in your condition.'

'I'm beginning to think you intend to keep me

a prisoner in a gilded cage until the child is born,' she'd responded with a sharpness to her tone he didn't recognise. He'd noticed also that she had taken to looking at him oddly these days, as though trying to figure him out. *And what would you think if you knew you were married to a cold-blooded killer?* he often found himself thinking when she asked him to pass her the marmalade at breakfast, or enquired over dinner how his day had gone.

He didn't see himself as a cold-blooded killer, not really; it had been a spur-of-the-moment thing, a swift and decisive response to a threat. And while a small part of him genuinely regretted snatching up that glass ashtray, he knew deep down that he wouldn't think twice about doing the same thing again. Very likely he would have to do something about that odious black-mailer; the man represented a threat that could only go on for so long. Dealing with him would be an act of self-preservation, no more, no less.

But he would have to be careful; it would have to be meticulously planned this time, nothing left to chance. Maybe he was a cold-blooded killer after all. But then so were all those men who'd donned a uniform to go and fight the Germans. Was he any worse than them? Or that wing commander who was at the funeral earlier and who had never left Romily's side? Whence had he sprung? His stepmother certainly hadn't been slow in finding a replacement for his father, had she? So much for dear old Jack being the great love of her life. People were such frauds.

From inside the drawing room, he finally heard Roddy getting down to the business of explaining Allegra's will.

★ ★ ★

When Roddy had finished speaking, Romily said, 'It really is as if Allegra knew what was going to happen.'

'I feel awful that I didn't take her concerns more seriously,' responded Hope. 'I kept telling her that whatever she was feeling was normal. But to my shame, and with her love for dramatics, I simply disregarded much of what she said and did.'

'I feel the same way,' said Roddy, removing his glasses and rubbing his eyes. 'On the day of her wedding, she expressed the view that she didn't see a happy future for herself. Which has to be the saddest thing a bride ever said on her wedding day.'

'But now we have to listen to her properly,' said Romily, 'and do what is right. Before she died, Allegra made me promise that I would look after Isabella while Elijah was away, and that's what I shall do. And just so we're clear on the matter, and in accordance with what she has stated only too clearly in her will, if Elijah feels he cannot be Isabella's father, or if he doesn't return from the war, I will be her legal guardian.'

'It's a colossal responsibility and not one to be undertaken lightly, my dear,' said Roddy. 'Are you quite sure?'

'I've never felt surer about a thing. Just as Jack

469

tried to do the right thing by giving Allegra a home as a child, an attempt I freely admit he may not have got entirely right, I want to make amends and do the same for Isabella. I promised Allegra that the child would not go to an orphanage; it's a promise I plan to keep.'

'In that case I shall write to Elijah and explain that you will be the child's temporary guardian in his absence, and that the bulk of his wife's estate will go to him, with the remaining money split between a trust set up for Isabella when she comes of age, and another for you, Romily, to be used specifically for the benefit of the child while she is in your care.'

Romily shook her head. 'I shan't touch a penny of it. I shall leave it for Isabella when she's older.'

'That's completely up to you,' said Roddy. He turned to Hope. 'There's one last thing I have to do.' From beneath the papers in front of him, he slid an envelope across the table to her. 'Allegra wanted to explain in her own fashion why she chose Romily and not you to act as temporary guardian to her child. I believe she didn't want you to feel overlooked in any way.'

Hope sighed. 'She really did think of everything, didn't she?'

'Indeed she did, agreed Roddy. 'Romily, I have a letter here for you as well. One for Kit also, and also one for Elijah. And now,' he said, reaching for his briefcase, 'I really ought to leave you and return to London.'

'I'll drive you to the station,' Romily offered.

★ ★ ★

Romily was glad that Arthur was nowhere to be found when she and Roddy set off. They neither of them relished the prospect of being in the car for any length of time with him. He could make his own way to the station.

They weren't even at the end of the drive when Roddy asked the question Romily had suspected he had been itching to ask the minute she had introduced Tony Abbott to him at the funeral.

'He's a friend,' she explained, 'one who adds a refreshing male presence to the house. He cheers us all up. I think we do the same for him.'

'He seems rather taken with you,' Roddy said, 'if you don't mind me saying.'

'I enjoy his company, no more than that, Roddy.'

'Jack wouldn't want you to be lonely, or to feel that life has to grind to a halt, you know.'

'I do know that,' Romily said with a smile, 'but Jack is going to be a hard act to follow. For any man.'

'Even one as charming and dashing as Tony Abbott?'

She tutted. 'Even him.'

'I'll wager he's a patient fellow.'

'Nobody is patient now,' she said with a shake of her head, 'not with this war. Everybody's in a terrific hurry; look how quickly both Allegra and Florence rushed to marry. But to put your mind at rest, I have no plans to rush into anything. Especially not now.'

471

After Romily had driven into the centre of the village, then turned onto Station Road, Roddy said, 'I do hope you won't think badly of me about keeping Allegra's wishes secret, but client confidentiality is at the crux of what I do; I was bound to remain silent. Moreover, I never thought we'd be in the position we now find ourselves.'

'Of course you couldn't breathe a word of what she discussed with you, I'd be shocked if you had.'

'Thank you for your understanding. And I'd like to thank you personally for agreeing to the terms of the will; it's not what everybody in your situation would do.'

Romily turned briefly to look at him. 'I'll be honest with you, Roddy, it's not what I ever thought I would end up doing. Especially as I had begun making plans for the future; I'd decided to apply to the ATA to see if they'd have me.'

'I see,' said Roddy thoughtfully. 'And now you feel you can't do it, that you're trapped by the promise you made to Allegra?'

'I wouldn't say trapped exactly, but certainly outmanoeuvred by such a tragic turn of events.'

'You could employ the services of a first-class nanny and still go off and do your bit.'

'No, I couldn't do that. I couldn't abandon Allegra's baby into the care of somebody else right away. And this may surprise you — it certainly surprises me — but I have to admit to possessing more feelings of a maternal persuasion than I would have ever thought possible.

Which all adds up to a desire to do the best I possibly can.'

'I applaud you for your altruism, and I have no doubt that Jack would too. But what about your writing? You will still keep that up surely? Your readers would be very disappointed if you stopped. Not to say your publisher.'

'Oh yes, I shall continue writing, and to that end I shall find a way that enables both Hope and myself to pursue our work.' Romily kept to herself that she thought she knew just the person to help in that respect.

'You have it all worked out by the sounds of things,' said Roddy.

'Not by a long chalk, but I feel that to a degree, Jack left me custodian of his family, so all I'm doing is trying to honour the faith he had in my ability to succeed where, of his own admission, he failed.'

★ ★ ★

After she'd waved Roddy off from the station platform, Romily returned to her car and started for home.

She was halfway there when she spotted Arthur in a taxi on the other side of the road, presumably heading towards the station and the next train for London. He gave her what she could only describe as a sardonic wave of the hand. She had exchanged no more than a few words with him and was sorry to say she didn't care if she never set eyes on him again. Her custodianship of Jack's family stretched only so

473

far. Yet even as she thought this, and acknowledging that Arthur had made the effort to attend Allegra's funeral, she had to consider the chance that there was perhaps a very small shred of decency to be found within Jack's eldest child.

She continued on for a few yards, then had a sudden change of mind. Instead of returning to Island House, she would go to Winter Cottage to check on the house.

She left the car by the gate and went round to the back of the cottage, knowing that Allegra had kept a key hidden under a flowerpot. But the key wasn't there. She looked around for another suitable hiding place, and then, out of curiosity, she tried the door. To her surprise, it opened. How strange, she thought. Had somebody been here before her and taken the key away with them? But seeing the key in the lock on the inside, she closed the door behind her and ventured further into the cottage.

'Hello?' she called out. 'Is there anybody here?'

There was no audible reply, but there was the unmistakable sound of movement upstairs. On the kitchen table there were signs of somebody having recently eaten there — an opened tin of corned beef with a fork sticking out of it, together with a half-empty glass of water, gave the impression of an improvised meal of sorts.

She moved towards the spiral staircase, picking up a china vase from the dresser, and called out again with fearless authority: 'I know there's somebody up there. Come down now and make yourself known.'

Footsteps sounded again over her head, and as she gripped the china vase, a grubby face appeared at the top of the staircase.

'Stanley!'

57

'Please don't be angry, miss, I didn't mean no harm. It's just that I missed Bobby. I missed Island House too. And school with Miss Flowerday.' His words tumbled out of him in a hurried rush.

'I'm not cross with you, Stanley, far from it,' said Romily. 'But you did give me a terrible fright just now. How long have you been hiding here? And how did you know the cottage would be empty?'

'I got here late in the night after getting the last train from London. I kept my fingers crossed that Miss Allegra would still be with you at Island House. I knew where she kept a key and I walked over the fields so no one would see me. Only trouble was, it was so dark I got lost and then I fell in a ditch and got all wet and muddy.' He grinned. 'I'd forgotten how bloomin' muddy the countryside is.'

Romily smiled too. 'Well, that certainly explains the filthy state of your clothes. We'll have to get those laundered, and then we're going to have to think what we're going to do with you.'

'You ain't gonna send me back to me mum, are you? You can't do that. I won't go back!'

Romily raised a hand to calm him. 'For now, let's not talk about that. Far more important to me is when did you last eat properly?'

'I found a tin of peaches and some corned beef in the larder last night. There weren't nothing else, other than some flour and sugar. 'ow's Miss Allegra? 'as the baby come now?'

Romily drew in her breath and braced herself. 'I'm afraid I have bad news,' she said at length. 'Allegra died after having the baby. We held her funeral today.'

Stanley's jaw dropped and his eyes widened. 'But she can't be. Not bleedin' dead! Not 'er!'

'That's how we all feel. We're in a state of shock.'

'What about the baby?'

'It's a girl and she's beautiful, just like . . . just like her mother.' Grief welled up inside Romily with a painful suddenness. All day she had kept her emotions in check, but now, explaining to Stanley what had happened, and seeing the look of shocked disbelief on his grubby face, it pierced the veneer of self-control she had mastered for the funeral. His reaction, so raw in its sincerity, brought home to her how close they had all become at Island House. Even a ten-year-old boy had been touched by knowing Allegra for so short a time.

'You all right, miss?'

She plucked a handkerchief from the pocket of her coat and dabbed at her eyes. 'Sorry about that,' she said, forcing a brightness to her voice. 'It's been a long day. Let's go home and see what Mrs Partridge has got to say when she sees you.'

Stanley grinned. 'She'll probably threaten to box my ears.'

'I doubt that very much,' said Romily with a

small smile, thinking that having the boy back with them would cheer them all up. 'We've missed having you around,' she added. 'Especially Bobby.'

At the mention of his beloved dog, the grin grew even bigger on Stanley's face. 'I can't wait to see him.' Then his expression abruptly turned serious. ''e won't have forgotten me, will 'e?'

For the first time in many days, Romily laughed. 'That's about as likely as Hitler admitting 'e's mad.'

''itler *is* mad, ain't 'e, miss?' Stanley said when they had locked up Winter Cottage and were in the car.

'Dangerously so,' she replied. 'And therein lies the true menace we're fighting. One can't reason with a madman. All Hitler understands is fighting to the bitter end, and at any cost.'

'Is that what you really think, miss?'

'Sadly I do. All this talk of the war being over before Christmas came to naught, and now there's no telling what will happen next, or how long we'll have to wait for an end to it.'

'Maybe the war will go on long enough for me to sign up. I reckon I'd make a good soldier.'

Regretting how honest she'd been, forgetting that she was talking to a child, Romily changed the subject. 'Now tell me the real reason you ran away from home.'

'I was 'omesick for 'ere,' he said. 'Like I told you.'

'Just that?'

'What else could it be?' he said, his tone belligerent.

'If it is only homesickness,' she said slowly, 'then I'm afraid you'll have to go back to your mother. It's simply not a good enough reason for you to stay with us.'

He folded his arms across his chest and stared grimly out of the window. 'I won't stay there if you do send me back,' he muttered. 'Nobody can make me stay.'

58

No sooner had Romily pulled to a stop than, in an uncanny display of canine telepathy, Bobby came tearing across the lawn barking loudly. The dog practically flew at Stanley when the boy leapt out of the car. Romily stood for a moment to enjoy the reunion.

When they eventually made it inside the house, with Bobby still barking excitedly, as though announcing to the world that Stanley was back, Florence was the first to appear in the hallway. The look on her face when she saw the cause of the commotion was priceless.

'I found him lurking at Winter Cottage,' said Romily. 'Could you rustle up something for him to eat, please? After he's had a wash, that is. A jolly good scrub behind the ears is in order, I think.'

'At the very least, I shouldn't wonder,' said Florence with a smile. She ruffled the boy's hair, then gave him a hug. 'Lucky for you we kept the clothes you left behind,' she said.

'How's Isabella?' asked Romily.

'She's fine. Hope is giving her a bottle of milk in the kitchen, with Annelise's help, I might add.'

'Can I see them?' asked Stanley.

'You can when I've scrubbed you with carbolic, young man,' said Florence. 'Come on, upstairs you go, and then you can tell me what on earth you're doing here.'

'I see you ain't stopped being a bossy-boots,' he said with a wink.

She tutted and rolled her eyes. 'And you're as cheeky as ever.'

'Can I sleep in my old room, please?' Romily heard him ask Florence as they reached the landing.

★ ★ ★

While Stanley was in the bath, with Bobby watching over him, Florence made up the bed in his old room and dug out a pair of pyjamas, along with the dressing gown Allegra had bought him for Christmas. Florence had suggested they kept everything in case they were allocated a new evacuee, but a small part of her had wondered if Stanley would run away from his mother and come back here. Question was, what were they going to do about it?

The bed made, she knocked on the bathroom door. 'Stanley,' she said, 'time for me to check how clean you are.' Earlier he had undressed on his own, making it obvious that he didn't want her to see him without his clothes, which could have been due to shyness, though Florence knew it wasn't. She'd felt how he'd flinched when she'd hugged him downstairs in the hall.

Not giving him the chance to protest, she went straight in. What she saw made her feel physically sick. The poor lad was in a terrible state. She suspected he'd been thrashed with a belt; there were long welts, and marks that could only have been made by a buckle. There were also small round livid circles on his back and stomach. She had the dreadful feeling they were cigarette burns.

'Who did all that to you?' she said when he was out of the bath and she was carefully wrapping the towel around him.

'I fell,' he said, avoiding her eyes.

She knelt in front of him and rubbed at his scalp with another towel to dry his hair, at the same time checking to see if he had brought any lice with him. He hadn't. 'You don't have to lie to me, Stanley,' she said when she'd finished combing his hair. 'Not to me of all people. Did I ever tell you how I ended up working for Mrs Temple-Devereux?'

He shook his head.

'My dad used to beat me something rotten; my brothers too if they'd had a skinful at the pub. It was like a sport to them. And do you know, the worst thing about it was that for years I blamed myself. I thought it was my fault they hit me, that I deserved it, and so I never told a soul; I was too ashamed. What I eventually came to realise was that I had to get away. Then one day, when I was preoccupied with figuring out how I was going to do that, I nearly got myself run over. The driver of the car was Mrs Temple-Devereux, and to cut a long story short, she offered me a job and the chance to escape. So I grabbed that chance and made a new life for myself.'

'I can't imagine anyone wanting to hit you, Florence,' he said quietly, while Bobby nuzzled in closer, as if sensing they were talking about something serious. 'You're far too nice and pretty.'

'Yeah well, often it's the nicest people who get treated the worst. Now tell me the truth: was it your mum who did this to you?'

He nodded. 'And 'er new boyfriend. 'e don't like having me around. I don't think she does much neither.'

'Why was she so keen to have you back at home, then?'

'She just wanted my ration book, I reckon. But I took it from the kitchen drawer before I left.'

Florence had heard that this sort of thing was now common; that people would go to any lengths to get their hands on an extra ration book. 'Well,' she said, 'tomorrow I'm taking you to see Dr Garland. I want him to look at those burns; they look infected to me. I'm assuming they are cigarette burns?'

With the smallest of movements, Stanley nodded again. 'What will 'appen to me? Will I have to go back?'

'Not if I have anything to do with it,' she said, 'I'll find a way to keep you safe if it's the last thing I do.'

His eyes brimmed, and near to tears herself, Florence gently slipped her arms around him, taking care not to cause him any pain. 'Put your slippers on,' she said, 'and let's go downstairs and see what Mrs Partridge has got for you to eat.'

★　★　★

That evening, after Annelise and Stanley had gone to bed, and after Romily had sat for an age giving Isabella her bottle and then put her to sleep in her cot, she held what she laughingly called a pow-wow in the kitchen.

With Mrs Partridge presiding over a big pot of tea, everyone gathered around the kitchen table, their faces wreathed in concern as though they were about to hear yet more bad news. Keen to put their minds at rest, Romily began.

'I'll keep this as brief as I can,' she said. 'It's been a long day for us all, but I wanted to thank you both, Florence and Mrs Partridge, for all your help with the funeral. I'd like to think Elijah would have approved of the way it went, and of your support. I'd also like to think that together we make quite a team, wouldn't you agree, Hope?'

Hope nodded. 'Absolutely.'

'Which leads me on to what I really want to discuss. We have to accept that life has changed yet again for us here, and I think we can safely say that not one of us could have predicted where we are now. And who knows what tomorrow will bring?'

'Who indeed?' murmured Mrs Partridge, pouring out their tea.

'The way I see it,' Romily continued, 'is that to keep the show going, we have to pull together even more, and perhaps our roles here at Island House will have to change accordingly.' She paused and looked around the table.'

'This sounds terribly ominous. What on earth do you have in mind?' asked Hope, taking her mug of tea from Mrs Partridge.

'We need somebody to be in charge of the children; somebody caring and dependable, and above all somebody the children will love.'

'You mean hire a nanny?'

The expression on Florence's face as she asked the question told Romily that she hated the thought of that happening. Hope didn't look too happy either.

'Not as such,' said Romily. 'What I have in mind is this: Florence, I'd like you to take on the job of caring for the children. Annelise and Stanley already adore you, and Isabella will — '

'But I'm not qualified,' interrupted Florence, clearly taken aback at the suggestion. 'I mean, I'm just a housemaid.'

'You're not *just* a housemaid,' said Romily with a frown, 'and don't let me ever hear you say that again. You're blessed with common sense, firmness, and a loving and kind heart, I don't believe there is anyone better qualified than you to be the children's official nursery nurse.'

Hope smiled at Florence. 'Romily's right, you'd be perfect. Annelise would hate the idea of a stranger playing with her or putting her to bed now.'

'But what about my other duties? I'm not lazy, Miss Romily, you know that, but there's only so much time in the day. As it is, there are things I have to skimp on.'

'I'll vouch for how busy she is,' said Mrs Partridge. 'She never stops all day.'

'I know,' said Romily, 'and that's why I'm going to advertise for somebody to take your place and carry out your old duties, Florence. I wouldn't expect you to look after three children, especially not a tiny baby, and do everything else as well. As you all know, I promised Allegra personally that her daughter would be loved and well cared for, and I fully intend to learn on the job and do my fair share of looking after Isabella. So it won't all be on your shoulders, Florence. But your help, should you agree to this, will allow Hope and me to continue with our work.'

Mrs Partridge patted Florence's hand. 'I'll help you all I can, love, you know I will.'

'Me too,' said Hope. 'We'll pool our resources, just as a family should. Because that's what we are, aren't we? A family.'

Romily smiled at Hope, who was suddenly blushing. 'I couldn't have put it better myself,' she said.

'Does this mean you think Stanley is going to stay with us permanently?' asked Florence.

'Permanently might be too strong a word to use, but after what you've told me this evening about the burns on his body, I shall move heaven and earth to keep him here with us for as long as possible. Don't ask me how; I haven't got that far yet. And who knows, maybe his mother won't come looking for him again.'

After taking a sip of her tea, she said, 'I have other changes in mind also. We have no idea how long the war will go on for, and with Finland now in the hands of the Russians, more rationing on the way and goodness knows what else to emerge in the coming weeks and months, I've decided that we should make more of an effort to economise and cut back on things. I'm sure it won't be long before coal is rationed, so we'll shut up any bedrooms not in use and we shan't use the dining room any more. That will mean fewer rooms to heat and clean. We'll eat our meals here in the kitchen — that's if you don't object, Mrs Partridge, this being your territory. It makes good sense to scale things back.'

'You'll hear no objections from me,' said Mrs Partridge, 'after all, it is your house.'

'It's *our* house,' Romily said firmly, 'our *home*.'

★   ★   ★

That night before she got into bed, Florence wrote to Billy. Her last letter had been to tell him about Allegra's death; now she wrote and told him that she was to be a nursery nurse and that Miss Romily was going to increase her wages. *I'll be able to save even more now for our home together when you eventually come back*, she wrote.

She also told him about Stanley running away from his mother and Bobby's joy at being reunited with him. *I swear that if that dog could sing, he would be singing from the rooftops how pleased he is to have Stanley back with us.*

She finished her letter by telling Billy to take care, and that if he saw Elijah, he was to let him know that Isabella was well and growing just as she should be.

Funny, she thought, when at last she got into bed and turned out the light, life just kept on surprising her. Every day seemed to bring something new for them at Island House. What would be next? she wondered as she drifted off to sleep.

59

'I see that evacuee is back, then,' said Elspeth Grainger, looking out of the window of the Cobbles Tea Room onto the busy market square. Her gaze was hooked on one passer-by in particular, the woman pushing a pram with a boy and dog at her side.

'You'd think his mother would have more sense than to allow him to return to such a household,' said Edith Lawton.

'It's the baby I feel sorry for, growing up in a house of sin. God help her,' joined in Ivy Swann. 'Motherless and as good as fatherless.'

'And of course Elijah Hartley isn't the child's father; heaven only knows who is.'

'Personally I'd say the child is better off without that flighty Italian piece as her mother.'

Their gaze still on the woman pushing the pram, Elspeth said, 'It didn't take long for Jack Devereux's widow to start making eyes at another man, did it?'

Nods of agreement followed, and then:

'He was at the girl's funeral,' said Ivy, 'bold as brass, I heard. You'd think she'd be more discreet.'

'Women of that sort are without shame. They just do as they please.'

'And look where it gets them.'

The three women tutted in mutual disgust.

Well aware that the coven was keenly observing her, Romily was on her way to see Dr Garland.

Florence had offered to take Stanley to the doctor, but Romily had thought it better that she do it herself; after all, it was she who was going to fight on behalf of the boy if his frightful mother came back for him. If possible, she wanted to have Dr Garland on her side, and she would also involve Constable Ashwood if push came to shove. Her hope was that Mrs Nettles would guess exactly where Stanley had gone and would be too lazy to make the journey a second time. She strongly suspected that by rights she should notify the authorities that Stanley was at Island House, but for now she was prepared to flout the law.

With Isabella fast asleep in the pram, Romily pushed it over the cobbled surface of the square and saw a familiar figure coming towards her. It was Tony Abbott. Stanley spotted him at the same time and called out to him.

'Well, well, well, look who's come back to us then,' Tony greeted the boy while patting Bobby on the head, the dog wagging its tail at top speed. 'Just visiting, are you?'

'I 'ope not. London's the last place I wanna be, that's why I ran away. Mrs Temple-Devereux says I can stay.'

Tony looked at Romily. 'I'm guessing that might not be as straightforward as it sounds.'

'You're right.'

'And how's Isabella?' he asked, peering into the pram.

'Sleeping like a baby,' replied Romily. 'Which thankfully she seems a dab hand at.'

He straightened up. 'I don't suppose I could tempt you into having a cup of coffee, could I? I have half an hour before I have to be back at base.'

'Are you going on a mission?' asked Stanley before Romily had a chance to reply.

Tony tapped his nose. 'That would be telling. All I'll say is watch the sky early this evening.'

'Coffee is a nice thought,' Romily said, when Tony returned his attention to her, 'but we're on our way to see Dr Garland.'

'Oh well, I shouldn't keep you in that case.' He hesitated. 'Look, I know it might not seem appropriate, but I don't suppose you'd like to come to a concert we're putting on at the cathedral in Bury St Edmunds in a few weeks' time, would you?'

'What sort of concert?' she asked.

'We have a surprising number of talented musicians amongst the chaps and WAAFs who frequent the Athenaeum, so we thought we'd put something together by way of entertainment, missions permitting, of course.'

'Are you performing?'

He smiled. 'I'm playing the piano. But don't let that put you off.'

'You never mentioned you were a pianist.'

'Probably because I wouldn't go so far as to describe myself in that fashion. I'm very much an enthusiastic amateur.'

'Can I come, mister?' piped up Stanley.

Tony laughed. 'I should imagine it will be past

491

your bedtime, old chap. So how about it, Romily? You could bring Hope along as well. I know it's not much to write home about, but it would be an evening out for you both.' His expression now solemn, he added, 'Especially after . . . well, you know . . . after Allegra.'

It sounded tempting to Romily. Very tempting. But she quickly checked herself. Her life was different now, she couldn't just abandon Allegra's child for the chance of an evening out. 'It's sweet of you to invite me,' she said, 'but another time perhaps. I would feel badly leaving Isabella.'

'Florence would look after the baby,' piped up Stanley again. 'You should go, miss, have yourself some fun.'

'Thank you, Stanley,' she said curtly. 'When I need your advice, rest assured I shall ask for it.'

He stuck out his lip, stuffed his hands into his pockets and shuffled his feet. 'I didn't mean nothing by it,' he muttered. 'Just seems rude if somebody invites you somewhere and you says no. I mean, I'd go if — '

'That's quite enough, Stanley. Now come along or we'll be late for our appointment to see the doctor.' She nodded goodbye to Tony and sped off with the pram, bouncing it over the cobbles.

'Are you cross with me, miss?' asked Stanley, running after her.

'Yes,' she said simply. 'You shouldn't have interrupted and butted in like that. It wasn't polite.'

'But it wasn't polite to say no when Mr Abbott

was being so nice. Don't you like 'im, miss?'

'Of course I do. Everybody likes him, he's that sort of a chap.'

'I reckon 'e likes you. A lot. And if — '

'And there you go again, Stanley Nettles, putting your twopenn'orth in when it's not required.

'But I don't understand. Why don't you want to go and listen to 'im play the piano? I bet 'e's good.'

It was a perfectly rational question, but for too many reasons Romily didn't want to dwell on, she knew she shouldn't go, even though in essence the idea had its appeal.

With Bobby tied to the pram outside the surgery, Romily carefully carried Isabella inside with them. Wrapped in a blanket, the baby was still sleeping soundly when they took their seats in the small waiting room while Dr Garland's receptionist, Cynthia Blackwood, dealt with somebody on the telephone. She was still speaking to the caller when Dr Garland appeared with his hat and coat on.

'I got delayed on my rounds,' he said. 'Have you been waiting long? Terribly sorry if you have. Nothing wrong with the baby, is there?' His face and tone of voice were the epitome of concern. He'd admitted to Romily how upset he'd been when he'd returned from his holiday and learned of Allegra's death.

'Isabella's fine,' she said, rising to her feet, 'although it might be prudent for you to check her over while we're here, just to be on the safe side.'

'Of course,' he said. Noticing Stanley as he

hung up his coat on the ornate rack beside the door, he smiled. 'Hello there, young man. So you've returned to us, have you?'

Suddenly looking anxious, Stanley took a step back. Romily put a gentle but reassuring hand on his shoulder, regretting now how abrupt she'd been with him.

'It's Stanley I've come about,' she said, her voice lowered, conscious that Cynthia Black-wood was all ears now that she had ended her conversation on the telephone.

'Well then, let's go through and have a chat, shall we?'

★　★　★

With his expression drawn into a frown, Dr Garland dabbed iodine on the burns on Stanley's body, the poor lad bravely gritting his teeth all the while and then relaxing when the dressings were applied. When he had finished, he called for Cynthia to take the boy and give him a glass of barley water and a biscuit.

'This is one of the worst cases of child abuse I've come across,' he said when they were alone. 'You did the right thing in bringing the boy to see me.'

'I can't allow Mrs Nettles to drag him back to London again; my conscience just won't let me,' said Romily. She was deeply shocked at what she'd just seen. How could a mother do that, or allow it to happen? 'And yet I know she's his mother,' she continued. 'It's her right to have him.'

'Why don't we cross that bridge if we need to?'

'We?'

'Having treated Stanley, I'll happily act as a witness that he's in more danger by being with his mother than he is with you.'

'She could claim she didn't touch him, that it was her boyfriend who did it. Or, heaven forbid, she could say I'm to blame.'

'I hardly think Stanley would let anyone believe that. Not for a second. Now then, let me take a look at Isabella.'

★ ★ ★

When they left Dr Garland, and still feeling guilty that she'd been so terse with Stanley, Romily offered to take him to the sweet shop to make amends. His face lit up. 'You ain't cross with me no more, then?' he said.

'No,' she replied, 'and I'm sorry for the way I spoke to you earlier. It was quite unnecessary.'

'So will you go and see Mr Abbott play the piano? I think 'e'd like you to be there.'

She laughed. 'You're a pushy little devil when you want to be, aren't you?'

The boy just smiled back at her and she suddenly thought: why not go? And why not take Hope with her so they could both have an evening out? A change of scene would probably do them good. And Isabella would be in safe hands with Florence, of course she would. But of equal concern to Romily was the feeling she knew she had to get over — that agreeing to attend the concert felt like a betrayal of her love for Jack. It was just a concert, nothing more.

'Now then, Stanley,' she said, her mind made up, 'our next port of call is the newsagent's, where we're going to place an advertisement to find a new housemaid.'

It was a task she didn't particularly relish. Whoever came to work at Island House would have to be exactly the right person. She didn't want the applecart upset in any way.

60

April 1940

It was nearly three weeks later when Stanley came careering into the kitchen one afternoon at top speed. He was panting hard and had Bobby hot on his heels.

'You ain't never gonna believe it!' he cried, dropping his school bag and gas mask case to the floor. 'Never in a million years!'

'And you'll never believe the sharpness of my tongue if you carry on hollering and banging,' replied Mrs Partridge. 'Florence has just got Isabella off to sleep, so hush with all your noise. Now wash your hands and sit down with a composure more befitting a gentleman. A gentleman who speaks properly too.'

Hope smiled at Florence as Stanley, scowling hard, went over to the sink. She watched him give his hands a cursory wash under the tap before drying them on the front of his jersey, causing Mrs Partridge to roll her eyes. 'There's a perfectly good towel right there on the hook behind you,' she said.

'Don't you want to know my news?' he said, ignoring this last reprimand and sitting at the table next to Annelise, who was chewing on a biscuit and looking adoringly at him. Given half a chance, she would follow round after the boy just like Bobby.

'I for one would like to know what's brought you home in such a lather of excitement,' said Hope.

'Me too,' said Florence, cradling the sleeping baby in her arms and adjusting her blanket.

'It's old Ma Foghorn,' Stanley said with undisguised relish.

'That's Lady Fogg to you, young man,' scolded Mrs Partridge.

'What's happened to her?' asked Hope.

'She's been taken off to the police station. Shoved into the back of a police car, she was. 'andcuffs . . . I mean Handcuffs and all!'

'No! She couldn't have been,' said Florence. 'She's a pain, but surely not a criminal?'

'Did you actually see it happen?' asked Hope.

Stanley wrinkled his nose. 'No, but that's what Mrs Bunch said happened. You ask her when she comes tomorrow; she was the one who was telling everybody about it. I was just coming out of the sweet shop and she was there with a crowd around her. She said Constable Ashwood had to push Ma Foghorn into the car, and all the while she was shouting that she was going to report him to his superiors.'

'So what is she supposed to have done?' asked Mrs Partridge, putting a glass of milk on the table in front of Stanley. Hope could see that despite the woman's high dudgeon, she was itching to know more.

'She's been accused of hoarding food, of buying stuff on the black market from a man in Sudbury. He sold her false petrol coupons and all and she's been hiding everything in the cellar.'

498

'How did the police find out about it?' asked Florence.

'Mrs Bunch says she fired one of her maids earlier in the week, accused her of deliberately smashing a teapot, and to get her revenge the maid told Constable Ashwood about the stash in the cellar, which Ma Foghorn thought nobody knew about.'

'Well,' said Mrs Partridge with a tut of disgust, 'so much for us all being in this war together. Some folk always have to think their need is greater and that they're above the law.'

'But what if it isn't true?' asked Hope, unable to believe that a woman of Lady Fogg's standing, a supposed pillar of the community, could behave so disgracefully. 'What if the maid told Constable Ashwood a pack of lies?'

'She has been driving around in the Daimler a lot more than you'd expect her to be able to, given the restrictions on petrol,' said Florence. 'Do you suppose Sir Archibald was in on it?'

'Nothing would surprise me,' said Mrs Partridge. 'They say wartime either brings out the best in a person, or the worst. Stanley Nettles, if I've told you once I've told you a hundred times, please don't slurp your milk.'

'Sorry, Mrs Partridge.'

'When you've finished, why don't you get out from under my feet and find something to do in the garden?'

When Stanley had gone, taking Annelise and Bobby with him, Hope asked Mrs Partridge if everything was all right. 'You don't seem your usual self today,' she said, refraining from

499

suggesting that Stanley had been lucky not to have his head bitten off, and for no real reason.

The older woman sighed and sat in her chair by the range. She took up a bundle of knitting. 'Oh, take no notice of me, I'm just a bit tired.' She sighed again. 'Must be getting old.'

'It's probably the extra work we're putting you to,' said Hope. 'With any luck after tomorrow, when we've interviewed those who have responded to the advert, things will get better. Trouble is, with so many girls leaving the village to go off and do their bit for the war, I don't suppose we'll have the best of the crop. Evelyn was saying that their latest maid at Meadow Lodge has just left to join the Land Army, and she'd only been with them a short while. She's the third girl to go in the last week.'

'In search of excitement, no doubt,' said Mrs Partridge. 'Young girls these days are all the same. Just don't you go getting any ideas, Florence; I don't know what we'd do without you.'

Florence smiled. 'Don't worry, I'm not going anywhere.'

Hope watched the girl run her hand over the baby's head, stroking her downy hair with a tenderness that brought a sadness to her. Poor Allegra, it should have been her sitting here with them and holding that dear little baby.

It still didn't seem real that Allegra was dead, and Hope continued to be haunted by the memory of being so short with her cousin that afternoon just before she had gone into labour. Romily had told her not to dwell on it, that it would have been the last thing on Allegra's mind once the baby had decided it was time to come. Hope knew she was right, as she was with so many things, but it was a lesson in learning to keep one's temper under control.

'I'll keep an ear out for Annelise,' said Florence, 'if you want to go and do some work.'

'Would you?' said Hope gratefully.

'Of course. It'll be no bother.'

'You're a saint, Florence.'

★ ★ ★

Upstairs in her room, the window open, Hope looked down onto the garden and saw Stanley pulling Annelise and Bobby along in the old wooden cart she and Kit had unearthed from the outhouse. As tempting as it was to continue watching the children playing, she tore her gaze away and sat down ready to start work.

Following Stanley's return to Island House, her children's book had gained a pleasing momentum, and it was now almost finished; both her agent and publisher were keen to see this new direction of her work. Stanley had no idea that he had become her muse; she hoped to surprise him with a copy of the book when it was printed.

To everyone's relief, there had been no reappearance of Mrs Nettles on the doorstep, and for the time being life at Island House had settled back into its previous rhythm. Maybe the ghastly woman was ashamed of the state her son had been in when he'd run away to them, although she didn't strike Hope as the type of woman who would be easily shamed.

★ ★ ★

She had been working for nearly an hour on a pen-and-ink drawing of Freddie and Ragsy ambling along a country lane on a bright and sunny summer's afternoon when she heard Bobby barking down in the garden. She leaned forward to look out of the window and saw the post boy pedalling up the drive on his bicycle with the last delivery of the day. Stretching her neck and easing the tension in her shoulders from sitting in the same position for so long, she watched Stanley dart across the lawn to take the post from the boy. He gave it to Annelise, who was still sitting in the wooden cart, then lifted her out and took her by the hand, walking her beside him towards the house so that she could deliver the letters herself. He often did this with her, knowing that at even so young an age she liked to be helpful.

A few minutes later, when Hope had resumed drawing, Annelise came into the room. 'Letter,' she said proudly, holding it out to Hope. At eighteen months old, she was acquiring a new word almost on a daily basis, though heaven help them all at some of those she would end up learning from Stanley! 'Letter,' she repeated.

'For me?' asked Hope.

Annelise nodded and pushed it into Hope's hands before scooting off with a giggle.

Hope recognised her brother's handwriting

instantly. Reaching for the penknife she kept for sharpening her pencils, she carefully slit open the sides of the blue airmail envelope, then the top. She smoothed the flimsy paper flat on her desk and settled down to read what Kit had to say.

Dear Hope,

I still can't believe the news about Allegra; it really doesn't seem possible that she's dead. I wonder if you feel the same way as I do, that it was only recently, since our father died, that I came to know — and like — Allegra. I wish we'd had more time to get to know each other properly, as adults; we spent far too much time bickering as feuding children, each of us, as I see it now, vying for our father's attention. It's such a shame we didn't find a way to forgive each other a very long time ago.

It's funny, but being so far away has given me a fresh perspective on life, and us as a family. As I see it, you and I have always got on — and don't be angry for me saying this, but after Dieter died, you turned away from the world, and from me, as if unable to bear anyone close to you. (Was it because you didn't want me to see you at your worst?) I have a sense that maybe that need to isolate yourself is behind you now. I do hope so; you have so much to offer the world. Dare I mention (and I do dare, because I'm not within hitting range!) Edmund's name at this juncture? He's a good man who I know cares about you, and given the right sort of encouragement, he could care for you a lot more. Life can be cruelly short, Hope, as you know all too well, so don't let the chance of happiness pass you by.

When I think about it, I suppose Dad's final wish for us to grow closer as a family has been achieved to a degree, thanks to Romily. The exception being an obvious one: Arthur. Do you ever hear from him? I haven't heard a word since I've been here. Did he bother to attend Allegra's funeral? Probably not.

I don't know why I'm asking you these questions as I shall be seeing you very soon — I now have my pilot's licence and am coming home! If all goes to plan I'll have a berth on the Arcadia departing from Halifax, Nova Scotia, in just over a fortnight's time — I should make Liverpool docks on or shortly after my birthday, depending how the crossing goes, so please be sure to ask Mrs P to have a cake ready for me when I eventually get to Island House! I'll try to put a trunk call through to you to let you know what train I'll be on. It would be nice, petrol permitting, if somebody came to meet me at the station, as I'll have my luggage with me.

Could you keep news of my return from Evelyn, please, as I'd like to surprise her when I'm back? So mum's the word, sister dear!

*I'm so looking forward to seeing you all.
I expect Annelise has grown in my
absence. I shouldn't think she'll remember
me, especially as I've grown a moustache!*

*Fondest love,
Kit*

Hope smiled, trying to picture her baby-faced
brother with a moustache. Annelise was not the
only one to have grown in the last few months; it
was obvious to Hope that Kit had too. Going to
Canada had evidently done him good, had
matured him, so it seemed, and made him
insightful as well. Not so long ago such a blatant
reference to Edmund would have maddened her,
but now it merely made her smile. She hadn't
seen Edmund since the night of the New Year's
Eve party, but they were regularly in touch, and
increasingly Hope found herself looking forward
to his letters.

But now she was looking forward to seeing
Kit. She longed to hug her younger brother and
say how sorry she was for treating him the way
she had. Thank God she would have that
opportunity, something she regretted not having
with her father.

Thanks to her many conversations with
Romily, the image in her head of the man she
had grown up believing at worst to be a
terrifying ogre, and at best distant and uncaring,
his mind always elsewhere, had altered greatly.
Now she saw a complex man she had never
understood, a man who had perhaps never really

505

understood himself. More and more she wished they had made their peace before he died and they had both been able to sweep aside the bitterness they had exchanged over Dieter. One thing she would say to her father now, if it were possible, was that she forgave him, that she knew grief had blighted his life just as she had allowed it to do her own.

Her flow of concentration now gone, she put away her drawing things and went downstairs to share the good news of Kit's return with Romily. Her brother's surprise would add to the enjoyment of the evening ahead of them, when they would be going to the concert Tony Abbott was playing in.

Downstairs, crossing the hallway, she could hear the sound of typing. Romily was in the throes of completing her latest novel and spent the afternoons cloistered away in the drawing room while Florence took care of Isabella. When it was the children's bathtime, Romily stopped work and took over from Florence. Often she resumed work later in the evening after supper, the sound of her feverish typing continuing sometimes until nearly midnight.

Hope knocked on the drawing room door and instantly the sound of Romily's typewriter went quiet. 'Whoever it is, I hope you've brought me tea and cake. I'm famished.'

'No tea and cake,' answered Hope, going inside, 'but good news from Kit; he's written to say he's on his way home. According to the date on his letter, he should be with us any day soon — perhaps even tomorrow for his birthday.'

'How wonderful. We shall have to arrange a party for him.'

Hope smiled. 'He's already put in a request for Mrs Partridge to bake him a cake.'

'In that case, we'd better not disappoint him, had we?'

61

Tony had offered to be their chauffeur, but having saved sufficient petrol coupons, Romily had opted to drive to the concert in her MG. It was a beautiful spring evening, and with the top of the car down and their headscarves tied firmly in place, she and Hope set off in good time to meet him at the Angel Hotel for a pre-concert drink.

'I still can't believe the news about Lady Fogg,' remarked Romily when they passed the entrance to Melstead Hall. 'What could the stupid woman have been thinking?'

'I almost feel sorry for her,' said Hope. 'She'll never live this down, she'll be the laughing stock of the village.'

'I suppose we should hold on to the old edict about not throwing stones in glass houses. I know for a fact that Mrs Partridge stocked the larder up in advance of war being declared. She won't have been the only one to do that.'

'Yes, but what goes against the grain is Lady Fogg lecturing the rest of us about doing one's bit, that it's all hands to the pump, while all the time she was doing quite the opposite and looking out for number one. How did she think she would get away with it? That's what baffles me, especially as she has such a poor reputation for the way she treats anyone who works for her. Did it really not cross her mind that one of them would try to get even with her?'

'I think we can safely call that a classic display of arrogance born out of inbred contempt for the lower orders,' said Romily, enjoying the sensation of freedom as she drove along the narrow lane, the sound of birdsong just discernible above the engine of her MG. 'It's the very thing I can't tolerate. Jack couldn't either. It was one of the many things that attracted me to him, his complete lack of airs and graces.'

Hope smiled. 'That's one of the things that Arthur always held against him, his unconventional desire to ignore the rules by which others played the game. On one occasion Dad turned up at Arthur and Kit's school for some play or other in a butcher's van. He'd forgotten all about the play, and when he did remember, he leapt into his car only for it to break down some ten miles from the school. He then hitched a ride from a local tradesman. Arthur was mortified and never lived it down. Frankly I thought it showed Dad in a good light; another father might have given up altogether.'

Romily gave her a sideways glance. 'That's the first time I've heard you recall your father with something akin to fondness.'

A moment passed before Hope replied. 'I think it's only now that I'm allowing myself to remember the good times with him,' she said. 'I'd buried them deep the day we fell out over Dieter. After that happened, I needed to hate him, which is a terrible admission.'

'But wholly understandable. I know without a shred of doubt that he would have given anything to put things right with you.'

'Dieter was much more forgiving of him than I was. He always believed that my father would come round to our marriage, that he just needed time. I can hear him now telling me that the memory of fighting in the Great War had of course left an indelible mark on Dad, and that we had to be patient.'

'He was right.'

'I know, but like Dad, I can be a stubborn devil when I want to be. I've certainly been stubborn over not wanting to relinquish Dieter.'

With a change of gear as she increased her speed, Romily said, 'I don't think you have to; more like you need to reach a stage of acceptance. Easier said than done, I know. It's something I'm going to have to do myself. I have to be grateful I had that time with Jack. Better that than nothing at all.'

'That's how I'm beginning to feel, whereas before I would have regarded a shift in my emotions like that as a betrayal. I would have punished myself for daring to think that way. The funny thing is,' Hope went on, adjusting her scarf, 'Kit more or less said that in his letter that came today. He knows me better than I thought he did.'

Romily took her hand off the steering wheel and patted Hope's forearm next to her. 'That's often how it is: we underestimate other people's insightfulness. Probably because we're so blinded by the dark to which we've subjected ourselves.'

'But you didn't strike me as being consumed by your grief for Jack,' Hope said after Romily braked hard and swerved to avoid a rabbit darting across the road.

'I came close to it,' she said, her foot pressing down again on the accelerator so that she had to raise her voice above the throaty roar of the engine, 'but there wasn't time to succumb fully to the pain, not with suddenly having a house full of guests. With hindsight, I can see it was a blessing having you all there, almost as if Jack knew it would help, knowing that unless I have a challenge to overcome, I don't feel whole.'

'I suspect that your charming wing commander might see you in a similar light: as a challenge. One has to admire his persistence.'

Romily tutted. 'And there you go again, Hope, busily fishing with your little net.'

'At least I'm not pretending to be subtle about it.'

'Well, and with equal frankness, I could ask if you are beginning to regard Edmund as more than just an old chum?'

A small smile playing at the corners of her mouth, Hope said, 'I might be.'

'Good.'

⋆　⋆　⋆

Tony was waiting for them at the entrance to the Angel Hotel. His hair was pushed back from his broad forehead, and he was wearing a white dress shirt and a dinner jacket, a white carnation in his lapel. Romily had to do a double-take to make sure it really was him; he appeared so very different.

'If a thing's worth doing, it's worth doing properly,' he said in response to Romily's comment about his attire. 'And if I may say, ladies, you both look jolly smart yourselves. Now then, what would you like to drink?'

Their drinks ordered at the crowded bar — sherry for Hope, and whisky and soda for Romily and Tony — he indicated a table in the window, but before they could reach it, a crowd of fellow musicians similarly dressed in formal evening wear intercepted him.

'No wonder you sloped off so fast,' joked a fair-haired man with a wink at Tony. 'You had these two beautiful ladies hidden up your sleeve. Which I call damned sly of you.'

'Allow me to introduce Guy Lance,' said Tony, 'the worst violinist your ears are ever likely to be subjected to, but not a bad pilot, I'm pleased to say.'

'You're too kind, old chap.' The man, who was younger than Tony, shook hands first with Hope and then with Romily, holding onto her hand for a moment longer than was necessary, at the same time letting his rakish gaze sweep over her — a thoroughly disagreeable gesture that did not go unnoticed by Tony, Romily noted.

There then followed, amidst much exuberant laughter, a round of enthusiastic introductions to the rest of the musicians, culminating in a toast. 'To an evening of fine music,' Tony said, holding his glass aloft.

'Or something close to it!' joked Guy Lance. Seconds later, and in a skilled manoeuvre that a sheep dog would have been proud of, he somehow managed to separate Romily from the group.

He offered her a cigarette from the packet he'd pulled from his jacket pocket. She declined and eyed him speculatively as he lit the cigarette and blew an ostentatious ribbon of smoke into the air, air that was already thick and hazy blue.

'Tell me,' he said, 'just how the devil does Tony know you? And are you the reason I can never find him at the airfield when we have time off?'

'I bumped into him in the snow earlier in the year,' Romily replied, 'and as to how he spends his time off, you'll have to ask Tony about that.'

He grinned. 'Are you sure *he* didn't bump into *you* on purpose? I suspect I might have done if I had chanced upon such a beautiful woman.'

A tremor of anger stirring within her, Romily gave him a cool look. 'Are you always this brazen?'

'Lord, no, I'm on my very best behaviour and restraining myself with great effort.'

'Then may I suggest you try a little harder. This brash act might work with girls your own age, but not with me, I can assure you.'

'Goodness,' he said lightly, 'I do believe you mean it.'

'I do. Now I really should talk to Tony, since I'm here as his guest.' She turned abruptly and, quietly seething, moved over to where Tony was talking to Hope.

'What an arrogant pig that man is,' she muttered.

'I'm sorry,' said Tony. 'I didn't get a chance to warn you about old Guy. He has a certain reputation when it comes to the ladies.'

'I have no idea why any woman with any sense would find him in the least bit attractive.'

'My word,' said Hope with a smile, 'he's really rattled you, hasn't he?'

Romily drained her glass of whisky and soda. 'Not in the slightest,' she said tersely.

★　★　★

The concert in the cathedral, which had attracted a large crowd, began with a frantically fast-paced rendition of Rimsky-Korsakov's 'Flight of the Bumblebee' played by a trio of tuba players who had everyone smiling and applauding enthusiastically when they took their bow.

Next up was a cellist bravely taking on the first movement of Elgar's cello concerto. He also received an enthusiastic round of applause and took his bow with an enormous look of relief, wiping the sweat from his forehead as he did so. When he'd carried his cello away, Tony appeared and sat at the piano. After a bit of fidgeting on the stool, he placed his hands above the keys, then began with the opening bars of a Chopin nocturne. He played well. Better than well. He had a sure but sensitive touch.

Romily responded to his playing by closing her eyes and letting the music wash over her. It was like a soothing balm, a warm blanket of comfort that made her realise how tense she had been, and how, quite out of character, she had allowed a few words from a stranger to upset her equilibrium. Motionless, she sat spellbound, her head lowered as if in prayer, giving herself up to the exquisite melody as it wrapped itself around her.

She stayed that way right until the very last notes died away. But when she did look up to join in with the applause, she found herself fighting off tears. She blinked hard, but the tears spilled over, and as she dashed them away with a hand, yet more flowed. To her very great consternation, she could do nothing to stop them. It was as if a tap had been turned on and there was no way to turn it off. She tried to swallow back the painful lump that had unaccountably formed in her throat, but that wouldn't work either. More than anything she wanted to flee, to be alone outside to compose herself.

No, that was a lie! She wanted to be back at Island House with Jack. She wanted her life to be how it was before she'd gone to Europe, before Jack had had his stroke. She wanted to wake up in the morning lying beside her darling husband, knowing the day would be full of fun and laughter, and above all, full of their love for each other.

'Are you all right?' whispered Hope beside her.

Unable to speak, she nodded and dug about clumsily in her handbag for a handkerchief. Was this some kind of delayed grief? she thought. Had Tony's beautiful playing unearthed a further layer of grief she had hitherto suppressed?

She dabbed her eyes and caught him looking at her with concern while taking another well-deserved bow as the audience continued to applaud him. With a frown on his face, he resumed his seat at the piano and was joined by Guy Lance, who, with a showy flourish, tucked his violin under his chin before throwing himself into a spirited rendition of Brahms's Hungarian Dance No. 5, with Tony accompanying him. He played far from perfectly, but it was easy to see why he had chosen this crowd-pleasing piece of music; it was showy and full of energy, a lot like Guy himself, Romily thought wryly.

The change of tempo helped her to pull herself together, and with her tears now checked, she slipped the screwed-up handkerchief back into her bag. Guy Lance was, she was forced to admit, the type of man to whom, in another life, she had once been attracted. But that other life now seemed as though it had been lived by someone else. Loving Jack had changed her forever. And for the better.

At the end of the concert, after a rousing and patriotic refrain of 'Land of Hope and Glory', which had everybody on their feet and singing along, refreshments were served. While Hope went over to join the queue for the fruit punch, Tony appeared at Romily's side.

'Now why,' she said, hoping he wouldn't ask about her earlier display of tears, 'did you never let on to us that you were such a talented pianist?'

He shrugged. 'I'm hardly that.'

'I beg to differ. You must have studied extremely hard to be that good.'

'Let's just say I had an encouraging teacher. But I have to say, you seemed upset by my playing. Or was it the music? Did the piece remind you of something, of . . . of your husband perhaps?'

'Sort of,' she said evasively, touched at his perceptiveness.

When she didn't expand, he said, 'What did you think of Guy?' He tilted his head towards the refreshment queue, where a couple of pretty WAAFs were hanging on the man's every word.

She smiled. 'I think you probably know what I thought.'

He smiled too. 'Beneath all the show, he's not a bad chap. He has a knack for raising morale within the squadron, and there's no better pilot. Hope was telling me that her brother now has his pilot's licence and is due home from Canada very soon. I'd like to meet him; it might be that I can help oil the wheels of getting him properly trained up now.'

'In that case,' said Romily, 'if you're free, you must come and join in with celebrating his return.'

'Excellent. I look forward to it.'

62

Crammed into his bunk, Kit lay on his back listening to the snoring men around him, each one of them seemingly oblivious to the roiling sea they were crossing. What a way to spend his birthday, he thought wryly.

The *Arcadia* had departed Halifax harbour five days ago as part of a convoy sailing across the Atlantic. The nearer they got to Britain, the worse the weather became and the slower the ship's progress. Kit did not make for a good sailor and had been sick more times than he cared to remember. Give him an aircraft any day! He'd be only too glad to have this treacherous voyage over with and to be able to stand on terra firma at Liverpool docks.

The weather wasn't their only problem, of course. The real threat they faced was being hunted down by a U-boat, or being blown up by a mine. God forgive him, but yesterday when he'd vomited for hour after hour, he'd felt so ill, a direct hit by a torpedo would have been a merciful release.

His outward journey had been nothing like this; the crossing then had been as smooth as sailing across the surface of the lily pond at Island House. But whatever hardship he was experiencing now was worth it, for he was return-ing home with his pilot's licence. It was the first thing he had achieved for which he felt genuine pride. He sincerely hoped his days of being a reservist might be over, that he'd now be accepted for immediate training.

As the ship heaved and gave the impression of tipping over to one side, he clung onto the sides of his bunk, and prayed fervently that he wouldn't be sick again. He tried to distract his thoughts to something other than being trapped inside the bowels of this enormous ship with sinister killers lurking beneath the waves. He thought of Island House, and of seeing Evelyn again.

Canada had been fun and he'd enjoyed every minute of his stay, especially when he'd been up in the air. Oh, those endless blue skies, just like being in heaven! He had tried to put his experiences into words in a journal, but his efforts had been less than impressive. He hoped his letters to Evelyn hadn't bored her too much.

He hadn't exactly been counting the days before leaving Winnipeg, but uppermost in his thoughts these last few days had been the prospect of seeing Evelyn again. Her letters had given him hope that she might have missed him and would be glad to see him.

When he'd received the news from Hope of his cousin's death, he'd been stunned. His father's death had shocked him less, perhaps because of his age and the hostility between them, but Allegra's passing just seemed unfath-omable and damned wrong. And now there was a child left behind. He felt oddly curious about this new member of the family — this child who would continue the Devereux line. All he knew from Hope was that the baby was a girl, and once his shock at Allegra's death had subsided, he had tried to figure out what his relationship towards the baby was; was he an uncle, or a second cousin?

He preferred to think of himself in the role of avuncular uncle, and at once warmed to the idea of playing a part in the child's life. A life he hoped would know more love and stability than poor Allegra had ever had. But how that would happen, he couldn't surmise. Who was going to look after the poor little mite? Would Elijah? Would he really want to take on the responsibility of a child that wasn't his? It would take a special kind of man to do that.

He closed his eyes, and at last tiredness overwhelmed him and he slept. He dreamt of Island House, not when he'd been a boy, but as his adult self; of lying on the lawn beside Evelyn — something he had never actually done — of leaning over and kissing her, of tasting the sweetness of her soft warm lips and —

The fantasy was rudely shattered by the loudest noise he'd ever heard. An explosion! Another explosion followed, and the ship rocked with such force Kit was catapulted out of his bunk. He landed with a thud on the floor, and after a few seconds of terrifying disorientation, he realised he was lying in water, freezing-cold water that was rushing in from somewhere. Pandemonium was now breaking out. Men were sloshing around in the water, grabbing life vests and shouting that the ship had been torpedoed.

In the ghostly pale-blue emergency lights, Kit

strapped on his life vest with fumbling hands, and followed behind the men already heading up the narrow metal staircase. He was halfway up the stairs when there was another explosion and the ship shuddered and lurched. Water gushed down from above him, and he was thrown back down the way he'd just come, banging his head as he fell.

Panic filled him as his breath was sucked from his lungs and he was forced under the icy blackness of the water. Down he went, deeper and deeper, tumbling over and over as if he were in the ocean itself. No longer knowing which way was up, he kicked his legs and clawed with his hands in the hope he would rise to the surface. Somehow he did, and he grabbed hold of a rail and banged his head again, seeing stars.

His chest heaving for air, he gasped and spluttered, registering he was just inches from the ceiling of where he'd been sleeping. With more water flooding in, he knew he had to get out, and quick. Adrenalin pumping through him, he swam with all his strength against the powerful tide and made it up to the next deck, where he staggered to his feet in water that swirled menacingly around his knees, threatening to drag him back the way he'd come. The instinct to survive propelled him through the chaos of twisted metal and bodies strewn like driftwood. He knew that there was no time to lose if he were to escape with his life, but he couldn't ignore the men who lay injured around him, so he heaved the one nearest to him over his shoulder, staggering beneath the dead weight.

During the course of the voyage, there had been several calm and orderly lifeboat drills, but nothing had prepared him for the real thing, or of the sheer terror of knowing that with the precipitous angle at which the ship was leaning, it would only be minutes before the vessel would go down.

Breathless and shivering, the man over his shoulder groaning, Kit had made it to the lifeboat deck when a volley of shouts rang out.

'Get back! Get back!'

A massive explosion erupted, sending a fireball shooting high into the air just yards from where he was standing. Thrown off his feet once more, he felt a searing white-hot pain cover him from head to toe. It was inside him too, scorching his lungs. To his horror, he realised he was engulfed in flames. He started to scream, his skin blistering, his hair alight, his nostrils filled with the sickening stench of burning flesh. Writhing in agony, and still screaming, he accepted that this was it: he was going to die on his twenty-fourth birthday in the ocean, never to see his sister, or Evelyn, again.

63

It was a lovely sun-warmed spring day and Florence was taking the children in her care for a late-afternoon walk before tea.

At one end of the pram Annelise sat happily humming to herself and pointing out things to Isabella, not caring that the baby was fast asleep and not paying the slightest bit of attention. Bobby was with them, and every now and then the dog would scamper off into the thickening fresh green hedgerows, sending birds flying with startled squawks into the air.

It was the kind of day when everything seemed perfect, when it simply didn't make sense that anyone would want to fight a war. Billy hadn't written for some time now, and Mrs Partridge reckoned that was because things were getting serious. Florence didn't want to dwell too much on what it might mean; she just wanted Billy home so they could begin married life properly. Miss Romily had said that maybe she and Billy could move into Winter Cottage when the war was over; that was if Elijah didn't mind them renting it from him, now that he was the new owner of Allegra's little house.

The interviews to find a new maid had not gone well yesterday — one girl hadn't bothered to turn up, and the two that did were not to Miss Romily's liking. 'Providence will provide,' Mrs Partridge had taken to saying, and Florence certainly hoped that was true.

'Goosie, goosie!' cried Annelise excitedly, bouncing the pram up and down. '*Goosie!*'

She was pointing towards Nut Tree Cottage, where Miss Treadmill, red-faced and muttering to herself, was digging in the front garden. Either side of her, and watching on with interest, were the two well-fed geese. Like many others in the village, the two women had dug up their flower beds and replaced them with productive vegetable plots.

On hearing Annelise's squeals of delight at the sight of the geese, Miss Treadmill stopped what she was doing. Dressed in brown corduroy breeches with patches at the knees and a leather jerkin over a baggy plaid shirt, she took off her cap and gave a cheery wave with it. There were some in the village who said less than generous things about Miss Treadmill, but Florence didn't care; so what if the woman dressed like a man? She brought the pram to a stop by the wooden gate. 'Is it all right if Annelise says hello to the geese?' she asked.

'Course it is!' Miss Treadmill said with a hearty bark, leaving a dirty mark across her forehead as she pushed a filthy hand through her head of greying curly hair. 'Lift her down from the pram and let her have a proper gander. So to speak,' she added with another laugh.

At first Annelise held back with a sudden bout of shyness as Miss Treadmill opened the gate, but when the two geese waddled over to take a look at their visitors, she forgot about being shy and went up to them, wobbling her head from side to side as if communicating with them in some way. Considering that the birds were taller than she was, Florence thought how fearless the little girl was. They bent their necks to take a closer look at her, and one of them, the one wearing a buttercup-yellow neckerchief, pecked at a button on the child's coat. Annelise giggled, and Miss Treadmill smiled. Then, turning to peer over the gate at the pram, she said, 'How's the littl'un doing?'

'She's the perfect baby,' said Florence. 'She sleeps well and takes her bottle from anyone who'll give it to her. She's not choosy at all.'

'Damned shame about the poor little beggar's mother. I can't claim to have known Allegra well, but she deserved better, and when you think of some folk who really have no right to have good fortune shine on them, it makes you wonder what this world is about, doesn't it?'

Before Florence could reply, Miss Treadmill hitched up her breeches, saying: 'I'm thinking of that Lady Fogg in particular. Ruddy cheek of the woman, lording it over the rest of us and all the time hoarding what wasn't hers to have. Makes my blood boil, people like that. I hope they throw her in clink and chuck the key away. But I'll wager that husband of hers will pull a string or two and she'll get off with no more than a warning. And we all know the likes of us wouldn't be so lucky.'

'Hello, dearie,' called a softer, bird-like voice. Miss Gant, carrying a glass of what looked like lemonade, came down the overgrown path in her slippers and handed the drink to Miss Treadmill.

'Good afternoon, Miss Gant,' said Florence. 'We just stopped by so Annelise could say hello to the geese; she seems to have formed quite a liking for them. How's Alfie, your pig?'

Miss Treadmill snorted, not unlike a pig herself. 'He's the damnedest laziest thing you ever set eyes on, lies in the sun all day waiting to be fed and have his back scratched — just like a man if you ask me!'

'He's very well, thank you,' said Miss Gant, clearly more kindly disposed to the pig, 'and Annelise is welcome to come and see him and the geese any time she wants. Would you like a glass of lemonade?'

'No thank you, Miss Gant. We'll be on our way soon. I didn't mean to disturb or impose.'

After taking a long swig of her drink, draining it in one, Miss Treadmill wiped her mouth with the back of her hand and passed the glass back to Miss Gant. 'What's the latest news then, Cissy?' she asked. She winked at Florence. 'Cissy here listens to the wireless more than she does to me. Glued to it she is, night and day.'

'How else are we to know what's going on?' Miss Gant said. 'I want to know if the German army is heading towards Melstead St Mary.'

Miss Treadmill smiled. 'Why, so you can be ready to talk them into submission?'

Miss Gant blushed. 'You shouldn't make fun of me for taking an interest, Philly dear,' she said with a flutter of hands. 'Rather you should spare a thought for the poor men on board that ship that's been torpedoed by a U-boat in the Atlantic. Another few hours and they would have arrived safely in Liverpool. To think of those poor souls from Canada now lying at the bottom of the sea, it's just too awful.'

Florence pricked up her ears and hardly daring to ask, said, 'Do you know what the ship's name was?'

'Oh yes, it was the reason I listened so attentively. We used to have a goose with the same name, you see. She was such a beauty. You remember her, don't you, Philly dear? She was utterly devoted to me, would scarcely leave my side given half a chance. Like a shadow, she was. Do you remember, Philly?'

Miss Treadmill rolled her eyes and resumed digging, pushing the spade into the earth with a large booted foot. 'How could I forget her,' she said, 'if for no other reason than the wretched bird hated me. The jealous fiend would peck me quite viciously. Until one day when I'd had enough and gave her a damned good shove up the backside. That soon taught her some manners, I can tell you!'

'And her name?' pressed Florence.

'Oh, so sorry, didn't I say?' said Miss Gant. 'It was Arcadia. I christened her myself. Such a lovely name, I always thought.'

'And was that what the torpedoed ship was called?' Florence asked with a terrible sense of foreboding. Yesterday, before Hope and Miss Romily had left for Mr Abbott's concert, Hope had asked Mrs Partridge if she would make a birthday cake for her brother as he was due to arrive at Island House any day. Until this moment, the name of the ship Hope had mentioned as being the one bringing her brother home across the Atlantic had slipped Florence's memory, but now she recalled with horrible certainty that it was called the *Arcadia*.

'It was indeed,' replied Miss Gant. 'You see now why the name stuck with me, don't you? It brought back so many memories.'

'Did they say on the wireless whether there were any survivors?' asked Florence.

'I'm afraid I didn't hear. I suddenly remembered that Philly was waiting for her drink and I rushed out here with it. She can be so very impatient, you know.'

'Oh for goodness' sake, you do exaggerate, Cissy, I'm the least impatient person alive!'

Florence rounded up Annelise and leaving the two women to bicker, and, with Isabella still sleeping soundly, she set off for Island House with a heavy heart. Surely the Devereux family didn't deserve yet another tragic loss?

★   ★   ★

Missing, believed dead.

The chilling words met Hope and Romily at every turn as they tried to find out what had happened on board the *Arcadia* and who exactly had survived. A naval vessel had responded to a distress call shortly after the ship had been hit, but only a handful of men had been rescued from the water before it went down. Christopher Devereux had not been named amongst the survivors.

It was possible, so Tony had said when he

called in to thank them for supporting the concert last night, that the naval ship had not hung around in case the U-boat returned, so other survivors might have managed to escape in a life raft from the *Arcadia*. Imagining her brother adrift in the treacherous waters of the Atlantic was the best Hope could come up with as a sickening alternative to him being dead. If he was lost at sea, there was at least the chance another naval or merchant ship might pick him up.

She prayed that night in bed that Kit would be found. She kept the same prayer going in the days that followed. Together with Evelyn, she clung to the faintest of hopes that he had somehow beaten the odds and would arrive at Island House any day wondering what all the fuss had been about.

But when a fortnight had passed and there was still no word of him having been picked up, Hope's faith in prayer faded. Her brother was dead; she had no alternative but to accept that she had lost another person she loved. And just as she'd wished she'd had the chance to apologise to Allegra before she had died, and to her father, so she wished she could have had the chance to say sorry to Kit for being such a poor sister to him.

To stop herself from dwelling on the last awful moments of what her brother might have suffered, she forced her heart to wrap itself around the memories of them wandering the meadows together as children, of him lying on his back in amongst the long grass and staring up at the clouds, of the times she had defied the orders of their nanny and sneaked into his room to keep him company when he was ill.

Dear Kit, he had been such a gentle, loving boy. Why had his life had to end so cruelly and so needlessly?

64

As April drew to a close, the news on the wireless and in the newspapers took on a chilling reality that left no one in any doubt that the phoney war was over. Hitler had now invaded Denmark and Norway. Norway put up a valiant resistance, but the Germans overcame them and landed seven divisions ashore within forty-eight hours, seizing the main ports.

'Could they do that here?' asked Stanley, his eyes wide as he ran his finger over the words of the newspaper in front of him on the kitchen table, his brow furrowed in concentration.

'Could who do what exactly?' asked Romily.

'Them Jerries. Could they invade us? Jimmy Powell at school today was saying it's only a matter of time before we're all speaking German.'

'Jimmy Powell is talking nonsense,' said Mrs Partridge, furiously knocking the lumps out of the potatoes she was mashing. 'Them Danes and Norwegians might not have been ready for that madman, but let me tell you, we are!'

'How do you know that for sure?'

Mrs Partridge spun round, the potato masher in her hand. 'That's just the sort of cowardly defeatist talk we can do without!'

'Mrs Partridge is right,' said Romily more gently. 'Hitler wants us all to be scared and to think it would be easier to throw in the towel and surrender.'

'But — '

'No buts, Stanley,' chimed in Mrs Partridge again. 'We're not going to let that Hitler get so much as a sniff of us. The navy will bomb the German warships clean out of the water or my name isn't Enid Partridge! Now why don't you put that newspaper away and go and play in the garden. You could help Mrs Bunch with the rugs if you want to be helpful. There's a spare beater in the scullery you can use.'

After Stanley had gone, Romily continued to give Isabella her teatime bottle of milk, marvelling as she always did at the baby's perfection, and the tug she had on her heart. She glanced over at Mrs Partridge giving the saucepan of potatoes hell.

'Does Stanley seem particularly anxious to you?' she asked. It had often crossed Romily's mind how scared the boy might be that his mother would show up here again and demand he return to London with her. Was it possible that his apparent growing fear of a German invasion masked the more tangible fear that his mother presented? So far their tactic of staying silent about him running away to be with them here at Island House was working; nobody from the authorities had been in touch, and better still, there had not been one word of contact from Mrs Nettles.

'I know what you mean,' said Mrs Partridge, 'but truth be told, we're all more anxious now, aren't we? These last months most folk have been grumbling about what they can and cannot do; now it seems more real, that any day the enemy could land on these shores.'

'I agree,' said Romily. 'There's a change of mood in the air; people are beginning to take things more seriously. Which might make finding a new maid even more difficult, unless I become a lot less choosy.'

'No, you mustn't do that,' the other woman said with a shake of her head. 'We're coping well enough as things are. Don't fret over it.'

'I had thought we might be able to poach one of the maids from Melstead Hall, but I hear they have their eyes firmly on pastures further afield.'

'We can hardly blame them in the circumstances. Oh, I nearly forgot to tell you, Mrs Bunch was saying earlier that Sir Archibald has gone to London and is remaining there for the foreseeable, leaving Lady Fogg to face her shame alone. Word is, she's not got a friend to turn to, she's been well and truly ostracised by the great and good of Melstead St Mary.'

'That seems a little unnecessary,' said Romily with a frown, picturing Lady Fogg alone and miserable in that great mausoleum of a house, and probably disappointing all and sundry in the village that she hadn't been sent to prison and put to work sewing mailbags.

'Some might say it's the least she deserves.'

'Well, I've never been an advocate of spite for the sake of spite.'

'That's because you're always so fair-minded.'

'I wouldn't say that exactly; probably more a case of having been spared the full extent of Lady Fogg's rudeness because I've had so little contact with her.' An idea suddenly came to

Romily. 'What say you we invite her for tea one day?' she added.

Mrs Partridge stared at her with an expression of alarm. 'Do you think that wise? Won't we be tainted by association?'

'Flirting with the enemy, you mean? What could be more delicious?' said Romily with a smile. 'In fact, a better idea would be to invite her to join me for tea at the Cobbles, that way the coven would either witness us together with their own eyes, or get to hear of it. Just imagine their shock and disgust! And who knows, it might go some way to help alter public opinion; after all, isn't there enough hostility in the world?'

Mrs Partridge smiled back at her. 'I can see the idea has put the sparkle back in your eye.'

'I wasn't aware it had gone.'

'You've been looking a bit peaky lately, if you don't mind me saying. I shouldn't wonder if it's all that time you've spent in the drawing room typing, barely seeing the light of day. Like a mole you've been while finishing that book of yours. It's not healthy. Not healthy at all.'

'Even by your standards that's quite an exaggeration. I sense, however, that you're leading up to something. What's on your mind?'

The potatoes now mashed, Mrs Partridge went over to the sink to wash and dry her hands before returning to the table. 'It's just that I can't help thinking that the handsome wing commander might help to put that sparkle in your eye on a more regular basis. Of course, it is only my opinion and one I'm sure you'll take no notice of, but why not have a little fun? Go to the pictures with him occasionally, or a dance in Bury St Edmunds. I've known you long enough to know that you weren't made to sit at home being idle.'

'I'd hardly call finishing a novel and helping to look after Isabella, Stanley and Annelise being idle.'

'You know what I'm getting at. You need excitement in your life, something to get the heart beating and the pulse ticking.'

'Mrs Partridge, I do declare you have been reading too many romantic novels lately!'

The other woman looked outraged. 'I've done no such thing! I much prefer a murder mystery like the books you write.'

The baby's bottle now empty, Romily carefully lifted Isabella up onto her shoulder and gently rubbed her back. 'I appreciate your concern for my well-being,' she said, 'but I regard Tony as a good friend and nothing more. He's accepted that position, too, and happily so. In a way I think he now regards me as a sister, which is much more to my liking.'

Her hands resting on the table, the fingers splayed out like a fan, Mrs Partridge looked at her steadily. 'Did I ever tell you about when my husband died?' she asked.

Surprised at the question, Romily shook her head and continued to rub Isabella's back. 'No, I don't recall you ever talking about him.'

'That's because I didn't carry him around with me like a millstone. Don't get me wrong, I loved him all right, loved him more than life itself, but I knew that when he was gone, he was gone. But what I also knew was that *I* wasn't gone. I was very much alive and wanted to enjoy life.'

'You never married again, though?'

'That's not to say I didn't want to, I just wasn't asked.' The older woman smiled. 'I wasn't that good a catch, I suppose.'

Romily smiled too. 'Perhaps you just didn't meet the man who was worthy of you. There's still time, you know.'

Mrs Partridge laughed and was about to say something more when they both heard the sound of barking outside in the garden, followed by the letter box being pushed open in the hall. Until last week, the arrival of the post each day had brought with it the hope that amongst the letters there would be one saying Kit was alive and well. But that hope had died, replaced with the certainty that he could not have survived the sinking of the *Arcadia*. They knew now that there had been a fire on board the ship before it went down, and every time Romily thought of that, she hoped that the end had come quickly for Kit, that he hadn't suffered.

With Isabella now asleep, Romily carried her upstairs to her room and laid her gently in the cot. Covering her with a blanket, and taking a moment to absorb the delicate perfection of her clear pale skin, she fell under the spell of the enviable innocence of the child. Just a few weeks old, and with no understanding of the tragic circumstances of her birth, or of the threat of Nazi Germany advancing towards them, she was

536

the most precious of things, a shining symbol of hope over adversity.

Downstairs, Romily went to see what the postman had brought. Please God, not more bad news, she thought. She took the two letters through to the drawing room, and opened the first one.

Dear Romily,

I'm not going to beat about the bush (as if I ever do), but I do so wish you'd hurry up and finish that dratted book of yours — YOU'RE NEEDED!

And no, I'm not exaggerating the case. We're all working flat out here with scarcely a moment to ourselves. The truth is, the RAF now realise they've underestimated just how many pilots they need to ferry training aircraft about the country, which means the ATA is crying out for girls like YOU! So please, get on and apply!

Love from your best friend who always knows best,
Sarah X

PS Appallingly rude of me to leave it as a postscript, but I was sorry to read in your last letter about Kit. How truly bloody awful! But it's another reason why you should join the ATA — how else will we win this war if you don't do your bit?

PPS Please don't think I'm being insensitive, I know you now have the additional responsibility of Allegra's baby, but surely your devoted maid, Florence, can deputise for you?

Typical Sarah, thought Romily amused, not so much avoiding the beating of any bushes as thoroughly flattening anything within a hundred-mile radius. The letter folded and put to one side, she picked up the silver paperknife on her desk and slit open the second.

Dear Mrs Temple-Devereux,

I'm sorry I haven't been in touch since Allegra's death, but the truth is I couldn't bring myself to put pen to paper. Each time I tried, I just couldn't put into words how I felt. It's like the last seven months has been a dream. I keep asking myself if Allegra really did come back to Island House. Or did I imagine it? Did I imagine our wedding day? But then I reread the letters from you and Mr Fitzwilliam telling me the awful news and I know it's all true.

Every day I wish to God I hadn't been so keen to sign up. I'm haunted by the thought that if I had stayed at home and been with Allegra, she might still be alive. I don't think I'll ever forgive myself for leaving her when I did.

Billy tells me that Florence writes often about the baby in her letters to him.

*Apparently she's beautiful, just like her
mother. I hope she is. This is hard for me
to say, but sometimes I think Isabella
would be better off not having me as her
adopted father. What can I give her when I
return home? Wouldn't she be better off
living permanently as a Devereux with you
at Island House? Please don't think I'm
trying to shirk my responsibilities; I'm not,
I just want Allegra's daughter to have the
best start in life and I'm frightened I can't
do that. What if she refuses to regard me
as her father?*

*In the meantime, I must thank you for
being Isabella's guardian. I wish I could
give her some kind of present, but stuck
here in the middle of nowhere, there's
nothing I can send, other than this lucky
four-leaf clover I found the other day when
I went for a walk during a short break
from duty. It's not much, I know, but I'm
sending it with my love to the daughter of
the woman I loved, in the hope that it will
bring her luck.*

*Kind regards,
Elijah Hartley*

Touched by how painfully honest Elijah had
been, Romily unwrapped the four-leaf clover he
had carefully included with his letter. It was such
a little thing, but the thought of him taking the
time and effort to preserve it for Isabella filled
her with sadness. She pictured him finding it

amongst the long spring grass and thinking of Allegra and her daughter. Just as soon as she could, Romily would have the lucky talisman pressed and framed as a keepsake for Isabella. Hopefully one day the girl would come to realise its significance.

65

'I just wish I knew exactly what happened to Kit,' said Hope. 'With Dieter there was certainty; as heartbreaking as it was, I was with him at the end and could say goodbye. But with my brother, there's so much uncertainty how he died. I can't stand the thought of him suffering alone, of not being there, when he needed me . . . ' Unable to go on, she put down her cup for fear of her hand shaking too much and spilling tea over the tablecloth.

'When he needed you most?' said Edmund quietly, his voice only just audible above the hum of chatter and busy activity around them. It was mid afternoon and the Lyons Corner House on the Strand where they'd arranged to meet was packed; there was a pianist playing, adding to the noise.

Hope raised her gaze and met Edmund's. 'It's the not knowing that haunts me.'

'I'd feel the same way. I'd want to know all the facts. As a doctor rooted in the laws of science, I always need physical proof of a thing before I can accept it. I think that's why I've never been drawn to religion; it all boils down to faith rather than actual empirical knowledge.'

'Sometimes I think faith is all we have,' she said with a heartfelt sigh.

'Do you remember that awful row we had as children,' said Edmund after a pause, 'when you announced that you were going to become a nun and — '

'And you said if I wanted to get dressed up in a stupid outfit I'd be better off running away and joining the circus as a clown,' she finished for him with a smile. 'I was very cross with you.'

'You were. You refused to speak to me for days afterwards, you said you didn't want to associate with such a heathen.'

Hope cringed. 'I had a tendency to be a frightful prig back then. I still can be. I'm ashamed to admit this, but the afternoon Allegra went into labour I'd been unnecessarily sharp with her, and for something so absurdly inconsequential, for which I can never apologise.'

'We all say things in the heat of the moment that we later regret.'

Her head tilted to one side, she smiled. 'You always try to make me feel better about things, don't you?'

'But do I succeed in doing that?' he asked, returning her smile.

'You do.'

'Good. Now tell me how things went with your publisher this morning.'

She told him about the meeting she'd had before coming here. 'They've asked me to make a start on a sequel,' she said. 'In fact they see it as a series of books for children.'

'That's wonderful. I assume that's precisely what you wanted to hear?'

'Yes. I feel oddly connected to the characters I've created, protective of them too, and in a way that I never have before with just my drawings. I say,' she said, as a waitress passed their table in her smart Nippy uniform, carrying a heavily laden tray, 'look over there, the table to the right of the pillar; it's my sister-in-law, Irene, and oh . . . ' Her voice broke off abruptly.

'What?' asked Edmund, turning in his chair to follow the direction of her gaze. 'What's wrong? Oh,' he said, echoing Hope. 'That's not Arthur with her, is it?' he added quietly, whipping his head back round.

'No it's not, and whoever he is, they seem awfully familiar with each other, don't they?'

'I think we can agree they're not strangers.'

Hope tried to tear her eyes away, but she couldn't and continued to watch in what could only be called fascinated horror as the man leaned in closer to Irene and stroked her cheek. She had no real fondness for her brother, but she felt a surprising pang of sympathy for him that his wife was betraying him this way. Or was Arthur such a terrible husband that this was how Irene coped?

'Would you rather we left so you don't have to witness what's going on?' asked Edmund.

At last Hope tore her gaze away from Irene and the man. 'No,' she said firmly, 'I'm not going to let them spoil our time together, not when I see so little of you. Shall we order another pot of tea?'

'Good idea.' After he'd attracted the attention of their waitress and requested more tea and a plate of crumpets, Edmund settled back in his chair. 'We needn't see so little of one another if you wanted to change things, you know.'

'Is that something you'd like to do?' Hope asked warily. 'See more of me?'

He picked up an unused teaspoon and turned it over in his hands. 'I think you know the answer to that, but I'm astute enough to accept that you might not want to, that your love and loyalty to Dieter would keep you from changing the status quo. Maybe for ever. Which I'm bound to say I think would be a great shame for you.'

'You're such a good and decent man, Edmund.'

He put the spoon down and drew his eyebrows together in a frown of obvious disapproval. 'How exceedingly dull you make me sound.'

'That wasn't my intention. Not at all.'

'Describe me in three words,' he said, once their waitress had brought their tea and crumpets and left them alone, though not before bestowing upon Edmund a wide and admiring smile. It made Hope appreciate that her childhood friend had grown into an attractive man, something she hadn't been aware of before. He was just Edmund, the boy with whom she had played when home at Island House for the school holidays.

But now she gave herself up to studying the intently serious expression across the table from her as Edmund waited for her response. How strange, she thought, that she had genuinely never really looked at him until this moment. Perhaps knowing him for so many years, she had taken him for granted in the same way she took her own appearance for granted. Which was ironic, for as an artist she prized what she viewed as her highly attuned ability to observe with an

544

acute eye for detail. If she were to paint him, she thought with renewed perspective, she would endeavour to capture the gentleness of his face, the blue of his eyes, the length of his eyelashes, the fairness of his hair, the deceptive strength of his jaw and the smoothness of his pale skin.

'You're staring at me,' Edmund said, pushing the plate of crumpets towards her. 'Does that mean you're struggling to think of something that makes me sound vaguely interesting? And for the love of God, please don't describe me as dependable. I cannot think of anything that conjures up dullness in a person more than that one word.'

'I'm thinking,' she said, hurriedly changing tack — dependable had certainly been on the tip of her tongue. Maybe it showed how dull *she* was that she had thought of that particular adjective to describe Edmund. 'Irritable might be one word I'd use,' she said with a flash of humour and a smile.

He smiled too. 'Go on. Your next word.'

'Insightful.'

He nodded. 'Explain why.'

'You understand people. Me in particular. I respect that about you.'

He groaned. 'Next you'll say that you admire me.'

'Certainly not!'

'Thank God for that,' he said with a laugh.

She spread some butter onto her crumpet. 'Gifted,' she said at length.

'In what sense?'

'As a doctor you have a gift for healing people,

and since we met up again last year, you've helped in some measure to heal me.'

He stared at her. 'Have I? Have I really?'

'You know you have.'

Her answer seemed to hang between them for a very long time.

'Those are your three words to describe me, then,' he said at length, 'irritable, insightful and gifted.'

'No,' she said, meeting his clear blue eyes, 'I'll take back irritable and replace it with the-person-with-whom-I'd-most-like-to-spend-more-time.'

He held her gaze. 'I make that a lot more than one word. But I strongly approve.'

'Good. Now it's your turn to think of three words to describe me.'

'That's easy.' He leant forward, rested his elbow on the table and placed his chin on the upturned palm of his hand. His eyes were clear and so very guileless, yet so intently searching. She felt he saw right into the depths of her soul, into the dark nooks and crannies where the worst of her lay hidden from view. 'Brave,' he said softly, 'and beautiful.' He raised a hand as she opened her mouth to dispute his description of her. 'Don't interrupt!' he said. 'And now I'm going to cheat the way you did. The words Brazil nut come to mind.'

'Brazil nut?' she repeated, puzzled. 'What on earth do you mean?'

'Difficult to crack, but worth it when one does. That's me being incredibly insightful by the way, in case you missed it.'

She laughed. 'It's not everybody's ideal

description of oneself, but I accept it's perfectly apt when applied to me.'

'And with that established, when can I see you again?'

'That's the difficult part, isn't it? You're here in London and I'm at Island House with Annelise.'

'Not so difficult at all,' he replied with a shake of his head. 'When I next have a day off, I shall come up and see you. It will be something to look forward to.'

'It'll be something I shall look forward to also,' she murmured, a warm glow spreading through her.

Again the words hung between them, making Hope realise just how very happy she was that not only had Edmund come back into her life, but that he should care for her so much.

'How do you think Evelyn is?' she asked when a few moments had passed.

'You mean with regard to Kit?'

Hope nodded. 'I feel there's so much she's not saying.'

'Evelyn plays her cards pretty close to her chest. Whatever feelings she may have begun to have for Kit, she hasn't shared them with me. In some ways she's quite like you, Hope, resistant to wearing her heart on her sleeve.' His expression earnest, he reached across the table and tentatively laced his fingers through hers. 'I meant it earlier when I said you were beautiful. I've always thought so. I'm just glad you've allowed me to say it.'

'I'm glad too.'

She was just relaxing into his touch when, out

of the corner of her eye, she spotted Irene rise from her chair and make her way towards the ladies' cloakroom. 'If I'm not mistaken, I'd say my sister-in-law is pregnant,' said Hope. 'You're an expert; what do you think?'

His eyes on Irene, Edmund said, 'About five months, I'd say. Presumably Arthur didn't tell you he was due to be a father?'

'Indeed he didn't,' answered Hope. 'But the question that springs to mind,' she went on, her eyes returning to the table where Irene had been sitting, and where her companion remained, 'is whether the baby is actually his.'

66

May 1940

Arthur was late leaving work that evening. He wasn't the only one; most of his department had stayed behind.

It had been this way for some days, the War Office finally stepping up a gear ever since Chamberlain had stood down as PM and Churchill had taken his place. When the announcement was made that Chamberlain was going, the women in Arthur's office did nothing but talk about Churchill and how he would now galvanise the nation and give Hitler the shock of his life.

The shock, however, was the other way around when on the twelfth of May, Hitler ordered the invasion of France. Within no time, German tanks had crossed the Meuse and sliced open a gap in the Allied front. The talk now was that it wouldn't be long before German troops would reach the English Channel. With Holland, Luxembourg and Belgium now gone, Arthur pitied the poor devils stuck with the British Expeditionary Force in France.

It was a pleasantly warm and mild evening, and so instead of using the Underground, Arthur decided to walk home. He was in no hurry. Irene's mother had descended upon them for a visit of an unspecified length, and every minute appeared to be spent discussing what would be needed when the baby arrived. The bloody Germans were practically banging on the door, and all Irene and her mother cared about was choosing the baby's layette and what colour to paint the nursery.

Arthur had noticed that as Irene's pregnancy progressed, his input, or even his opinion, had grown exponentially less important, as though he were now redundant. To put it crudely, he had sown the seed and now he simply wasn't required. Was this how all fathers-to-be felt? And if he were honest, wasn't this how he would prefer it? For now, at any rate. But once the child was born, he would see to it that things were very different. He would not be pushed aside then.

Whitehall now well behind him, Arthur slowed his pace yet further. Above him was one of the many barrage balloons protecting London from an attack by the Luftwaffe. The women in the office twittered on about how pretty the silver balloons were, but he saw them differently. To him they were great sinister beasts hovering high in the sky waiting to devour their prey.

He was just passing the open door of a pub surrounded by sandbags, catching the invitingly tantalising smell of warm beer and the acrid tang of cigarette smoke, when he spotted something across the road that stopped him in his tracks. For a moment he could have sworn he was seeing things, or that the woman simply bore an uncanny resemblance. But then, looking at the man who had his arm linked through hers, his jaw quite literally dropped.

The blood pounding in his eardrums, his chest tight, he set off in pursuit, keeping his distance until he could be absolutely sure of what he was seeing.

But he *was* sure! He might only have vision in one eye, but as he trailed in their wake, watching the amorous manner in which the woman tilted back her head and laughed at what the man was saying, he'd wager his house and every penny in the bank that he wasn't mistaken.

By God, he'd pulled some stunts of his own, but this was beyond anything he had ever dreamt up. How gullible he'd been! What a ruddy great imbecile the pair of them had made of him. Not for a single second had he suspected he was being duped. Well, now their little game was over. It ended as of now. They'd had their sport; it was time for him to turn the tables. What was more, he was going to damned well enjoy himself while exposing the pair of them.

The blaring of a car horn had him jumping back onto the pavement. So intent had he been on pursuing his quarry, he hadn't noticed that he'd stepped into the road. The man behind the wheel of the car seemed to think his recklessness worthy of another blast of the horn, which had the effect of attracting attention from passers-by. Including those he was following. Not ready yet to confront them, he pulled his hat down low and ducked into a shop doorway in Jermyn Street. When he deemed it safe to continue, he set off again at a faster pace in order to catch them up. Seeing them stop in front of the Ritz then go in, he counted to a hundred and followed them inside.

After leaving his coat with the cloakroom assistant, he went through to the bar. Sure enough, there they were, large as life, just making themselves comfortable at a cosy little table. And all at his expense no doubt.

'Well, well, *well*, isn't this just fine?' he said, pulling out a chair and joining them. 'And my word, Pamela, how well you look. I don't believe Lazarus himself could have risen from his tomb looking better than you do right now.'

The look of shock on the woman's face could not have been more satisfying. The same was true of her companion, the odious little man, David Webster, who had visited Arthur at home to blackmail him. To her credit, Pamela regained her composure faster than he did.

'Darling,' she said, leaning forward and filling the air between them with a waft of the perfume she had always worn, 'I do hope you're not going to make a scene.'

'Perish the thought,' said Arthur. 'I'm going to be wholly civilised. Now then, have you ordered something to drink? Mine's a gin and tonic. Stick it on your bill, why don't you?'

When on a sticky wicket and not calling the shots, Webster clearly had none of Pamela's chutzpah, and looking decidedly pale, he grasped the armrests of his chair and made to get up. Arthur shot out his hand and restrained him with an iron grip. 'Stay right where you are,' he said, his voice low and threatening. 'You're not going anywhere, not until I say so.'

The last remnants of colour drained from the

man's face, but proving again that she was made of stronger stuff, Pamela merely smiled and acknowledged the approach of a waiter. 'We might as well hear what Arthur has to say, Davey,' she said quite calmly.

Their drinks ordered, Pamela directed her attention towards Arthur. 'It wasn't nice what you did, hitting me like that. I lay unconscious on the floor for ages. I could have died. I'm surprised I didn't.'

'After today, you might wish you had,' said Arthur. 'You too, Davey,' he added, enjoying the sight of the pathetic man practically quivering in his chair.

'Don't be like that, Arthur,' said Pamela. 'It's hard for a woman to make her way in the world; I only do what I can to get by. You can't blame me for that, can you?'

He had to admire her nerve, but he kept the thought to himself. 'Given our surroundings, I should say you're more than getting by.'

When the waiter had returned with their drinks and once more left them alone, Arthur swirled the ice around in his gin and tonic and took a long sip. 'When did the idea come to you to play dead and blackmail me from the grave, in a manner of speaking?' As furious as he was that he'd been played for a fool, he was curious to know more.

'When I was in hospital later that night having six stitches put in my head,' Pamela answered him. She raised her hand and touched her head. 'I still have quite a lump there, thanks to you.'

'And I have quite a lump of money missing

from my bank account thanks to you and your friend here.' He gave Webster a contemptuous glance.

Another question came to Arthur's mind, and in the mood to have every i dotted and every t crossed, he said, 'We hardly move in the same circles, but how is it we haven't bumped into one another before now?'

'Davey and I have been away.'

'How nice for you both. Doing what? Setting up a new scam somewhere?'

'We've been finding ourselves a lovely new home in the country, just as I've always dreamt of doing. Now, darling, why don't we be reasonable about this and call it quits? What do you think, Arthur, bygones?'

'You're not in any position to bargain with me,' he snapped, sickened by the audacity of the woman.

'I think you'll find I am,' she said. 'One word from me to your pretty little wife and she'll know just what a vile man she's married to.'

'And I'll see that you go to prison for extortion.'

'Would that be worth losing your good name for? I don't think that's something you're prepared to do.'

He leaned in closer to her. 'What a damned shame I didn't hit you harder that day.' Such was the menace in his voice and the look of hatred he gave her, she actually backed away from him. 'Here's what you're going to do next,' he said. 'You're going to hand over every photograph, negative and any other evidence of my association with you in your possession.'

'And if I don't?'

'I shall make you wish I'd put you out of your misery when I had the chance. Have I made myself clear?'

Pamela exchanged a glance with Webster, who hadn't touched his drink and now looking positively green about the gills. What a contemptible specimen of a man he was.

'Perfectly clear,' muttered Pamela.

67

It had taken considerable effort and persistence on Romily's part to persuade Lady Fogg to agree to have tea with her at the Cobbles Tea Room. Not for a minute did Romily underestimate the amount of courage it must have cost the woman to sit here with her, or what a blow to her pride it had to be.

But here they were, centre stage and the focus of just about everybody's attention, this being Lady Fogg's first public appearance since going into hiding at Melstead Hall. Nobody had actually been rude to her, or even directly snubbed her, but it was obvious from the glances and not-so-discreet mutterings emanating from the tables around them that her crimes were a long way from being forgotten. For many it would be a case of delicious *Schadenfreude*, of enjoying the spectacle of seeing how the high and mighty could be felled. Probably their only disappointment was that Lady Fogg had been saved, very likely at her husband's intervention, from a spell behind bars.

Romily's insistence on meeting here in a public place was not based on some kind of perverse pleasure in seeing the woman suffer, but more from a desire to try and help repair the damage Lady Fogg had inflicted on herself. She really did believe that there was enough hostility in the world right now, Melstead St Mary didn't need to have its own private war going on. She also believed that meeting publicly would send out an unambiguous message that Romily Temple-Devereux was not the type of woman to kick a person when they were down, or hold a grudge. Her hope was that others might follow her example.

'Any news from your husband as to when his business commitments might allow him to return?' she ventured to ask Lady Fogg. She strongly suspected it wasn't business keeping the man in town, but she was prepared to go along with the pretence if it saved Lady Fogg a little more face. She couldn't help but feel sorry for the poor woman, looking as she did, a shadow of her former self, discernibly older and greyer, her skin sallow and powdery. She had lost weight too.

After dabbing her mouth with her napkin, Lady Fogg shook her head. 'It's all very tiresome. People make such demands upon him and he's too good-natured to say no. As a consequence, he's constantly rushed off his feet.'

'Quite,' said Romily, thinking that what she had encountered of Sir Archibald provided her with scant evidence to support such a claim about his nature. She further suspected that far from rushed off his feet, he was hunkered down at some prestigious club enjoying innumerable whisky and sodas while hiding behind a newspaper.

She steered the conversation on to the latest news coming in from across the Channel. She had it on good authority from Tony that a small armada of vessels of various sizes was being amassed on the south coast in order to help with a massive rescue operation to bring home the stranded troops of the British Expeditionary Force. Florence was frantic for news about Billy; many others in the village were also waiting anxiously for the safe return of their loved ones.

With the household still in shock after the sinking of the *Arcadia* and Kit's death, a small piece of good fortune had come their way in the arrival at Island House of seventeen-year-old Lotte Gelder. The moment Romily heard about the Jewish refugee through an agency in London that had been recommended to her, she had known in an instant that she would employ her as a maid. The girl was in need of work, but more importantly, she was in need of somewhere she could call home.

Lotte had arrived in England last year, leaving behind her family in Austria, and for various reasons had been shunted from pillar to post as a result of misfortune, as well as a series of appointed guardians failing in their responsibility to take proper care of her. With the help of a Quaker couple who had befriended her in St Albans, where she had been housed in a hostel for refugees, she had managed to obtain a domestic work permit. She had only been with them for a few days, but already Romily knew that she fitted in perfectly. Mrs Partridge had taken an immediate liking to her, as had Florence. She was a quiet girl, thoughtful too, but a willing worker, and always spoke politely in her clipped English, learnt, she said, from listening to the wireless since arriving in England.

'You haven't heard a word I've been saying, have you?' said Lady Fogg from across the table, a flash of her old feisty and scolding spirit surfacing.

'I'm sorry,' said Romily. 'I was just thinking about how events have turned out recently, one really doesn't know what's around the corner, does one?'

Lady Fogg's brow creased and she lowered the cup in her hand to its saucer. 'You're right, and I must confess to being more than a little surprised by your invitation.'

'I'm sure you were. Doubtless you suspected my motives.'

'I did. I thought perhaps you just wanted the opportunity to gloat over my unfortunate fall from grace.'

'I'm sorry you would think that of me, but I do understand why you might have done. I assure you that wasn't why I invited you. I don't like seeing anyone down on their luck, or condemned out of hand; after all, let he cast the first stone who is not guilty of some crime or other. We've all had a lapse of conscience and done things we shouldn't have and then had to face the consequences. But after that,' she added, 'in an ideal world it should be an end to the matter.'

'I don't think anyone here is going to let me forget what I did. My actions were selfish and very, very wrong, and counter to all that we'd been told.'

'You don't have to explain anything to me,' said Romily.

'But I'd like to, since you've gone to the bother to ask me here today.' Lady Fogg took out a handkerchief from her handbag and gave her nose a long, hard blow.

'You probably won't believe this,' she continued, 'but I didn't mean it to happen the way it did. I just thought it would be sensible to stock up on a few crucial items, things I know Archie is fond of, but before I knew it, it had all got out of hand and I couldn't stop myself. It became so easy. And worse still, justifiable.' She dabbed at the corners of her mouth with a shaking hand, as though the confession was costing her dear.

'The petrol wasn't for me,' she went on, 'it was for Archie; he does so grumble when he can't use the Daimler. I just wanted to see him happy. So little in life pleases him these days. Least of all me. And now I sound as if I'm looking for sympathy, which I'm not.' She took a sip of her tea. Then: 'You're an intelligent woman, Mrs Temple-Devereux, so I'm sure you don't believe a word about Archie having business commitments in London.'

Romily nodded, but didn't say anything. She sensed that Lady Fogg wanted — maybe even needed — to unburden herself yet further.

'He's gone there to get away from me,' she said, her voice low. 'I have no idea when he'll be back. He . . . he says I should stop badgering him and be grateful that he managed to pull the necessary strings to avoid me being punished as I ought to have been. He says he's ashamed of me.'

'How very pompous of him,' remarked Romily, 'and also, if you don't mind my saying, how cowardly of him to run off to London. He should have stood by you. Jack would have stood by me no matter what I did.'

'I admire your certainty,' said Lady Fogg with a sniff.

'But you don't believe me, do you?' said Romily. 'You think Jack would have abandoned me in the same way as your husband has you.'

Lady Fogg shook her head. 'I've learnt over the years that there are very few people in life one can rely upon fully.'

'That's probably true. But one would hope one's own husband would be included in the few.'

'You're young; you still believe in the inherent goodness of others, don't you?'

'Now you're making me sound as naive and gullible as a child who believes in the tooth fairy.'

'In my experience, youth fills a person with far too much hope.'

'I'm hardly youthful,' Romily countered with a smile. 'But I do believe there's more goodness in the world than bad.'

'Is that why you invited me here today, because you believed there might still be a spark of decency in me?'

'No, I invited you out of friendship.'

'*Friendship?*' repeated Lady Fogg, recoiling from the word as though Romily had called her a harlot. 'I don't believe that for a minute; more likely I'm a charity case for you to be pitied. A pet project. Maybe something for you to put in

561

one of your penny-dreadful books!'

Her voice had risen to its customary strident pitch, and in the confined space, there was no chance of people not hearing. Or even pretending they hadn't caught every word and weren't loving it.

'Well,' said Romily, amused, 'I'm glad we've cleared that up. Anything else you'd like to get off your chest now that you're back to your usual malevolent self?'

The tea room had fallen completely silent, and with her back ramrod straight, her chin up and her nostrils flaring, Lady Fogg glared furiously at Romily, her lips pursed.

'Go on,' urged Romily. Ironically, she welcomed the exchange; she preferred Lady Fogg in full flight than the beaten woman she had allowed herself to become. 'You can do better than that,' she taunted her. 'I guarantee there's a lot more bile in that poisonous spleen of yours to pour out yet.'

Audible gasps were heard, and if it were possible, Lady Fogg's nostrils flared even more. And then the most extraordinary thing happened. Laughter rang out, and it didn't come from the surrounding tables; it came from Lady Fogg herself.

Even more extraordinary, the laughter continued, and in turn Romily began to laugh too. As did those around them. It wasn't cruel, mocking laughter; it was genuine high spirits at the absurdly comical situation in which they'd found themselves.

When the laughter finally died down, Lady

Fogg rose from her chair. She looked horribly like she was about to make a speech.

'I know there's been a lot of talk and speculation in the village about me recently,' she began to say, confirming Romily's fear, 'all of which I thoroughly deserve. I behaved appallingly and I couldn't be more ashamed of what I did.'

She hesitated and looked down at Romily, and as if sensing she needed encouragement, Romily nodded up at her. Why stop her when actually she was doing a pretty good job of explaining herself?

'I'm well aware that because of what I did I've lost your respect, and — '

'You never had mine,' someone muttered sotto voce.

'*Shh!*' said somebody else. 'Let the old dragon speak.'

'No, no, that's quite all right,' went on Lady Fogg, putting a hand in the air. 'I understand, and I know I have no right to ask this of you all, but if you could find it in your hearts to forgive a very foolish old woman who still has some way to go in learning to be just a fraction as generous-hearted as this woman sitting here with me, I'd be most grateful. There, that's it. That's all I have to say.'

She plonked herself back down heavily in her chair, rattling the cups and saucers on the table as she did. A brief hush followed, and then it was broken by the sound of somebody clapping. Another person joined in, and then another, until everybody was applauding.

'I think that's your answer,' said Romily above the noise. 'You're forgiven.'

Lady Fogg's lip wobbled and she reached for her handkerchief again. 'Thank you,' she murmured. 'Thank you so very much.'

68

Reluctant to attract further criticism, Lady Fogg had not dared to drive into the village as she would normally, and now, having set off for home together on foot, Romily parted company with her at the divide in the road, where to the right Melstead Hall lay half a mile distant, and to the left Island House about the same.

A good day's work, Romily decided, with Lady Fogg's words of gratitude still playing in her head. She knew from personal experience what it felt like to be the focus of gossip — the tongues had barely stopped since she'd made her first appearance in the village — but whereas it was water off a duck's back for Romily, it was very different for somebody of Lady Fogg's ilk. Her standing in the community mattered to her, and only time would tell if she would change her behaviour to ensure she was no longer a figure of fun and disrespect.

At the sound of an engine behind her, Romily glanced over her shoulder. Seeing an RAF staff car approaching, she moved over onto the grass verge of the narrow lane to give it room to pass. But it didn't pass; instead the driver gave the horn a friendly pip-pip and brought the Austin 10 to a stop alongside her.

'Darling, I'd know those elegant legs and determined stride anywhere!' came a voice from the open passenger window. It was Sarah, with

Tony next to her behind the wheel of the car.

'What on earth are you doing here, Sarah?' asked Romily, taking in her friend's shorter haircut and smart blue uniform, thinking how transforming it was. She looked quite debonair and very at ease in the well-fitted tunic, but then Romily would have expected nothing less. In Sarah's hand, resting on the sill of the car window, was a cigarette — smoking was a habit neither of them had taken to in the past, but evidently her friend had now adopted the habit.

'Coming to see you, of course,' said Sarah. 'Hop in!'

'I hope it's not a bad time to land on you like this,' said Tony, looking at Romily in the rear-view mirror once she was settled on the back seat.

'Of course it's not a bad time,' said Sarah, answering on her behalf. 'Never is between chums. Am I right, darling?'

'You're right as always,' said Romily with a smile, happy to see her friend. 'But presumably you haven't come all this way just to see me, and more to the point, what are you doing hitching a ride in an RAF staff car?'

'I flew in a couple of hours ago. Had to deliver a trainer to the good wing commander's airfield. Makes a welcome change from risking hypothermia on the usual run up to northern parts. But today was a doddle: breakfast in Hatfield, lunch in Suffolk, and dinner at Island House, I'm rather hoping,' she added with a laugh. 'During which I plan to lure you away from your country idyll. You did get my last letter, didn't you?'

'Indeed I did.'

Sarah twisted in her seat to look at Romily in the back of the car. 'I wasn't kidding when I said the RAF underestimated the number of pilots they require to move training aircraft around the country. Just ask Tony here. And trust me, it won't stop there; before too long, demand will be such that us girls will be needed to ferry operational aircraft too.'

Romily exchanged a look with Tony in the mirror as he slowed his speed and turned into the driveway of Island House. 'It's true,' he said simply.

★ ★ ★

'Sarah, I can't,' said Romily later that evening when Tony had returned to the airfield and it was just the two of them sitting in the boathouse. They'd brought their tumblers of whisky with them, and though the day had been warm, the night air had a chill to it, and so they were wrapped in woollen blankets as they looked out over the still moonlit water of the lily pond. 'You know I can't leave Island House,' she reiterated, 'I have commitments here now. I'm responsible for a child; I'm her guardian.'

'But as you said, that's only the case until her father returns.'

'And who's to say when Elijah will return? Moreover, he can't just abdicate his duty as a soldier because of Isabella.'

Sarah tutted. 'I'd never have imagined that you of all people would pass up the chance to do something of such importance, not to mention throw yourself into the adventure of it all. Don't you want to prove to those absurd men out there who think we women are fit only for knitting balaclavas and scrubbing floors that we're capable of a damned sight more?'

'Don't you think I would if I could?'

'But darling, you can! Isabella is a baby; she doesn't have a clue who you are. Leave her in the care of those who can do just as good a job as you, if not better. Then when the war is over, you can coo and fuss over her to your heart's desire.'

Romily smiled. 'God help any child you have, Sarah.'

'Phooey! Best way to bring up a child is with a good dose of healthy neglect. It didn't do either of us any harm, did it?'

Thinking of Jack's family, and how they had suffered from being denied the two things they needed most as children — love and stability — Romily sipped her whisky thoughtfully, savouring its agreeably peaty taste. But as important as it was to her to do her duty by Jack's family, the temptation of doing something new — something exciting and challenging — had its appeal.

Was Sarah right? Was she stagnating here? Could Hope manage the household without her? After all, she wouldn't be alone; she would have Florence, Mrs Partridge, Mrs Bunch and now Lotte to rely on.

'I can hear the cogs grinding inside your head,' said Sarah. 'You're tempted, aren't you? And don't lie to me.'

'Even if I was tempted, what about the next book I'm expected to start writing?'

'Good God, surely I don't have to remind you there's a war on? If the Germans make it across the Channel, as they're planning to do, reading will be the last thing any of us will be doing! You know the situation is dire right now, don't you? Or have you lost sight of what's going on beyond the parameters of your cosy life here?'

With emotion rising in her chest, her face reddening with outrage, Romily knocked back the last of her drink in one furious swallow. When she could trust herself to speak, she said, 'I certainly have not lost sight of what's going on. Far from it. But whereas you have no commitments to bind you, I have plenty. I'm needed here.'

A moment of quiet passed between them.

'This isn't you, darling,' said Sarah finally. 'Not the Romily Temple I know of old. The girl I know would have enlisted for war work at the first opportunity.'

'And just what would people think if I hightailed off the way you want me to?'

Sarah turned sharply. The look of shock on her face was writ large. 'Since when did you care what people thought of you?' she said. 'Oh my poor Romily, that I've lived to see this day! It really is time you left here, before it's too late and you're unrecognisable to me.'

Romily tutted. 'Don't be so dramatic, and if you're trying to rile me, you're doing an excellent job of it.'

'But I know you, Romily. Okay, marriage,

widowhood and domesticity might have changed you superficially, but none of that can change the essential nature of a person. I know you need more than this mundane existence is giving you.' She extended a hand, the one holding her glass of whisky, to encompass the lily pond and the garden beyond, all of which was enchantingly bathed in silvery moonlight 'Isn't this worth fighting for?' she demanded. 'Or would you prefer to stay here and do nothing, and wait for some bloody Nazi in jackboots to wrench it from you? Do you think that's what Jack would want you to do?'

* * *

After they'd gone inside to get ready for bed, Romily gave Isabella her midnight bottle of milk and wondered at what Sarah had said. She knew her friend's comments were not designed to upset her but to make her think. Really think.

Was there a chance she had lost an essential part of her character in carrying out Jack's wishes to unite his family? Was she no longer the same woman who had smuggled the Friedberg heirlooms back from Europe to keep them safe? Was that the last act of true courage she had accomplished? Had she allowed her grief for Jack to diminish her, letting it rob her of her innate self?

No! That wasn't true. Not entirely. Admittedly, it had taken courage of a different sort to carry out Jack's last wishes here at Island House, but that had not been without its challenges, and was continuing to throw up more almost on a daily basis.

But was this really how she saw the months and years ahead, simply taking each day as it came, dealing with the mundane? Had she become complacent with her lot, happy to let others shoulder the responsibility of keeping the country safe? Just a few hours ago, she had referred to her part in today's act of atonement by Lady Fogg as being a good day's work. The thought appalled her now. When there were those dying to safeguard Britain, could she really claim that saving Lady Fogg's honour was some kind of achievement?

And what would Jack think of her settling for so little?

The baby's bottle now empty, Romily placed it on the table beside her. After rubbing Isabella's back to be sure there was no danger of her waking with wind, she put the contented and sleepy child back in her cot, her eyes already closed, then kissed her forehead and quietly left the room, closing the door after her.

Too restless to sleep, she went downstairs to make herself a hot drink. To her surprise, she found Sarah quite at home in the kitchen, dressed in the nightclothes Romily had loaned her, and standing at the stove heating a pan of milk.

'There's enough here for two small mugs of cocoa if you want,' her friend said, as though she had been expecting Romily.

'I hope it's a guilty conscience that's keeping you awake,' remarked Romily, reaching into the cupboard for another mug.

'Certainly not. I've never suffered with one of those before and I'm not about to start now.'

Romily watched Sarah pour the milk and took the proffered mug. They sat at the kitchen table. 'Actually,' said Sarah, 'and since I have you on your own again, there's another matter I want to discuss with you.'

'Oh yes?'

'It's your handsome wing commander.'

'I wish people would stop referring to him in that way,' Romily muttered irritably. 'It quite gets on my nerves.'

'In that case,' said Sarah, 'perhaps I can help you out on that score. I rather like the fellow, so what do you say to me tossing my cap into the ring, so to speak? Be honest. Would you be offended if I were to make a play for him?'

Romily laughed. 'Sarah, of all the things you could have asked me, that would be the least offensive thing ever. Especially after everything else you've thrown at me today.'

'You mean you wouldn't mind? Not in the slightest? Not even the teeniest-weeniest bit?'

'Not in the slightest. He's a lovely chap, but not for me.' She blinked and blew on her cocoa. 'Not after Jack. So go right ahead and make your move.'

Her lively eyes dancing, Sarah smiled. 'I will, rest assured. Although heaven only knows when we'd be able to meet up.'

Romily smiled back at her friend. 'Knowing you, you'll find a way.'

'I have one more thing to say, something I

want you to promise. I want you to think very hard about what I've said. The war needs women like you, Romily, women who can rise to the challenge and who aren't afraid to leap into the unknown. Do you promise?'

'I do. If only to keep you quiet.'

'Good. Now then, how about a tot of something in this cocoa to help us sleep well?'

69

June 1940

Florence had not heard from Billy in weeks. Nor had anyone heard from Elijah or Tommy.

The news on the wireless about the evacuation of Dunkirk frightened her half to death. There were reports of boats of all sizes, some just small fishing boats, rescuing soldiers, and worse still, there was talk of returning soldiers being in a dreadful state. Eric Mallow, a reservist from the village and one of the first to be rescued and sent home on leave, had arrived back two days ago. Mrs Bunch had spoken to him and said he barely opened his mouth to her and flinched at the slightest noise. 'I've known him since he was a cocky boy in shorts, and I swear I've never known him so quiet,' she'd said.

Yesterday, on her day off, Florence had taken the bus to Sudbury to treat herself to some new shoes, and had got chatting to a couple of soldiers who'd made it back from Dunkirk. They'd told her it had been hell on earth, with nowhere to hide while the Luftwaffe dropped bomb after bomb on them. They said they'd seen dozens of soldiers blown up before their eyes. It had been a terrible sight when one of the lads had begun to cry, and once he'd started, he just didn't seem able to stop. Florence's heart had gone out to him, and had she been braver, she would have given him a hug, but as it was, the other lad, whose head was swathed in a bandage, put his arm around his pal like he would a brother.

The lad with the bandaged head didn't have a good word to say about the Belgians, who'd surrendered without warning and left the BEF soldiers stranded. 'Bloody King Leopold,' he'd said furiously, 'declaring the Allied cause lost — well, it's not bleeding surprising when you've got cowards like that in charge. And where was the RAF in all this?' he'd gone on. 'Where were they when the Germans were slaughtering us and we were trapped like bleeding rats in a barrel?'

A po-faced woman in the seat behind Florence had tutted and said there was no need to use such coarse language, and at that the soldier had turned away to look out of the window, his lips moving with some inaudible response. Florence had plucked up the courage to ask if either of the soldiers knew anything about Billy Minton and Elijah Hartley, seeing as they were from the Suffolk Regiment, but neither of them could help her.

Florence didn't think she would ever forget the bitter anger and bleak despair of those two young lads. She could picture them now, as she opened the windows at Winter Cottage to let in the fresh morning air, their grim, tired faces staring blankly out of the bus at a world that probably didn't seem real to them any more.

Ever since the evacuation of Dunkirk had begun, just over a week ago at the end of May, and the small seed of hope had grown within her that Billy might be brought home to safety and given a few days' leave, Florence had been coming here to ensure the cottage was ready for them to stay in as man and wife. She hoped Elijah wouldn't mind; that he would be happy for the little house to be kept clean and tidy rather than left to its own devices. She had also made a daily trip to Clover End Cottage to air it ready for Elijah's return, using the key he'd left behind for Allegra so that she could come and go as she pleased.

Going up the narrow winding staircase to the floor above, the wooden boards creaking beneath her feet, the words of the gypsy woman from last summer played in her head — *You'll find love and you'll lose love.* From the moment they had learned of the news about the evacuation, the words had taunted Florence cruelly. It was the last thing she thought of before going to sleep at night, and the first that she woke to.

The rosebud-patterned curtains swaying in the warm breeze, she stood at the open window in the bedroom that had been Allegra's and looked down on to the overgrown garden. Brambles and weeds and grass as high as her knees had quickly taken hold since the cottage had been left empty. If Florence had more free time, she would do something about it, but she had her hands full with looking after Annelise and Isabella. Bob Manners, their gardener at Island House, had said he might have the odd hour going spare, but since the Local Defence Volunteers had been formed, he'd been too busy.

To everybody's surprise, Lady Fogg had offered the volunteers one of her barns to use on a permanent basis so that the platoon of men didn't have to share facilities at the village hall. Billy's dad, George, had signed up with the LDV and had told Florence that Lady Fogg made them all a hot drink at the end of their meetings, even inviting them into her house, although she did make them take off their boots before crossing the threshold. The new Lady Fogg was a definite improvement on the stuffy old one!

Without a doubt, the war felt so much more real now. Hope had told them that Dr Flowerday was working round the clock in London treating hundreds of returning soldiers who were badly wounded. Some, she said, were in a shocking state, with limbs blown off, or their insides hanging out; it was a miracle they'd made it back at all.

In complete contrast to the horror of what those poor soldiers had gone through, Florence rested her elbows on the windowsill and watched a pair of swallows merrily darting through the air, swooping up and down as if they didn't have a care in the world. Which they probably didn't.

She hadn't really wanted to visit here today, not again, not when it would bring another day of disappointment that Billy wasn't one of the thousands of soldiers evacuated to safety. But Miss Romily had insisted that she come every morning to air the cottage, then return in the evening to close it up. Perhaps it was a way to keep her mind busy; to stop it dwelling on Billy.

While the pain of hoping against hope that

Billy was alive wore her down, Florence knew that it was nothing compared to what those two soldiers on the bus yesterday had gone through. It worried her how altered Billy might be if he did make it back. Would his mind be so badly affected he'd no longer be the same man? It had happened to countless men returning from the Great War — some never recovered from the horrors they'd witnessed; they went clean off their heads.

Yet so long as Billy came back to her, Florence would take care of him no matter what. She loved him and would help him to mend. She had meant it that bitterly cold January day in church when she'd said the words, for better or for worse, and that was what she would do.

But what of Elijah? What if he returned badly injured; who would take care of him? And what about Isabella if he didn't survive the carnage the Germans were inflicting on the Allies as they pushed relentlessly forward?

At Miss Romily's instruction, all Allegra's personal things, such as they were, had been carefully stored at Island House for when Elijah wanted to go through them; he would be the one to decide what to keep, in particular what to keep for Isabella when she was old enough to want to know about her mother.

When Florence had helped with the sad task of packing up Allegra's belongings, she had wondered about Isabella's real father in Italy, a man they knew nothing about other than that his name was Luigi. Some might say he had a right to know about his daughter. Some might even say he had the right to claim the child as his own and take her back to Italy with him.

Florence hoped that the man would never get to hear of Isabella's presence in the world; she couldn't imagine not having the baby around. The same was true of Annelise and Stanley. Three children who had unexpectedly come to them, and, like a blessing from God, brought joy into their lives at Island House. But each, she saw now, could be taken from them in the blink of an eye by their rightful parents.

There she went again, as Mrs Partridge would say, fearing the worst. And hadn't Mrs Partridge been proved right when she'd said that providence would provide when it came to finding a new maid? Lotte couldn't be a better addition to the household; everything she did, she did quietly and efficiently, without a single word of complaint. Not that she was ever asked to do anything Florence had never done herself.

Much to Florence's amusement, Stanley had taken a real shine to the girl with her pale porcelain skin, striking blue eyes and dark hair that fell in a cascade of corkscrew curls when it wasn't pinned up beneath her maid's cap. Bless him, he could often be found following her around, offering to help her beat the rugs, or put the washing out.

But there was a sadness to Lotte; a burden of sadness she kept very much to herself. She slept in the small room next to Florence's, and more than once Florence had heard her crying herself to sleep at night. It wasn't surprising really when you thought about the family she had left behind in Austria, who had probably been interned in one of those awful camps Hope had told Florence about, where Jews and just about anyone else Hitler didn't like were put to work like slaves. That was if they were lucky.

Luck, thought Florence as she walked back to Island House — or providence, as Mrs Partridge liked to call it — had brought Lotte to them; would it also bring Billy and Elijah safely home? Please God it did.

70

Later that evening, long after the children had gone to bed and Miss Romily had taken herself off to work in the drawing room, Florence and Lotte were listening to the news on the wireless while washing up together. They had just heard that the operation to evacuate Dunkirk was over, which filled Florence with sick misery. What if Billy wasn't among the last of the soldiers to be brought back? What if she never knew exactly what had happened to him, just as Hope would never really know how her brother had died?

Behind her, Bobby suddenly gave a low growl and raised himself from beside Mrs Partridge, who was snoring gently by the range. Within seconds there was a knock at the back door.

'That's odd,' said Hope, who was sitting at the kitchen table darning one of Stanley's socks. 'We don't normally have callers at the back door at this time of night.' With Bobby following closely behind, she went to see who it was.

At the sink, Florence carefully lifted a corner of the blackout curtain and craned her neck to try and catch a glimpse of who it might be. It was probably Bert Cox, the ARP warden, here to tick them off for some blackout misdemeanour. She knew it was his job, but really, he was such an old woman about it; the slightest bit of light from any house and he relished the opportunity to take people to task.

At the sound of barking and men's voices — voices she recognised — Florence turned away from the window and watched in stunned amazement as, through the open kitchen door, in walked not Bert Cox, but Elijah, and there was Billy right behind him. She let out a cry and flew across the kitchen.

He held her so tightly in his arms she could barely breathe. But she didn't care; all that mattered was that he was safely home. Tears of joy streamed down her cheeks and she clung on to him, never wanting to let him go ever again.

'Gawd bless us,' said Mrs Partridge, awake now and rubbing at her eyes. 'Am I dreaming, or are you both really back!'

'We're back,' said Billy, releasing his hold on Florence.

'How long for?' asked Florence, wiping the tears from her face. 'And where will you be sent next? Not back to France, I hope. Was it very awful? We've heard such dreadful things! Oh my goodness, I can't believe you're actually here!'

'One question at a time, Flo,' he said, exchanging a look with Elijah. 'We have to report to barracks tomorrow afternoon, then we'll have a better idea what happens next.'

'Well in my opinion,' said Mrs Partridge, 'there's just one question that needs asking. How hungry are you?'

It was Elijah who answered. 'Starving, Mrs Partridge, and that's God's own truth.'

'Just as I thought. Now sit yourselves down while Florence and I rustle up something for you. There's some leftover shepherd's pie in the pantry; it's not much, with all this wretched rationing, but it'll have to do. Lotte, perhaps you'd like to fetch that for me. I dare say Miss Romily won't object to you two boys having it.'

'Talking of Romily,' said Hope, 'I'll go and fetch her. I'm sure she'll be delighted to see you both.'

Billy frowned and rubbed at his grubby unshaven chin. 'We're not really in any fit state to be — '

'Billy Minton, don't talk nonsense,' interrupted Mrs Partridge, tying on her apron. 'Nobody here cares a fig if you're filthy dirty and look like a couple of tramps. Florence, are you going to just stand there gawping at your husband, or are you going to help feed him?'

Florence laughed. 'You see, Billy, some things never change. Mrs Partridge is still just as much of a dragon as she ever was.'

⋆　⋆　⋆

But some things had changed. Billy was not the same happy-golucky lad Florence had waved goodbye to in January.

Alone in the dark as they walked to Winter Cottage, where they were to spend their first night together, he scarcely spoke, and when he did, it was to utter just a few short words before lapsing into brooding silence. With sadness Florence remembered how Billy had always joked around and chatted nineteen to the dozen.

He's exhausted, she chided herself, just as the ugly screech of a barn owl filled the night stillness, followed by the swoosh of its wings as the bird swooped across the lane in front of them. The next thing Florence knew, she was being thrown to the ground. The air knocked out of her, it was some moments before she realised that she was lying in the ditch with Billy on top of her. He was breathing hard, the weight of his body crushing her painfully.

'Billy,' she said, trying to wriggle free, 'what is it? Are you all right?'

When he didn't answer, just began to shake, she recalled the sobbing young soldier on the bus on the way to Sudbury and the state he'd been in. In a degree of shock herself, she held Billy in her arms. Minutes passed as she did her best to comfort him, and when eventually his body stilled, he rolled off her and struggled to his feet. He held his hand out to her and helped her up.

'I'm sorry,' he muttered, avoiding her gaze. 'You must think I've lost my mind, turned into one of those pathetic ninnies who jumps at the slightest noise.'

'I don't think anything of the sort,' she said softly. 'I know what a terrible time you must have had.'

He shook his head and at last levelled his gaze with hers. 'No you don't. Unless you were there, you can't possibly understand what it feels like to see men all about you blown to bits. To wonder if it's your own head about to be blasted off your body and left to roll around on the sand.'

'You're right,' she said, doing her best not to flinch at the unfamiliar harshness of his tone. 'But I just want you to know that I love you no matter what.'

They walked the rest of the way to Winter Cottage in a silence punctuated by their footsteps, the heavier sound of Billy's boots and Florence's lighter step.

'I'm not sure I can do this,' he mumbled when they reached the cottage and Florence produced the key from her handbag.

'What can't you do?' she asked him.

'Be here with you tonight.'

'What do you mean?'

'Perhaps it'd be better if I went home, to my parents. I should see them before I return to barracks.'

'I thought you said you'd see them in the morning?'

He turned his head to one side, then the other, looking anywhere but at her. 'I'm tired,' he said flatly.

'Even more reason to stay the night here.'

'But . . . but it'll be our first night together and I don't think I . . . and you're probably hoping . . . ' His voice trailed off.

She put a hand on his forearm, suddenly understanding what was worrying him. 'It's okay, Billy. We're just going to sleep. That's all.' Before he could say anything else, she put the key in the lock and pushed open the door. 'Come on,' she said. 'Let's get you to bed so you can sleep.'

★ ★ ★

But they didn't sleep. Trying to put him at ease, Florence gently encouraged Billy to talk, to share with her what he had gone through in the last

585

few days, days that he could never have imagined he'd ever experience. In the darkness, lying side by side in bed, their bodies only just touching, he told her how he and Elijah had become separated from the rest of the men; how after sleeping rough they'd managed to steal a German motorcycle. Their commanding officer had told them to head to the coast, to Dunkirk, where the rescue operation would take place. They thought they were doing well, even joking that they were escaping to Dunkirk with the aid of enemy fuel, but when they reached the coast and hid in the sand dunes along with all the other soldiers waiting to be rescued, that was when they encountered the full might of the Luftwaffe strafing the skies above them. With bombs raining down on them, they were convinced they wouldn't make it. Even after they had waded out up to their chests in seawater and finally made it onto a rescue boat heading for England, Billy had been certain he would die.

'What about Tommy?' asked Florence when at last he fell quiet. 'Did he make it home?'

Billy slowly shook his head. Then he turned and burrowed his head into her neck and cried silently, his body shaking violently within her arms.

Florence cried with him, for the boy he'd once been and for the man he now was.

71

On a warm and sunny morning in July, a little over a month since the night Billy and Elijah had arrived home safely, Romily was up early with Isabella. After changing and feeding the baby, she carried her outside to the garden.

At a slow, unhurried pace she walked across the dewy grass, leaving behind her a trail of footsteps. She paused to drink in the heavenly smell of the stocks and the sweet peas that were climbing rampantly up the canes she had placed in the flower bed with Bob Manners' guidance. It was such a simple pleasure, breathing in the sweet perfume of the flowers, but one that seemed almost symbolic of everything the country was fighting to protect and preserve. The sheer loveliness of the garden on this perfectly glorious morning confirmed what Sarah had said, and what Romily had always known to be true — she could not remain here while a ruthless regime that was hell-bent on destroying all that was just and beautiful in the name of fascism marched ever nearer.

With Italy now at war with Britain and the Nazi swastika flying from the Eiffel Tower in Paris, the fight to defend themselves had escalated dramatically in the last month, and there was genuine fear amongst many in the village that a German invasion could actually now happen. No longer did anyone speak of a phoney war. Two days ago, Norwich had been bombed and one of Bob Manners' nieces who worked at the Colman's factory had been lucky to escape with her life.

There had been losses closer to home. Wally Bryson who used to work in the butcher's shop hadn't made it back from France, and Billy and Elijah had seen with their own eyes their old friend Tommy mown down by enemy gunfire. They had tried to carry him to safety, but he'd died in Billy's arms.

Elijah had told Romily how he and Billy had been rescued on the beach at Dunkirk, and she could only wonder at the matter-of-fact way he spoke of what must have been a hellish ordeal. His stoicism had touched Romily and left her thinking how proud Allegra would have been of him.

She had tentatively asked Elijah, that night he had arrived back, if he wanted to go upstairs and see Isabella asleep in her cot. His expression had changed instantly to one of pained emotion, and she had regretted her question. Mrs Partridge had stepped in and said perhaps he might prefer to see the child in the morning after a good night's sleep. He'd agreed quickly that that might be better, then said it was time he set off for Clover End Cottage.

He'd returned the next morning and, with what Romily could only describe as a look of heartbreak on his face, had made Isabella's acquaintance in the garden as she lay in her pram watching the leaves in the apple tree dancing above her.

'She looks like Allegra,' he'd whispered. It was the first utterance he'd made of Allegra's name.

'That's what we all think,' Romily had said. 'She's beautiful, isn't she?'

He'd nodded. 'I've never seen a baby so small before. Is she . . . you know . . . quite well?'

'Oh yes, quite well, and with the sweetest temperament. She sleeps like a charm and rarely cries.'

'Allegra was so sure she would have a girl,' he'd said wistfully.

Romily had suggested he might like to hold the baby, and he'd looked shocked.

'Me?' he'd said.

'Why not?' she'd asked.

'Because . . . because I might drop her.' He'd held up his large rough hands as though this was evidence enough to prove his case.

'You'll be fine,' Romily had encouraged him. And without giving him a chance to back out, she had reached into the pram and carefully placed Isabella in his arms. 'See,' she'd said, 'nothing to it.'

But there was everything to it, and when Isabella's soft hazel gaze had met his and her lips curved into what had become her trademark lopsided smile, Elijah's eyes had misted over and Romily could see he was struggling to keep his composure. Expecting him to want to give the child back, she had put her hands out, but he'd shaken his head and turned away, slowly walking the length of the garden, his head lowered as if

589

deep in conversation with Isabella.

Since then Elijah and Billy, as members of the 1st Battalion of the Suffolk Regiment, had been sent to Frome in Somerset to begin what they had been told would be a lengthy period of intensive training. Elijah wrote every week, always asking after Isabella and often sending her a small present. In return Romily also wrote every week, and occasionally she would include a sketch that Hope would draw of Isabella as a keepsake for him.

Now, as Romily picked a handful of fragrant sweet pea flowers to take inside, holding the bunch so Isabella could look at them, she thought of Elijah's willing involvement in the child's life and felt sure that before too long, providing he survived this bloody awful war, Isabella would come to know him as her loving father, just as Allegra had wanted.

Deep in thought and retracing her steps across the dewy lawn, Romily looked up to see Hope standing at the French doors of the drawing room. She was dressed in a sombre dress of dark green, a colour that drained her of what little colour she possessed, and it reminded Romily that she had better get a move on. Today they were holding a memorial service at the church for Kit. Hope had put off organising it, perhaps refusing to let go entirely of her younger brother.

★ ★ ★

If ever there was a man who enjoyed the sound of his own voice, it was the Reverend Tate.

Perhaps it wouldn't be so bad if he'd actually known Kit properly, but as it was, he was merely gushing one insincere platitude after another. It was one of the reasons Hope had not rushed to hold this service; she had not trusted herself to sit through an hour of her brother being wholly misrepresented. At times like this, she thought with caustic irreverence, it seemed to be the prerogative of the living to canonise the dead.

Positioned in the pew at the front of the church, with Arthur to her left and Romily and Roddy to her right, she longed for Reverend Tate to bring a halt to his monotonous drivel. But there seemed to be no end to his verbosity. Kit was now being held up as a shining example of bravery, an example the young boys in the village should live up to.

No! Hope wanted to scream. It wasn't bravery that had led Kit to his death; it was a desire to prove to their father — even if he was dead — that he was as much a man as Jack Devereux had ever been. Poor Kit, so desperate for approval all his short life, he had made the ultimate sacrifice.

Tears filled Hope's eyes as she recalled the last letter her brother had written to her, and she dashed them away angrily. From nowhere she was suddenly consumed with a white-hot anger. Anger that Kit had felt the need to prove himself. Anger that their father could not have shown that he loved Kit for the boy he was. Anger that a madman in Germany had plunged Europe into a war that was going to claim many more lives yet. She was angry too that loving

591

another person could make one feel so vulnerable to the pain of loss. First Dieter, then her father and Allegra, now her brother. How many more would she lose? Otto and Sabine? Edmund? Oh please not Edmund!

Not for the first time that day, Hope wished Edmund had managed to find the time to get away, but he was still frantically busy in London treating all those poor horrifically injured soldiers who had returned from France and Belgium.

She leant forward just a couple of inches and turned discreetly to look at Evelyn, who was sitting in the pew across the aisle from her. Hope had never known Evelyn to show an excess of emotion, and she wasn't showing any now. Staring ahead, her gaze fixed on the stained-glass window behind the altar, she gave the impression of being oblivious to Reverend Tate droning on. The only sign that she was upset was the handkerchief that was poking out from her hands on her lap.

* * *

Thank God that fiasco was finally over, thought Arthur as he followed his sister out of the church and into the bright summer sunshine. Another minute and they'd all have fallen asleep, or died of sheer boredom.

With no grave to stand around, people were gathering in small groups on the gravel pathway, unsure what to do next other than avoid the peril of getting stuck talking to Reverend Tate; in that purpose they seemed entirely of one mind.

'I can't think for a moment that Kit would have approved of that,' said Evelyn Flowerday as she approached Hope and Romily.

'I couldn't agree more,' replied Hope. 'It was truly ghastly. I hardly recognised the person Tate was talking about. What did you think, Arthur?'

Surprised at the question, that his opinion mattered to his sister, he said, 'I couldn't agree more. The whole show was deplorable and plumbed depths of sentimentality that even Kit would have baulked at. Please swear on all you cherish that you won't allow my send-off to be so soppy.'

Hope gave a half smile. 'The same goes for me. Just have a choir to sing 'How Great Thou Art' and then get on with having a drink.'

The exchange surprised Arthur. He had thought his sister might have lapped it all up, a ready convert to Kit's new status as courageous hero who could do no wrong.

'Talking of which,' said Romily, 'do you suppose we ought to put everyone out of their misery and tell them it's time to move on to Island House for refreshments?'

'Why not?' said Hope. 'Having survived the awfulness of that toe-curling service, I certainly think we all deserve a drink.'

'A very large one at that,' said Roddy. 'Shall I do the honours and round everybody up? Not that I think they'll need much encouraging.'

★　★　★

Roddy was right; it didn't take long for people to get the message and begin the short walk to Island House, the sombreness of the last hour evaporating in the warm sunshine as they strolled along the footpath. By the time they reached the house, the mourners had adopted an air of cheerful revelry, as if on a pleasant day out. A flash of irritation had Arthur wanting to tell them to show some bloody respect, but his annoyance was so insignificant that frankly he didn't have it in him to criticise, not when he himself had been feeling in such good spirits lately.

Ever since he'd discovered Pamela was alive, that he hadn't actually murdered her, he had felt different, almost as if he had had a close shave with death itself and survived. In many ways he had, for if he really had killed the woman and had somehow been found guilty of doing so, he would have very likely been hanged for it. Until that day when he'd encountered Pamela and David Webster together, he hadn't understood just how heavily that threat of discovery had weighed upon him. Yes, the news that he was going to be a father had cheered him considerably, but as the weeks had gone by he had realised just what he might lose if the police did come knocking on his door to arrest him. The thought of never knowing his child had made him sick to his stomach.

Yet for all that, his threat to Pamela, should she not do as he'd demanded in handing over all evidence of their association, had not been an empty one. It was now not only his own skin he was out to protect, but that of his unborn child.

Thanks to Mrs Partridge and Lotte, everything was ready for them when they arrived back at Island House. Florence had accompanied Stanley to the funeral, the boy having surprised them by wanting to attend. His interest in the war had grown since Billy and Elijah had returned from Dunkirk, and she worried that he saw life as a soldier or a pilot as one big adventure, a bit of a lark. He'd taken to quoting Churchill's speeches at the kitchen table while they were eating, mimicking the prime minister's gruff voice, which confused Bobby no end. Miss Romily had said that maybe attending Kit's memorial service might temper the lad's enthusiasm. After Reverend Tate's eulogy, Florence doubted that.

With Isabella fast asleep in her pram and Stanley amusing Annelise with Bobby, Florence was free to help Lotte serve drinks. The guests were gathered on the terrace, making the most of the lovely day, and she went outside with a tray of sherry glasses and moved amongst the villagers, most of whom she knew. There had been a good turnout, larger than they had expected, but then people here had known Kit when he was a young boy. Billy's parents had closed the shop to be in church, as had several others. Florence was glad for Hope that so many had wanted to show their respects. She went over to her in-laws and offered them a drink. Ruby declined, but George took a glass of sherry, his large hand wrapped clumsily around the small, delicate glass.

'Seems hard to believe that this time last year none of this had started,' he said with a shake of his head.

'I know,' said Florence, thinking how she hadn't really got to know Billy properly until last August Bank Holiday at the village fete.

As if reading her mind, George smiled. 'We only knew you as a customer back then, and now you're our daughter-in-law.'

Florence glanced anxiously at Ruby, waiting for one of her cutting remarks, but the woman remained tight-lipped. Things had very slowly improved between them, but Florence was always on her guard. 'Just another fortnight and Billy will be home for two days' leave,' she said. 'I can't wait to see him. I was wondering if you'd like to come to Winter Cottage for Sunday lunch when he's home.'

'That'd be very kind of you,' said George, 'but we wouldn't want to put you to any trouble.'

'It's no trouble at all. It'll be nice to use the cottage properly, as a real home, now it's all official like and Elijah's letting us rent it from him, and so cheaply too, since I spend most of my time at Island House.'

'Must be fair odd for you toing and froing between here and there,' said George, looking back up at the house behind them. 'Like having two homes.'

'That'll all change when you have a baby,' said Ruby with a meaningful look, 'and stop working.'

From nowhere, the arrival of a grandchild had suddenly become important to Ruby, as though she saw this as Florence's sole purpose. She made no bones about hinting that they should get a move on and produce one. A baby was the last thing Florence wanted any time soon, especially now that Miss Romily had confided in her about her plans for the future. But she wasn't about to admit any of that to her mother-in-law.

Nor was she prepared to admit that she and Billy had yet to get anywhere near making a baby. Poor Billy had been too shattered by what he'd seen at Dunkirk to want to have sex with her. While a part of her had felt just a little bit rejected when he'd wanted to do nothing more than hold her, she'd known better than to push him.

'A baby will happen soon enough, I expect,' she said brightly to Ruby, and before the conversation could go any further, she left her in-laws and went to serve the other guests.

★ ★ ★

With only a handful of guests left now, Hope studied Arthur, unable to figure him out.

Her brother was a different man to the one who had spent a week here last year to fulfil the wishes of their father's will. Not a vindictive word of scorn or criticism had he directed at Hope or Romily today. Could it be that the prospect of fatherhood was having a positive effect on him?

But when Hope thought of the day in London with Edmund when they had seen Irene with another man, she experienced the unknown sensation of actually feeling sorry for her brother. If Irene had been indulging in an affair, Hope wanted to believe that it would be short-lived. But more importantly, she wanted very much to believe that the child Irene was expecting was Arthur's. Even after the extensive catalogue of terrible things he had done over the years, Hope couldn't bear the thought that he could be made a cuckold in so cruel a fashion. Particularly so if it meant that unknowingly he ended up raising a child that wasn't actually his.

And who, she thought with a stab of incredulity, would ever have thought she would feel a trace of sympathy towards her elder brother? Maybe it was because with Allegra and Kit gone, it was now just the two of them left.

She was about to answer Arthur's question regarding the publication of her children's book — he'd said he wanted to be the first to have a signed copy, for his child — when in the distance she noticed the figure of a man slowly limping across the lawn. The brim of a peculiarly large floppy hat hid his face; it was the sort of hat an artist might wear to protect his eyes from the glare of the sun while painting. She owned one not unlike it herself.

There was something oddly familiar about the man, and as he came nearer, the sensation of familiarity grew stronger, but at the same time every ounce of her reason told Hope she was mistaken. But suddenly, when the figure raised a hand in the air as if in acknowledgement of her, she knew she wasn't wrong.

It was Kit, her dear, dear brother!

72

With the guests all magically gone, and exhausted and overcome by the reaction his appearance had caused, Kit sank gratefully into a chair in the shade of the apple tree, and dabbed lightly at the sheen of sweat on his face with a handkerchief.

He'd been told not to overdo it, and now he saw the sense in the advice he'd been given, and which he'd chosen to flout in his haste to return to Island House. He was used to people staring, especially strangers, but it was hard to bear the scrutiny of those who knew him — those who knew how he used to look. He didn't blame them for being shocked, or even repulsed; it was, as he'd been told, something he would have to learn to live with for the rest of his life. A life he was lucky to have, he'd also been repeatedly told.

'I still can't believe it's really you,' said his sister, kneeling on the grass in front of him. Her face was flushed, her eyes still shining from the tears she'd shed. In the chair next to Kit, Evelyn sat very still. He hadn't yet looked her directly in the eye, knowing that he would see a brave attempt on her part to hide her revulsion.

'I can't believe I'm actually here,' he said to Hope.

'But why didn't you let us know you were on your way, or more to the point that you were alive?'

'I did. I sent you a letter.'

'When?'

'A few weeks ago.'

Hope tutted. 'It must be that new lad who's taken over from Will Capper; didn't I say he looked decidedly wet behind the ears? Your letter has probably ended up in a hedge somewhere.'

'Never mind the post boy,' said Arthur, seated in the wicker chair to Kit's left, and as a result, the one closest to the grotesquely scarred flesh of his face. 'Tell us exactly what happened to you. How the hell did you survive the sinking of the *Arcadia* and then not surface until now?'

It was a question Kit had often asked himself: just how the hell *had* he survived? With painfully deformed hands — his fingers had practically melted and fused together when the flames had engulfed him — he took the glass of barley water Romily passed to him from the tray on the table. 'My memories are still patchy,' he said, 'and it's anybody's guess whether I'll ever remember everything. My last memory is of being blown off my feet and feeling I was being burnt alive. The next thing I knew, I was waking in a hospital bed covered in bandages. Apparently I'd been as near to death as one can be without actually being dead.' He took a sip of the refreshing drink, placing the glass against what remained of his lips, keeping to himself how he'd screamed with pain every time the doctors and nurses had moved him. Or how he'd cried like a baby when his dressings were changed, despite the gentleness of the nurses who took care of him.

'I'm told an American merchant ship on its

way back to New York picked me out of the water,' he continued, 'and took me to a hospital when they reached port. They did their best to dress my burns, and to treat the infection and raging temperature I then had, as well as try to figure out who I was, but I had total amnesia. They said it was the shock; my brain had shut down. It's working better now. For instance, I know I went to Canada to learn to fly, but I have only fleeting memories of doing so. And I have no memory of the *Arcadia* sinking, or of being in the water. That part's a blank.'

'Perhaps that's just as well,' said Evelyn quietly.

Kit turned his head and from beneath the brim of his ridiculous hat — which he wore not so much to hide behind as to protect his damaged skin from the sun — forced himself to look at her, to see how pitifully the girl he had hoped might one day come to love him now regarded him. He knew that wish would never come true now. Nobody in their right mind would love or marry him. He found Evelyn's gaze fixed on his, cool, assured and unflinching. Its directness was unnerving; he'd grown more used to people not being able to look him in the eye. Had come to expect it.

Throughout his long journey back to England, he had encountered any amount of stares, and on his way here from the train station, a couple of young boys with fishing rods slung over their shoulders had gawped at him in fascinated horror, then sniggered when they'd passed by. At least they hadn't run off screaming that they'd seen a monster, which was how he'd thought he looked when he first saw his face without bandages. His right hand profile was not much altered, but the left side of his face was hideously distorted. The doctors had carried out skin grafts to try and salvage what remained of his ear, cheek and jaw, and all the time Kit, still suffering from amnesia, had viewed the disfigured face in the mirror as that of a stranger. His body had suffered too, particularly his legs, which was why he now walked with a limp. Once he'd been able to get out of bed in the hospital, the nurses had helped him to regain the use of his legs. Initially the pain had been so great he had been overcome with nausea and exhaustion. It would all take time, the nurses had encouraged him, he would have to be patient.

'I think you're right,' he said finally in answer to Evelyn's remark. Then in an effort to lighten the intensity of the mood, he said to the group as a whole, 'Well then, tell me about this memorial service you held in my honour. I do hope nice things were said of me. Do you suppose people will feel cheated that they gave up their valuable time for a fraud?'

'My dear boy,' said Roddy, 'that will be the very last thing they'll feel.'

'We'll get your old room ready,' said Romily. 'You must stay with us for as long as you want.'

'Yes,' agreed Hope. 'No rushing back to London. I won't hear of it.'

Kit thought of London and his old life there. While he could not remember the sinking of the *Arcadia*, he could recall in detail how bored he'd been working at the Imperial Bank and how excited he'd been to embark on the journey to Canada to learn to fly. If only he'd listened to his sister and been patient enough to bide his time as a reservist and wait for the RAF to call him up. But no, his foolishly eager need to jump the gun, to be seen to be doing something, coupled with the need to impress Evelyn, had been for naught.

As often happened when he was exhausted and began to rue the day he'd left England for Canada, he felt the dark cloud of depression descend, bringing with it the familiar feeling that he was as good as useless now; that it would have been better had he died in the Atlantic with the rest of the men on board the *Arcadia*.

Part Three

The New Chapter

*'Never in the field of human conflict was
so much owed by so many to so few.'*

Winston Churchill, 20th August, 1940

73

December 1940

It was Boxing Day afternoon and Romily was home on a three-day pass. She hadn't expected to be able to get away, but fortunately the rota had enabled both her and Sarah to have a short break; it was the first Romily had had since joining the ATA. Her friend had warned her that the hours were long and tiring, and so they were, but despite existing in a state of perpetual exhaustion, not for a very long time had Romily felt so energised or alive.

She had joined the Air Transport Auxiliary exactly a year to the day since Jack's death, and she liked to think he would approve and be cheering her on. Her initial training period had coincided with the Luftwaffe targeting airfields in southern England, followed by an all-out attack on London when bombs rained down on the city. It had started with more than three hundred German bombers, escorted by over six hundred fighter planes, coming up the Thames and bombing Woolwich Arsenal and the docks, a gasworks and a power station, leaving hundreds dead and many injured. Since then the East End of London had suffered nightly bombing raids, while thousands of people crowded into Underground stations to sleep in safety.

Last month Germany had undertaken a new

tactic, that of bombing provincial cities in order to wipe out British industry and a number of ports. The devastation and death toll served to confirm that Romily had done the right thing in leaving Hope in charge of running Island House, with Florence taking care of the children. It had not been an easy decision leaving Isabella; after all, she was the child's guardian while Elijah continued to serve in the Suffolk Regiment, but her conscience simply would not have allowed her to remain living a life of comfort and ease while so many were suffering, not when she had a genuine skill to offer.

Weekly letters from Hope and Florence had kept her abreast of life in the village, how the LDV had become the Home Guard, and how Stanley's mother had written to say that she knew exactly where her son was and that they were welcome to him — good riddance to bad rubbish was the general gist of her scribbled note, according to Hope. The spite of her message was kept from Stanley; instead he was told that his stay at Island House was now official and came with his mother's blessing. Not that Stanley gave a hoot. As far as he was concerned, Melstead St Mary was his home; he was happy there, especially as he now had a new friend, an evacuee from the East End who'd arrived with a new influx of children. The village school was full to bursting and Hope was helping out with art classes, as well as listening to children read.

Now, as Romily circulated amongst the guests at the party Hope had organised for the village, she came across Roddy alone by the fireside. 'You look thoughtful,' she said, squeezing past Miss Gant and Miss Treadmill to join him.

'I was thinking of the transformation you've wrought here,' he said.

'Me? Oh no, Hope is responsible for putting this party together. I didn't do a thing.'

'That's my point,' said Roddy. 'Poor Hope was so deeply mired in her grief for Dieter and her bitterness towards her father, she would never have been able to do something like this, not until you came into her life.'

'I refute that entirely. It's down to the passing of time, nothing to do with me.'

Roddy shook his head. 'No, my dear, you must take your share of the credit. Take a look around you; the evidence is plain to see. There's Arthur with his wife, and now the proud father of a fine baby boy. And there's Kit in front of the Christmas tree with Evelyn and her brother. Admittedly Kit's not yet fully back from the brink, but that girl is working her firm but loving magic on him, just as I suspected she would. Hope too is allowing herself to fall in love again, with Edmund. Just look at the expression on her face. I don't think I've ever seen her looking more confident and assured of herself. This is all down to you, Romily; you brought this family back together — back to life — just as Jack wanted.'

'They did it themselves, Roddy. I merely welcomed them to treat Island House as their true and proper home, so perhaps it's the house that should be thanked. I know that for myself it was a great comfort being here after Jack died. I wish he was here to see this,' she said, her voice suddenly sad and her gaze falling on Elijah with Isabella in his arms. He could not have looked a more proud father as he showed the little girl off to Billy and his parents. 'Allegra should be here with us too,' she said quietly.

Roddy sighed. 'Poor Allegra, all that radiant beauty and shining talent. I still rail at the unfairness of her death. I was so very fond of her. I saw in her something I felt we had in common, that we were only ever on the periphery of the family, outsiders looking in.'

Romily looked at him, shocked. 'Oh Roddy, you can't possibly mean that. Jack never regarded you as an outsider; you know jolly well he thought of you as a brother. More so than his actual brother.'

'I know that, but Allegra and I were adopted into the family, and that makes a difference to how one sees oneself within it.'

'Then maybe the same goes for me. After all, I'm only a Devereux by marriage.'

'You always have an answer for me, don't you?' Roddy said with a smile. 'But talking of marriage, what do you think to your wing commander and Sarah announcing their engagement earlier today?'

Romily glanced over to where Sarah and Tony were talking to Lady Fogg and her husband — Sir Archibald having finally returned to Melstead Hall when the Blitz took hold of London. Romily knew from Mrs Partridge that there had been mutterings in the village that the man had only come home because he was a rotten coward and was afraid of being bombed at his club.

'I couldn't be happier for them,' Romily said quite truthfully. 'And really, it's high time you, and everybody else stopped referring to the poor man as *my* wing commander; he was never any such thing.'

Roddy stared at her thoughtfully. 'You don't think you might have been happy with him yourself?'

She laughed. 'Goodness, no. Not so soon after Jack. I'm happy as I am, Roddy, really I am. You don't need to worry about me.'

'Somebody has to,' he said with a gentleness to his voice that touched her. 'I shouldn't say this,' he went on, 'but I will anyway, since it's Christmas, a time I always think is made for heartfelt confessions. The thing is, if I had met you before Jack did, and had I been younger and more dashing, and not a dull old solicitor, I might have tipped my hat in your direction. But alas, compared to the dazzling brightness of Jack's star, I would not have stood a chance. But then the strength of Jack's character had the ability to eclipse most men, so I hold no grudge towards him in that respect. I still miss him, you know.'

Romily slipped her arm through his and kissed him affectionately on the cheek. 'I know you do, just as I do. You're the dearest man alive, Roddy, and for that I'll always love you. And for being such a loyal and supportive friend, not just to Jack and his family, but to me. Which I hope will always be the case.'

He patted her hand. 'In that, you can be absolutely sure. You only have to say the word, Romily, and God willing, I shall be there for you. Now tell me some more about your work with the ATA. Jack would be so proud of you. And jealous too!'

'Oh, he would have leapt at the chance to join, and long before I did.'

'Much good it would have done him when he couldn't fly.'

Romily laughed. 'Do you suppose a little thing like that would have stopped him?'

They were both laughing as, over on the other side of the drawing room, one of the guests wound up the gramophone player and the sound of Al Bowlly's soft-toned voice singing 'The Very Thought of You' filled the room. The first time Romily had ever danced with Jack, it had been to this song. Holding her firmly against him, their bodies almost as one as they moved together, he had brushed her ear and neck with his lips as he sang along. It had been one of the very many intensely sensual moments between them.

Now, hearing those same words, her heart grew heavy with longing for Jack.

The very thought of you and I forget to do
The little ordinary things that everyone ought
*   to do,*
I'm living in a kind of daydream
I'm happy as a king
And foolish though it may seem
To me that's everything

But rather than give in to the grief that without warning still had the power to creep up on her and strike her down, she cleared her tightening throat. 'Roddy,' she said, 'there's something I need to discuss with you. It's something I should have arranged with you a long time ago. Do you remember the jewels and the Rembrandt sketch belonging to the Friedberg family in Austria that I brought back from Europe before Jack's death?'

'Yes.' Roddy nodded. 'I remember thinking how you really shouldn't have taken such a tremendous risk.'

'Tish and tosh, it was hardly any risk at all! Now what I want to ask you is this; those items have been in the safe upstairs ever since I brought them back with me. The original plan was for Sarah to have them in London, but when war broke out we decided it would be better for them to stay here in what we believe is comparative safety.'

'That makes sense, yes. Although a bank vault would be quite secure, I'm sure.'

'You're probably right, but transporting them anywhere now could put them at risk. A risk I'd rather not take. Currently, apart from me, only one other person knows the combination to unlock the safe, and that person is Florence.'

'Florence?'

'Don't look so surprised, Roddy; I've trusted that girl implicitly since the day she came to work for me. Just as Elijah and I have trusted her to look after Isabella in our absence.'

'Fair enough. What do you want me to do?'

'I want you to know the combination also, in case anything happens to me or Florence.'

'Nothing is going to happen to you,' he said with a frown. 'You'll live forever, Romily. You're indestructible.'

Romily recalled saying a similar thing to Jack. 'But in the event of your optimism being misplaced,' she said, 'I'd like for you to have the combination. It would give me peace of mind. I think it would give Florence peace of mind too, knowing she wouldn't have to shoulder the responsibility completely alone if for some reason I did fall out of the sky or something equally careless. We also need to have a document drawn up stating very clearly who owns the contents of the safe. Of course none of this really seemed necessary when I carried out the favour for Sarah, as we didn't think the war would go on for too long. Now we know better.'

'I'll do whatever is necessary,' he said. 'Will you have time to sign the paperwork before you and Sarah leave?'

'Sarah's leaving first thing tomorrow morning, but I'll be here until the afternoon. I'd also like to make a new will. Again, it's something I should have done before now. Will you have time to prepare everything?'

'I shall make time.'

'Thank you, Roddy, what would we do without you?'

'You of all people would manage.'

★　★　★

614

'Well, Hope, this is quite the party you've thrown,' said Arthur, coming over to join her and Kit. 'If you're not careful, the good people of Melstead St Mary will expect this every Boxing Day.'

'Would that be such a bad thing?' replied Hope. 'I enjoyed organising it, so why not?'

'Why not indeed?' With a nod to Kit, Arthur said, 'You're looking in pretty good health, all things considered.'

'I'll take that as a compliment coming from you,' said Kit. 'Fatherhood seems to be suiting you,' he added. 'Ralph is a regular chip off the old block and no mistake.' He exchanged a look with Hope. Not long after his return to Island House, his sister had confided in Kit what she and Edmund had witnessed in London: Irene playing fast and loose with another man. A year ago Kit might have taken grim satisfaction in telling Arthur that his wife was making a fool of him, if only to settle an old score, but he had no appetite for such juvenile games now. What was more, when Ralph was born there was no question of his parentage. The child bore an unmistakable likeness to his father; he was a Devereux through and through. The poor devil even had his father's temper if he couldn't get what he wanted. As a consequence, both Kit and Hope had decided that maybe all marriages had their share of secrets, and if Irene was unfaithful to Arthur, it was frankly none of their business. Sleeping dogs and all that.

Absorbed in his own thoughts, he hadn't realised his brother had drifted off to talk to somebody else, not until Hope nudged his arm.

'You all right?' she asked with a small frown on her face. 'Are you weary of being sociable?'

'I'm fine,' he lied. Tiredness was a permanent problem for him. He rarely slept for longer than a couple of hours at night, frequently woken by terrifying nightmares of being consumed by a raging inferno, the flames licking at his body. He would wake bathed in sweat and more often than not screaming loud enough to wake the entire household.

But he was determined to get better, to focus on leading as normal a life as he possibly could. As Evelyn never stopped telling him, he just had to be patient with his recovery. He looked across the room to where she was talking to Romily. He smiled to himself, thinking he could look at her for hours, given half a chance.

When the revulsion and rejection he had anticipated from Evelyn had not happened, he had assumed her feelings for him were based on nothing more than pity. She had soon put him right on that score, telling him that as far as she was concerned, he was still a work in progress, an undertaking that she had every intention of seeing through to the end. She caught him staring at her now and smiled. It was the kind of smile that made him believe in miracles, that anything really was possible.

'She loves you very much, you do realise that, don't you?' Hope said softly beside him.

'She could have any man she wanted,' Kit murmured, still staring at Evelyn.

'True. But she's chosen you, so don't you forget that.'

'I won't,' he said, turning to look at his sister. 'The same goes for you and Edmund.'

She smiled, reminding him of when they were children and she had corrected him over something, only then to concede that he hadn't been wholly wrong. 'I suppose we have to count ourselves lucky,' she said, looking around the crowded room until her gaze found Edmund.

'Perhaps you should go and rescue him,' said Kit, seeing him cornered by Lady Fogg.

'I'm sure he can take care of himself. Besides, there's something I've been wanting to say to you.'

'Oh, that sounds ominous. What are you going to take me to task over this time? I've said I'll agree to see that skin-graft specialist friend of Edmund's in the new year; you don't need to cajole me any more over that.'

Kit would prefer never to see another doctor or hospital again for the rest of his life; any visit to one usually resulted in excruciating pain. But if he were to have any semblance of a normal life, including a way to earn a living, it was something he would have to endure for a long time ahead. He'd do it for Evelyn's sake, if not for himself.

'Kit, you always make me sound such a tyrant,' his sister said disapprovingly. 'I only nag you because I want the best for you.'

He smiled and put his arm around her. 'I know. And you know what, that was probably what Dad thought when he was screaming blue murder at us.'

'Lord, now you're likening me to our father, of all people!'

'But isn't it true? Aren't we all a bit like him, just trying to make the best of a difficult life? More and more I've begun to see what a challenge it must have been coping with us four children on his own. Yes, he often got it wrong, spectacularly wrong, but by God, can we say we'd have done any better? If nearly losing my life has taught me one thing, it's to walk a mile in another fellow's shoes before I judge him.'

'You've become quite the philosopher,' Hope said with a smile.

'No I haven't, I've grown up. Now then, what was it you wanted to say to me?'

'Something I should have said a long time ago. You're the best brother I could ever wish for.'

'Is that it?'

She laughed. 'You want more?'

'Always!'

74

Later that night, over at Winter Cottage, Florence lay wrapped in Billy's arms. It would be their last night together for goodness knew how long, and she was determined not to miss a second of it.

My husband, she thought dreamily, listening to the rise and fall of Billy's breathing, as well as the steady thud, thud, thud of his heart as she lay with her head on his chest. My handsome, wonderful husband. How lucky I am!

It was funny, they'd been married for almost a year, but it was only now that Florence felt she was truly his wife. Was that merely because at long last they had made love?

With my body I thee worship, she thought with a smile.

Well, since Christmas Eve they had certainly committed themselves to the joy of worshipping each other with their bodies! Their initial attempt had not gone too well, but now they had really got the hang of it and Florence could see what all the fuss was about.

She raised her head very slowly so as not to disturb him as he slept, and looked up at his handsome face, tracing his features with her eyes, wanting to run a finger along his smooth jaw, but again not wanting to wake him.

Florence had confided in Miss Romily and Mrs Partridge, and both women had assured her that it was only to be expected that Billy would need time to recover from the awful things he'd experienced in France; that she was not to worry, as it would only make things worse. She didn't kid herself that Billy was the carefree, light-hearted boy he had once been, but he was definitely easier within himself now, and his old sense of humour had returned, and for that she would be forever grateful.

As if sensing she was watching him, Billy stirred. 'Go to sleep, Mrs Minton,' he murmured sleepily, his eyes fluttering open. 'Or otherwise I'll have to have my wicked way with you again.'

'You're all talk, Billy Minton,' she teased.

'Oh yes?' he said, his voice less sleepy now. Then with one strong, effortless movement, he rolled her over and stared down into her eyes. 'Say that again.'

She laughed and kissed him happily on the mouth. 'You know what, Billy, I love you even with all your many faults.'

'Of course you do. It's because I'm so irresistible.'

'And so modest.'

'You'd have me no other way. Come on, we'd better go to sleep, we both have to be up early in the morning.'

'I can't sleep,' she said, not wanting to think of tomorrow when she would have to say goodbye to him again.

'Yes you can.'

He was right. Eventually she did sleep, a deep restful sleep.

75

'There she goes.'

'Just look at those awful mannish trousers she's wearing. It's not natural, women dressing that way.'

'I've said it before and I'll say it again, what she's doing is not a proper job for a lady. Not a real lady.'

'Which only goes to confirm what we've always thought.'

'I disagree.'

Edith Lawton and Ivy Swann abruptly lowered their teacups and turned away from the window of the Cobbles Tea Room, through which they had been observing the driver of the red sports car stride at a hurried but elegant pace into the newsagent's shop. The two women looked quizzically at Elspeth Grainger, each convinced they must have misheard her.

'I admire her,' said Elspeth boldly, putting down the mince pie she was eating. 'What she's doing shows she has backbone. Real backbone.'

Her comments were met with shocked disbelief.

'Backbone is all very well,' said Edith stiffly, 'but as I've said before, what about her responsibility to the children?'

'Yes,' joined in Ivy, 'what's to become of them while she's playing at being a pilot? It's shameful, that's what it is. It's the men I feel sorry for. Women like her are stealing their jobs. Jobs that would be better done by a man, a man who — '

'I hear the children are very well cared for,' interrupted Elspeth. 'And heaven only knows, with the nightly bombing raids on London, the RAF needs every bit of help it can get. If that means women are needed to ferry aircraft about the country while our brave boys in blue can get on with the business of combat, I for one am all for it.'

'Well,' said Ivy with a scandalised shake of her head, 'I never thought I'd hear you take that woman's side. Are you feeling all right, Elspeth? Are you running a temperature? Was it all too much for you over Christmas?'

'I've never felt better, thank you very much,' said Elspeth. 'And I'll tell this for nothing. That Mrs Temple-Devereux's a darned sight more patriotic than some people I can think of round here. What's more, if I were her age, I'd be doing a lot more than knitting and digging for victory. I'd be . . . I'd be driving an ambulance or manning a canteen at the very least!'

A stunned silence fell on the table, and not knowing what else to say, the three women turned to look out of the window again. The object of their discussion was emerging from the news-agent's with a newspaper tucked under her arm. Her stylish long fur coat, worn over her ATA uniform, accentuated the swift grace of her step as she approached the open-topped car and slipped nimbly behind the steering wheel.

Still without speaking, the three women

watched her secure a silk scarf around her head and pull on a pair of cream fur-trimmed gloves. She then started up the engine and pulled away from the kerb. She drove round the square, and as she passed the tea room, she seemed deliberately to slow her speed before waving at the three women. Elspeth Grainger waved back with pride and respect, earning herself a wide smile from the driver and a cheery toot-toot of the car horn.

Then with a throaty roar of engine, Romily Temple-Devereux was gone.

We do hope that you have enjoyed reading this large print book.

Did you know that all of our titles are available for purchase?

We publish a wide range of high quality large print books including:
Romances, Mysteries, Classics
General Fiction
Non Fiction and Westerns

Special interest titles available in large print are:
The Little Oxford Dictionary
Music Book
Song Book
Hymn Book
Service Book

Also available from us courtesy of Oxford University Press:
Young Readers' Dictionary
(large print edition)
Young Readers' Thesaurus
(large print edition)

For further information or a free brochure, please contact us at:
Ulverscroft Large Print Books Ltd.,
The Green, Bradgate Road, Anstey,
Leicester, LE7 7FU, England.
Tel: (00 44) 0116 236 4325
Fax: (00 44) 0116 234 0205

Other titles published by Ulverscroft:

THE QUEEN OF NEW BEGINNINGS

Erica James

Clayton Miller's life is a mess. One of the country's best comedy scriptwriters, his career has stalled. His girlfriend has left him for his ex-best friend and ex-writing partner. When he commits a spectacularly public fall from grace and is hounded by the press, his agent banishes him to a remote country house until the dust settles . . . Alice Shoemaker is a voiceover artist who habitually avoids telling the truth. She's agreed to help a friend, by shopping and cleaning for the unknown man staying at Cuckoo House. She suspects that Clayton has something to hide. But equally, so does she . . . As they discover the truth about each other, an unlikely friendship is formed and secrets are revealed, until Alice discovers the worst kind of betrayal.

TELL IT TO THE SKIES

Erica James

Venice has been Lydia's home for many years. Living there has given her a sense of peace and fulfilment. But one day, in a heart-stopping moment, the glimpse of a young man's face in the crowd threatens to change everything: long banished memories of a dreadful secret come flooding back . . . As a child Lydia and her sister were sent to live with their grandparents. There in a cruel, loveless world Lydia grew up fast. She learned to keep secrets and to trust sparingly. And through it all she was shadowed by guilt and grief. Now, twenty-eight years later, Lydia is persuaded to leave behind the safe new life she has created and return to England to face the past. And maybe her future . . .